Accolades for America's greatest hero Mack Bolan

D0957089

NO ORDINARY MAN

No matter how hard Mack Bolan tried, no matter how many dealers went down, no matter how many couriers were torn to bits by their own greed, the problem just kept getting worse. It spread like a cancer, and Bolan felt he was out there on the front line all alone.

But he could step back and look at what he had done with a matter-of-fact acceptance that it was important work, and that he had done it well. There was the odd night, though, when he could not *help* but wonder whether he made a difference. If he were to die during the night, would the world be a worse place when the sun rose?

Bolan didn't know.

"Mack Bolan stabs right through the heart of the frustration and hopelessness the average person feels about crime running rampant in the streets."
                    —*Dallas Times Herald*

DON PENDLETON's
MACK BOLAN.

Backlash

A GOLD EAGLE BOOK FROM
WORLDWIDE.

TORONTO · NEW YORK · LONDON · PARIS
AMSTERDAM · STOCKHOLM · HAMBURG
ATHENS · MILAN · TOKYO · SYDNEY

First edition September 1990

ISBN 0-373-61420-9

Special thanks and acknowledgment to
Charlie McDade for his contribution to this work.

Let us have faith that right makes might,
and in that faith let us to the end dare to do
our duty as we understand it.

—Abraham Lincoln

I realized a long time ago what had to be
done and dedicated my life to doing it.
Regrets? Only that the fight rages on and
that America still needs men with my skills.

—Mack Bolan

CHAPTER ONE

Mack Bolan killed the engine of the small launch, letting it drift with the swells for a couple of minutes. Finally it came close enough for him to get a rope around one of the channel markers. The freighter loomed up ahead, a slab of mat-black against the dark blue sky. Smears of phosphorescent algae washed against Bolan's launch, momentarily glowing a dull greenish-yellow, then darkening as the next wave carried them past.

Using a pair of powerful Zeiss glasses, he swept the deck of the big freighter, the SS *Panamanian Queen*, from stem to stern. Her running lights were out, and only two small lamps glowed high in the superstructure. As best as he could tell, the deck was deserted except for a single sailor, leaning over the aft rail. The red tip of the man's cigarette waxed and waned like some distant star as he alternately puffed and dangled the butt over the water. Each time he flicked it with a snap of his finger, a shower of sparks fell toward the water far below, winking out long before it reached the sea.

Bolan was playing a hunch, and he crossed his fingers, hoping he wasn't wasting a whole night on a wild-goose chase. Talking the DEA into lending him the boat hadn't been easy. Even so, the effort was nothing if it paid off as he suspected it would. But the warrior was trapped between a rock and a hard place. Alone on the water he was sure to attract attention from the Coast

Guard if he was spotted by a patrol boat or a surveillance chopper. And if the Guard didn't spot him, there was still a chance the smugglers might. There was no place to hide.

The drug trade off the Florida coast was a lot worse than most people suspected, the dealers themselves were twice as brutal as the newspapers reported. The wholesale slaughter of families, a practice imported from Colombia, had made the old days of Mafia heroin trafficking seem sedate in comparison.

This new world was a jungle, and those who drifted through it were unlikely to be missed by society, a fact that hadn't escaped the cartel's notice. Burn them, or even think about it, and chances were that you disappeared without a trace. Your family—if you had one—wasn't going to run to the cops. And your friends—if you had any—were probably run through the same meat grinder. True blue right to the very end.

Bolan had deliberately chosen the launch for its low profile. It had been customized for speed by its previous owner, specifically for high-speed runs, before being confiscated by the DEA. Like most of the fast boats used by drug runners, it was more stable at fifty knots than it was dead in the water. The sea was running high, and an occasional swell slapped high enough on the gunwale to slosh a little water into the bottom of the boat. Bolan bailed it out enough to keep his ankles dry, but resigned himself to the discomfort of kneeling in an inch or two of water.

It was one o'clock in the morning, and the rendezvous, if it was to take place at all, would have to be in the next hour or so. They were more than an hour out, and the early-morning fleet of sport boats full of tourists would start its run around four. Bolan's man would want to be well clear of the waterfront by then.

He checked the deck of the *Panamanian Queen* again. The smoking sailor was gone.

The screws of the freighter turned slowly, its huge engines confined to fighting the ebbing tide. At one-thirty Bolan heard the first distant rumble of the courier. It came and went, rising and falling like the tide itself, and Bolan knew its engines were whining every time the screws came out of a trough, then growling as the blades bit on the downswell. The sporadic bursts of sound grew longer and more frequent as the runner approached at high speed.

Bolan stared into the darkness, trying to fix the sound of the racing engines. Any high sign would be by light. With everyone from the Coast Guard to the competition monitoring frequencies from one end of the marine band to the other, radio was out of the question. Bolan grabbed the glasses and swung them in the direction of the sound. He waited what seemed like an eternity before switching back to the freighter. Still nothing.

The droning of the engines grew louder, then slacked off. There had still been no signal, but Bolan realized the runner must be in visual contact with the freighter. In the glasses the mainland bobbed in and out of sight as his own boat rose and fell. Like a huge mound of gray and glitter hovering on the tide, Florida seemed to be a live thing or a floating island out of some Japanese fable. The first light came from the freighter, and Bolan almost missed it. At first he thought it was a cigarette lighter, but it was too perfect for an open flame. It flashed once, went out, then flashed twice in rapid succession.

Bolan swung the glasses in the direction the torch had been aimed and caught a single answering flash. Quicker than the wink of a firefly, it came and went. Like a kid waiting patiently with a jar, Bolan watched, hoping for another glimmer, but there was nothing more. The engine slacked off still further, dropping to a low rumble.

It was too risky for the warrior to start his own engine yet. He'd have to wait until the drop had been made and the runner pushed off. Even if someone on the freighter heard him, there would be no attempt to warn the runner. By unwritten law, once the drop was made, the couriers were on their own. To guarantee their own safety, they relied on their knowledge of the coastline and enough horsepower to outrun nearly anything on the water but a hydroplane. It was a risky job, but it paid well, and most of the couriers were in it as much for the kicks as for the money.

Bolan saw one last flash from the freighter, then heard the slap of a rope ladder being dropped over the side. He picked it out after several seconds and watched as two men climbed over the rail, heavy canvas bags strapped to their shoulders. The slender shape of a Cigarette bobbed over the tops of the swells, its engine burbling as the exhaust tubes rose and fell. In the glasses Bolan could just make out the shape of the man at the wheel. As far as he could tell, the runner was alone.

The engine noise died altogether, and the driver reached out to grab the end of the ladder to hold himself steady. The nimbleness of the sailors was almost admirable. The bottom man, his feet no more than a yard above the side of the Cigarette, clung to the ladder and leaned back to drop his package into the bottom of the boat. Even at this distance Bolan could hear the dull thud as the sack hit. The sailor reached up for his partner's bag, then dropped it onto the first. This time Bolan heard nothing as the first sack cushioned the impact.

As the two men scrambled back up the ladder, the pilot pushed off with a boat hook, maneuvering himself far enough away from the freighter's hull to risk the rising swells, turned his engine over and swung in a sharp arc. The phosphorescent algae swirled behind him, momentarily agitated and marking his passage with a glowing wake.

The engine rumbled, and the boat took off like a dart. The two sailors were long gone, and Bolan untied his own craft. He cranked it up, the big Chevy 454 engine growling like an angry dragster. By the time he opened the throttle, the Cigarette was little more than a dot, barely visible without the binoculars.

It was a race for the coastline now, and the Executioner had nothing to lose by opening it up all the way. His boat seemed to stand on its twin screws, its hull sliding over the waves instead of cutting through them. He knew he could get fairly close before the courier heard him over the roar of his own engine. And if the Cigarette made it into the tangled canals and lagoons along the coast, he'd be long gone. This was a one-shot opportunity. If he spooked the courier and didn't nail him, he'd never get a second chance.

Bolan adjusted the Uzi hanging from his shoulder and made sure the safety was off, while steering with one hand. It was a heady sensation, one he hadn't had in a long time. There was something about high speed on open water that appealed to him. Despite his normally cautious nature, he was more than willing to sit back and enjoy the ride.

They were approaching the outer banks at better than eighty knots. Bolan was closing the gap, but it was going to be close—closer than he liked. He could see patches of white water now. The turbulent wake of the Cigarette still fizzed and bubbled as he ran parallel, about twenty yards to the left.

The shimmer of light on the mainland began to backdrop the speeding courier, and Bolan could see his quarry starkly etched against the glow. Any moment, the Cigarette could pick him up, and he shifted the Uzi again, anxious to have it at his fingertips.

The courier began a broad turn to the left, and Bolan was forced to change course. The Cigarette was dead ahead, broadside, no more than one hundred yards away when the courier spotted his pursuer. He tightened the curve, swinging sharply south, and the warrior caught the flash of an automatic rifle almost at once.

It was impossible to hear anything over the roaring engines, and his windshield shattered with the second burst. Slivers splashed over him like a shower of solid rain. Dustlike particles powdered the skin of his hands and forearms, causing them to glitter as if he had been coated with metal-flake paint. Letting go of the wheel with one hand, Bolan waved the Uzi in the general direction of the Cigarette. He wanted to keep the courier honest, not kill him. If at all possible, he wanted the man alive.

Gouts of water rose in the air a few yards ahead of the fleeing boat, then Bolan stitched a tight line across the courier's stern. But the guy wasn't ready to go belly-up just yet. He jerked the wheel and came about, now barreling straight toward the Executioner under a full head of steam. Bracing his assault rifle on the top of his windscreen, he opened up, the hail of fire digging chunks of fiberglass out of the launch's prow. Long, irregular canals chipped the paint and sent splinters flying in every direction. Bolan, trying to keep his balance and to avoid the charging Cigarette, returned fire reluctantly, but the courier gave him no choice.

There was a sudden deep rumble, and a plume of fire spouted up behind the driver. One of Bolan's slugs must have hit a fuel line. The warrior waved, trying to get the courier to turn around, but the man was too busy reloading. The flame spurted forward suddenly, then expanded like a desert flower blooming in a Disney nature film.

The Cigarette roared past, and Bolan jerked his throttle back and dived for the deck. He could see the courier's face frozen in that brief instant of understanding, when the full, fatal imminence is first comprehended.

Bolan had his head and arms covered as the boat went up. He scrambled back to his feet in time to see the courier spiraling head over heels, like a puppet tossed out of a speeding car. The boat was hidden by an orange ball, some of its pieces cartwheeling end over end before landing back in the sea.

Then the concussion slammed into the warrior, knocking him back on his heels, deafening him for a moment.

In the sudden quiet Bolan stared at the flames. Black smoke billowed off the water where the fuel burned a brilliant orange. As the swells passed through, the fire rose and fell, writhing like a living thing, twisting and turning as if it were trying to get away from the sea. Bolan listened for the courier, but he heard no call for help. Cutting back on his throttle, he skirted the blaze, letting his boat come as close as he dared. He could feel the heat on his skin. Gusts of wind covered him with oily soot that smeared under his fingers as he tried to wipe it away.

The Cigarette had been shattered. A few scraps of foam rubber and splintered wood drifted on the swells. Some, like rafts, spun away from the blaze, their tops coated with burning fuel. The launch's prow bumped against something soft, which was hidden by the water. He slowed to a crawl, then stopped the engine altogether, letting the boat drift. He plowed his hands through the water, leaning far over the side. He felt it for a second, then it slipped away. The warrior found the boat hook lying in the bottom of his boat and stabbed into the dark waters.

He felt it strike something, then whatever it was drifted away under the force of his probe. He tried again, this time lowering the hook gently. He got lucky.

Low in the water, almost the full length of the pole, he found it again. Twisting the boat hook, he managed to sink the single sharp tine into the fabric. Slowly he tugged the heavy object back toward the surface.

It was a canvas bag. As Bolan tugged it into the boat, streaming from both sides as water gushed out from under the flap keeping it closed, he felt the boat strike something. He dropped the bag and moved to the front, grabbing the boat hook from the deck pallet and moving cautiously to keep his balance.

He dropped the pole into the water, moving it slowly from side to side. When he found nothing, he moved to the opposite side of the boat. This time he felt something almost at once. The pole struck a soft object, and he twisted the hooked end, then jerked upward. The item wasn't as heavy as the first, and the pole came up easily. He leaned over the side, reaching down at the same time, plunging his hand into the water up to his elbow. Again he felt cloth under his fingers. He grabbed hold and pulled it to the surface.

It was the courier's arm. Torn away by the blast and charred by the burning fuel, it was snarled in the remains of the man's shirt. Bolan brought the limb on board, placed it gently in the bottom of the boat and went back to probing. Five minutes later he found a second sack, hauled it in and dropped it beside the first.

The flames had begun to die down now. The fuel burned quickly, and as the water continued to spread it to a thinner and thinner layer, the blaze had begun to exhaust itself. Bolan used the glasses to scan the area surrounding the fire. He didn't want to leave the courier's body in the water if he could help it—not so much for humanitarian considerations as for identification. He thought he knew whom he'd been following, but things changed so suddenly—and so illogically—in the world in which he found himself that nothing was certain.

He restarted the engine, taking the wheel loosely and steering through one more slow circuit. Then he grabbed a powerful flashlight, and trained its beam on the water just ahead of the boat.

He was ready to pack it in when he saw what he was looking for. Face up, his eyes staring, the courier drifted slowly past, his remaining arm as listless as seaweed. His bare chest, obvious even in the murky water, had been charred and blistered by the flames. Bolan killed the engine and grabbed for the hook. It seemed almost sacrilegious, but there was no other way to do it. Snagging the hook in tattered clothing, the warrior held the pole straight in the air, maintaining enough pull to keep the body from floating free.

Leaning over the side, he grappled for the belt and pulled the corpse into the boat. He dragged the dead man aft and covered him with a greasy tarpaulin. The last of the flames flickered out as Bolan turned the big Chevy engine over.

So far he'd been lucky. He'd been able to trace the courier, and that, regardless of whether the man under the tarp was the man he thought he was, was the next link in the chain. With that link in place, the chain came almost full circle, trapping the kingpin inside a loop he couldn't possibly wiggle out of. That made the night's work worth it. All he had to do now was to get back to port without being spotted. He didn't need the hassle of trying to explain the man under the tarp, not to vice cops who'd heard every theme and variation, and not to the Coast Guard, who'd just as soon not be involved at all, and were running short of patience with the whole sordid business.

When the light winked on to his left, Bolan glanced at it briefly, then kicked the engine full out. If the chopper spotted him, it would certainly look him over. If it was the Coast Guard, the best he could hope for was a night in jail. If it was anybody else, he'd be lucky to spend a night anywhere. Frustrated by the escalating violence, the cops and the DEA were beginning to shoot first. It seemed the only way to avoid being shot themselves.

The chopper climbed another hundred feet, then banked in his direction. Bolan cursed and pushed on the wheel as if that would make the boat go still faster. The chopper was closing fast, and he still had two miles to go before the tangled swamps of the south Florida shoreline would offer him some protection.

The warrior kept glancing back over his shoulder as the chopper narrowed the gap. It was a Huey and could belong to anyone. It was little more than a black shape in the air, a smear on the grayish sky. He couldn't see any markings in the quick glimpses and couldn't take the time for a longer look.

When the chopper was five hundred yards behind him, he heard a low thump and turned to see a puff of smoke ripped in the prop wash. Without thinking, he jerked the helm, and the boat nearly capsized as it sawed through the ragged swells.

The 2.75-inch rocket slammed into the sea less than fifty feet away. It went off with a muffled roar, hurling a column of water high into the air. Bolan goosed the boat again, this time zigzagging to keep the chopper guessing. A second rocket sailed over his head, slicing into the water without detonating, leaving a dull silver spout behind as it sank out of sight.

As it drew closer, the chopper's engine began to roar even louder than Bolan's own. It climbed higher and swerved to the left. Bolan could just make it out, hovering like a giant insect over his left shoulder. Juking to the right, he opened the throttle and drove for the shoreline. The first burst of machine gun fire sailed high over his head, and he spun the wheel desperately, trying to keep the gunner off balance.

Recognizing the distinctive sound of an M-60, he was convinced now that it wasn't a Coast Guard ship, and it seemed unlikely that it could be local police, who didn't usually resort to such impressive firepower, preferring to let the Feds handle the heavy combat offshore. Bolan had only a hundred yards before he'd reach the tangled undergrowth of the shoreline.

Slowing a bit, he searched for an opening to one of the swampy channels that crisscrossed the marshes. Mangroves and cypresses grew farther inland, away from the brackish water, and they were thick and covered with fronds of moss. But he'd have to find a way inland before they would do him any good.

Bolan spotted a break in the underbrush as a second burst of 7.62 mm gunfire sprayed the tail end of his boat. The heavy slugs ripped at the fiberglass hull, and the warrior had a sinking feeling as he jerked the wheel to the left. The speeding boat leaned way over, slipping sideways on the water as it skidded toward the opening.

Branches and leaves whipped the hull as he narrowly avoided running aground. Righting the boat with difficulty, he slowed, jerking the launch back toward the center of the channel. The undergrowth grew ten or twelve feet in the air on either bank, offering him some cover. The chopper would have to fly right over his head to keep him in sight.

He could hear the chopper somewhere behind him, its engine straining as it climbed higher to look for him. A quarter mile inland, the swamp forest took over, and he could hide.

But first he had to get there.

A sunken log slammed into the hull, sending the boat into a skid. Bolan jerked it back toward the center of the channel. Water spurted through a crack in the hull. He could feel his pants getting wet, but he pushed the boat harder.

A few scraggly trees hung over the bank on the left-hand side about fifty yards ahead. He could just make them out against the dark gray sky. He thought for a moment of trying to conceal the boat under their dangling branches, but if he tried to stop, he might overshoot the cover. The channel was too narrow for him to turn, and he decided to bypass the opportunity.

Bolan considered taking to the land, but the swamp was treacherous and the footing all but impossible. And he couldn't abandon his cargo, at least not until he knew what it was. Evidence hadn't been that easy to come by, and he'd be damned if he'd let a boatful get away without a fight. Since his Uzi was no match for the chopper's firepower, flight was the only viable option. As much as it galled him to turn tail, there were times— and this was clearly one of them—when it was better to stay alive to fight another day than to make some showboating gesture and stand ground. He didn't need to fight a battle he knew he couldn't win.

The warrior pushed the boat into a sharp turn, feeling the hull slide toward the far bank. The trees were only thirty yards ahead, and the chopper was right on his tail. The machine gun opened up a third time, this time tearing hell out of the rear end of the boat. He killed the engine and let the boat coast the last twenty yards, jerking the wheel toward the spongy bank. The boat struck at an angle, glanced off, and Bolan fought to hold his course as the trees closed over him. The chopper climbed straight up, probably waiting to see which way he ran.

Bolan climbed onto the bank, hauling a rope after him and wrapping it around the nearest sturdy bush. He quickly tied the back end to a second shrub, then backed away, keeping under the thickest foliage.

He could still hear the chopper's rotor thumping overhead. After a minute, when it was obvious he wasn't going to cut and run into the open, the Huey swooped down, the M-60 opening up and tearing into the forest canopy. The gunner emptied a belt, paused to slap another one home, then sprayed left and right. Bolan could hear the slugs chewing into the boat's hull as he crawled into a tangle of vines draped over a fallen tree. The trunk was rotting, but offered him a little cover. He couldn't afford to be choosy.

Then the thunder stopped as the chopper climbed again. Bolan realized he was holding his breath. The sound of the rotor gradually died away, and the warrior crawled back into the open. He was lucky there hadn't been a place for the Huey to set down.

The boat was useless. It lay on its side, canted away from the bank. Water geysered through the shattered hull, and as the boat filled, it listed even farther. Bolan climbed aboard and went through the courier's pockets, tucking a wallet and some loose papers into his shirt. Then he secured the man's corpse in the small forward cabin.

Hoisting the canvas sacks over his shoulder, he glanced at the sky for a moment, then stepped onto the spongy shore. It was going to be a long walk home, but he was still alive. And in Mack Bolan's line of work, that was success.

CHAPTER TWO

Gil Hoffman had seen worse troops before, but not lately, and never with so little interest in what they were supposed to be learning. He shook his head in exasperation. It was too damn hot to have to put up with this, and he cursed under his breath. Then, as if the whispering had been a trial run, he shouted the same insults at the top of his lungs. "You pussies look like a bunch of assholes. You want to get your head shot off? Stay the hell down."

He turned to Ricardo Vargas, who watched him with a curious smile. Hoffman rolled his hands, indicating that Vargas should translate for him. "And I want it word for word."

Vargas grinned, repeated the taunts in Spanish, then waited for his superior's next move. The men grumbled, glaring at Hoffman while lying prostrate on the broken, yellowed grass.

"Tell them to take fifteen. We'll start all over when I recover from the shock."

When Vargas repeated the instructions, he turned back to Hoffman, watching him with a mixture of amusement and curiosity. Hoffman, kicking dust with every step, walked out of the harsh glare of the sun and flopped down under a tree. He gestured for Vargas to join him.

"How long they been here, Ricky?"

"Four weeks tomorrow."

"Four weeks? Are you kidding me? Four weeks, and they can't even keep their butts down? Jesus..."

"You want miracles, amigo?"

"No, just soldiers."

"Maybe you're in the wrong country."

"No maybe about it. I'm getting too old for this shit. I just don't have any patience anymore."

"You better find it, Gil. This is about as good as it gets."

"Shit!"

Vargas laughed again. "What do you want? It's your first day. This isn't like the old days. This is a whole different thing. Shit goes on down here you wouldn't believe. They hate the Sandinistas, call them beggar dogs, which is a lot bigger insult than you might think. I'm telling you, man, you won't believe it, even when you see it."

"Ricky, there's nothing I haven't seen. You oughta know that by now. Hell, this is what, our fourth gig together?"

"Fifth."

"There you go, fifth. So you should know nothing surprises me."

"Just wait. This is the worst. These guys hate the Sandinistas, but they won't fight them, because the brass sits on its ass in Tegoose while the campesinos grunt and sweat. Then they get fed up, they go home pissed off, and they hate everybody."

"I thought Angola was bad. Remember that?"

"You just don't understand the Third World, Gil."

"What's to understand? They're people like anybody else."

"Not really. You're too damn American to see how different it is."

"And you're not?"

"I was born in Cuba."

"Big deal. I was born in Wisconsin. So what? You got farms. So do we. You got cows. We do, too. Your problem is you romanticize everything. As long as it's *not* American."

"Just remember what I said," Vargas said. His grin faded for the first time. He leaned closer. "Something's screwy here, Gil. I've only been here a month, but I can smell it. It's there all the time, like a dead rat in the basement. It stinks."

Hoffman waved it away. "We're getting old, amigo. Too damn old for this crap. You know how I can tell?"

"How?"

"I miss my wife. Every place I've been—Laos, Angola, all the way back to Guatemala, before the Bay of Pigs—I never missed her. Not that I didn't love her. But there was all this stuff out there, you know. And I wanted some of all of it. A piece here, a piece there. Not just the broads, either, although that was part of it, but the excitement, man, that was the real kick. It was like I was gonna live forever. Now I don't think so. Now I know I could buy the farm anytime at all. The thrill is gone, Ricky. I'm not immortal anymore."

"If you feel that way, Gil, you shouldn't be here. Especially not here."

"Here's not so different, Ricky."

"Yeah, amigo, it is. That's what I'm trying to tell you. It *is* different. You wait. You'll understand. Then we'll talk about it."

Hoffman ripped at the handful of grass with his teeth, chewing at the blades with a thoughtful expression. "Maybe I think too much. Maybe that's what it is. I didn't use to do that. There wasn't time."

"There was time, Gil. But we weren't interested. Things were going so fast and we went right along with them. Now we know better. It's like a pitcher, you know? The great ones, they lose a little off the fastball, they find some other way to get you out, like Seaver did, and Guidry. We can't all be flamethrowers all our lives like Nolan Ryan. The trouble is, you start thinking, you start understanding. You think too much, you second-guess yourself, Gil. That's what's happening. But that might not be so bad, huh? Maybe we'll be lucky. Maybe we can bail out before it catches up with us."

"Maybe." Hoffman chewed another mouthful of grass. "Maybe we better get these assholes started again. What do you say?"

"Beat's thinking, amigo." He wasn't kidding, and Hoffman knew it.

HOFFMAN WAS FLIRTING with disaster. He sensed it but kept trying to push the thought away. The day's heat had drained him, sucking the life out of him as surely as the mosquitoes sucked his blood. He sat under a tree looking up at the stars. The constellations weren't familiar. Guatemala was a long time ago, and he hadn't been in this part of the world much since then. As he stared at the sky, trying to make sense of it—and of his life—it occurred to him that he was fighting a losing battle. There was no sense to either, not at the moment. He was exhausted, and he was too close to the edge.

He couldn't understand why he kept making the same mistake, trying to take social misfits, torturers and criminals, mix them with green recruits who would rather be sitting under a tree somewhere, and make an army out of them. And it was always the same thing.

Always the snakes took over. The poison ran too deep, and boys will, after all, be boys. There was no way fighting for some elusive idea of freedom would change a man who was used to murdering for profit and raping for fun. But that was what they gave him to deal with, time after goddamn time.

He knew he needed sleep, but he also knew there was little chance of getting any, even if he tried to force himself. Things were too much out of his hands at the moment. The sound of a distant engine caught his ear, distracting him for a moment. At first he thought it might be a truck, but that seemed unlikely. This far out, so close to the border, nobody in his right mind moved very far from camp. Then, as the distant buzz saw whine drew closer, he recognized it as the sound of an airplane. He didn't know about any scheduled delivery, but the Sandinistas weren't likely to launch a night raid, not with a single plane, anyway. They might be infuriating, but they weren't stupid.

Part of him wanted to go and check it out, and part of him just wanted to get some shut-eye. Maybe, he thought, fate would settle it. He climbed to his feet, brushed off his clothing, then reached into a pocket of his fatigue pants and fished out a coin.

Hoffman held the coin close to his eye for a moment, recognized it as a half-dollar, then tossed it into the air. "Heads I go to sleep, tails I walk over to the airstrip." He whispered it, but his voice startled him in the quiet night. "Tails it is."

He glanced at the sky for a moment, then shuffled across the dry ground into the hundred yards of forest between the main camp and the airstrip. When he reached the far side, he noticed a jeep, its engine running, sitting against the trees at the far end of the runway. The plane was close now, and coming in low from the east. The headlights of the jeep blinked once, then twice and stayed dark.

The plane banked to the left, and its engine noise was almost swallowed by the forest for a minute, then it snarled back, again from the east, this time touching down. The pilot handled the small Cessna push-pull easily, keeping it steady as it bounced over the rough strip. He taxied to within twenty yards of the waiting jeep, spun the plane around, then throttled back.

Hoffman eased through the trees, keeping just inside the underbrush until he was at a point almost even with the plane. As he watched, the cabin door swung open and the pilot jumped down. He waved to the jeep, and someone sprinted toward him. Together, the pilot and the jeep driver lugged a heavy canvas bag toward the plane.

The driver climbed in, tugging the bag as the pilot pushed. A moment later the driver reappeared, and the cabin door closed. Hoffman was baffled. What could possibly be in the bag that required a night landing on an unlighted strip in the heart of the jungle? It didn't make sense. Especially since whatever it was was being shipped out, not in.

The plane started to roll, bounced back down the runway and lifted off, a fine haze of dust trailing behind it. Hoffman watched the jeep driver, who hustled back to his vehicle and started the engine. Moving quickly, Hoffman sprinted through the trees toward the motor pool. The camp kept its fifteen vehicles under a thatched roof supported by raw saplings, and Hoffman was sure the jeep was one of theirs.

The driver had to run the length of the runway, then loop around to get back to the motor pool, and Hoffman waited in the shadows as the jeep, using only its parking lights, coasted toward him. The vehicle rolled to a stop just under the roof, and the driver killed the engine. Hoffman waited until the driver climbed out, then whistled. The man stopped in his tracks.

"Who's there?" he whispered.

Hoffman recognized him now, a tall, sinewy ex-Green Beret named Chuddy Johnson.

"What's in the bag, my man?" Hoffman asked.

"Who's there?" Johnson repeated.

"Does it change what's in the bag?"

"Shut the fuck up, man. Who the hell are you?"

Hoffman stepped toward him, reached into the jeep and clicked on the headlights. "Recognize me now, buddy?"

"Oh, it's you, Hoffman."

"What's in the bag, Chuddy? I'm not going to ask you again."

"Same old shit."

"Which is?"

"Why don't you ask ol' Vinnie? He knows all about it."

"I'm asking you."

Johnson sighed with exasperation. "Look, Gil, you're new here."

"What's that got to do with anything?"

"It's a long story."

"I can't sleep anyhow. Why don't you tell me a long story? It might help."

"I doubt it."

"Try."

"All right." Johnson sat on the jeep's rear bumper. He fished a cigarette out of his shirt pocket and lit it.

After a long drag, he exhaled a thin stream of smoke. "It's coke."

"Where'd you get it?"

"Hell, man, where does anybody get it? Colombia."

"How'd it get here?"

"Cardozo brings it in from Choluteca on the coast."

"Where's it headed?"

"Miami."

"And?"

"And what?"

"Tell me the rest of it. The money. Where's the money go?"

"Hell, I don't know. They turn it around, buy ammunition and shit. Hell, half the stuff we use, we pay for with the dope."

"You mean to tell me we're smuggling dope to pay for weapons?"

"Pretty funny, isn't it?"

"The hell it is."

"Hey, man, I don't make the rules."

"And you're telling me Vince Arledge knows all about it?"

Johnson nodded. "It was his idea, I think. I mean, he's the one who told me about it when I first got here. Shit, everybody knows. No point in gettin' your nose all out of joint. It's covered. The shit flies into Homestead Air Base. We've got permanent clearance. It turns into cash overnight. Five days later we've got more ammo, more guns, you name it. And the taxpayers don't even have to pick up the tab."

"You think it's that simple, do you?"

"Hey, man, it isn't my war. I just do what they tell me. I'd suggest you think about that. Talk to Vince before you go off half-cocked."

Hoffman realized he was in a bind. "Yeah, I guess I'll do that."

"I didn't like it much at first, either. But, you know, it's what you get used to. I've been here awhile. I'm used to it. You will be, too, before you know it."

"I don't think so, Chuddy."

"Don't get involved, man. Go along with the program. It's better for everybody. Safer, too."

"You threatening me?"

Johnson shrugged. Hoffman leaned into the jeep to shut off the headlights. He heard Johnson move and turned just as the taller man barreled into him. Hoffman fell back, slamming his hip into the side of the jeep. Johnson grabbed for his throat, digging his wiry fingers into Hoffman's windpipe. The older man tried to wriggle free, then jerked his legs high into the air. He was able to lock one knee around his opponent's neck. He started pulling and Johnson let go of his throat.

Hoffman jerked harder, and Johnson sank his teeth into the flesh just above the knee. The merc reached for the survival knife hanging from his garrison belt, and Hoffman jerked a third time. The snap sounded louder than it was in the darkness, louder still compared to the sudden silence.

Hoffman disentangled, then climbed to his feet. His throat was full of fire, and he rubbed at the raw skin on his neck where Johnson's nails had dug in.

It was the end of the line, and he knew it, knew that he had felt it coming. Well, now it was here, and he had a decision to make. It wasn't going to be easy, and he didn't even have a clue where to start. But he knew he'd better find one, and quick.

CHAPTER THREE

The traffic of early evening had long gone. An occasional eighteen wheeler roared past, taking advantage of the unwritten law permitting highballing truckers to bury the needle if they kept to the straight and narrow.

Bolan listened to the whine of heavy tires way off in the distance, the powerful diesel humming steadily, the pitch of both rising slowly until the truck barreled past like a freight train, then slowly faded away. In some ways it was like his own passage through the world. He was a bolt out of the blue, gone before anyone knew he'd been there.

Restless, Bolan sat up, grabbed a light jacket and slipped it on to hide the Beretta 93-R holstered under his arm. He opened the door to the room and stepped onto the chipped concrete sidewalk that ran the length of the motel. Leaning against the frail column supporting the roof, he watched the night. It was dark and motionless, except for the blinking red arrow under the dim blue Vacancy sign.

He noticed a car two stalls up from his own, a man at the wheel puffing on a small cigar. He stepped out from under the roof into a soft mist drifting through the air. The man in the car opened his door and climbed out, the dome light briefly lighting his face. Bolan kept his body turned slightly, watching the man close his car door and toss the cigar butt over his shoulder, almost as if it were a ritual.

Bolan had reached the tree line at the edge of the parking lot when the man started toward him. He waved and shouted something the warrior couldn't hear. A bright flame told him why. The man had another cigar jammed into his teeth and was trying to talk around it while he fired it up.

The man continued to walk toward him, barely watching where he was walking. Bolan leaned against a tree, concealing his left side and pulling the Beretta. The man was fifteen feet away now, still not quite satisfied with his light. But he stopped and looked at the cigar.

"Who are you?" the warrior asked.

"That's my line, buddy. But you asked first, and I'm polite, so I'll tell you. Name's Byron Wade, Lieutenant Byron Wade." There was no emphasis on the rank, Bolan noticed. Wade had merely added it as an afterthought. "Miami Police Department. You got a minute?"

"You have any identification?"

"Sure." He tossed a small leather card case. Bolan snatched it out of the air and checked it. "Okay. What do you want?"

"A friend in the DEA told me where to find you, Mr. Belasko. I've got a few questions." Michael Belasko was the cover name Mack Bolan was using for this mission.

"Shoot."

"Want to tell me what happened out on the water?"

"No."

"Are you responsible for the stiff in the boat?"

"No."

"Should I believe that?"

"I guess I wouldn't, if I were you. But you do what you have to."

"You have any idea about the hornet's nest you kicked open here?"

"I'm working on it."

Wade turned his back and struggled with the cigar again. This time he got it lit. Wreathed in blue smoke, he turned back to Bolan. "I've got a proposition for you, Mr. Belasko."

When Bolan didn't respond, Wade puffed twice, then waved the smoke away with the back of his hand. "It goes like this—I'll tell you what I know if you tell me what you know. I could use a hand from a hotshot Justice agent on this thing."

"I don't know if I can do that." Bolan didn't bother to inform Wade that he wasn't a Justice agent. The information could put a whole new complexion on the situation.

"I could haul you in."

"Maybe you should."

"Wouldn't be fair to you."

"That bother you?"

"Yeah, it does. There's not enough fairness to go around. And since I know something I'll bet you don't, I have a slight advantage at the moment."

"All right, let's have it. If it makes any difference to me, I'll tell you what I know."

"Fair enough. The stiff? He was a spook. Part-time, contract man, true, but a spook is a spook, am I right?"

"Tell me more."

"C...I...A. Clear? Understand what I'm telling you?"

"Yeah, I do."

"You boys from Justice didn't know that, did you?"

"No."

"Your turn."

"What do you want to know?"

"All of it, if you can. If you can't, I want to know why you can't."

"Okay. I was following a tip on a drug run. The dead man was a mule. He hooked up with a freighter off the coast about thirty miles or so. Coming back, I was on his tail and he spotted me."

"I thought you said you didn't waste him."

"You want to hear it all or not?"

"All right, I'm sorry. Forgive my inquisitive nature. I'm a cop, after all."

"He turned on me and started shooting. I fired back to keep him off me. His boat caught fire. I tried to warn him, but he didn't understand until it was too late. The boat blew."

"And out of the goodness of your heart you fished him out so the sharks wouldn't get him."

"Not really. He was all I had. I wanted him alive. But I figured I might learn something if I knew who he was."

"So what's the rest of it?"

"You want more?"

"A little, yeah. Like what happened to the DEA's launch that you left sitting on the bottom of the lagoon out there. He do that or did you?"

"Neither. I don't know who did it."

"Did you know he was full of bullet holes from a big mother of a gun, probably an M-50 or M-60? We're still waiting for the M.E. to report."

"Yeah, I knew that."

"But you didn't do it."

"I already told you that."

"You fish anything else out of the drink?"

Bolan didn't answer.

"I'll take that as a yes. It wouldn't be dope now, would it?"

The warrior remained silent.

"You mind telling me what you did with it?"

"Would you believe me if I did?"

"Try me."

"I flushed it."

"All right, I'll tell you what I'm going to do, pal. But I'm only going to do this because I have a hunch about you, a gut instinct, if you will, the kind I often end up regretting, but can't afford to ignore. There's been no official ID on the corpse yet, but I know who, and what, he is. I haven't told anybody because I don't want a fucking headache two miles wide, which is exactly what I'm going to get as soon as somebody else figures out who he is. And they will do that very shortly. You can bet your ass. As far as I'm concerned, spook or no, one dead mule is fine, although not as good as two dead mules. And so on. So I'm going to sit on this for a while, provided you tell me who you are. And I mean exactly. Right now!"

"Got a pencil?"

"What for?"

"I'll give you a telephone number. Let them tell you."

Wade scrounged a stubby pencil out of his raincoat pocket. He licked the point, then said, go ahead. He jotted the number down with short strokes. When he was finished, he said, "I see by the area code that we're into some heavy shit here. Looks like that headache will be a three miler.

"Let me tell you just one more thing, then," Wade went on. "Miami is full of spooks. We got semi-spooks, semipro spooks, retired spooks, reactivated spooks, has-beens and wannabe's. They keep some strange company, and I wouldn't mind if they all killed one another one Sunday while I was in church. But it ain't gonna happen. I guess what I'm trying to say is, I don't know who this guy was working for, not really. So watch your ass, because anybody, and I do mean anybody, could be a friend of his. It might even be a friend of yours. *¿Comprende?*''

Bolan understood only too well. ''There's a phone in my room.''

''Let's go make that call.''

WHEN WADE WAS GONE, Bolan lay down on the bed and stared at the ceiling. He had no choice but to hold out on the cop; he needed the kind of information Wade wasn't likely to have. He knew that if Wade did have access to it, others might know somebody was looking. It was safer, for him and for Wade, to hold a little back.

Lost in thought, he stared at the fly-speckled ceiling. A question haunted him—why? Bolan knew only too well it was the one question a scientist never permitted himself, and the one question which, more than any other, concerned men in his line of work. Understanding human behavior, the reasons for it, motive, was the most difficult aspect of his job.

Yet without it he was paralyzed. On the other hand, staring the question in the face was enough to short-circuit every nerve. It could numb the brain, freeze the hand halfway between thin air and a holster, even get you killed.

Looking too closely at the things men did to one another was bad enough. Trying to understand why they did them, what it was that made men willing and able to do them was all but impossible. But of all the crimes that he had encountered, the warrior had never been able to understand why a man could turn his back on the things he professed to believe in just to line his pockets. Clearly money was part of the answer, but only a part, perhaps the smallest and least significant.

Selling drugs to innocent kids was about as evil as a man could get, but how much more evil was a man whose obligation was to prevent that evil and, instead, abetted it? Lining his pockets in the process, true enough, but why did money turn some heads and not others? The drug lords had money to spare, rolling hundred-dollar bills into tubes, snorting coke through them as casually as a kid sucked soda through a straw, so casually that it was an insult to anyone who ever needed a buck.

And no matter how hard Bolan tried, no matter how many dealers went down, no matter how many couriers were torn to bits by their own cupidity, the problem just kept getting worse. It spread like a cancer, and at times Bolan felt he was out there on the front line all alone. Knowing he wasn't didn't make him feel any better. Knowing that there were men who served two masters made it feel a whole lot worse.

Bolan closed his eyes reluctantly, as if he were betraying some commitment he felt but didn't understand. He knew he was taking things too personally. He knew, too, that he couldn't change if he wanted to. But sometimes he felt so tired that he wondered if he could go on, even for another day. And then, when he thought about comrades who had refused to give up, he didn't see how he could stop. He owed it to them not to, as much as to himself, as much as to any sense of duty.

It was easy for a man to deceive himself, to let self-importance, ego, take over. But Bolan was no ordinary man. He had an ego as much as anyone else, but unlike most men, he kept it under tight rein. It served him. He was its master. He did what he had to, not what self-aggrandizement would tempt him to do. No showboating, no grandstanding, just the plodding, incessant weariness of anonymity.

And he could step back and look at what he had done and nod, not with pride, but with a matter-of-fact acceptance that it was important work, and that he had done it well. It was the quiet satisfaction of a master, almost zenlike in its egoless purity. There were nights, though, and this was one of them, when he couldn't help but wonder whether it made any difference. If he died during the night, would the world be a worse place when the sun rose? Mack Bolan didn't know.

But he had to keep fighting.

CHAPTER FOUR

Byron Wade sipped the cold coffee on his desk. He made a face, took another sip, then reached for the phone. Its blinking light was distracting him even more than the insistent buzz of the intercom.

"Yeah, Wade," he snapped. "All right, yeah. I'll be right there."

He'd been expecting the call all morning. Longer, in fact. Once he eyeballed the stiff, he knew there would be a lot of very low-profile—but intense—interest. He thought back to his meeting with Belasko and the phone call to some high-muck-a-muck Fed in Washington. But the big man was bona fide, so he'd keep his part of the bargain solid. As long as he could.

The hall was empty when Wade stepped through the open door. The phone rang, this time a bell, indicating an outside line, but he ignored it. Three offices down Captain Randolph Parsons waited in the doorway.

When Wade reached him, Parsons stepped back enough to make room for his subordinate to pass, then closed the door.

"Sit down, By." Parsons was using his syrupy voice, and Wade ground his teeth.

Taking a chair across from Parsons's desk, Wade crossed one leg over the opposite knee, glanced at his dangling foot just long enough to notice his shoes needed shining, then rubbed a hand over his red-rimmed eyes.

"I know it's late, but this was too important."

"That's all right, Randy. It's not like I have a home life anymore. Go ahead. What is it?"

"That stiff we got in last night."

"What about him? He's not really dead, or what?"

"Oh, he's dead. That's not the problem. It's not what he is. It's what he was."

Wade sat there, chewing on his lower lip. He knew what was coming but had to pretend he didn't. He hoped he could pull it off. When it became apparent Parsons wanted him to ask, he took a deep breath, then did what he always did. "What was he?" he asked.

"He has friends in Langley. You tell me."

"Shit!" Wade stood and ran a hand through his unruly hair. Parsons watched in fascination, trying to decide whether Wade wanted to straighten the tangles or make them worse. The problem with Wade, who was a good cop and a better friend, was that you were never sure, not just about his hair, but about everything he did.

Finally Wade expelled his breath in an explosive rush. "You know, Randy, I read a book once, about Bugsy Siegel. You know what it was called?"

"No, what?"

"It was called *We Only Kill Each Other*."

"So what's your point?"

"My point is, every time we turn over a rock, we find one of these assholes with a hole in him. We turn over another rock, and we find the guy who put it there. And every time, we find everybody has the same damn uncle. It's getting old. I wish to hell they would all go to Guatemala or some fucking place. Then they could shoot each other to pieces for all I care."

"You sound bitter, By."

"Who, me?" Wade laughed. "Bitter? No way. I love trying to investigate a homicide with all these Feds stepping on each other's dick. I only get pissed when they step on mine."

"We've already got a bite on this one. Guy named Arledge. He'll be here in fifteen or twenty minutes."

"What's he want? Too late for mouth-to-mouth."

"I gather he wants to apprise us of the federal interest."

"You mean he wants to orchestrate the cover arrangements, don't you?"

Parsons spread his arms wide. "Hey, I don't like it any better than you do. But what can we do about it?"

"We *could* tell him to go fuck himself. Just this once."

"What good would that do?"

"Make me feel better."

"Look, I know how you feel. But you know how it is. There's a lot of shit going down out there." He gestured vaguely toward the street. "We don't know all the details."

"Secrets. You know what I think? I think every time one of their cowboys goes off the deep end, they just pump the lake out and pretend nobody drowned. That's what I think. If they kept a tighter rein on these goons, it would be a hell of a lot better for everybody." The glass rattled, and Wade looked at the door. "That him?"

"Beats me."

"He know how we got the good news?"

"No."

"You gonna tell him?"

"If he says pretty please, then maybe. Hell, it was only an anonymous tip, anyway, but let him sweat a little. All right?"

"Suits me."

Wade got up and opened the door. A tall man with the sharp features of a hungry weasel stood with his knuckles poised for another rap on the glass. The lieutenant stepped back, and the visitor walked into the office. "Shut the door," he said to Wade over his shoulder.

Wade made a face, then sat down. The visitor glared at him, turned and grabbed the door by the knob.

"Don't slam it," Parsons said.

"You Parsons?" the visitor asked.

"Says so on the door, doesn't it?"

The visitor jerked a thumb at Wade. "Who's he?"

"Whatever happened to hello?" the lieutenant asked. "Kids..." He shook his head as if he'd never understand.

"I'm Vincent Arledge." The guy spoke his own name as if it should mean something to his hosts. When neither man said anything, Arledge continued, "You want to tell me what happened?"

"We don't really know what happened," Parsons replied. "We've got a stiff. A check of his prints rang a few bells in D.C. That's all I can tell you."

"What happened to him?"

"If you want my opinion, it looks like he lost an argument with a dragon." Wade smiled sardonically.

"Who the hell *are* you?" Arledge demanded.

"Byron Wade. It's my stiff."

"You find him?"

Arledge stared at Wade for a long moment. His lips moved like those of a man having a seizure, but nothing came out. Finally he said, "Let's take a ride. Show me where."

Wade looked at Parsons, who shrugged. "Why not?" Wade said. He got up slowly, shifting his muscular shoulders to fit more comfortably in his jacket, then opened the door and left without waiting to see whether Arledge followed him. There was no doubt in his mind.

In the garage the lieutenant climbed into the two-year-old Plymouth and left the door open while he started the engine. Arledge tried the far door, but it was locked. Wade leaned over, opened it and closed his own door.

Out in traffic Arledge seemed to relax a little. He lit a cigarette, then waved it at Wade. "You mind?" When the other man shook his head, Arledge took a drag. He opened the window to let the smoke out. When the cigarette was no more than a stub, he pinched off the light and tossed the filter out the window. "How'd you find the body?" he asked.

The question took Wade by surprise. "Phone tip."

"Anonymous?" The lieutenant hesitated. Before he could frame his answer, Arledge said, "Thought so. That's always the way."

"It happens a lot."

"Yeah, it does."

"What was McDonough working on?" Wade asked.

"I don't know."

"Don't give me any of that need-to-know crap. I've been that route more than enough."

Arledge sounded earnest. "I really don't know. He was just a contract agent, a local asset. He wasn't real Company."

"He's real dead, though. I'll tell you that."

Arledge nodded, then, as an afterthought, said, ''I didn't know him. Never met him, in fact.''

Wade thought about that, turning it over in his mind like a man looking at something that might be gold and might just be pyrite. He wasn't sure he could tell the difference, and he wasn't sure he cared.

They were on the open highway now, and Wade drove easily, letting one arm dangle out the window. Arledge stared into the marsh grass that stretched as far away as he could see, ending in the blunt, black tree line. Above it the stars glittered wickedly, flashing like a villain's teeth.

''This could have waited until daylight,'' Wade suggested.

''No time. I have to get my report in.''

''You guys don't really give a shit about this, do you?'' Arledge kept silent. Wade sighed in exasperation. ''You know, if you guys gave us a little more cooperation, it would be a lot easier. This damn city's a cesspool. It's full of little boys running around playing games, playing by the rules you guys taught them. They have the toys, and they want to play. If there's no game, they make one up.''

''It's not that simple,'' Arledge said.

''Oh, but it is.''

''It's a two-way street, Wade. You know that. If you were a little more flexible, maybe we would be, too.''

''Flexible my ass. We have people running around here with more artillery than some Third World countries. What you didn't give them, you taught them how to get for themselves. Half the shit that goes down in Miami leads back to your Bureau of Public Roads.''

''No more.''

''The hell it doesn't.''

"No, I mean the sign. It doesn't say that anymore."

"What's it say now? Little Red Schoolhouse?"

Arledge started to answer, then, realizing the lieutenant was in no mood to listen, snapped his jaw shut.

Wade spun the car into the gravel shoulder, braking a few feet from a Bronco sitting by the roadside on big balloon tires. It bore the Miami-Dade shield on the front door and sported a huge light rack.

"What's this?" Arledge asked.

"We have to go back aways. This is the best way." He opened his door and waved to a uniform leaning against the front fender. "Got to borrow the buggy, Tito. You mind?"

The officer shook his head. "How long?" He glanced curiously at Arledge, but Wade made no attempt to introduce him. Tito turned away.

The 4X4 rode high over the swampy water, rocking and rolling through small streams and over hummocks. Wade pushed the Bronco as hard as he dared, enjoying the queasy look on Arledge's face.

When the remains of the launch exploded into view, Wade nudged the Bronco as close to the orange tape as he could, then jumped down onto to spongy grass. Arledge followed reluctantly.

"Watch out for snakes," Wade warned, his smile clearly visible in the headlights. But Arledge didn't react. The policeman was starting to suspect that this guy was no desk jockey. He reached back into the Bronco and snatched a large flashlight. Clicking it on, he ducked under the tape and moved to the channel bank.

"I don't know what you expect to find here," Wade said. "We went over the boat pretty thoroughly."

"Maybe nothing. But you know how it is sometimes. If you know what to look for, something turns up."

"Oh, and what should we look for?"

"I don't know. What did you find?"

"The body, an arm, lots of bugs. The usual."

"That's all?"

"Far as I know." Wade hedged a little and hoped Arledge didn't notice.

"And somebody called it in, you said?"

Before Wade could answer, Arledge stepped over the gunwale and down into the boat.

"Yeah. And don't fuck around with anything down there. I don't think the lab boys are finished."

"Don't worry. The lab isn't going to have anything to do."

"What do you mean?"

"I mean, we're taking this one ourselves."

"You don't have jurisdiction. No domestic action. Remember the Church Committee, the Pike Committee, the—"

"It's cleared through the Justice Department. Captain Parsons has been apprised. And now so have you."

"Shit!"

Arledge turned to grin at Wade. "Gotcha!" He laughed.

"Maybe," Wade replied, clicking off the light.

"Hey, Wade, what the fuck are you doing?"

"Saving the citizens of Miami a couple of cents. Use your federal batteries if you want to see anything else."

"You son of a bitch, Wade."

"Gotcha!"

CHAPTER FIVE

Bolan sat at the table, peering through a fog of cigarette smoke and clouds of dry ice. The nearly impene-
trable air, tinted blue, pink and yellow by swirling lights
mounted high overhead, was what passed for atmo-
sphere in trendy clubs in Miami. The music, loud and
bottom heavy, made the ice in his drink rattle steadily
against the glass.

The band occupied a platform swathed in dense car-
bon dioxide wreaths. Their flashy outfits, liberally
sprinkled with sequins and rhinestones, glittered inter-
mittently whenever the fog cleared enough for some
light to get through. Elevated above the dance floor, the
bandstand loomed up like an iceberg out of the sea of
smoke and darkness.

Down below, those who had nothing better to do
milled around on the dance floor. The dancers, wearing expensive clothes and as much gold as they could
carry, seemed to fall into two groups, more or less
evenly represented among the swirling throng. Half of
them had no sense of rhythm, and the other half seemed
oblivious to everything, including the heavy backbeat
laid down by two full drum kits and a trio of leggy
blondes rapping on everything from claves to tam-
bourines. The music made up in volume what it lacked
in subtlety. On the other hand, the narcotized dancers
probably wouldn't have noticed if everything went dead
at once.

Bolan hated places like this. They represented a kind of mindless hedonism, too lame to pass for the end of civilization, and too boring to interest anyone but the most masochistic sociologist. But Wade had told him to try Chico's Pub and to look for a Hispanic Mr. Clean. It would have been nice to have more to go on, but small favors were better than none. With the courier a dead end this was where he had to start again, this time hoping for a better break on the back end.

Glancing at his watch, Bolan realized he'd been there for a half hour. He saw the waitress eyeing him, downed the last of his ginger ale and hoisted the glass. She smiled, then pushed through the crowd, moving slowly, as if afraid the least exertion might raise what little there was of her skirt above the limit.

"Another one?" she asked.

Bolan nodded.

"Sure you don't want to try something a little stronger?"

"No, thanks."

She walked off, tapping Bolan's empty glass against her tanned thigh, and disappeared into the melee. Bolan turned his attention back to the empty table in the corner. The warrior had seen the burly skinhead, a thick-necked Hispanic with a Fu Manchu mustache, but the guy had vanished almost as quickly as he'd materialized.

Until Bolan got some feedback on the dead man and the papers he'd been carrying, there was time to kill, and this was the best place to do it in. If the skinhead panned out, he might get another thread to pull on, maybe unravel a little more of the dense fabric that seemed to shroud the drug ring so tightly.

The band took a break, announcing it with a brassy fanfare and a drumroll that was both too long and too loud. Before the musicians hit the floor, the sound system switched to a DJ who grinned out over the crowd from a booth behind the bandstand.

The waitress was back, another ginger ale in hand. She set it on the table with a crack, then smiled. "No way to drown your sorrows, honey. Not with that stuff."

Bolan slipped her a five. "Keep the change," he said. She smiled more broadly, tucked the bill into her back pocket and disappeared.

When Bolan turned back to Skinhead's table, it was occupied. The Hispanic wasn't there, but two men, one in an expensive suit, the other in a lime-green leisure suit, sat stiffly with their backs to the wall. Leisure Suit scanned the crowd, stretching his neck to raise his head as far as he could. The thick tendons on either side of his Adam's apple looked as if they would snap if he turned too quickly. Business Suit was less obvious in his survey, but no less attentive.

Bolan sipped his drink, trying not to stare. A reeling blonde, on heels too high and too sharp to keep her stable, grabbed on to Bolan's table. "Can I have this?" she asked, jerking one of the three empty chairs by its back.

The warrior nodded, and she staggered off, towing the chair behind on two of its legs. She had momentarily blocked his view, and when he could see Skinhead's table again, the man in the business suit was gone. Bolan stood casually, as if to stretch, but it was impossible to see anything in the sea of whirling bodies. Rather than call attention to himself, he elected to sit back down and wait for Skinhead.

Five minutes later the man in the business suit was back, followed by Skinhead. Bolan nursed his ginger ale while the three men leaned their heads over the center of the table. Hearing anything was out of the question, and trying to read lips was pointless. But it was apparent that Skinhead was unhappy about something. He kept shaking his head. Once, he slammed a fist onto the table. The glasses and ashtray on the table jumped, but in the deafening roar of the nightclub, it was like watching a silent movie.

Skinhead seemed to direct the bulk of his anger at the man in the business suit. Whenever the third man ventured to say something, Skinhead waved the words aside angrily, with impatience and contempt clearly visible in his face and the dismissive casualness of the gesture. As he grew more irritated, the scar on his scalp seemed to glow, as if molten metal coursed through a transparent vein.

After a half hour, Skinhead stood so abruptly that his chair tipped over. He kicked it aside angrily, shattering one of the struts and sending the chair skidding out onto the dance floor. Then he left.

Bolan was on his feet before Skinhead got halfway across the floor. By the time the burly man reached the front door, the Executioner was fifteen feet behind him, moving like a man who had just remembered something important.

Skinhead was outside a moment later. When Bolan pushed through the crowd in the doorway, all he could see of his quarry was the dull glare of neon on the polished scalp. Bolan slowed down as Skinhead waved a hand. A moment later a stretch Cadillac pulled up. The back door swung open and the man ducked inside. Through the tinted glass, it wasn't possible to see who else occupied the vehicle. Bolan started moving toward his own car, pausing just long enough to note the license plate on the big car. He had expected it to be a local rental, but it was neither. The big car had Louisiana plates, and they were customized.

Bolan sprinted through the fringes of the crowd and skipped through a side alley to the parking lot behind the building. His car was flush against the back wall between two cars. It was a tight fit and maneuvering out of the squeeze took precious time. By the time he got loose, the limousine was a block away.

He raced the light, just beating it, then slowed to fall in behind the limo. The Cadillac moved slowly, its body seesawing awkwardly over each hump and pothole. Bolan let a van and a convertible full of kids slip in between him and his quarry, then settled back to see where Skinhead might be going. Heading east on Calle Ocho, they passed through Little Havana, but the limo kept rolling at a steady clip, working its way through the congestion toward the east side.

Bolan nearly lost the Caddy once, just squeaking through an amber light. The convertible was long gone, but the van still hung in there. The warrior started wondering whether the van might be as interested in the limo as he was.

The van slowed for a turn, and halfway through the vehicle stopped. Bolan hit the brakes and jerked his wheel to the left, narrowly missing the van's rear fender. As he started to move around it, the vehicle backed up, braked and spun to the left. A moment later the brake lights flashed on again, and Bolan cursed as he was forced to swing wide. By the time he realized the limo was gone, the van had disappeared behind him.

Bolan slapped the wheel angrily, then doubled back to the previous block. At the corner he had two choices. He could go right, toward the ocean and the estates down along the shore, or he could take the left toward the shabby south side. It didn't take much to convince him which way the limo would most likely have gone.

A pair of taillights winked on and off about two blocks ahead, and the Executioner pushed his car to narrow the gap. If it was the limo, he couldn't afford to come up on it too quickly. But if it wasn't, the sooner he found out the better. He roared through another amber light, narrowly missing a Corvette that jumped the green on the side street. The sports car's horn blared behind him, and Bolan glanced in the mirror just as the gray van screamed out of an alley and rocked toward him.

The van swung sideways, blocking his way. Bolan jammed the Buick into reverse. A cloud of burnt rubber swirled around him through the open window as he backed up, but the Corvette had swung into the side street now and stood astride the white line. There was little room on either side. The warrior slammed on his brakes and sat for a second, listening to his engine idle. Two men scurried out of the van and dropped to their knees in the middle of the street. Bolan didn't have to see the guns to know they were there.

Kicking the vehicle into low, he swung up onto the curb between two parked cars and headed straight for the van. One man scrambled back into the vehicle while a second took aim over the hood of a parked car.

Bolan hoisted the .44 Desert Eagle and braced it on the windowledge, steering with his right hand. The warrior fired wide, narrowly missing the gunner, who fell backward out of sight.

At the corner his vehicle jumped off the curb, just missing a newspaper delivery truck, idling at a newsstand across the street. He fishtailed back into the side street and hit the gas hard. The van was no match for his speed, but there was no way he could hope to outrun the Corvette, not if the man behind the wheel had the faintest idea how to drive.

At the next corner he slowed just enough to check out the traffic situation, then barreled through a red light. The street ahead was empty now, except for the telltale red of the Caddy's taillights far in the distance. The mirror was empty, too. The van had vanished once again, and the Corvette—if it even was involved—had also chosen to disengage.

Flooring the gas pedal, he roared after the limo, hearing at the back of his mind Byron Wade's voice. *You have any idea about the hornet's nest you kicked open here?*

He did now.

CHAPTER SIX

"Fuck you, man. I'm getting tired of this shit! You tell that asshole Gardner it's not his war. Not anymore. It's mine, and I'll fight it the way I want to."

"Calm down, Willie, calm down. All I said was Gardner's getting a little antsy about the press."

"You think I give a shit what's in the papers?"

"That's easy for you to say. You don't have the *Washington Post* on your ass. Or the Intelligence Oversight Committee."

"There's ways to handle the press. The committee, too."

"Your ways are a little, shall we say, rough-hewn. I don't think Mr. Gardner can get away with that sort of thing. Look, we've got an election coming up in Nicaragua. The Arenas plan is a big deal on the Hill. And I don't think you ought to push so damn hard right now. Lay low on the drug shit."

"Politics is Gardner's problem. I've got to raise money any way I can. If he can't handle Congress, *I* can handle my end. As far as the papers are concerned, he should take a lesson from Nicaragua. In my country if we don't like what the papers say, we shoot the editors. Hell, Somoza did it for years."

"But it isn't your country anymore, is it, Willie?"

"And whose fault is that? You think *I* let that happen? Oh, no, my friend. Not me. It was your Mr. Carter who was afraid of a little blood. Human rights, he said." Guillermo Pagan spit in disgust, grinding his foot on the floor and turning to face Arledge for the first time since the interview began. "Human rights. For a little thing like that he cuts off the money. He doesn't do that, no way we lose. But he did, and we lost. Now look—"

"That's old news, Willie."

"Well, I got some new news for you, Arledge. For you and your Mr. Gardner. I don't need your money anymore. I can pay my own way."

"But that isn't necessary."

"But I want it that way. You think you own me because you send me your pitiful money, money Congress can cut off any time some pansy congressman hears about a beating? What good is your money?"

"It's not about control, Willie, and you know that. It's about restoring some semblance of order to Nicaragua."

"Non-Communist order, don't you mean?"

"Well, that goes without saying."

"*Nothing* goes without saying. Nothing."

"So what do you want me to tell Gardner?"

"Tell him whatever you like. I don't care."

"He won't like that. How am I supposed to explain what happened to McDonough? That was a stupid thing to do. Don't you know better than to use an easily traceable asset for something like that?"

"It is of no consequence. Besides, you handled it."

"He can stop you, you know."

"Let him try."

"I'm warning you, Willie. Don't do something you're going to regret."

"I already have, Mr. Arledge. I listened to your Mr. Gardner once too often. Now it's time to do it my way."

"Look, Bartlett is already pissed. He's trying to convince Gardner to cut you off."

"Let him. Maybe I cut him off first."

"I didn't hear that."

"Of course not. And I didn't say it."

"Look, I think I should warn you. You're not exactly the fairhaired boy at the Agency anymore."

"I can live with that."

"But can you live with Rivera?"

Pagan laughed. He collapsed into his chair, his head thrown back, and tears came to his eyes. "That old man? He's a buffoon. If Gardner prefers him to me, he deserves to lose his job."

Arledge was quiet. "I'm perfectly serious, Willie. They've already floated a trial balloon with the State Department. If it flies over there, Bartlett's going to suggest we go with Rivera. We want somebody up front, somebody we can get behind."

"The old man will never go along. He has no heart. All he wants to do is play tennis and watch the little girls. You think a man like that can conquer a country? Overthrow a government?"

"He can if we help him. Besides, all we have to do is give him a boost in the election. He can win with our help. Hell, almost anybody can beat Ortega right now."

"If the election is held. If it's held and if it's fair. Maybe. But don't count on that. And, anyway, you never know what might happen. Maybe Ortega will die before then. Who knows?"

"That option's been squashed."

"By who?"

"By Bartlett, who else?"

"Then unsquash it, damn it. What the hell do I pay you for?"

"I'm working on it."

"What does Gardner say?"

"He's thinking about it."

"Fuck it. It doesn't matter what he thinks, anyway. I can handle it. And leave Rivera to me. I know him like the inside of my own head. I know how he thinks, and I know what makes him weep in the night. He won't be a problem."

"If Bartlett pushes for him, I won't be able to stop it."

"Bartlett is a fool. He, too, is an old man. I met him four years ago. He came to Tegucigalpa with an entourage. It was like a king's progress. All the ceremony, the attendants, the stupid questions. He doesn't have any understanding of what's happening in Nicaragua."

"Don't underestimate him. He's DDO now, and he's a quick study. He's also a bit of an idealist. Anticommunism is fine, but not at any price. He has limits, and as far as he's concerned, you've already transgressed them."

"And I will continue to do so. Nicaragua is *my* country, not his, and not Gardner's. Mine. I was born there, and I intend to be buried there."

"You have to die first."

"I will, my friend, but not for a long, long time. There is too much to do. And Rivera can't do it. Only I can. Pastora, Bermudez, rank amateurs. Boys playing at politics. But politics is a man's game. It's not for the faint of heart. Not in Central America. You should understand that, Vincenzo."

"Will you at least promise me you'll exercise a little discretion in the meantime?"

"Ah, I understand. You still worry about the newspapers. That was unfortunate, but it can be handled.

And I'll make sure it doesn't happen again. But you have to keep your own house in order."

"What are you talking about?"

"I'm talking about the threats to my life and to my property. I'm talking about your Mr. Hoffman. He seems to have disappeared altogether. I don't think that's good news, do you? If Hoffman's been captured by the *piris*, which I doubt, he could be real trouble for us. If there's one thing I know, it's that a caged bird eventually sings. He has nothing else to do."

"We're working on that."

"You'll keep me posted?"

"Of course. I'm on your side, Willie. You must know that. But you have to be on my side, too. You have to work with me. I'll do everything I can, and so will Gardner. Just don't make things harder than they have to be."

"I wouldn't think of it."

Arledge rose to go. "I hope not. I can't do much for you if you do."

Pagan said nothing. He watched Arledge leave, then sat back in the chair. Things were getting complicated. He talked a good game, and he had Arledge worried. But he was worried himself, and he wasn't used to the impotence, the feeling of things slipping out of control. He didn't know what had gone wrong, but he was determined to find out and to fix it, no matter what.

Gardner worried him most. The CIA had been generous, and they had gotten him going. But he now felt as if he'd been used. They had made a fool of him in some way he couldn't quite define, but the knowledge chewed at him like some live thing in his gut. He worried that to kill it he'd have to risk his own life, and he didn't like that one bit.

Pagan knew, too, that he had himself to blame. He'd been too trusting, too naive. The Yankee promises came so easily, and they were just what he wanted to hear. He should have known early on that nothing was that simple. No one was that good to a perfect stranger, not unless there was something in it for him. He should have seen it, and he hadn't.

But as much as he blamed himself, Guillermo Pagan knew how to make himself feel better. Only a fool whipped himself when there was someone else to whip, and there was no shortage of candidates. He could start with Gardner, then move on to Bartlett, Arledge. One by one he could knock them down like clay pigeons. But that would solve nothing. So, even though he could do it, he wanted to find something better, a more perfect revenge, one that wouldn't call attention to him, not until he was beyond retribution.

But first he had to neutralize Rivera. If Gardner and Bartlett thought they had a viable alternative, the ground would begin to move under him. But if he was the only viable alternative to the Sandinistas, they would have to stand by him. That meant Rivera had to be out of the picture.

Pagan had a sneaking admiration for the old man, not least because he was everything that the younger man wished to be. Cultured, educated, handsome, even dignified. These were all attributes that Pagan could merely pretend to. And Rivera had been loyal without sacrificing his principles. This was the one thing Pagan envied above all else. He, too, had been loyal, but he'd never had to sacrifice principles because he had none. And, except in the darkest heart of the night, he was proud of it.

But maybe Rivera wasn't the problem. Maybe it was Bartlett. And if something happened to Rivera, wouldn't Arledge immediately suspect him now? He could have Arledge killed, of course, but that would be a shameful waste. Arledge was useful. He could get Gardner's ear, and if he had that, he had the ear of the President, the only ear that really mattered in the final analysis. So there had to be another way.

That he would find it, Pagan didn't doubt. That it would be easy, he wasn't as sure. But it was important to make a beginning. Once the wheels started to turn, things would happen, and he liked that. He was a man who made things happen, and he liked to be known as such.

But there were other, smaller matters to attend to. There was the missing shipment. There had to be some way to find out what had happened. He wanted to ask Arledge, but not tonight. He couldn't afford to show weakness at the moment. He'd have to find some way to work on Arledge to get what he needed, even if it was just a scrap of information, a rumor, anything that might lead him where he wanted to go.

After all, he thought, he was paying the man. Why should he hold out? What were these little things? These facts? They were nothing to get upset about. They were, after all, just bits of information, things you could reduce to holes in a card, or numbers on a magnetic tape. Arledge shouldn't be so stingy. Or was that all there was to it? Maybe Arledge had his own agenda. If he took money from two masters, why not three?

Why not?

CHAPTER SEVEN

Gil Hoffman sat in the motel room, staring at the bottle in his hand and half listening to the radio's blaring Muzak. He needed a drink, needed one badly. He'd already had a few, but this was no time to be particular. He snatched angrily at the smeared water glass on the table in front of him, tilted three fingers of the cheap whiskey and downed it in two quick gulps. He winced as the rotgut flamed down his gullet like lava, choked back the impulse to gag and wiped a hand across his tearing eyes.

His nerves were gone, and the whiskey would do nothing to restore them. All it would do was kill the awareness. He could function on autopilot for a while, until the need for his next dose of anesthetic became too insistent to ignore. When the DJ announced the time as 2:00 a.m., Hoffman set the glass down slowly and watched his hand for any sign of the shakes. The glass descended smoothly, and he managed to make contact with the table without a sound. He was ready.

It was still drizzling when he stepped outside, locking the door behind him while glancing at the empty parking lot across the street. He might have been wrong about the car he'd seen earlier, but it didn't pay to get sloppy, not now, especially. He climbed into the beat-up Ford and fumbled for the ignition. Despite its ratty exterior, the Ford was a crackerjack, and the full-throated rumble of the bored engine made the whole car quiver like a skittish horse.

He backed away from the motel, letting the car coast, then jerked the wheel and eased up on the clutch. First gear was a mother, and the car jumped, its tires hissing on the slick pavement. The squish of puddles sounded like Niagara to his sensitized ears. He was certain every one in the motel was peering through the curtains, as if they weren't used to late-night goings-on.

He was going to have to go to Bartlett sooner or later. But when he went, he wanted more than guesswork and innuendo. He needed something solid, something he'd seen with his own eyes at the very least. The web of intersecting rumors was more than enough to convince him, but Bartlett was another matter. Too much logic and not enough instinct in the man, as if tweed somehow prevented your sixth sense from picking up signals.

Hoffman had the most tantalizing of leads, but he was walking a tightrope. There was a chance, one he didn't even want to consider, that Bartlett was already aware of what was going on. If that turned out to be true, and if he called attention to it—and to himself— he was cutting his own throat. But he couldn't believe, didn't want to believe it. Bartlett wasn't that kind of man. About Gardner he was less certain, but, in all fairness, he didn't really know the new DCI. Field agents seldom got to hobnob with the big boys, and Hoffman wasn't kidding himself. He was the quintessential field hand.

On the other hand, guys like Vince Arledge were all too common in the Agency. High-strung, impatient, smarter than everybody else—or so they thought—they got tired of the restraints. They saw the goal, and they wanted it quick and—if necessary—dirty. Getting it done was all that counted. Unfortunately they were so tightly focused that they lost sight of the big picture. He'd known Arledge in Angola. The man had a reputation for a short fuse and rather loose interpretation of the rules, such as they were.

That Vince Arledge was sitting on Guillermo Pagan's shoulder, like some perverse Jiminy Cricket, didn't look promising. The meet was scheduled in less than an hour. Hoffman wasn't entirely pleased with himself for his suspicions, but the one thing he knew so far was that drugs were coming into Homestead under Agency cover. And somebody had to know about it. Chuddy Johnson said it was Arledge, but Johnson might have been bluffing. In any case, Johnson was dead. That meant he had to find the next rung on the ladder, or somebody who knew who it was. There wasn't a better candidate than Vince Arledge.

Homestead was a secure base, but it was wide open if you knew where to look. And Gil Hoffman was in the know. The Allpoints Transport hangar was tucked away in a far corner, only fifty yards from the chain-link fence surrounding the far reaches of the base. There were patrols, but they wouldn't pose a problem. Hoffman didn't have to go over the wire to see what he wanted to see. Night glasses, a telephoto lens and some infrared film were all he needed. He patted the camera case on the seat beside him, letting his fingers drum on the soft leather.

Route 821 took him right past the base. The marshland on the perimeter hadn't been developed because Uncle Sam owned it. Hiding the low-slung Ford in the tall grass wouldn't be a problem, either. All he needed was a little luck, and it was about time for some to come his way. It was more than overdue.

The highway glared back at him, the wet surface picking up his headlights and smearing them across the pavement. He turned off 821 into the opening to a service road, a narrow strip of asphalt that was seldom used. Few people knew of its existence. Hoffman had used Allpoints Transport before, and knew of the road because it had concerned him as a possible security problem. He left the engine running but killed the lights.

Hoffman opened the door, reached into the back seat and jerked the heavy bolt cutters off the floor. He looked both ways, but the highway was dead, nothing moving in either direction. A steel chain held the levered gate shut, but it was no match for the cutters. He ripped the chain off, then tilted the gate open. It didn't want to move at first, but finally, squealing every foot of the way, it tipped up enough for him to get the Ford past.

He dumped the cutters into the back, then nosed the Ford, still lightless, past the bar, scraping the roof on its underside. He coasted twenty-five feet or so past the gate, then went back to tug the bar back into place. Covering every base, he rapped the severed chain around the post, then sprinted back to the car.

The CIA man went the rest of the way without lights, goosing the engine once in a while, just enough to keep the car rolling forward. A mile off the highway the roof of the Allpoints Transport hangar rose above the tall grass between the road and the invisible fence. Hoffman got out of the vehicle to look for a safe place to stash it. In the unlikely event of somebody passing by, he didn't want the car spotted.

Testing the soggy ground carefully, he found a patch that seemed a little more solid than the rest and stomped around to make sure it was broad enough to take the whole car. If he had to leave in a hurry, the last thing he wanted was to get bogged down and have to escape on foot.

He nudged the Ford off the road rear end first and let it roll, ready to brake at the first sign that the car was sinking. The tail dipped once, but rose again almost at once. When he had it far back enough to conceal behind the tall grass, he got out, tugging the camera bag after him and leaving the keys in the ignition.

Easing into the grass across the road, he moved forward. The blades towered over his head, in some places reaching a dozen feet into the air. Every step sent small rivers of water rushing toward him. The footing was less than perfect, and he slipped once and fell to one knee. He'd broken his fall with one hand, but it sank into muck well past his wrist. The grass was tough, its edges sharp and spiny. It tore at his exposed skin and sawed at his clothing as he struggled toward the fence.

The flight was due in any minute, and Hoffman knew he'd have only the tiniest of windows. If he wasn't in position when the plane touched down, he mightn't get anything conclusive. Pagan wasn't about to waste time. The muck sucked at his boots, and thick clots clung to the textured soles, making every step that much harder.

Hoffman heard an engine in the distance, but it was too early to tell whether it was the Allpoints Transport. The sound grew louder as he floundered through the grass, which was beginning to thin a little as he approached the fence. It was a twin-engine plane, but he still couldn't tell what kind. The Air Force didn't use many prop jobs anymore, but Homestead was used by

Air National Guard units, and the Coast Guard kept a handful of patrol planes in its own hangar.

The red lights of the hangar roofline bobbed in and out of view then Hoffman broke through the last stand of tall grass. He was in waist-high weeds now, and mosquitoes swarmed up out of the standing water and settled on his bare skin like soft down. He'd forgotten to put repellant on and cursed himself.

The sound of the plane continued to grow, and he saw its landing lights to the southeast. The pilot wasn't wasting time on a flyby, and the aircraft swooped down out of the mist and rain. It touched down with a squeal of rubber, hitting an auxiliary strip and rolling out of sight on the far side of the hangar. He heard the muted rumble as the pilot feathered his props, then settled into a steady taxi.

Two minutes later, as he scrambled to thread the long lens in place, the plane reappeared, rocking over the expansion strips in the concrete. The lens screwed home, and the CIA man let the camera dangle from his neck while he used the night glasses.

Two men stood in front of a gray van left of the hangar, one almost totally obscured, the other visible only from the back. All he could tell was that the man was massive and that his head was shaved.

Hoffman switched to the camera and snapped two quick shots of the van. He knew he was skating on thin ice, because he was no photographer, but he needed something he could slam on Bartlett's desk, something to wave in front of his nose to make him sit up and take notice.

Through the viewfinder, he watched as the bald-headed man turned slightly and he clicked the shutter. Almost as if he'd heard the noise, the man turned to face him, and Hoffman snapped a second shot. Baldie tapped his companion on the shoulder, and Hoffman smiled when he recognized Vince Arledge. He snapped two more, then switched back to the night glasses.

The aircraft lumbered to a stop, and the pilot opened the cockpit door. He jumped down as Hoffman switched back to the camera, then he reached into the plane for a bag.

Hoffman was disappointed that Pagan himself wasn't there, but it would have been too much to hope for. He shot the rest of the film, then dropped to one knee to take the lens off. He was so busy fumbling with the heavy lens that he didn't hear the grass rustle until the man was almost on him. The CIA agent turned just as the gunner stepped out of the tall grass, a Galil in hand. He seemed surprised to see Hoffman and looked around as if some kind of practical joke had been played on him. In that split second of hesitation Hoffman hurled the camera, then dived to the left, slugs from the Galil hot on his heels.

He scrambled to his feet, dodging to the right, then to the left, hoping the guy chased him instead of emptying his chip. Hoffman tugged his own weapon free, but plunged on through the grass for several yards before turning to face his pursuer.

The man bulled his way straight through the eight-foot-high growth, and Hoffman could track him by the surging rasp of the jagged grass. He took dead aim on a spot just ahead of the charging man and was about to fire when he heard a shout. He hesitated for a second, and the guard stopped. Another shout echoed overhead, then sifted down through the grass.

Hoffman recognized the voice of Vince Arledge. Taking advantage of the diversion, the CIA agent backed through the grass as quickly as he dared, heading in a straight line toward the road. He heard the fence rattle and realized that Arledge or the bald guy, maybe both, had climbed the fence and joined the pursuit.

He sprawled headlong as he left the grass, tripping over the sharp incline and landing heavily. The wind was knocked from his lungs, and he lay there for a few seconds, sucking at the air and trying to shake loose the swarm of shooting stars slicing through his head. Then he crawled up the short bank and dashed toward his car. A jeep was angled across the road, but it was empty.

He darted around the vehicle and made for the Ford, hoping it hadn't been found. He was in luck.

The uproar behind him continued as he ripped open the door. The engine rumbled to life, and Hoffman forced himself to take a deep, calming breath before hitting the gas.

The tires slipped on the grass and mud for a second, then dug in. The car slewed sidewise but kept moving forward. When the front wheels reached the pavement, Hoffman jerked the wheel and hit the gas. The rear wheels spun furiously, then caught as he backed off on the pedal. The car lurched onto the roadway as two men charged past the jeep, one on either side.

Hoffman floored it as the first volley took out his rear window. The Ford jerked ahead with a squeal and a second burst of gunfire raked the roof. Hoffman kept his head below the dash, steering blind for a few seconds. He braked, slipping toward the edge of the pavement. Like a wise guy teasing a hitchhiker, he turned and looked back over the trunk.

When the tall guy got close enough, Hoffman fired three times, the big Browning 9 mm almost too much to handle in that awkward position. He saw the guy stumble then fall to one knee. The man's face, still wearing that surprised look, glowed an eerie red in the glare of the taillights. Baldie dived off the roadway into the ditch. Hoffman emptied the Browning and saw the red face disappear in a deep ruby geyser.

Arledge careered out of the marsh grass twenty feet behind the dead man. Hoffman saw him glance at the twitching corpse for an instant, then swing his pistol up into a two-handed grip. "Hoffman," he shouted as the bald guy turned and ran back toward the jeep. Headlights speared through the darkness, and Hoffman kicked the Ford into low and put the pedal to the floor. Arledge opened up, and Hoffman bent his head below the dash.

He knew he could take the jeep, but he had to stay alive long enough to open a little distance between the two vehicles. He was in third gear and doing sixty when he reached the wooden gate. He ducked his head and plowed through the barricade, jerking the wheel left and fantailing across the four-lane highway. He floored it again and stared at the rearview. He was a quarter mile ahead and widening his lead when the jeep lurched onto the highway.

He'd won this round, but he'd lost the camera—and the proof he needed.

CHAPTER EIGHT

The peeling paint on the weather-beaten sign read Showtime Freight Forwarders. The limo Bolan had been following was parked near a corner of the building, its roof glistening with rain. Steam rose into the humid mist, coiling up off the hood. The faint metallic ping of a cooling engine tolled like a tiny bell.

Bolan could hear nothing from the building as he listened at the door. He hadn't seen the men leave the car, but they had to be here somewhere. He pressed his ear to the door, but still heard nothing but the soft hiss of the swirling drizzle.

He tried the door, but it was locked. He slid along the wall, keeping one hand on the damp cinder block, and turned the corner. Down toward the water, a steel ladder, set in the wall and raised out of reach, led to the warehouse roof.

The warrior tried to reach the ladder by jumping, but it was too high. He looked around for something to give him an edge. The side of the building was clean. Bolan headed down toward the water and found himself confronted by a loading dock. A stack of empty freight pallets occupied one corner, nudged against a corrugated freight bay door. The warrior climbed onto the dock, hauled one of the pallets to the edge, then dropped back to ground level.

Lugging the splintery skid to a spot beneath the ladder, he leaned it against the wall. The lumber was rough and old, smeared with tar and spiny with splinters, but it looked sturdy enough for his use. Checking with one foot to make sure it was solid, he dug his toe into a crevice between two slats. Bouncing twice to get his rhythm, Bolan leaned toward the wall and strained upward. Quickly shifting his feet, he got a foothold on the top of the pallet. His balance was thrown off by the proximity to the wall, but he was high enough to reach the ladder. As he started to fall backward, his fingers closed around one rung.

Letting the ladder take his full weight, he swung free, feeling the metal give a little under him. Bolan dangled for a few seconds, then pulled himself up to the next rung. One more, and he was able to get a foot on the bottom rung. Scrambling up the ladder, he tumbled over a low retaining wall and landed on his knees on the roof. The broad, flat expanse sprouted a sparse thicket of pipes and conduits near its center. The cupolas of half a dozen skylights sat like a row of small garages along the back edge of the roof.

The uneven asphalt was covered with puddles. An odd collection of refuse littered the tar, probably tossed up by kids. A few beer cans sat in a pile, and broken light bulbs, bottles and assorted tin cans poked up out of the puddles, along with a healthy sample of the local geology.

Bolan picked his way carefully toward the nearest air vent, a black cylinder two feet in diameter that was topped with a metal lid. Inside, Bolan could just make out the slowly turning blades of the fan, moving in the slight breeze. Leaning close, he listened to the interior of the warehouse, which was just as quiet as it had seemed from the ground.

The glass of the skylights was grimy, but two of them glowed faintly with a dim light from far below. The warrior tiptoed to the nearer of the two, but he was unable to see anything in the interior. Dampening his hand in a nearby puddle, he rubbed at the dirt, reducing it to a muddy smear. He dipped his hand again, and this time succeeded in rinsing away some of the mud.

Directly below, columns of pallets poked toward the ceiling. A forklift was just visible in the shadows off to the left. To the right, a block of light lay on the floor, but he was unable to see where it came from. Moving to the next skylight, Bolan cleaned a four-inch circle and found himself staring down into a dimly lit cubicle.

A man sat in a chair in the center of the cubicle, his head lolling to one side. The Executioner shifted his position a little, enough to see the last few coils of rope that bound the man to his chair. One sleeve of his shirt was dark, possibly bloodstained. Other than the motionless prisoner and his chair, the cubicle was empty.

In an adjoining cubicle, a little more brightly lit than the first, three men huddled in conversation. Two of them sat on a leatherette lounge, the third, standing in front of a desk, stood over them, shaking a finger under their noses. The angle should have made identification impossible, but he had no trouble spotting the bald head and the atrocious lime-green leisure suit. As far as he could tell, the third man was a new player. Bolan moved to the other side of the skylight, hurriedly wiped another peephole, but still couldn't see any of the faces.

He ran his fingers over the metal edges of the skylight frame, looking for a joint. He knew that at least one of the panels would open outward. If he could find it, he might be able to pry it open. The waterfront side came up empty, and Bolan moved around to the opposite side. The middle panel had a double frame. He tried to get his fingertips between the edges, but the fit was too tight. With a utility knife, he was able to drive the point in far enough to risk trying to pry it free. The blade slipped off the soft metal on his first try, and he drove the point in farther before trying again.

This time he managed to wedge it open far enough to slip the blade all the way through. As he leaned into the handle, the frame began to squeak open. The warrior held his breath, working the panel with painstaking slowness, a quarter inch at a time. Each time the metal began to protest he had to stop. The panel hadn't been open in a long time, and grit and dirt filled the seam like brittle putty, making it harder to move the glass.

As the skylight opened farther, he could hear mumbled conversation. The glass was too filthy to see through, and he couldn't afford to take his eyes off the panel to peer through the broadening crack. To make matters worse, some of the grit was beginning to fall into the warehouse, a thin sheet of sand cascading over the freight piled to within ten feet of the ceiling.

The lock hinges finally clicked, and Bolan could let go of the glass. He dropped to one knee and peered into the gloom below. The men were still talking. Leisure Suit sat behind the desk, waving his arms with short, choppy strokes, their movement a stiff parody of a barroom braggart describing a recent brawl. The warrior tried to catch the words, but they were unintelligible.

Two of the men stood abruptly, Leisure Suit taking Skinhead by the arm and tugging him toward the door of the twelve-by-twelve cubicle. A moment later both men had disappeared into the shadows. The remaining man, so thin that looking down on him was like staring at the top of a post, slumped in his chair, a grim reminder of the posture of the man in the adjoining cubicle.

Bolan swung one leg through the opening, letting his weight balance on his hips as he swung the other leg in. Allowing his arms to take the weight, he lowered himself until they were fully extended. He felt for secure footing but couldn't reach the pallets stacked beneath him.

He was about to let go when he heard the sudden rumble of an engine. He realized one, and perhaps both, of the two men had left the warehouse and had already reached their car.

He looked back over his shoulder, trying to judge the gap. it looked to be only a couple of feet, not very far. He had no idea how securely the pallets were stacked, how well balanced they might be. If he threw that balance off with his full weight, he could send the whole stack tumbling to the floor, perhaps burying himself in the process.

As near as he could tell, he was off center. Pushing away from the wall, Bolan let go and braced himself for the impact. His feet went out from under him, and he threw his arms wide to keep himself from rolling off the pallet. The fall knocked the wind out of him, and he lay flat, listening to the echo of his fall bounce back from the far corners of the warehouse.

Gulping air into his lungs, he scrambled to his knees. Neither man seemed to have heard him. The prisoner remained motionless, while the second man stared at his own hands, as if he, too, were tied to his seat. Bolan peered into the shadowy pit below him. The pallets were banded, and the stack seemed reasonably stable, but getting down wasn't going to be a picnic. Getting down without any additional noise might be out of the question. But he had no choice. He couldn't reach the skylight, and the only way out was through one of the warehouse doors.

The third man finally moved, getting to his feet and walking toward the cubicle door. Bolan waited until he disappeared, then swung over the side of the tower of freight. Groping with his feet in the darkness, he found the next skid. It offered him a perfect foothold, and he secured both feet, then bent to grab one of the metal bands to steady himself while he felt for the next skid down.

Five layers down he finally felt the solid floor beneath his feet. He let go and let the floor take his full weight. He felt just a little unstable, like a seaman used to an unsteady foundation suddenly confronted with the weighty motionless of the earth after a year at sea.

He heard a door latch click and pulled out his Beretta. Setting the weapon for a 3-round burst, he moved toward the nearer of the two cubicles. A door slammed, and the vibration of the cubicle walls rattled glass all over the building. He reached the near corner of the cubicle and reached out with his free hand.

Easing along the wall, he felt for the doorframe. Just as his fingers closed over the metal molding, he heard a gunshot. It was the last thing he expected. Two more shots echoed through the warehouse as he leaped for the door.

Wrenching the knob, he nearly tore it loose as the door swung open. Bolan stepped into the room, his eyes adjusting to the changing light. The tall, thin man stood over the prisoner in the chair, his pistol pointing vaguely over the guy's shoulder. He turned as the door slammed into the partition, bringing the gun around slowly, as if he were underwater.

"Don't!" Bolan warned.

But the man ignored him. The gun, a Russian-made automatic, continued its lazy arc, and the warrior dived into the small room. He heard the next shot as he was coming out of a roll, brought up the Beretta and squeezed. Each of the three shots found its mark, leaving a ragged line of holes in the man's chest. His gun hand seemed to wave at Bolan as his fingers lost control of the weapon. It tilted forward, pivoting on the loose curl of his trigger finger, then fell. His body followed, collapsing on the floor.

Bolan stepped over the dead man and knelt next to the chair. The prisoner's head was thrown back, his eyes open but already sightless. An ugly hole, like the socket of a third eye no longer there, stared at Bolan from the center of the man's forehead.

Starting with the pockets of both dead men, Bolan searched the warehouse, working quickly in case one of the other men should return. Neither body yielded any documents, not even a driver's license. He left the bodies in the dim light and moved into the warehouse proper. Examining the freight by match light, he was stunned to find most of it consisted of weapons, primarily from the Eastern Bloc. There were stacks of Czech-made assault rifles and hundreds of thousands of rounds of ammunition.

One entire column of pallets contained crates of Soviet RPG-7s, another of grenades, both American M-59s and Yugoslavian M-69s. There was enough to wage a small war. What he couldn't figure out was the connection between an arsenal like this and a drug operation. Most of the cocaine cowboys favored automatic weapons such as Uzis and Ingrams. They were easier to conceal and, at the close range in which most burns took place, were accurate. Assault rifles were for some other kind of war.

In the second cubicle Bolan rifled the desk. A jumble of papers and notebooks filled the bottom drawer, and he sifted through them. It wasn't possible to make sense out of the crabbed notations, and the ledgers were neat but cryptic. It would take more time than he had at the moment to ferret out any secrets.

The warrior stacked the papers on top of the desk, then went back to the cavernous storage area. A minute's rummaging turned up a small canvas bag. It was heavy, and when he undid the drawstring he found phosphorous grenades. He dumped most of the grenades onto the floor, sprinted back to the cubicle, crammed the papers into the bag and ran for the door. He'd have to tell Wade about the bodies, but he wanted to piece a few things together before he made the call.

CHAPTER NINE

Emiliano Rivera allowed his body to sink into the soft leather of the chair. Leaning back, he adjusted the earphones more snugly and raised the volume a notch by remote control. The first notes of Chopin's Sonata no. 2 weren't loud enough to suit him, and he bounced the remote button twice more until he had a level he liked. Martha Argerich, the pianist, seemed confident and negotiated the tricky dynamics without apparent effort. It was interesting to hear a woman's approach to music he had always considered to be vigorously masculine.

But it was Chopin who was important. Chopin made him think of Paris, and Paris was where he had been happiest. He didn't know why, although he had thought about it often. Perhaps it was simply a matter of geography. Being so far from the turbulence of his native country might have been more soothing than he wanted to believe. But what would that say about his patriotism? Would it mean that, deep down, he loved his country less than he wanted to believe?

He sank deeper into the chair, letting the music swell around him, wrapping himself in the cascading sonority as if in cloth. He shrugged his shoulders to find the closest fit with the chair, heaved a deep sigh and reached for the television remote. He clicked on the set, then the VCR. The picture squiggled once or twice, then settled down.

The tape, addressed simply "To General Rivera," had been left on his doorstep several days ago. He had intended to watch it, but something kept interfering. After a while he started to suspect there was some reason he shouldn't watch it. But curiosity was an overwhelming force.

Fortifying himself with a dose of Chopin, he sucked in his gut and forced himself to watch. The tape started simply, the fuzziness and blurred focus evidence of the amateur status of the photographer. Then, as if someone else had taken control of the camera, the picture became crystal-clear, the camera rock-steady. The cloudless blue sky filled the screen, then trees appeared at the very bottom. As the camera moved slowly earthward, he realized why the tape had been sent to him. His father's house appeared to the left. The cameraman panned left, then zoomed in on the house, as if to say, "Yes, old man, it is what you think it is." As if he had to be reassured.

The screen went blank for a moment, and when the picture returned the vantage point was far closer to the house. A statue, formerly a nymph pouring water from an urn into a fountain, occupied the left of the screen now, and Rivera remembered how often he had sat on the grass beside the fountain, reading, listening to his tutor, even playing chess with his grandfather, who had built the house and had mortared the fountain with his own hands.

The nymph no longer had the urn. She no longer had arms with which to hold it, no longer had a head. The wistful smile with which she had watched the cascading water had been replaced by an ugly stump of broken stone, all that was left of her neck. Such destruction made Rivera shake his head. But he went livid when the camera pulled back and the cameraman moved left to reveal the graffiti spray-painted on the delicate breasts of the ruined statue. Even under the paint it was easy to see that some animal had defaced them, too, had chipped away the nipples, leaving lunar craters where the mounds had been. But the graffiti was the worst. In crude letters and cruder Spanish it said, "Fuck you, and your mother."

Rivera, his hands shaking so that he could hardly control them, pressed the freeze-frame button. Who had done this? And who had sent him the tape? Were they one and the same? But more than any other question, the ones that raced around his head again and again, like daredevil motorcycles in a wire basket, was why? Why do it and why tape it?

He closed his eyes and leaned back. He grasped one shaking hand in the other, as if the trembling of each would cancel that of the other. The music seemed a distraction now. He ripped off the headphones and tossed them across the room. Arrested by their wire, they stopped dead in the air, then fell to the floor with a crack.

Slowly Rivera allowed his eyes to reopen. He peered at the screen through a haze, not knowing yet that it was tears. Fluttering his lids, he felt the water collect in the corners of his eyes and wiped at it with the back of his hand. He clicked the play button.

A small yellow smear appeared in the background. The lens twisted and the blur sharpened, catching the arsonist in the act of withdrawing. The sudden rush of flame held Rivera's eye. He leaned toward the screen, holding his breath as the portico was bathed in a ghastly orange. The cameraman was shrewd. As if he had known Rivera's reaction, he zoomed closer, fixing first on the walnut doors, then on the hand-carved lintel, pulling back, lingering on the Doric capitals a moment, then pulling back farther. The entire house was awash in flame now. Presoaked and just waiting for the match, it went up like a refinery, soon all but hidden behind the inferno that consumed it.

Rivera searched backward, watching intently as the flames grew smaller and smaller and the house emerged once again intact from the flames. Again and again he watched as the holocaust devoured the last link to his homeland, then rematerialized as if refusing to die. Over and over again the house defied physics, defied time itself as it grew from the ashes without benefit of carpenters or masons then, in the blink of an eye, was reduced once more to a swirl of orange and a wreath of black.

He watched until he could stand to watch it no more, all the while wondering who had done it with such delicious malice and such deliberate cruelty, filming the entire thing. He froze the picture again, at the very moment when the last vestige of the stately mansion vanished in smoke and flame. The fire, even in its motionless state, seemed to flicker and swirl, the smoke to billow toward a heaven for which there was no room on the screen. Who had sent him the tape? He had to know.

The two questions swirled in his head like the flames that transfixed him, whirling faster and faster until they joined into a seamless blur of confusion. Without realizing it, he began to scream the questions aloud, over and over in an unintelligible howl. The door to his study burst open, but Rivera didn't notice. Two men, their fatigues smartly pressed, their weapons held at the ready, stood frozen in the doorway as their general slowly rose, still screaming words they couldn't understand.

Rivera shook his head, slowly at first, then faster, harder. Her hurled the remote control at the television, showing the final horrific throes of the ancestral mansion. The control shattered, bouncing off the glass screen. He wanted the screen to shatter, to fill the room with a sudden, acrid smoke billowing from a yawning hole in the set like the last breath of a dying man. He wanted to smell the flames, to feel their heat on his skin, to feel himself consumed with the same fury. Instead, he watched helplessly as the pieces of the remote control bounced soundlessly on the rug.

In helpless fury he kicked at the wreckage of the control, catching his foot in the wire of the headphone and pulling the jack loose. As if by the filmmaker's own design, the third movement of Chopin's sonata, the Funeral March, began to swell from the speakers, booming out at him in all its luxurious solemnity. He stared in disbelief at the headset that had given way, raised a booted foot as if to crush the offending device, then held his rage in check. Slowly he bent to retrieve the headphones, placed them back on his head, plugged them in again and sank back into the chair.

He reached for the CD player remote, then looked at the two men in the doorway. They stood stock-still, uncertain what to do. Then, as Rivera continued to stare at them, they began to fidget. He said nothing, his arm extended, the fingertips just pressing the metal remote.

Realizing that he wanted them to leave, but that he didn't wish to say anything, the taller of the two lowered his weapon and took a step backward, then another. The second man turned his head and watched his companion back slowly out of the room. When the first guard was gone, the second snapped a crisp salute, turned smartly on his heel and closed the door as he passed through.

Only then did Rivera pick up the remote control. It was as if someone watching him had punched a freeze-frame, trapping him there in all his pain, frozen forever in the agonizing moment. Then, freed momentarily, he moved quickly, uncertain whether he might yet be suspended in that hell another time.

He punched up the third movement again, then increased the volume, sinking back into the soft leather to enjoy the exquisite melancholy of Chopin's masterpiece.

The television screen was blank now, the freeze-frame long since having automatically shut down. He got up, not bothering to straighten, and took a second remote control from the television cabinet. He rewound the tape and started it over, watching one more time. This time, when the house was gone, he didn't try to make it reappear. He let the fire burn, as out of control as the fire in his blood.

And then, as if by magic, the smoke and flames were gone. On the screen, seen as if from a mountaintop, a figure moved in from the left, so small that it was impossible to tell whether it was that of a man or a woman.

The camera began to zoom in one more time, closer and closer, until the figure grew larger and then the focus shifted and zoomed again, this time zeroing in on the face. And all his questions were answered in a single instant as the lips moved and a hand waved a casual salute before the screen went black.

Then, the last notes of the piano fading away, he tossed the earphones aside and reached for the telephone. He had plans to make.

And vengeance to exact.

CHAPTER TEN

Byron Wade was a fountain of information. Unfortunately most of what he had was more suggestive than conclusive. He had tantalizing hints and fascinating coincidences, but nothing more than that to go on. Hampered by a lack of manpower, constrained by laws designed to protect the best of society and easily abused by the worst of society, he was more than happy to share his information—sketchy as it was—with his visitor.

Mack Bolan was back to square one. The warehouse wasn't exactly a dead end, but it would take a few days to unravel the tangle of notes and coded entries. Until that had been done all he could do was troll.

"So what can you tell me about this guy Pagan?"

Wade laughed. "Oh, hell, I could play Scheherazade, if you want. There's a thousand and one stories, easy. Let's start with the bare bones. Pagan was a colonel in the National Guard under Somoza. Sometimes I think half the people in Miami have some connection to Somoza. 'Somocistas,' they call 'em. Animals would be more appropriate. I watch the tube, I see these revolutions all over the globe, and you know what? Half the time I don't blame the people. Anyway, Pagan got here around 1980, maybe early '81."

"Why would he have all those arms in the warehouse? It looks more like something for a war than drug running."

"First of all, running drugs in this part of the country *is* a war. We've got factions and splinter groups. We've got the boys from Medellín. We've got the Mafia. Hell, we've got Panamanians, Colombians, Bolivians, Salvadorans, Peruvians, Ecuadorians, Uruguayans, Paraguayans. Stop me before I forget somebody. We call it the OAS, the Organization of American Smugglers. Pagan's a shark, but there are lots of sharks, so you protect yourself. If you're in Pagan's shoes, you don't trust anybody."

Bolan sipped at the coffee. "I think there's more to it than that, Lieutenant."

"Why?"

"It's the kind of weapons. Sure, assault rifles, submachine guns, maybe even a few rockets of one kind or another. That I can buy as a smuggler's arsenal. But case after case of grenades, assault rifles by the hundred, hundreds of thousands of rounds of ammunitions? Come on, Wade, you don't believe that's just an ordinary stockpile any more than I do."

Wade stood and walked to a cupboard over the sink. He opened the door and moved a few items around on the shelves, looking for something. When he found it, he turned back to the table. He sat down heavily, unscrewed the cap from the bottle and poured about an ounce of J&B into his coffee. He held the bottle out to Bolan, who declined.

"All right, look, I have my suspicions, same as you. But I can't do anything about them. Policy, you see."

"Whose policy?"

Wade shook his head. "I don't know."

"But you can guess."

"Yeah, I can guess. We're talking mid-Atlantic here, Delmarva Peninsula."

"CIA?"

"Maybe, maybe not. Look, there's more subterranean types running around this city than you'd believe. When I worked vice, every time I got close, some asshole with a federal shield would show up, flap his leather in my face and walk off with the perp—*and* the dope *and* the guns. You name it. Hell, it wouldn't surprise me if one of them was working on a nuke, for Christ's sake. I got fed up and asked for a transfer. By that time, they were more than happy to oblige me. I guess I was getting to be a pain in the ass."

"You ever find out what was really going on?"

"Not for sure, but I got a hunch or three. Now let's focus on Willie boy. That's who you're after, anyway. See, he's got some juice in D.C. I don't know how much, and I don't know what kind. But I know it's real juice. Because I had my wrist slapped the one time I went nose to nose with him. And I'll tell you this…that scumbag's got a rep for nasty shit. Barbaric, inhuman actually."

Bolan took another sip of his coffee. "You were telling me about Pagan."

"Look, the guy you took down, or ripped off or whatever the hell you did to him, was a Pagan gofer. He had one foot in Pagan's camp, one in free-lance and a hand in Langley's pocket. I don't know what he did with the other hand. Counted his money, I guess. Anyway, I did some digging, rattled a few cages, called in a few chits. Whatever. Seems your boy McDonough was a regular courier for Pagan *and* was wired to a bunch of spook types for years. I don't know whether he was spying on Pagan for Langley, or watching Langley for Pagan. Maybe both. So some asshole from Uncle shows up and tries to pick my brains. He was curious about what happened, but he didn't seem surprised. If I had to guess, I'd say he knew more than he let on, but you can't always tell, because they try to make you think that whether they do or not. It gets on my nerves."

"Lieutenant, I'd appreciate any help you could give me on this."

"Look, Belasko, I don't know why I should help you, but I'm already doing what I can. I been looking through files, checking where I could, that sort of thing, but I can only do so much. I know you're plugged in up north, and that's great. You take a little scum off the pond, that's even better. But there's just so much I can do to help without getting my own ass in a sling. And I know your clout doesn't extend far enough to catch me when I fall. I've got a family, and they come first. Anything I can do, I will. But you've got to be patient, and you've to let me decide how far I can go."

"Fair enough."

Bolan stood to go. Wade poured a little more booze into his coffee, finished the cup and walked Bolan out to the front yard.

STANDING in the full-length window overlooking his garden, Guillermo Pagan ran a hand through the tangled black curls cascading down the back of his neck. He was on edge, and his head ached. It was always like that for him. The ache would come when things got rough. It had been that way as long as he could remember. In the old days there was something he could do about it. Now it wasn't so easy.

He knew, deep inside himself, that getting to that place again, where he had that kind of power, was the only thing that mattered. He was getting impatient, but he was afraid of overplaying his hand. He had the fools right where he wanted them. All he had to do was wait. Everything was falling into place.

Turning away from the window, Pagan sat down at the huge mahogany desk set well back away from the window. The glass was bulletproof, of course, but he still didn't like to sit too close. He opened the draperies only at night when it was too dark to see inside, and he never put the light on when the draperies were open. He knew that some people called him paranoid. They whispered behind his back that he was too suspicious, that he trusted no one but himself.

It was all true, but it wasn't paranoia. It was wisdom. It had been a long time coming for him, but it had arrived, and he wasn't about to forget a lesson so painfully learned. He had trusted others before, and look what had happened—he was a thousand miles from home, a stranger, at the wrong end of the power, dependent on its indulgence instead of exercising it, dispensing it with a stingy hand or a gracious largesse, as the spirit moved him.

But all that would change soon. He could feel it in his bones, the way an arthritic senses a coming rain. It was coming, and he was determined to be ready. This little misfortune with McDonough was too bad, but it wasn't fatal, not by a long shot. What disturbed him was not knowing who had done it. Usually he was able to obtain such information. But not this time, and he didn't like that at all.

Pagan leaned back in the huge leather chair and touched a button set in one of its arms. The draperies closed with a soft whirring sound. He touched another button and a light went on. It was too low at first, and he pressed another button to make it brighter. Slowly the room came into focus, and he jabbed the button once more to bring the light up another notch.

On the left-hand wall a map of Central America glowed under a pin spot. Pagan spent long hours in this chair, staring at the map. He wondered what was wrong with him, why he would want to go back to such a backward place as Nicaragua. He had it soft here, more money than God and anything he wanted. But somehow it wasn't enough. Somehow he felt as if he had been cheated out of something that was rightfully his.

Somoza had always told him that he would one day be in a position to take control of the National Guard, and he had looked forward to that day with great pleasure. It would have been a dream come true to have total control of such a machine. But Somoza, the clown, had screwed up. Unable to read the handwriting on the wall, he had dragged his feet too long and ruined everything.

If he had been willing to let go, to step aside and let a better man take charge, he could have kept his prestige and his money. All he would have lost was the power. But Pagan understood now—that was the rub. Power was more important than money to some men. Somoza had been one of those men, and he knew that he was one, too.

But there were still some things to be attended to. He had a business to run, after all. And there were things to arrange, plans to make. He was getting impatient, and his headaches were getting worse. He couldn't wait much longer. Arledge kept saying to go slow, to hold his horses. Warning him that too fast would ruin everything, Arledge kept dragging him down. The man was a deadweight. But for the time being he was useful. One day he wouldn't be, and then . . .

But that day wasn't now. There were still many uses for Vincenzo. It was hard, sitting and talking to the man, hard concealing what he really thought of him, hard to keep from reaching out and squashing him, the way one would squash an unpleasant but harmless insect. For that was all Arledge was—harmless and unpleasant. He'd been very helpful in the beginning, but that was a long time ago. Some people would say that he was ungrateful to feel that way about Arledge, but a powerful man had to have a cold heart.

Pagan intended to rule Nicaragua. And it wouldn't be long now.

CHAPTER ELEVEN

The house sat back among the palms, nearly hidden by a profusion of tall shrubs. The building itself was large and rambling, spreading out from a central courtyard in every direction. Like an amoeba unsure which way it should go, it probed this way and that with no apparent plan. Like many of the large homes in southern Florida, it was an architectural mishmash. The basic contours of imitation Spanish had been blurred by frequent additions, as bogus as the original, but with less concern for preserving appearances.

Overhead, a helicopter seemed to hang in the air. A pair of searchlights speared down at the house, their beams dancing on the orange tiles of the roof. The chopper's dual exhausts belched small flames and plumes of gray smoke. The strands quickly unraveled in the prop wash and were little more than a dull haze before they cleared the chopper's fuselage.

Pete Banazak shifted uncomfortably in the tree. His backside was sore from three hours in the branches, and the ants kept getting into his clothes and ripping pieces of his flesh away as if they'd been invited to a feast. All he could think about was the old Charlton Heston movie where the ants ate plants and livestock, peasants and pets, everything, in fact, except Charlton Heston.

He let the glasses fall to his chest and raised his partner on the small handset. Danny Weston came back with an edge in his voice, as if Banazak had a lot of gall to bother him.

"What now, Pete?" he snapped.

"You got anything on that chopper yet?"

"Negative . . . I'll let you know. See anything interesting?"

"Nope."

"Not even the *señorita*? It's long past show time, isn't it?"

"Maybe she takes Monday's off."

"Too bad. That tree's a bitch. That stuff I gave you do anything for the ants?"

"I think it just pissed them off."

Weston laughed. "I'm glad I let you try it first."

"You son of a bitch. You mean you haven't used the stuff yet?"

"Hell, Pete, the head of the FDA doesn't try anything on himself until somebody tests it first. Why should I?"

"Fuck you."

"Talk to you later."

Banazak grunted into the mike, then clicked off. He lifted the glasses again and trained them on the chopper. He didn't see anything he hadn't already seen a hundred times. He swept the house from end to end. Most of the windows were dark, and it looked as if everyone had gone to bed.

He wondered how Pagan could sleep with that racket. He thought maybe it was something you could get used to, but he knew he never would, and he doubted if Pagan would, either. There were times when he wished he was back home in Maryland, working the bay for clams. Hell, it was good enough for his old man, why did he have to be different?

He swept the glasses the width of the house again, just to have something to do. The man he was supposed to be watching, Guillermo Pagan, was about as elusive as Bigfoot. It seemed there were a dozen stories for every sighting, and a dozen sightings for every story. The trouble was, everybody talked about him and nobody ever really saw him. They thought they saw him, or they talked to somebody else who claimed to have seen him. And that was about it. A mystery man, for sure, but what else was Guillermo Pagan? All Banazak knew for sure was that if only one story out of ten was accurate, Guillermo Pagan ought to be skinned alive and staked out on an anthill.

Once second-in-command of Somoza's private army, Pagan now spent his time, if the rumors were true, running drugs to finance an overthrow of the Sandinista regime. But Byron Wade wouldn't confirm or deny any of it. All he wanted was someone to watch. He wouldn't even say what to look for. Since Wade was his boss, he did what he was told. And that's why Pete Banazak found himself sitting in a tree. Six years on the Miami police force had brought him this far, and no farther.

Watching the chopper without the glasses, he fidgeted nervously in the tree. Bracing his back against the trunk, he stretched out his legs and let them dangle on either side of his perch to relieve the cramping. The worst part of the assignment was that he and Weston were forbidden to do anything but watch. No matter what happened—and their orders were explicit on this point—they were there to gather information, and only that. Both men knew it was because Pagan was rumored to be well connected, to have friends in high places. And by high, it was understood, they were talking about something considerably more lofty than the mayor's office.

Danny Weston, ten years Banazak's senior, shrugged it off. He had four years to go for a pension. That was his primary goal in life, and the less he had to exert himself in the remaining four years, the happier he was. Banazak, on the other hand, chafed under the restriction. He had heard enough stories, and placed enough credence in them, to know that Pagan was probably responsible for half of the cocaine run through Florida. The word on the street was that Pagan was plugged into Medellín. On a wire between Colombia and Washington, drawn tight and razor-sharp, Señor Pagan tiptoed over Miami like a black angel. It would give Pete Banazak genuine pleasure to rap that wire once or twice with a stout stick to see just how good a dancer Guillermo Pagan might be.

The hypnotic rhythm of the chopper's whirling blades suddenly faltered, and the engine roared. The searchlights went out, and the bird began to climb. A pair of lights erupted from the southeast like spears of fire and raced straight at the chopper. Banazak couldn't see past the bright light, but it had to be coming from a second helicopter.

He got Weston on the horn, then shinnied down the tree and raced to the wall surrounding Pagan's compound. When he topped the wall, he paused as if frozen. A lance of brilliant orange raced toward the struggling chopper. The ball of flame was abrupt and total. Banazak knew enough about munitions to recognize a Stinger missile. The chopper, its parts starkly outlined against the bright ball of fire, now looked like a blowup schematic. All that was missing were the little numbers and arrows. The flames disappeared, as if sucked back into the tube from which they'd come, and Banazak heard the tinny racket of wreckage scattering on the terra-cotta roof and sliding to the ground.

He raced toward the house, drawn as much by his own excitement as by any thought that he might be able to do something useful. All the lights in the house went out. Someone had thrown a master switch, or cut the main power line. Even the floods were dark. Small pools of fire trickled down the roof where puddles of the chopper's fuel had spilled. They ran into the flashing and oozed along the gutters, outlining the roof in bright orange, like Christmas lights in July.

The floodlights flashed on again, but the rest of the house remained dark. Banazak heard a shout behind him and stopped in his tracks. The shout came again, louder, and he heard footsteps. Weston burst out of the darkness, racing toward him. "What the fuck happened?" he shouted.

"I don't know. Something blew the chopper right out of the sky. A missile, I think. The house is on fire from the chopper's fuel. That's all I saw."

Headlights slashed through the dense shrubbery to the right of the house. The squeal of tires was almost drowned out by the roaring engine as a limousine swerved around the corner and headed straight for them, bouncing across the lawn and through the carefully tended flowerbeds. A searchlight appeared in the sky, then swept across the lawn, tracking the limo. It picked Weston out, swept past him, then came back. Banazak shouted, but Weston didn't hear him. A minigun on the second chopper opened up, and Weston turned back toward the wall. Gouts of turf spouted around him as the gunner walked his 7.62 mm fire toward the stunned cop.

"Dan, get down!" Banazak shouted. "Hit it!" But Weston kept running. When the gunner found his range, Weston jerked like a drunken puppet, his arms thrown up over his head. He turned twice in an awkward pirouette. The gunner let go with a tight burst, and Weston was slammed backward. Chunks of flesh were torn from his body, and Banazak, hugging the ground twenty feet away, felt the sticky splatter of blood rain down on his neck and hands. Something stung his cheek, and he reached to wipe it away.

A sliver of bone protruded from his face, and he tugged it free, wincing with the pain. He realized the bone was Weston's, and he knew his partner was dead. The chopper roared past overhead as the limo dodged under the trees and skidded into the stone wall. With a tortured squeal, the big car sprinted along the wall, a geyser of sparks arcing up over its roof until the driver managed to get away from the jagged stone.

Banazak scrambled to his feet and rushed toward the motionless body of Dan Weston. The cop lay on his side, curled into a ball. His left arm lay alongside of him, splayed at a crazy angle, and looked as if it belonged to someone else. Banazak felt for a pulse, but there was nothing. Only then did he realize Weston's arm had been shattered at the elbow, the forearm still attached by shreds of cartilage.

Then he turned toward the wall and saw the limo sitting motionless under the heavy foliage. The leaves burst into a bright green as the helicopter tried to find it with the searchlight. Banazak climbed to his feet, looking stupidly at the automatic in his hand, then shook his head. A sharp hiss snapped him back to reality, and he looked back toward the limo as a rocket slammed into the wall just behind it. A second rocket whooshed away from the chopper, and Banazak raised his 9 mm Browning. He fired once, then just kept squeezing the trigger until the clip was empty. He started to run as a third rocket slammed into the limo.

An orange balloon inflated around the car, then it seemed to fold in two like a pocketknife. Its body, a flat shadow at the heart of the ball of fire, stood on its bumpers, like an awkward letter *A*. Banazak slammed a new clip into his Browning and dropped to one knee. He fired more methodically this time, chewing on the tip of his tongue and smiling as he saw the sparks where several of his slugs had glanced off the engine housing.

The chopper seemed to pivot on its rotor shaft, then started to climb. A pair of rockets screamed overhead, and Banazak heard them slam into the house before he could turn his head. The aircraft continued to climb, and he emptied his second magazine, then tucked the pistol into his waistband. He sprinted toward the house, now burning from end to end. Two huge holes gaped in the terra-cotta tiles where the last two rockets had torn into the building. Smoke spiraled up through the holes, catching the orange color of the fuel still burning in the copper gutters.

When he was within fifty yards, a second car roared around the corner of the house, this time heading straight for the gate. Banazak hollered for the car to stop, but if the driver heard him, he paid no attention.

The first siren moaned off in the distance, and Banazak was dimly aware that the world didn't end at the stone wall behind him. For a moment the thunder and the hellish glare of the burning limousine and building were the only things his mind had room for. Then he remembered Danny Weston. He wanted to turn back to his dead partner, as if it might make a difference, but he knew there could be people trapped in the blazing house. And he knew Weston, if he could, would tell him to help the living. That was what they got paid for. It was what they did best.

Or at least it used to be.

He didn't see the two men racing toward him from the wall. Banazak sank to the ground as the first burst of gunfire sailed over his head. If he hadn't gone down, it would have torn his head off. He turned in bewilderment. He spotted the shadows and started to bring his gun around. The two men had stopped in their tracks, machine pistols held at waist level. The loud report of another gun jerked his head to the left.

When he looked back, one of the gunners had gone down. The second seemed confused. He was yelling in Spanish, then jerked his gun around to fire into the darkness. A second shot cracked, and that gunman, too, went down. Banazak, galvanized by the sudden quiet, leaped to his feet.

"What the hell's going on?" he shouted.

"That's what I want to know," Mack Bolan said, stepping out of the shadows.

"Who the hell are you?"

"That's not something you want to know."

Bolan watched Banazak race toward him. The young cop seemed confused, his gun half dangling and half trained on the warrior. The big guy ducked back into the shadows. He could hear Banazak calling to him, but his work wasn't finished. The second limousine darted past him, its tires spinning on the slick lawn, then bounded toward the main gate and was gone.

Bolan vaulted the wall, landing lightly on the balls of his feet. He raced to his Buick. The engine was still running and the driver's door hanging open like an amazed mouth. The warrior kicked it in gear before the door closed and roared past the main gate, now a garish orange where the ruined limousine still spewed flames and sooty smoke into the night.

It was time Byron Wade came clean.

CHAPTER TWELVE

Hoffman sat for a long time watching Bartlett's house. When all the lights but one went out, he slipped from his car and crossed the road. The split-rail fence was no obstacle, and the long climb uphill through the knee-high weeds was tiring but negotiable.

He could kick himself for having lost the camera, but he knew what he'd seen, and that would have to be good enough. If he couldn't persuade Bartlett to at least investigate, he might as well pack it in. There was no way in hell he could ever turn his back on another Company man.

He approached the house carefully but without the usual paranoia. He knew Bartlett well enough to know that the man was a throwback. He still lived in the age of gentleman spies. No bodyguards, no television surveillance. Hell, he'd be surprised if Bartlett even remembered to throw on the hard-wired burglar alarm. But Winston Bartlett wasn't a fool, despite his affectations.

And Hoffman had seen the DDO on the shooting range. Executives at his level were excused from the semiannual qualification rounds, but Bartlett insisted on taking his turn. There were stories about him, some of them no doubt apocryphal, behind the Nazi lines. Wild Bill Donovan himself was said to have presented him with a special citation, and Bartlett, like a dwindling handful of other OSS boys, still worshiped at the old man's church.

Hoffman knew he was on slippery turf. All he could ask was a fair hearing, and if he didn't get it from Winston Bartlett, he wasn't going to get it at all. It was a fool's errand, but he couldn't walk away from it. Under his carefully cultivated veneer of cynicism, Gil Hoffman cared about the Agency that had been his life for twenty-five years.

Stepping over the low stone wall separating the meadow from the tailored lawn, he was startled by the sound of an automobile engine in the distance. He froze for an instant, then turned toward the sound, seeing headlights bobbing among the trees. It couldn't be that Bartlett was expecting anyone, because the house was all but dark.

When the car slowed, as if searching for something, Hoffman dropped down alongside the wall, pressing himself into the grass, not daring even to raise his head to look toward the driveway. The beams swept over him for a second, splashing a slice of his shadow against the stone, then lighting the redwood wall of the house. When the car's tires crunched on the gravel, Hoffman peeked over the wall for an instant. A light went on in the first-floor foyer.

The vehicle halted a few feet from the porch. The driver extinguished the headlights and turned off the engine. The man got out, but his face was averted, and Hoffman couldn't tell who it was. He crossed in front of the car, then mounted the steps. The porch light went on, but it was still impossible to see the driver's face. Hoffman could hear the door chimes, then the door opened.

Bartlett stood there, his suit coat off, but still wearing his vest and pinstriped trousers. He stepped aside to admit the visitor, then closed the door, pausing for a second to look out over the lawn as if he sensed something out there in the darkness.

Another light went on. Hoffman stared across the lawn into what must have been Bartlett's study. Books in leather bindings lined the wall opposite the window, then Bartlett blocked his view. He closed the draperies, and Hoffman was cut off, still not knowing who had come to call.

Hoffman waited patiently, debating whether to approach the house. He kept vacillating. It seemed odd that the man would have an unexpected guest at this hour, then he realized that it was no odder than his own purpose. And there was a distinct possibility of some connection between his presence and that of the caller.

What the hell, he thought, getting to his knees. He stepped over the stone wall, then sprinted straight toward the window of the study. It would be too much to ask for it to be open, but he still might be able to hear something useful. Pressing himself flat against the house, he paused to catch his breath, then rose on tiptoe until his ear was just below the windowledge.

Mumbled conversation rose and fell. Little scraps of words, pieces of sentences, seemed almost audible, but he realized he was interpreting the mumble by interjecting his own purpose and resolved to be more objective.

Moving the length of the wall, he reached a corner and found another window into the same room. This one was curtained but closed just as tightly as the first. Straining to get his ear to the glass, he nearly lost his footing. The voices were more animated now, not louder, but more insistent in their exchanges. Bartlett seemed to be angry, the visitor even angrier. But Hoffman still couldn't hear anything specific. It was all a matter of tone.

The voices died away, and he strained harder, then heard the click of a door latch. He heart Bartlett's voice around the front of the house, and realized this was his chance. The alarm would be off with the door open, and he tried the window. It resisted at first, but he dug his fingers under the sash, squeezing them in until their tips burned. He jerked upward and the sash rose.

He had to get inside before the door closed and the alarm went back on. Hauling himself up, he ducked his head through the opening and rested his chest on the sill. Using his shoulders, he shoved the window wider, then tumbled through, landing with a thud on the hard wooden floor. He got to his knees and tugged the sash back just as he heard the front door close.

Hoffman felt for his pistol, just in case, then got to his feet. The light was still on, which meant that Bartlett would be coming back. He stepped to the door, flattening himself against the wall just inside. He unholstered the pistol and released the safety. The knob on the study door squeaked, and he held his breath. A moment later Bartlett stood in the doorway.

Hoffman waited for the DDO to step through, then jabbed the pistol into his ribs.

"Are you alone?"

Bartlett turned slowly until he could see Hoffman's face. "So soon?"

"I said are you alone?"

"Yes."

"Good."

"I've been expecting you, Gilbert. I've been worried about you."

"Don't bullshit me, Bartlett."

"Bullshitting isn't a suitable pastime for a gentleman, Gilbert. Surely you know that. I wish I could say I'm surprised to see you, but unfortunately that's not the case."

"We have to talk."

"I should say we do. Why don't you put the gun away and act like a civilized man for a few moments, eh?"

"Come on, Bartlett, don't run that number on me. I'm not some jerk fresh off the farm."

"Of course you're not. That's why I assume you know how to use a chair. Sit down, Gilbert." Bartlett lowered his arms. He didn't seem the least bit nervous, and that made Hoffman suspicious. He was wired to begin with. And if Bartlett wasn't surprised to see him, then he might have his own surprise in store for Hoffman.

"You're somewhat of a desperado, I've been given to understand. Is that right?"

"I suppose."

"Then Mr. Arledge was telling the truth?"

"I don't know what he told you."

"Why not let him tell us both?"

Hoffman jerked his head toward the door, but Bartlett laughed. "No, no, no. He's gone. But his words are still with us."

The older man walked toward his desk. "Come over here where you can see me. I don't want you to get anxious and shoot me unnecessarily. Unless that's why you came?"

"No, I said we have to talk."

"All right now. Just be patient." Bartlett reached under his desk and pulled a small drawer open. He pressed a button, and Hoffman heard the whirring of tape. "Sit down," Bartlett said. "This will take no longer than it just took, eh?"

He pressed a second button, and Hoffman heard the hum of an amplifier, then Bartlett's voice, telling Arledge to sit down. Ignoring his superior's advice to sit, Hoffman stood rooted to the spot while he listened to a replay of the conversation that had just taken place. This time he could hear it all plainly. Too plainly. And he was almost amused to realize he hadn't unfairly been projecting himself into the middle of the conversation. He was, in fact, the principal topic.

The two men raised their voices as the tape wound on, then reached an abrupt conclusion. There was the sound of forced pleasantry, then a brief pause as the voices faded away. Finally there was the unmistakable sound of a window being raised and the hard thump of bone on wood. "I trust you did no permanent damage when you landed," Bartlett said.

Stunned by what he had just heard, and not knowing what else to do, Hoffman answered the question. "No, I'm all right."

"Good . . . now, will you please sit down?"

"You don't believe that garbage, do you?" Hoffman demanded, beginning to recover.

"How can I know what to believe, Gilbert? I have, after all, just heard a most extraordinary set of allegations. You're accused of an interesting variety of crimes. And by a man in my employ. What *am* I to think?"

"I'm in your employ, as you put it, too. The question, it seems to me, isn't what, but whom?"

"Fair enough. Why don't you let me hear your side of things? But first let me ask you one question."

"All right . . ."

"Did you or did you not leave Honduras without authorization?"

"Yes, I did."

"And I assume your reason for doing so is at least one of the reasons you've come to see me, as well?"

Hoffman nodded.

"Very well, Gilbert." Bartlett sighed, then collapsed into a chair. "Get on with it."

Bartlett leaned back in his chair, perfectly at ease. He listened intently, nodding from time to time, but he didn't interrupt. When Hoffman concluded, Bartlett stroked his chin thoughtfully. "You say our proprietary is being used to smuggle cocaine?"

"Yes."

"And that Guillermo Pagan is masterminding the scheme, with help from Vincent Arledge? That's a pretty tall tale, Gilbert. Do you have any proof?"

"Only what I saw. Just my testimony. And, of course, Chuddy Johnson's body, and that of the man at Homestead."

"It may interest you to know that Johnson is simply missing, according to the official version. And there has been nothing at all on this other business."

Hoffman shrugged. "What can I say? I know what I know."

Bartlett paused to light his pipe. He hummed softly while he packed the tobacco, then lit it with a wooden match. When the first real curl of smoke spiraled over his head, he said, "Do you know a man named Donald McDonough?"

"No. Should I?"

"I suppose not. It just seems odd that he's now dead, that he's a former contract agent, and that he was killed while attempting to deliver a rather large quantity of cocaine from a freighter offshore. Odder still are the rumors that hint at a connection to Señor Pagan."

"But, of course, Vince Arledge is COS in Miami," Hoffman said. "So..."

"Exactly. I want you to do something for me, Gilbert, if you will. Unofficially, of course. I want you to talk to a man named Byron Wade, a Miami policeman."

"What about?"

"I'll give you all the details. But I want you to understand that this doesn't mean I'm totally convinced of the truth of your story. Although, in all fairness, I must tell you I'm inclined to accept it. And bear in mind that, as far as the Agency is concerned, you're absent without authorization, so be careful. No matter what happens, report to me, and only to me."

Hoffman shook his head. "I don't suppose I have any choice in the matter?"

"No, Gilbert, I'm afraid you don't. By the way, you don't know anything about an attack on Señor Pagan's home, do you?"

"Only that it sounds like a good idea."

"I'm beginning to think the same thing. Convincing our esteemed interloper is another matter, however. But that's not for you to worry about. Now here's what I want you to do."

CHAPTER THIRTEEN

The C-47 looked like an early casualty in a demolition derby. The only things new about the plane were the freshly painted logo on both sides of the fuselage and the registry number low on the tail fin. But Allpoints Transport didn't exist and the number wasn't real. That didn't bother Tony Gregory. He'd been living in a surreal world for fifteen years. It was the only place where he was comfortable.

He sat on an oil drum and watched the cargo roll aboard. A dozen men in fatigue pants and khaki undershirts wrestled the wheeled pallets up the cargo ramp and into the hold. Gregory had no idea what was in the crates, and he didn't want to know. The less you knew the better off you were. He'd decided that early on, and the intervening years had done nothing to change his mind.

Gregory waved to Juan Corona, one of the two kickers who were making the flight with him. Corona stumbled toward him through the dust cloud kicked up by the freight handlers, a crooked grin not quite at home under his bushy mustache.

"You're late," Gregory accused.

Corona laughed, even though he knew Gregory wasn't joking. It was what Juan did; it was how he got along in the world. He stuck a big cigar in under the mustache and clicked his lighter. He tugged on the flame, sucking it into the cigar for a few seconds, then tucked the lighter into his pant pocket. He took a couple of puffs, then sat down next to Gregory's barrel.

"It's just a job, amigo. You shouldn't be so serious all the time."

"The day I'm not serious is the day we don't come back, amigo."

Corona shrugged. "Fine, then you be serious. I want to come back here, for sure. I'd miss the lavish appointments, the luxurious accommodations, the elegant dining. Most of all, I would miss the beautiful *señoritas* lounging around the pool. I guess you would, too, eh, Tony? I guess that's why you're so serious."

"Fuck you, Juan."

Corona glanced at his watch. "We still lift off at eleven?"

"Supposed to."

"No way. These guys are too damn slow. More like noon."

"You got something else to do, Juanito?"

"Sure, amigo. I've always got something else to do. I'm only here for the money. Just like you."

Gregory laughed. "Money? That what you call it?"

"Don't kid a kidder, Antonio. You think I don't know what you do when you get back here? You think I don't know what goes on the plane before you go back to Miami?"

"I think you better *not* know. That's what I think. And I also thing you should keep your lip buttoned. This isn't like that. This is special. This shit isn't for the contras, amigo."

Corona seemed interested all of a sudden. "What, then?"

"I don't know. But it's different. Something's shakin', and I can't figure it. Besides, you're not supposed to know about the other shit, either."

"Why shouldn't I know what everybody else knows?"

"Because everybody else has sense enough to pretend they *don't* know. But not you. You have to flap your gums to every fucking whore in Honduras. You have to hang out with newspapermen and tease them. You think you're smarter than they are, but you're wrong, amigo. You drop one damn stitch and they pull the whole fucking sweater apart with you inside it. And you know what that leaves you, amigo?"

"What?"

"It leaves you naked, buddy. And nobody, especially not politicians, wants to help a naked peon. Not you, not me, not any of us. Believe it, Juanito, if the shit hits the fan, we take it all."

"You're too cynical, Tony."

"You think so? Just wait."

"Wait for what?"

"For somebody to turn on the fan."

Gregory stood and stretched. At six-two and 210, he was carrying more weight than he was used to. It was solid weight, but he felt slow, sluggish. Under the tan, he felt as if he were slowly melting, turning into that worst of all relics, a hard man gone soft. And he had a bad feeling that it was about to catch up with him.

He ran one thick finger across his upper lip, feeling the raspy stubble of his vanished mustache. It itched, and he thought about letting it grow back, but he needed to see something different in the mirror for a while. "I'll see you later," he called over his shoulder. "I'm gonna try to build a fire under these clowns."

Gregory shuffled through the dust until he found the chief of the freight crew. The two men argued, and Corona watched with detached amusement. Then Gregory waved a finger pointedly under the chief's nose and stormed off. Corona closed his eyes and lay back on hands clasped behind his head.

The next thing he knew, Gregory was back, kicking the soles of his boots. "Come on, Juan, let's move it."

Corona shook his head to clear it, then scrambled to his feet. "What time is it?" he mumbled.

"Noon."

Corona grinned. "See, I told you, amigo."

Gregory walked toward the open bay of the C-47 and climbed the ramp. Pedro Ramirez, the other kicker, waited just inside the bay door, sitting on a pallet. When Corona climbed the ramp, he pushed a red button to close the door. The whine of the servo made the plane vibrate, and the skin of the plane seemed to hum. A transport version of the DC-3, the C-47 had been around for more than forty years. But it was a good plane and, if you treated it fairly, a reliable one. This one had seen better days, but he'd rather be in a worn-out plane he knew than a classy-looking fraud with bells and whistles.

Gregory walked forward to the cabin and dropped into the pilot's seat. He draped the headset around his neck and set his controls before kicking over the plane's twin engines. The old Douglas looked like a piece of crap, but the maintenance was halfway decent and the engines were in good shape. As soon as the engines caught, and the stuttering cough settled into a steady rumble, Gregory felt the tension drain away. This was where he was happiest. It made all the rest of it bearable.

The plane started to roll over the grassy strip, and he barked a warning over the intercom. Corona and Ramirez were pros, and they would take care of themselves, but Gregory liked to follow a routine, and a warning was part of it. The strip was short, and Gregory had the engines going flat out. Even so, they barely cleared the trees at the far end of the tiny airfield.

He remembered somebody telling him that it cost a 150 dollars a yard to clear a jungle strip. For this particular job they must have been on a tight budget. Another hundred yards would have made it a lot more comfortable.

But they cleared the canopy, and he made a tight circle around the strip before setting a course toward San Mateo de la Cruz. It was his first flight to that particular base. In fact, he'd never even heard of it until two days ago.

The rolling terrain beneath the plane was a challenge. As with all clandestine flights, the primary concern was avoiding detection. Gregory knew that it was even more important than getting the freight to its destination. Better that it not arrive than that its existence be discovered. The problem with flying under the radar was that it brought the plane within range of dozens of potential hazards. Even a lucky rifle shot could bring down the aircraft.

Gregory liked to go for the direct route. Instead of heading along the coast and then zigzagging back inland to his drop, he made straight for it. He worked on the theory that the less time you were in the air, the less likely you were to get shot out of it. It was a hazy day, and little wisps of morning fog still clung to the high canopy. The absence of bright sun was a blessing, making it easier on the eyes, easier to see whatever might be happening below.

He couldn't use his own radar, because it would betray his presence, so he was forced to rely on instinct and eyesight. Patches of jungle jutted up higher than the surrounding canopy, and as he broke over the Montañas de Colón, the trees thinned and he could see the forest floor. The dozens of streams and lakes looked like patches of gray. An occasional village flashed by, animals scurrying in fright. Used to the bizarre traffic just over their heads, the villagers no longer bothered to look up.

The cabin door opened, and Corona dropped into the copilot's seat.

"Easy flight, huh?"

"So far."

"Relax, amigo. Today is like every other day. Someday soon you'll retire with a fat bank account. You'll find some *chica* with big tits and buy a house in Brazil or someplace, eh?"

"I already have a family."

"Me, too. So what? A little change never hurt nobody."

"Juan, you're one callous son of a bitch, you know that?"

"Hey, I do my job. I don't hurt nobody. That's all a man can be asked to do, right? Leave other people alone? I'm entitled to have a little fun once in a while."

"You and Pedro ready?"

"What's to be ready? We open the door and kick the shit out. Nothing to it. This isn't rocket science we do, amigo. We're burros, that's all. Except that the pay's good."

"I take it you're ready, then?"

"We're ready. How long?"

"Ten minutes, maybe fifteen. We just passed Santa Rosa. I just hope I can find the drop. There's supposed to be three fires in a triangle three miles downriver."

"They'll be there. If not, we dump the stuff, anyway. It's not our fault if they fuck up, no?"

"We have to. We don't have enough fuel to get back with a full load."

"So..." Corona lifted his leg and flexed the knee. "See that, already warmed up, amigo."

"Oh-oh."

"Don't kid around, amigo."

"I'm not kidding, Juan. Look..." He pointed dead ahead. "There, see them?"

"No man, I don't see...wait, yeah, yeah. Holy shit!"

"I don't like it. We haven't even gotten to the Rio Segovia. The border's five miles past that. What are they doing here?"

"Maybe they're Honduran."

"No way. Wrong profile. Those are Russian-made choppers. Got to be Nica."

"So what? They won't do nothing, man. They know better."

"Sure. Just like we know better, right?"

"What are you gonna do?"

"I don't know. You better go tell Pedro to nail his ass to the floor."

Corona left the cockpit, and Gregory jerked the plane into a sharp bank, heading west. The two choppers must have seen him, because they climbed up off the canopy. In the gray-white sky it was easy to peg them as MI-24s. They changed direction, also heading for the coast. Gregory knew he could outrun them, and he could outclimb them. But if the choppers carried air-to-air missiles, he could do neither.

The pilot of one of the choppers tried to raise him on the radio, but Gregory ignored the question, opening the throttles to eighty percent. The old engines grumbled, and the plane shuddered under the strain. So far he could still see the choppers, and he'd seen nothing to indicate hostile intent. In another minute he'd be far enough ahead that he could no longer see them through his canopy. The trailing chopper was almost out of sight already, the lead Hind a little closer.

A small bright flower grew toward him on a long gray stem. The missile streaked across the jungle, and he jerked the stick, trying to haul the C-47 into a climb. But the freight was heavy and the plane sluggish. There was no way he could outrun the missile.

He heard the explosion, and the plane shook like a rat in a terrier's jaws. He tried the intercom, but got no answer. His controls were gone; the plane no longer responded to his directions. He clicked on the autopilot, but nothing happened. Climbing out of his seat, he opened the door to the cabin and pushed through. A small hole—no more than a foot across—in the left of the fuselage was echoed by a much larger hole on the other side.

For some reason the missile hadn't detonated on initial impact. It didn't blow until it was inside the plane. Corona lay on his back, one arm flapping out of the plane. Pedro was nowhere. The explosion had taken him—and the pallet he'd sat on—right out of the plane. Only the jumbled cargo crushing his legs had kept Juan Corona from following Pedro out into the wild blue yonder.

"Holy shit!" Gregory shouted. He sprinted to where Corona lay, but knew, even before kneeling, that the kicker was dead. He checked for a pulse, found nothing, then raced to the far wall for a parachute. He slipped it on as the plane nosed into a shallow dive. One engine coughed, and a plume of black smoke waved along the fuselage, shrouding the hole in a dense cloud.

Gregory clicked the chute harness closed, then threw several heavy crates aside to get Corona's body free. Picking the dead man up by the arms, he clasped the body to his chest and staggered toward the hole in the fuselage. Gripping the rip cord in one hand, he jumped, dragging Juan with him. Choking on the black smoke, his eyes burning from the oil, he jerked the cord.

He only hoped they'd gotten far enough above the ground for the chute to open. The wind whipped at him, and his vision, still blurred, gradually returned enough for him to see the canopy below him. He turned as the chute opened and watched as the plane broke up, the tail tumbling end over end, the rest of it skipping like a flat rock on water, trailing a long, thin stream of black smoke behind it.

The chopper came out of nowhere. He could see the pilot waving to him, and he shifted his grip on Corona's body. The two men, one living and one dead, broke through the leaves and plunged into the jungle. What he first took for a distant clap of thunder was the first fuel tank of the C-47 rupturing.

He didn't hear the other.

CHAPTER FOURTEEN

Bolan answered the phone with a curt "Hello."

"It's me, Wade. I've got a man here I think you ought to talk to. Seems like you're both tryin' to wear the same pair of pants."

"They fit him?"

"Yeah, I think they do."

"Bring him over."

He hung up and walked to the bathroom. Splashing some cold water on his face, he rubbed at his eyes, heavy with lack of sleep. They looked bloodshot, but he was used to that. There were times when the mirror was his worst enemy. He could see the toll his crusade was taking.

Sitting down on the edge of the bed, he finished cleaning his guns. The Beretta was already reassembled. He had the Desert Eagle broken down. The springs seemed sluggish to him, the action a hair too loose. He tinkered with the bigger gun, replacing one spring and oiling it carefully. As he locked the slide back in place, he heard a car roll up to the motel. It's lights splashed through the flimsy curtains.

Bolan walked to the window, slipping the .44 into its holster. At the window he kept his hand on the pistol butt and leaned forward to look between the cloth and the window frame. He recognized Wade as the dome light went on. The lieutenant puffed his cheeks out as he climbed out of the car, then leaned back into say something to his passenger.

The warrior let his hand slide off the pistol and walked to the door. He stood there, as was his habit, back against the wall, with one hand on the knob. At the first knock he turned the knob and pulled the door open. Wade stepped in, glancing around the room as if he'd never seen it. Bolan watched his eyes. The way they danced was something that couldn't be taught. Only the best cops had it, checking a room once, then again, then a third time, every time seeing something new. Three cops for the price of one. The best bargain in public safety.

The lieutenant waved to his companion, who was standing beside the passenger door of Wade's vehicle. Bolan watched him move toward the door. Jaundiced by the tinted bug light under the awning, he still gave the impression of a man in his prime. A little shorter than Bolan, and maybe ten pounds lighter, he was still an impressive specimen.

Without preamble, Wade jerked a thumb toward the man in the doorway. "Gil Hoffman," he said. "He already knows your name." Wade lowered himself into the molded plastic chair as Hoffman closed the door. "You got something cold?"

Bolan shook his head.

"Figures," Wade said. Rubbing his hands together, he looked at each man in turn. "Let's cut the cards." The smile was a foot wide and as cold as dry ice.

MACK BOLAN DIDN'T suffer fools gladly, and he had no patience for stuffed shirts. When he found himself confronted by one of the former wearing one of the latter, he was prepared for a bad day. Gil Hoffman had prepped him on Winston Bartlett, and he was prepared for the worst.

Bartlett paced back and forth behind his desk. His carefully sculpted, brilliant white pompadour waved the tiniest bit with every measured step. His skin, betraying the slightest, fashionable hint of a tan, was as smooth as a baby's butt. For someone like Winston Bartlett stubble was bad form. He voted against Nixon, not once but three times, all because of the famous five o'clock shadow.

He was a type, a career man, the type who seemed to weather every change in administration, and to be immune to every shifting in the philosophical winds. Bartlett had made his mark early, and had been dragging it along to stand on ever since. He was as immovable as if his shoes were glued to the floor.

The man's style was almost a parody. More English than American, it was as if he dressed out of a style guide from Downing Street. The Savile Row suit and white on white shirt, so crisp that it rustled when he moved an arm, cost more than the average working man's whole wardrobe. Bartlett would be the last one to deny it.

His Italian oxfords were the only deviation from the sedate luxury Bartlett permitted himself, not exactly daring but still adventurous. When he finally stopped pacing, he planted himself behind his leather chair. "This isn't easy for us," he said.

Bolan nodded, waiting to find out what wasn't easy and, more to the point, who Bartlett meant by "us." The answers would be forthcoming, of that he was sure. But he was equally sure that it would be in the same stately pace that was the hallmark of all bureaucracy, even one where daggers hung in the cloakroom. In a

world where outsiders perceived the clocks to have thirty
hours to the day, and no ends to mark their passage,
patience wasn't a virtue—it was a necessity.

But Mack Bolan's patience was wearing thin.

"We don't like to go outside, you know," Bartlett
continued. "But these are strange times."

"You mean desperate times, don't you, Bartlett?"

"I'm sorry?"

"As in 'desperate measures'?"

"Oh, yes, quite. I don't know that I'd go quite that
far, but still..."

"How far would you go?"

Bolan's persistence was beginning to ruffle the fa-
bled Bartlett calm. He looked as if Bolan had just spit
on the carpet, then sighed heavily before turning his
chair far enough to the right to allow him to sit down.

"I suppose there's no point in beating about the
bush, is there?"

"None."

"Very well, then. Here it is...we seem to have
something of an impasse in the Isthmus. Central
America, that is."

"You mean Nicaragua?"

"Yes."

"And?"

"And we have a rather delicate situation. We believe
a change in government to be essential to stability in the
region."

"That's been apparent for some time."

"Of course, but we may have been a bit hasty. Gotten off on the wrong foot, so to speak. But there may be
another way."

"Why don't you come to the point?"

"In due time, young man, in due time. There are certain...delicate matters to be considered first."

"You've already made up your mind, or I wouldn't be here. Why don't you lay it on the table?"

"How much do you know about Central America, Mr. Belasko? Oh, I don't mean the contras, Somoza, the Sandinistas. That's ancient history. We're concerned about the future, not the past. It's in the future, after all, that the solution lies."

"If there is one, you mean."

Bartlett leaned back in his chair. He snatched a pencil from the blotter on his desk and tapped it, eraser down, on the arm of his chair. "You're rather one for plain speaking, aren't you?"

"It's the only way to stop talking and start doing. How many times around the bush is enough?"

"All right. We've considered all our options. It's obvious that the current plan has outlived its usefulness."

"You mean it didn't work, so it's time to chuck it."

Bartlett ignored the reformulation. "We've decided on an alternative. We believe it can work, and we mean to give it every chance to. And that's where you come in. Does the name Emiliano Rivera mean anything to you?"

"Not really."

"General Rivera was deputy chief of staff of the Nicaraguan army before the arrival of the Sandinistas. He's a brilliant and cultivated man, a graduate of the Sorbonne and of our own War College."

"And you've anointed him as the heir apparent. Now all you have to do is arrange the coronation. Is that the picture?"

"That's merely a rough sketch, Mr. Belasko. The final picture is considerably more sophisticated than that, and much harder to paint."

"How can you expect Rivera to succeed where Pastora and the others have failed?"

"The others were merely children looking through a candy store window, their noses pressed against the glass and nickels clutched in their grubby fists. In retrospect we should have realized they had no chance of succeeding. It was rather contemptuous of us, and insulting to the Nicaraguan people, to expect such a plan to succeed. But we've learned from our mistakes. We're big enough men to admit them, and intelligent enough to push on without repeating them. But this time we'll do it right. It will first be necessary to prime the pump, so to speak, but once that's accomplished, the desire of the Nicaraguan people for self-determination will take over. We have every reason to expect General Rivera will do well in the upcoming election."

"So they can freely choose the man you've already chosen."

"No, of course not. But if given the opportunity to choose, we believe they'll choose correctly. That's all we want to do—give them the opportunity."

"And, of course, Señor Ortega will offer his full cooperation."

Bartlett bristled. "He doesn't speak for the Nicaraguan people."

"And you do?"

"That's hardly the point. We believe that General Rivera does, and all we intend to do is give him a chance to be heard. It's in our best interest, and that of the hemisphere. I needn't tell you how important stability in Central America is to our own national security."

"And if I say I'm not interested?"

"We do have alternatives. Although, in all candor, I must tell you that you were our first choice for this sensitive and critical assignment. You've got a certain swashbuckling flair, I understand. But don't decide now. Why don't you meet General Rivera first? I think you'll find him a most interesting and honorable man."

"I don't think there's any point, Mr. Bartlett. I'm not interested."

"May I ask why not?"

"Because I came here expecting the truth, and all you've given me is the Agency newspeak. You and I both know that Guillermo Pagan, your most recent white knight, had rather soiled armor, as it turns out. You didn't even mention his name. You didn't mention his drug dealing, which was conducted under the willfully blind eye of the Agency, if not outright complicity."

"That's not your concern."

"The hell it isn't. You're a fool, Bartlett, if you think Pagan will roll over and play dead. You anointed him, and he wants to pull the sword out of the stone. He's a man who wants to be king, and you'll have to kill him to keep him from it."

"I see..."

"Do you?"

"Better than you think, Mr. Belasko. I think we should explore this matter a little further."

"It's your nickel."

CHAPTER FIFTEEN

Mack Bolan stood in the window for a moment, watching the street. A handful of windshields shone dully under the block's solitary lamp. The scattered cars, a few on either side of the street, looked more like monuments to a bygone age than vehicles still in use. Hoffman was late, and Bolan was getting concerned. Time was too damn valuable to waste, and they both knew it. Bolan let the curtains fall back, turned off the small light on the night table and sat on the edge of the bed.

The dial of a cheap clock radio glowed a dim green. Every minute the clock works clicked, and another number showed, and Hoffman was another minute late.

Hoffman was supposed to be his guide to the intricate underworld of Central American politics that flourished in Miami. There were Nicaraguans and Salvadorans, Guatemalans and Panamanians. It was a world where Emiliano Rivera and Guillermo Pagan stood like icons of the extremes, monuments to indifference and vengeance. They would start with Rivera and, if all went well, they would use him as a bludgeon to bring Pagan down.

If all went well. If Rivera was agreeable. If Bartlett could pull it off.

Unable to remain still, Bolan stood and walked to the window.

Another car had done its bit to fill in the emptiness of the street. Dust-streaked and battered, an ancient Volvo had pulled in between two cars directly across the street.

Beyond the Volvo, an alley, black as the mouth of hell, gaped between two buildings that had seen better days. Faded art deco facades were a sad reminder of a time when this part of Miami had nothing to fear, and nothing but a brilliant future to look forward to. One of the buildings was vacant, the other boarded up on the ground floor, probably to keep the junkies out. This was one area tourists would never see.

Something caught his eye in the mouth of the alley, but it was gone almost before it registered. Letting the curtain close to a narrow crack, he watched the shadowy opening, but nothing moved. He noticed a fifth-floor window in the building directly across from him and tried to remember if it had been open the last time he looked. He didn't think so, but couldn't be sure.

He was feeling uneasy. Hoffman was late and hadn't called. That in itself wasn't completely unexpected. Traffic was just one of a dozen variables, any of which could have held Hoffman up. But in Bolan's line of work, you learned to go with your gut. Hesitation was risky; ignoring the tingling of sensitive antennae could be riskier still, even deadly.

Bolan shrugged into his jacket and walked to the door. He paused just long enough to slip the safety off the Desert Eagle, then opened the door. He clicked the overhead light on as he left, letting the door close softly. Down the hall the elevator creaked and sighed as it struggled up its shaft. In the quiet hallway Bolan could hear the turning pulleys squeaking and the cables rattling as they strained to pull the car up to the top floor.

At the far end of the hall a fire door sat halfway open in defiance of fire regulations. A small block of wood, visible even half a hall away, had been jammed in at floor level, keeping the door from closing all the way. Bolan moved quickly over the frayed carpeting, his shoes scraping at threadbare patches the color of old sawdust. He paused for a moment at the door, listening to the moaning draft in the stairwell before pushing the door open. Slipping through the opening, he left the wood block in place and quietly closed the door as far as it would go.

Bolan leaned over the rail and looked down the six flights. The rectangular well was lit by a small red bulb on every landing, bathing the stairs and painted railing in a bloody glow. Other than the slight echo of the moaning wind, the stairwell was quiet. Bolan started up the stairs toward the roof. He stopped on the eighth floor, one flight below the door to the roof. He couldn't see anything through the dirty skylight overhead.

With one hand on the rail he moved quickly up the last flight. He held the big .44 in his left hand, keeping one eye on the door which, like the door on his own floor, had been left open a crack. It seemed odd that only two doors had been blocked, as if it were a signal to someone. On the top landing he paused to listen, placing his ear close to the narrow opening. The wind whistled through the gap. He strained to hear over the steady droning, but nothing seemed out of place.

Dropping into a crouch, he pushed the door gently. It gave immediately, and he ducked through, keeping the door open with a shoulder. Once on the roof, he dropped flat onto his stomach and wormed his way across the tar toward the yellow brick wall that encircled the roof. When he reached the wall, he rolled to his right, stopping just before a small drainage opening in the brick.

Bolan kept his head down and tried to get a look at the opposite roof, but saw nothing out of the ordinary. He still wasn't satisfied, though, and rolled past the opening to the next. Looking at the building from a different angle, he noticed that the open window had been raised still higher. The room beyond it was black, but someone was definitely there.

Bolan lay prone again, staring impatiently at the window. He heard a soft whisper behind him and turned to look toward the rear wall. A black knit cap bobbed just above the retaining wall. Its owner was too far below the wall to see him, and he scrambled to his feet and ducked behind the elevator housing. Peering around the housing, Bolan realized the man was talking to someone below him, while hanging on to a fire ladder.

The man suddenly darted up the ladder and threw one leg over the wall. A second man followed him, also wearing a black cap. They moved smoothly, as if they were used to working together, and Bolan watched as they huddled together on the roof, then moved toward the opposite wall. The first man, who was taller than his companion, mumbled something into his hand, and the warrior realized he was talking to someone on a small handset. The small antenna bobbed on its spring as the man tucked the unit into his pocket.

At the far wall the man waved to someone across the street, confirming Bolan's guess that there was a connection between the open window and the threat he had felt in his gut. Both men were armed with Galil submachine guns fitted with stubby sound suppressors. The hit team crossed to the stairwell, and Bolan was glad that he'd left the wooden block in place. The temptation to nail them while they were still setting up was great, but he was curious. He wanted to be certain they were after him before making his move. A fleabag dive like the Excelsior might house a half-dozen drug dealers, and the hit might be intended for one of them. If it wasn't, it would mean that he'd been compromised in some way. There were only a handful of possibilities, but he didn't want to go off half-cocked, finding a leak where there was none.

One man slipped down the stairs while the other positioned himself in the open doorway. He held the radio to his lips and whispered something, probably to a man in the building across the street. From his vantage point Bolan could see the open window, where a shadowy figure now moved about five feet back from the wall. The man on the roof fiddled with the volume control on his handset. It crackled and squawked loudly, then died to a burry whisper. Bolan couldn't make out the words.

The squawkbox crackled again, and the man leaned in and snapped off a quick count. "Five...four...three...two...one..." There was a throaty whoosh across the street, and Bolan saw the telltale smoke trail of an RPG as it darted across the street and screamed through the wall of the hotel a few stories below. A burst of autofire echoed up the stairwell, followed by shouts from at least three different voices.

It was time to move.

Bolan edged around the elevator housing. "Easy," he barked. "Just put it down." The gunman at the head of the stairs cursed. His head swiveled, looking for the source of the command.

"Easy," Bolan repeated.

But the gunman didn't listen. He swept his Galil in a quick arc across the roof, and Bolan dived under the snaking lead. He landed hard on his side, steadied the Desert Eagle and snapped a quick shot toward the door, now yawning redly where the gunman had kicked it all the way open.

Bolan raced toward the stairs, firing twice more to keep the gunner off balance. Back to the wall, he listened for a moment to the clatter of footsteps on the stairs. As he ducked through the open door, he saw the other man's head disappear below the landing, and he started down the steps.

The gunner shouted something in guttural Spanish, but the words were swallowed by their own echo. At the next landing Bolan stopped, expecting to see the gunner on the stairs. Peering around the railing, he saw the hat again, and again it disappeared down the next flight.

A burst from the Galil swarmed like bees up the stairs, pocking the walls and scattering paint chips and pieces of plaster. Bolan waited a moment before starting down the next flight. He heard running feet far below as the other man raced for the street. The warrior stopped halfway down and leaned over the rail. He waited for the gunner to swing around and start down from the sixth floor. Bracing the .44 on the railing, he held his breath for that split second, caught the moving shadow and fired three quick shots.

The shadow stumbled, then Bolan heard metal on stone and raced down the stairs. Turning the corner, he saw the gunner lying on his back, the Galil clutched against his stomach and pointed back up the steps. The warrior fired again, and this time there was no doubt.

Rushing past, he kicked the Galil away from the twitching fingers, slipped on a pool of blood and nearly lost his balance. Bracing himself against the wall, he plunged off the landing and headed down the next flight.

The thudding feet had stopped. Another shout, this time in English, boomed up the stairs, echoing and distorted in the hard, narrow well. It was erased almost immediately by the sharp crack of a pistol. A quick burst erupted from the Galil. Then there was dead silence.

The running feet picked up again; they were coming back his way. Bolan moved to the next landing and crouched, with his back against the wall. He could hear the hoarse rasp of the man's breath as he strained to climb back the way he had come.

The second gunner appeared, looking back over his shoulder, and Bolan shouted, "Hold it right there."

The startled head swiveled. The man looked down the stairs, then up at Bolan and back down again, as if trying to choose between heaven and hell. He shrugged once, took a step up and swung around his Galil.

Bolan fired once. The heavy .44 slug sent the knit cap spiraling down the stairs. Its owner threw up his hands, then vanished in an ungainly back flip. The submachine gun arced up in a graceful half loop, then dropped straight down the center of the stairwell. Bolan heard the heavy thud as the body hit on the stairs and stopped dead. A second later the gun slammed into the concrete far below, went off once, then died.

The Executioner stopped halfway down the flight, just long enough to check the man's pulse. He heard footsteps on the landing below and slipped another clip into his big weapon. Bracing himself for another assault, he found himself aiming at a surprised Gil Hoffman.

"I thought this was a safehouse," Bolan said.

Hoffman shook his head. "We've got trouble. Let's get out of here. I'll tell you about it on the way."

CHAPTER SIXTEEN

Guillermo Pagan sat behind a scarred metal desk, the gray paint veneered in cigarette tar, which gave it a dull bronze finish. He chewed thoughtfully on a cigar, a Cuban, which he allowed was the only reason he had never killed Fidel Castro. Pagan liked to talk big. Everything about him was outsize, including his paunch, which seemed premature on a man just past forty.

Pagan affected a military demeanor, and his fatigues, which had been custom-tailored, did battle with the advancing stomach. Trained at Fort Leavenworth, a lieutenant colonel in Somoza's National Guard, Pagan had been noted for his sharp mind and quick temper. When he fled Nicaragua, he had left neither behind.

Swarthy complexion darkened further by his favorite tanning salon, Pagan looked like a caricature of the Central American dictator gone to seed—which was exactly what he was. Unfortunately he had never quite managed to rule Nicaragua single-handedly, like his mentor, Anastasio Somoza DeBayle, but that had done nothing to prevent him from acquiring all the gestures and, perhaps more importantly, the attitudes.

Now, years away from any real influence in his native country, he still stung from the insulting haste with which he had been forced to leave. His cheeks still burned whenever he thought about it, and it was never very far from his mind.

He had sold himself to the Americans, and now they wanted to throw him away like a used tissue. But they had no idea who they were dealing with. He would show them, and they wouldn't forget it for a long, long time. They were "rethinking their options," figuring that soft-bellied pig Rivera could take his place. Well, he thought, let them. He had options of his own, options they'd never dreamed of.

Vincent Arledge, who had known him when he was the bright young star, skyrocketing through the rather murky firmament that was the National Guard, waited patiently for Pagan to frame his next thought. It was likely to be a while, since Pagan never said anything he didn't mean. And he never meant anything he hadn't thought about carefully.

Finally, when the silence had thickened noticeably, Pagan cleared his throat. "I think we have no choice, Ernesto."

"I already told you that." Arledge smiled at the use of his old *nom de guerre*. It had been a long time since anyone had used it, but he still relished its irony, chosen in mocking salute to the late Che Guevara, at whose demise he had been in conspicuous attendance. "I've already put somebody on it."

"Somebody good?"

"Somebody who can get the job done."

"Hoffman was a good man once," Pagan said, his voice tinged a little with a regret he didn't feel but recognized as appropriate.

"Past tense is appropriate."

"When?"

"The sooner the better. I already spoke to Bartlett about him. He was receptive."

"I lost a shipment a few days ago."

"I heard. But that wasn't Hoffman."

"How can you be sure?"

"He didn't know anything about it. He couldn't have."

"How do you explain it, then?"

Arledge shrugged. "There's a dozen possibilities. Who knows?"

"I don't want it to happen again."

Arledge nodded. "Naturally. But I don't control the whole world, you know."

"Then get me to the man who does." Pagan laughed, but he was serious.

Arledge watched him for a long moment. When he spoke, there was an edge to his voice that made Pagan's skin crawl. "You know, Willie, you're not the only duck in the pond. Miami is full of Somocistas. We thought you understood how things work and were willing to play by our rules."

"Haven't I?"

"Bullshit like you just gave me isn't going to go down too well."

"Ernesto, this is a game to you. That's why you talk about rules. But we're talking about my country. I'm a patriot and I'm concerned with things you know nothing about."

"Bullshit! Willie, all you want is to be the man who cuts the pie. The plain truth is, all we want is someone to cut it the way we want it cut. If not you, then somebody else. It's our pie and our knife, Willie. You better sleep on that a day or two. Let it sink in, amigo. You can't live with it, then it'll be *adiós*, and ain't nobody I know gonna lose a minute's sleep over it. Bartlett's pushing hard for Rivera. Gardner is leaning, but I can prop him up. But not forever.''

Pagan shifted in his chair. His weight came forward and the chair creaked under him. Suddenly conscious of the extra weight, he sucked in his gut. "You know, Ernesto, you gringos just don't understand. You have all these guns, lots of money, and still you have to come to me. You have to use *my* money. And you don't even give a damn where I get it as long as I do. Maybe *you* should sleep on that for a day or two..."

"Willie, don't fuck with me, understand?" Rubbing his palms together with a look of distaste, Arledge continued. "A bug, Willie, that's all you are. A bug. We can crush you and scatter the pieces to the four winds."

Pagan grinned. "You think so, Ernesto?"

"I know so, pal."

Pagan snapped his fingers. A door opened behind Arledge, and he turned to glare at the interruption. Two men, dressed in the same tight fatigues, cradling Israeli Galils in crooked arms, stood passively in the open door.

"You see these men, Ernesto? These men do what I say. I say cut off your balls, they do it. I say put a hole in your head, all they ask is how big I want it. Understand me?"

"Don't threaten me, Willie. This is five-and-dime theatrics. You don't have the clout here. You might kill me, but your ass will roast over an open fire if you do. I can guarantee it."

"Hey, Ernesto, guarantees don't mean anything. You remember the last guarantee you made me? Do you? How Somoza would be back in six months? That was, what, eight years ago? How's that guarantee coming? Still in effect?''

"The game changed when Somoza bought it. You know that.''

"That's my point, Ernesto. The game's changed. Now the rules are my rules. It's my ball. If I don't want to play, there's no game. ¿*Comprende?*''

"You're like all the others, Willie. Small time. You want to be El Jefe so bad, you got a garage full of sunglasses.''

"Which I bought with my money, Ernesto. Everything I have, I bought with my money. You used to tell me how your Congress was a bunch of assholes in your hip pocket. You could do what you wanted, regardless of what they said. I don't see that anymore. I don't hear you even suggest it anymore.''

"A small glitch, no more than that.''

"A small glitch. I don't know this word *glitch*. But I know your puppet shows play to empty houses now. Chamorro, Pastora, Bermudez. Faded stars, all of them, Ernesto. They have come and gone. But I'm still center stage. I play to packed houses.''

"There's still Rivera.''

"Rivera's nothing more than a straw man. He can do nothing.'' Mocking Arledge, Pagan rubbed his palms together. "Rivera's a little bug. I can crush him. Anytime and anyplace I choose.''

"If memory serves, it was your house that got blown up the other night, not Rivera's.''

"A small 'glitch,' no more than that. And I will find out who did it. I will take care of it in my own way.'' He nodded, and the two guards withdrew, closing the door softly. When they were gone, Pagan leaned forward, whispering conspiratorially. "You didn't happen to have anything to do with that, by any chance, did you, Ernesto?"

"If I did, you wouldn't be here now, Willie. No way."

"Big talk, amigo. Very big talk."

"Look, let's get down to it. We've got to take Hoffman out of the picture."

"How much?"

"Fifty K."

Pagan nodded slowly. *"Mucho dinero."*

"We've got to make it clean. Surgical. No fuck-ups. I've already told you that I got the best. The best doesn't come cheap."

Pagan reached for a drawer in the desk. Arledge tensed noticeably. Pagan laughed. "Nervous, Ernesto?"

Arledge shook his head. "A little. Things are too crazy lately."

"Roll with it, amigo. We don't want to be too predictable, after all. This is serious business."

"Yeah, it is."

Pagan jerked a brown envelope out of the drawer. He opened the flap and wet his thumb. Counting quickly, he stopped at fifty, pulled the rest out of the envelope and shoved it back into the drawer. He licked the flap, closed it, then pressed it flat with his palm. Tossing it across the desk, he said, "Don't spend it all in one place, Ernesto."

"Money tight?"

"No. But I'm a simple man. I come from peasant stock. I'm frugal, to a fault perhaps. But then I, too, don't like how crazy things have become. Poor management, Ernesto. We'll have to do something about that."

"I'm trying. But there are problems."

"Anything I can help with?"

"Not that kind of problem. Bureaucratic shit. But I can handle it. It'll shake out okay."

"Soon, I hope."

Arledge nodded. "Soon, yes."

"Take care of Hoffman. But remember, Gil was a friend of mine. I want it quick and painless."

"I understand that. And I'd be the last one to blame a man for developing a conscience, even if it *is* rather late in the game."

"Too late, it would seem."

Arledge didn't answer. He stood, tucking the envelope inside his shirt. "I've got a meeting with Akhmani. He's going to supply two thousand assault rifles. Czech AK-47s."

"How much will you need?"

"We're going to hash that over tonight. I'll let you know."

"Don't let him hold us up."

"I won't." He turned and left without saying goodbye.

Pagan sat there, listening to the sound of Arledge's footsteps on the concrete floor of the warehouse. There seemed to be tiny voices whispering high in the girders, as if someone were gossiping about the man walking by. He wasn't happy with the meeting, but he wasn't sure why.

There was something bothering Arledge. Pagan couldn't put his finger on it, but the man was coiled like a rattlesnake ready to strike at anything that moved. This wasn't the old Vincent Arledge, the man he'd known for a dozen years.

Arledge was under a lot of stress. That was clear. But stress was part of his life; he should be used to it by now.

Maybe there really was something to the threat that Rivera would supplant him in the affections of Charles Gardner. It didn't make sense, but then very little in the boiling caldron of Miami made sense.

He could find out, of course. He could find out anything, if he had enough time. There were no secrets in Miami. It was just that some stories had higher prices than others. He could ignore it, ignore Rivera, ignore Arledge and his dancing eyes. He had noticed that Arledge couldn't even keep his hands under control. In his lap the fingers had squirmed, and Arledge had knit them together to keep them still. But even then the muscles had twitched, as if something alive had been trying to get out through the skin.

Pagan tossed his cigar away and pulled a fresh one from his shirt pocket. He unwrapped it slowly, running it under his nose and inhaling deeply. He smiled at the aroma, so pungent, so fresh. Then the smile vanished. He was in danger of becoming fat and sloppy.

Too complacent already, the good life weighed him down like lead in his pockets. Maybe it was time to strike out on his own, instead of letting Arledge do all the legwork. He had begun to feel more and more like a canary in a cage. But the safety was deceptive.

After all, didn't they take canaries into the mines? And weren't they the first to die?

CHAPTER SEVENTEEN

The security was heavy. Bolan drifted to a stop at the main gate and rolled down his window to hand over his ID and a note from Rivera to a guard. The man walked to the front of the car while another, armed with an Uzi, took his place beside Bolan's window. The tall man held the documents in front of the car's headlights, then backed into the shadows. Through the open window, the warrior could hear him talking to someone on a transceiver. Bolan drummed his fingers on the steering wheel while he waited.

Five minutes later the tall man reappeared, passed the papers back to Bolan and waved him on. A winding drive, lined with cypresses on both sides, led off into the darkness. Fifty yards inside the fence, he spotted an open jeep, half hidden in dense shrubbery. Two men sat in the vehicle, one at the wheel and one at the gun mount in the rear. As Bolan passed, the jeep fell in behind him.

A dull halo surrounded a bank of trees, cutting across his line of vision, then disappeared as the drive swerved abruptly left. In a series of sinuous curves the tree-lined lane covered another hundred yards, then the lights reappeared as it swung back to the right into a thirty-yard straightaway. A three-story house, dwarfed by the trees, appeared in snatches, its walls bathed in light from hidden floods. The gravel under his tires crunched loudly as he swung into a circular driveway and braked.

A glance in the mirror showed him the jeep was still on his tail.

A broad stone patio, roofless and lined with sparkling white planters, led up to a massive doorway. Two armed men dressed in fatigues stood at attention, one on either side of the door. Through the thick glass of the door, Bolan spotted several more men in a dimly lit foyer. He walked to the door and handed his papers to the guard on the right, who glanced at them. He rapped on the glass, then handed the papers back. A man inside unlocked the door and pushed it open for Bolan to enter.

The door closed behind the warrior, and he was immediately surrounded by men who proceeded to pat him down. They found the .44 and confiscated it. The inner door was opened and Bolan passed through. A short man, his bent back and gnarled hands evidence of crippling arthritis, shuffled ahead, waving Bolan to follow him. The stooped gnome led him up a winding staircase into a long hall.

The man paused at an ornately carved wooden door, which he pushed open after a sharp double knock. Then he bowed to usher Bolan through. The door closed behind the big man with a soft thump.

Emiliano Rivera sat on a leather couch, a book open in his lap. Bolan looked around in surprise. All four walls were lined with books from ceiling to floor.

"You look confused, Mr. Belasko," Rivera said, getting to his feet.

"A little. I didn't expect this, I guess."

"El Caudillo isn't supposed to be contemplative, is that it? A man of action who knows Clausewitz and Machiavelli, maybe Sun Tsu if he's trendy, but not a scholar?"

"Something like that."

"Stereotypes, Mr. Belasko, are dangerous. And not only to those who are typed. It's important to confront the world with an active, unprejudiced intelligence."

"Sometimes, yes."

"Would you be more comfortable if I put on mirrored sunglasses and a uniform?"

"Don't patronize me, Rivera."

"Of course not, but if we're to be colleagues, I think we should speak plainly. I think we should understand each other as fully as any two men who share a common problem can."

"We don't share a problem, General. It's your problem, not mine. I've volunteered to help you solve it, no more than that."

"But no less, either, eh?"

"That goes without saying."

"*Nothing*, Mr. Belasko, goes without saying, not as far as I'm concerned. In a way, my fate will be in your hands as much as in my own. That makes it of grave importance to me to know what you're thinking at all times. That, and my natural curiosity."

"I don't give a damn about your natural curiosity."

Rivera bent to retrieve his book from the couch. He held it toward Bolan. "Spinoza. Do you know him?"

"No."

"He says that statesmen are esteemed as more crafty than learned. That's a stereotype, and it seems to me that, insofar as you're concerned, it applies to me. That may have been true at one time, but no more. The sooner you accept that, the sooner we'll get along."

"We don't have to get along. I don't have to like you or to respect you. I have a job to do, that's all. Don't waste your time trying to impress me. I've done a little reading of my own. I know more about you than you think, and there wasn't much there to like or respect."

"Another life, Mr. Belasko. Another era. Let's take a walk in the garden. I find it tranquilizing."

Without waiting for an answer, he crossed the library and opened the door. By the time Bolan reached the doorway, Rivera was halfway down the hall. The warrior trailed behind and caught up to him at the top of the staircase. He was conscious of the men below watching him. He was even more conscious of the empty holster on his hip. They descended the steps in tandem, neither man saying a word.

Rivera rapped on the glass of the inner door, and one of the guards opened it. The general stepped through and Bolan followed. The guard was about to open the outer door when Bolan stopped him. "My gun," he demanded.

The guard shook his head. "Sorry, *señor*," he said, looking at Rivera.

"It's all right, Carlos. Give him his weapon. He'll have ample opportunity to kill me, if that's what he wants to do. And I suspect he doesn't need a gun to do it."

Grudgingly Carlos jerked the .44 from a cubbyhole in the wall and handed it to Bolan, muzzle first. The warrior got the point, and he didn't like it. "Next time you do that you better pull the trigger, Carlos."

"Perhaps I will, *señor*," the guard replied.

Bolan holstered the Desert Eagle and followed Rivera outside. The general walked swiftly, as if he were anxious to get away from the house. He turned a corner of the building and waited for Bolan under an archway carved in a thick hedge. When Bolan caught up to him, he led the way through the arch into the garden, which was lit more dimly than the rest of the grounds.

"I find it restful here," he said.

Bolan didn't comment.

"All right, Mr. Belasko, you seem to be a man who values plain speaking. Since I also appreciate unflinching honesty, perhaps we should indulge the one trait we seem to have in common. I know my reputation. I also know that much of it is unjustified. I'm a military man, and I took orders. That's what a military man does. I know you can appreciate that, because it's obvious to me that you wouldn't be here if the choice were strictly left to you. But you must realize that a soldier doesn't always agree with his orders. If he was permitted the luxury of conscience, the army, any army, would come to a screeching halt."

"There's a limit to how far a man should go, no matter how dedicated," Bolan reminded him.

"That's true. But if you read the files carefully, you know that I separated myself from Somoza before he was deposed. That was conscience, Mr. Belasko, my conscience. I didn't have to do that. In fact, I did so at a considerable risk."

"Then why do you run cocaine into this country?"

"That's a lie. I don't. I know who does, and I also know that some people in your government benefit from the traffic."

"You could stop it."

"How?"

"Turn them in."

Rivera laughed. "You're not only honest, you're naive, as well. Do you think one man could accomplish what dozens, hundreds, even thousands, have been unable to do?"

"Every little bit helps."

"Perhaps..." Rivera paused thoughtfully. He seemed to be considering Bolan's remark. He reached up to scratch his cheek. The rasp of his nails on the leathery skin was the only sound in the garden. "Do you want to know why I'm planning to go back to Nicaragua?"

"For the power."

"No, Mr. Belasko. For the money. Unlike many of my superiors, I never had the luxury of a Swiss account. I wasn't adept at pillaging the treasury. In fact, I never had access to the conduits, which, by the way, your government knew about and even protected. But I know where a considerable fortune has been hidden in the currency of several countries and more in gold and jewels."

"Are you offering me a cut?"

"Would you like to take it? Don't bother to answer that. I already know. But I've become a practical man. Your country wishes to restore a palatable order to my country. I'm willing to do what I can to assist that restoration, but I'm equally interested in my own well-being. If participating in this little adventure is the price, then I'll pay it. By the way, you needn't think this is our little secret. I have said as much to Mr. Bartlett, and I'm sure he's told anyone else who might need to know."

"So, you're a statesman after all, General Rivera."

"Touché. But I—" Bolan knocked him to the ground before he could finish.

He held a hand over Rivera's mouth and whispered into his ear. "Quiet." He removed his hand. Pointing to the far edge of the garden, he whispered, "Over there...two men."

"Guards," Rivera replied, trying to sit up against the pressure of Bolan's arm.

"Your guards don't wear black, General. Wait here."

Bolan crawled off among a tangle of azaleas. A moment later a burst of automatic weapons fire chewed at the shrubbery, and the warrior heard a shout. He tugged at his coat to get at the Desert Eagle and pushed a clump of bushes aside. One of the two gunmen was struggling to get over a low fence all but hidden by the tangled greenery. His pants were caught on the sharp wire. Bolan called to him to stop, but the assassin tore free and plunged over the fence. Bolan charged toward the fence, keeping his head below the line of shrubs. He heard another shout, in Spanish, and took the fence at a leap, landing on his shoulder and rolling back into the crouch in one fluid motion.

He could just make out the shadow of the fleeing gunman. Bracing his wrist he fired twice. The gunman stumbled, and Bolan charged after him, zigzagging through the wild greenery beyond the fence. The gunman clawed his way through thickening undergrowth, and the warrior fired again. This time he knew by the groan that his shot had found its mark. He'd aimed low, hoping to take the gunman alive.

Another shout, this one more distant, was unintelligible. Behind him, the compound was in an uproar as men poured out of the house and rushed toward the garden. Bolan found the gunman, sprawled on his back, his head twisted at a queer angle against the trunk of a tree. Blood flowed down the man's chin. In the dim light Bolan could just make out the sticky gleam of the blood soaking into the gunman's black cotton turtleneck. Despite the warrior's intentions, the bullet had hit him squarely in the chest.

Bolan felt for a pulse, but the thickly muscled neck was still. He heard footsteps behind him and turned to see Rivera charging toward him, a borrowed rifle clutched in his right hand, his left warding off the clinging branches of the undergrowth.

"He's dead," Bolan said as Rivera ran up. The general wasn't even breathing hard. He must have been in better shape than Bolan imagined.

"Who is he?" Rivera asked, leaning forward to get a better look at the dead man's face.

"I was hoping you could tell me."

Rivera shook his head slowly. "Never saw him before."

Bolan checked the man's clothing but, as he expected, found the pockets few and empty.

"It seems our association hasn't gone unnoticed," Rivera said.

"It could just be a coincidence," Bolan replied. "A man like you has more enemies than most."

"Perhaps..."

CHAPTER EIGHTEEN

Winston Bartlett was famous for his love of horses. He raised quarter horses on a five-thousand-acre farm in the Virginia hills. As a deputy director of the CIA, he couldn't afford such an expensive hobby. But it was no trouble at all for the son of the senior partner of the prestigious Wall Street law firm of Bartlett, Dean and Eccles.

Bartlett was also a member of a syndicate that had made millions in Thoroughbred stud fees. Langley was full of rumors that horses were Bartlett's life, and the Agency was someplace to go when the weather was too wet to ride. Bartlett knew the rumors, had even fed them deliberately, in his cold-blooded, humorless way. It was the kind of revenge that could be appreciated only by a man rich enough to take a hike anytime he felt like it.

Lately Bartlett had started to wonder whether that time might not be far off. The world was no longer the civilized place it used to be. Henry Stimson, secretary of war under Roosevelt, had once put a stop to U.S. intelligence gathering with the observation that "gentlemen do not read each other's mail." Well, it might have been true in 1935, but it was no longer even close to the truth. This was a world in which a gentleman like Henry Stimson would have been hard-pressed to find a trace of civility.

There was too much ugliness in the modern world for a man like Winston Bartlett to feel comfortable. It was a world where heavy metal had taken the place of light verse. Poetry was dead, or at the very least, breathing its last gasp. The piano had been electrified and mass destruction institutionalized. The have-nots of the planet no longer wanted charity; they wanted revenge—the bloodier the better.

In short, Winston Bartlett was a man without a planet. He no longer belonged on earth. At sixty-four he had already seen more than he could bear of human cruelty. It was no longer possible to measure a man's thought by his conduct. Dissembling and hypocrisy were the hallmarks of the era. If people were unwilling, or perhaps even unable, to tell the truth, then there was no such thing as truth. Every man had his own, and even if he didn't, he'd make himself a truth he could live with.

Trying to be the voice of reason in the lunatic asylum that was Central American politics was slowly corroding him. At night Bartlett would sit in a chair, his unlit pipe dangling from a clenched fist, trying to make sense of it all. So far it had been a losing battle. This morning he had to be by himself, get away from everything that confused him. It was a morning to clear the air, and his head, try one last time to see a truth that, for everyone he knew, was right in front of their noses, but slipped away from his eager fingers like quicksilver. No matter how he tried to grasp it, the truth kept darting away from him, leaving him bewildered and angry. A ride in the country would be just the thing, perhaps the only thing, to clear his head.

But there would be no ride in the country today. There hadn't been one for weeks, and unless things took a turn for the better, something he didn't really expect, there would be none for a while. Bartlett closed his briefcase with a loud snap, a gesture that was as close as he came to swearing in public. He closed his study door behind him and walked across the hardwood floor, careful to keep his heels from cracking on it and waking his wife.

Outside, in front of the house, the car was already waiting. A fine mist was drifting through the air, and Bartlett glanced at the sky for a moment, frowned at the thick, swirling gray, then ducked his head to climb in.

The driver closed the door after him, then climbed into the front seat. He glanced in the rearview mirror. "All set, Mr. Bartlett?"

Bartlett shook his head absently. "Go ahead, Mr. Perry."

Taking the obvious hint, Perry closed the privacy glass before starting the engine. The big car, an unfashionable Cadillac, so determinedly out of step with the Mercedes-Benz favored by many of the younger bigwigs around the capital, purred softly, its huge tires rolling easily over the clean, freshly raked gravel drive. It was an hour's drive, traffic permitting, and Perry checked the clock on the dash as he always did to see how close to schedule he could keep. It was 6:32. If their luck held, he'd make the final turn into the long approach to the Dulles Building by 7:25. Mr. Bartlett liked to be in the office by 7:30.

Staring at the muted green of the meadows, Bartlett thought with distaste of the day ahead. His schedule was all arranged, as it always was, but unlike most days, this one promised to be anything but routine. The midnight phone call from the DCI had guaranteed that. Charles Gardner had been nearly apoplectic. He'd spluttered so much that Bartlett had been unable to decipher what he was saying. He was angry, and he was frightened, but about what Bartlett hadn't a clue. But he was certain to find out first thing. Gardner was going to see him at eight o'clock.

Bartlett was a team player, but working for Charles Gardner was rapidly forcing him to reconsider the wisdom of loyalty. Gardner was a political hack, whose only claim on the directorship had been the pivotal role he'd played in the last presidential election. He'd been the point man for the President's campaign committee, a job in which he had served more as a lightning rod than a strategist.

Like most longtime Company men, Bartlett thought of the CIA as a club rather than an arm of government. It was a place of soft voices and expensive suits. Oh, there had always been a few cowboys, and they had had a role to play, but even the cowboys had known just how far to push their luck.

Unfortunately, as Bartlett saw it, this was a new age, and a new breed of cowboy. It was fast cars and shiny suits now; hair triggers had replaced the hair shirts. Instead of biting your tongue and climbing back on board for another go, the new fashion was to second-guess your superiors and see just how much you could do without anyone knowing. Free-lancers at heart, if not in fact, the younger men had no patience for careful planning. It was as if they had all grown up on James Bond or Bonnie and Clyde. Instead of measuring their net worth by reference to bank accounts, they were more inclined to calculate firepower, megatons instead of mutual funds.

At the worst of it was that Charles Gardner, whether he realized it or not, was just like them. Fattened on his own rhetoric, Gardner had swaggered into town like a drunken gunslinger and started picking fights with every Third World movement to the left of Attila the Hun. It was useless warning him that the world was too volatile a place for Dodge City theatrics. Gardner wanted action, and action meant covert operations. He'd pushed Bartlett from day one, despite repeated warnings that caution was not only desirable, it was necessary.

Bartlett had wanted to quit early on, but he'd allowed himself to be talked out of it by longtime friends, both in and outside the Agency. If he left, they'd told him, Gardner would have a free hand. If he stayed, he could mitigate the walking disaster. Maybe not totally, but at least enough to salvage something of the Company. Hacks came and went, they insisted. No fewer than four former DCIs had separately implored him. In the end he had caved in. He had done the right thing, made the noble sacrifice. He only hoped it was worth it.

His office was already lit. Allison Hodges, his administrative assistant for seventeen years, seemed to live in the office. She was there when he got in every morning, and she said good-night to him when he left. This morning she waited for him as usual, standing guard over a mound of files, all with the distinctive blue stripe. He glanced at the stack before smiling at her.

"Good morning, Allie."

"Morning, Mr. Bartlett. The director has been calling. He wants to see you as soon as possible."

"I thought the meeting was scheduled for eight?"

"It was, but I gather something's come up."

"I suppose it would be too much to hope it's his IQ?"

Allison smiled indulgently. "Now, Mr. Bartlett..."

"I know, but I can't help it." Bartlett placed his briefcase on the floor beside his chair, reached for the pipe on his desk, already packed by Miss Hodges, and lit it. Through a cloud of blue smoke, he said, "You know where I'll be."

The walk was longer every time he took it. At nights he sometimes dreamed that the building was stretching and stretching, and in the dream he started walking the hall. As Gardner's office receded faster and faster, he began to run. Every time, he woke up with his heart pounding, a cold sweat on his brow.

And every time he took the walk, he relived the dream.

But he made it, and Gardner was there, waiting. Bartlett stepped in, resolving to maintain his customary calm and knowing he would break that resolve in short order. "Morning, Charlie," he said.

"Sit down, Winston, please." Gardner was using his most statesmanlike delivery. "We have a serious problem on our hands. I suppose you know about the screwup already."

"You mean the plane?"

"What else?"

"You don't really want the full menu, do you?"

"Not today, Win, please. I need you with me on this one, not against me."

"Of course, sorry. Go ahead, Charlie."

"The Venezuelans have delivered a message from Ortega. It seems they have the pilot."

"Impossible!" Bartlett bolted from his chair. "You don't believe that?"

"Oh, but it's true." Gardner picked up an envelope from his desk. It was bulky, but seemed rather light. He tapped it against the opposing palm for a moment. "There's proof, you see. A videotape."

"It's genuine?"

"No question. Tech Services confirms it's the real thing."

Bartlett sat back as if the wind had been knocked out of him. "I see." He sucked thoughtfully on the pipe for nearly a minute. "What do they want?" he asked.

"They don't want anything. They plan to put him on trial. His name's Gregory, I believe, and he's already confessed. That's what the tape is, his confession."

"Coercion, of course."

"I don't think so."

"What do you want to do?"

"I want to nuke the smug little bastards, that's what I want to do. Let SAC finish what the earthquake started. Send Managua back into the fucking Stone Age. But that's one option I don't have. What I need to know are the options I *do* have. We're going to hash this out. We aren't leaving until we've got a proposal I can send to the President."

Bartlett took another pull on the pipe. "Tall order."

"I know." Gardner ran a hand through his already unruly hair. "You've really dug us a deep hole on this one, Win."

"*I* have? What do you mean *I* have? I've been telling you for four years that we ought to pull the plug on this one. Pagan was a bad choice, but you insisted. Times have changed, Charlie. Times have changed, and we haven't kept up with them."

"What the hell does one thing have to do with the other?"

"Everything." Bartlett stood and walked around Gardner's desk. He sat on the end of the desk and riffled a stack of papers in Gardner's in tray. "Look at this, Charlie. You know what this is? This is garbage. It's smoke. It's hot air, damn it. And you sit here and you read it and you believe it. People are telling you what you want to hear, and by God you eat it up."

"We're in the intelligence business, Win. You can't argue with the need for information."

"I don't. What I argue with is the use of partial information. Case in point—Guillermo Pagan. We've given this man the benefit of every doubt. We've given him money, we've given him access to information, we've given him material support. And he thumbs his nose at us, Charlie. Gives us the old bird. But you don't want to see it because this paper here tells you he's anti-Communist."

"Well, he is, damn it." Gardner was getting hot. His cheeks already had the telltale rosy glow. His neck had begun to turn red. "I gave you the go-ahead on Rivera. What the hell else do you want?"

"I want Pagan out of the picture. If you don't disavow him, we lose credibility."

"Handle it, then, damn it."

"You'll stay out of it?"

"Until you fuck it up, yes. But on one condition."

"What?"

"Do whatever you have to to solve this Gregory mess. Buy him out of there. Kidnap him. Hell, shoot him if you have to. But I don't want a trial. Understood?"

It was Bartlett's turn to rumple his hair. He puffed on the pipe, but it had gone out. He shook his head slowly. "Understood."

"What do I tell the boss?"

"Tell him we'll use agents in place to negotiate his release. No fanfare. No publicity. Just a nice, quiet resolution."

"What if he wants to know what agents?"

"Tell him he needs deniability. Tell him we can't risk compromising them. Just tell him we'll do it."

"Can you do it?" Gardner asked.

"I don't know. But that's what he wants to hear, isn't it?"

Bartlett stood down from the desk. He looked Gardner in the eye.

The director blinked first.

CHAPTER NINETEEN

Vince Arledge sat at the breakfast table, staring at undercooked bacon. It was getting cold, and the grease had already started to congeal and turn white. He scraped some of the mess away with his fork, then picked up a napkin. Laying the three strips of bacon on the crinkled paper, he folded the napkin around the rashers, pressed the napkin flat with his palm and tugged each strip out of the paper. Each strip fell onto the plate with the dull thud of a large bug hitting a windshield. Angrily he jabbed the yolks of both eggs with his fork, watching the yellow fluid ooze from under the whitish skin like blood from a dying alien.

His appetite was long gone, but he ate, anyway, mechanically. The coffee, at least, was hot. He didn't know when he had lost his taste for the job, but it had been some time ago, and probably he'd suppressed it for a while before that, not letting himself face a truth about himself that he had always feared.

His nerves were gone.

He liked to tell himself that anyone would get tired of dealing with the lowlifes he had to work with day in and day out. And while working with them was bad enough, he had to do even more—he had to trust them to do what they were told, when they were told and how they were told. Not only that, he had sometimes to place his life in their hands. It was that last glitch that had worn him down.

There were times—and they were more and more frequent lately—when he felt as if every nerve in his body ended in a small flame, each one burning like a drop of molten steel. Late at night he had taken to imagining that his skin glowed with the collected fire, and he made shadow figures on the ceiling, fluttering his hands like moths with broken wings, fashioning distorted alligators and ducks with monstrous beaks. He was losing it, had probably already lost it.

But he couldn't quit. Not yet. He had this one last op, the one that would make it all worthwhile. It would take some doing; he knew that. There were some things you just couldn't kid yourself about. It was like a game, really, seeing if he could pull it off, if the old flair was there.

He was worried, though. He thought of all the times he'd won because the asshole on the other end had fucked up, sometimes big, sometimes little, but fucked up all the same. And that was his edge. He was always looking for the dropped stitch, the rust spot in the metal. And he'd always found it. But everybody has rust spots; everybody, sooner or later, drops a stitch. That was why he had to do it now—get out before it caught up with him.

Doing drugs had helped at first, letting him move like a madman through the shadow world where he was forced to spend every waking minute. But the drugs no longer worked, not even in the massive doses he had begun to use. All they did was keep him awake, staggering from rendezvous to meeting to appointment. At night, in some nameless armpit of a motel in some town whose name he couldn't remember, he'd roll a joint, light up and lie back, trying to unwind.

He'd lie there, too tired even to close his eyes. He'd stare at the ceiling and think of the slime on his hands, the slugs he dealt with, things that crawled out from under rocks, so strange they had no names, some new species for biologists to puzzle over. His idealism was the first casualty, a victim of pragmatism. He found himself doing things that repulsed him to get the job done. It was the job, after all, that was paramount. And after a while some inner anesthesia kicked in and he didn't feel the pain anymore, or the queasiness in his stomach when he took the next rung down the ladder to hell.

Arledge wanted it to end, but he didn't know how to take his own life. He'd spent too long keeping himself alive to throw it all away that easily. But if he couldn't take his life, at least he could take it into his own hands.

He had thought he could fake it for a while. But he couldn't do it anymore, not any of it. He had to get out. He was coming unglued, and it was starting to show. He thought Pagan had already noticed it, and if Pagan had noticed, others had, too. That made him too risky to keep around. Sooner or later one of them would come for him. They'd take him out and tell themselves they were doing him a favor.

Like a man who's just been told of a terminal illness, Arledge had started to count his days. He didn't know when it would happen, how long he had. All he could do was cross each day off the wall, draw an X through it and stare at it, congratulating himself for another twenty-four hours of drawing breath.

Unless he could pull off the long shot, hit one out in the bottom of the ninth. His whole career, even his whole life, had been a preparation for it. Now it was crunch time. He didn't know whether he still had it, but he was still man enough to give it a whirl. Hell, even the mighty Casey got three strikes. Why not Vince Arledge?

Why not go for it?

The first few steps had already been taken. He hadn't stumbled so far. What the hell? If he blew it, at least he'd go out smoking.

WINSTON BARTLETT didn't like being alone. With the kids on their own, he had grown closer to his wife, and felt incomplete when she was away. The demands of his job seldom came between them, but there were times when she needed to be away from the strain. The midnight calls, the meetings at all hours, the strange men on the other end of the phone all took a toll. She had been drinking on and off for years, but Bartlett sensed a change in her drinking habits in the year since his promotion to DDO.

For her own good he had packed her off to her sister's. A month in the California sun would do her good. They both knew it, and they both knew why it was necessary. Even so, Bartlett felt a little let down. He couldn't help blaming her, just a little. Lois hadn't expected her life to turn out the way it had. For that matter, neither had he. But a man did what he had to do, what was expected of him. That was the way he'd been raised, and he felt he had a right to expect the same acceptance from his family.

But Lois couldn't handle it all that well. Sitting alone in his study, he wondered whether he ought to resign. It was the best thing for Lois, of that he had no doubt. Whether it was the best thing for himself, he wasn't so sure. Despite his prissy exterior, there was something deep inside him that relished the sleaze, the seaminess of the job. He knew it said something about him, but he wasn't quite sure what.

He had days when he wondered whether anything he did made the slightest bit of difference in the world. He wanted to believe it all mattered, that it all helped, and if it did, even a little, then it was worth the trouble. But lately he had begun to doubt the wisdom of recent policy decisions. They seemed ill advised and badly thought out. Precision was something he valued highly. Decisions couldn't be made in a vacuum. You didn't change the world overnight just because you wanted to. You had to recognize realities, you had to deal with what was, not with what you wanted to be there.

And Gardner was such a dolt that it made life impossible, especially for the old-timers, the thirty-year men. Maybe it was the wisdom of experience, or maybe it was because they prided themselves on being above doctrine. They were hardheaded realists, pragmatists, these men he had worked with for three decades. Collectively they had a wealth of wisdom, hard-won and costly, that you ignored at your peril.

Now Gardner wanted to chuck it all. The days of retrenchment under Carter had been brutal. But this was something else again. People were leaving by the half dozen, fed up with the nonsense, frightened by the impetuous, unreasoning rush to remake the world overnight.

He cleaned the table, stacked the dishes in the washer, then slipped into his suit coat, tugging the silk vest into place with an impatient shrug. With Lois away, he had elected to spend a few days in the District at their apartment. It would do him some good to be away from the empty house, he had thought. He wasn't so sure now, but it was too late to do much about it.

The car would meet him in ten minutes. He browsed through the last couple of paragraphs of an article in the *Post*, folded the paper three times and stuck it in the garbage. The August sun was already heating up, and the humidity was certain to be brutal. Closing the door to the apartment, he rubbed idly at the back of his neck. It had been stiff for three or four days in a row, a sure sign of the stress he was under. He arranged for a car and took the elevator down, standing up front, against the control panel, as he always did.

It was amazing to him how neatly ordered his life was, how many habits he had, and how many things he was able to do without even thinking. In some ways, he thought, he was more than a creature of habit—he was an automaton. Dulles had always teased him about it, even once suggesting that too many habits made a man too predictable, and therefore unfit for being a spy. Dulles had actually used the word very seldom, and it was the only sign that he wasn't perfectly serious in his warning. Even so, Bartlett had taken it to heart, only to find that he was hopelessly bogged down in trivia if he had to think about everything he did. Better to lead an automated life on some level in order to free his mind for more complicated affairs.

Stepping into the morning heat, he was pleased to see that the car was on time. The driver stood by the door, leaning against the front fender, his back to the traffic. He recognized Bartlett immediately and opened the rear door with a nod. The DDO dropped into the seat with a sigh, then rolled his window partway down to enjoy the breeze as the car rolled out of the city. Langley was just a short hop away, and anything to salvage the morning before Gardner ruined it was welcome.

The driver slowed on the approach to the main gate, waved to the attendant, who waved him on through after glancing into the back seat to see who was in the car. The driver dropped him at the main entrance. "What time shall I pick you up, Mr. Bartlett?"

"Not before seven, I'm sure. I'll have to let you know."

"Very good, sir."

Bartlett stood beside the glass door and watched the car pull away. When it turned the corner and disappeared, he puffed his cheeks with an escaping sigh, then turned to push the smoothly pivoting panel open. The polished floor, still unmarked by the morning's heels, gleamed softly under the indirect lighting. He glanced at the CIA seal on the wall as he went by, then opened his pass case to show his ID. Once he was past the guards, the building looked distressingly anonymous. It was more like the headquarters of a giant insurance company than the home of cloak-and-dagger men.

He took the elevator to his floor, unlocked his office and dropped the briefcase in a chair just inside the door. Allison Hodges had the day off, and he thought he just might decide to cancel a few appointments. He clicked the light switch and walked to the window. Pulling the draperies aside, he wished again, as he had every morning since the Agency had moved into the building, that he could open the window. But the architect, ostensibly on orders from Dulles, had made no provision for open windows. It was suggested that Dulles was afraid secrets might escape. That was probably not that far off the mark, Bartlett thought at the time, and again this morning.

For a moment he considered wandering down the hall to see if Gardner was in yet. A few words alone before the meeting might save them a lot of time and aggravation. But Gardner seldom got in before the time of his first meeting, if then. Sloppy to a fault, in his habits and in his dress, the man was a walking disaster, but neither Bartlett nor any of the remaining holdovers had the heart to complain. They were all either too afraid for their jobs to risk offending the new man or, like Bartlett himself, so appalled by so much else wrong with the man that they saw no point in interfering. It would be like repainting a condemned building—far too little and way too late.

Dropping into his chair, Bartlett watched the green numbers on the clock change minute by minute, almost numb. He was burning out, and he knew it. What he didn't know was whether there was anything he could do about it. Perhaps it was time to step aside.

In the center drawer of his desk he kept a folder. He opened the drawer now and took it out, carefully opening the flap and adjusting the single sheet of paper inside. It was a neatly typed letter of resignation. All it lacked was a date and his signature. He'd kept it for years, and only Allison Hodges knew it was there. Every six months she retyped it for him. He never changed a word.

Bartlett read the letter over and nodded at the economy of its language, the elegant simplicity of it. He thought of it as an insurance policy of sorts. Retyping it was like paying the premium. It was always available and always paid in full. He thought about signing it more frequently of late.

But he had one more job to do. Nicaragua was too much on his mind. And as bad as Rivera was he was preferable to Guillermo Pagan. Bartlett knew that now, and knew that if he left, Gardner would manage to mess things up.

One more operation. That was all.

CHAPTER TWENTY

The plane banked to the left, and Bolan looked out the window at a moonscape. Managua looked like something out of a postapocalyptic extravaganza. The ruinous earthquake more than a decade before had left its mark.

The flight down had been uneventful, but Bolan found it unsettling. He'd had time to think, and he didn't like the results of his own analysis. The operation had all the hallmarks of a classic disaster. There were too many cooks and nowhere near enough broth. Rivera was the hub around which it all wobbled, and the warrior still hadn't gotten a fix on the eccentric general.

But having to leave the planning stage to avert disaster was not a good sign. Bartlett had been adamant that nothing go forward until Tony Gregory was recovered. That he sat in a rural jail in the highlands was cold comfort for the man who had to get him out. He would meet Hoffman here, and they wouldn't have to pull it off alone. But he'd had such assurances before. The most unsettling aspect of the whole affair, however, was the idea that one man knew enough to sink the Rivera ship before it even got out of dry dock. Either that man knew a hell of a lot more than usual in the compartmentalized world of special operations, or the whole mess was a house of cards, vulnerable to the first sneeze. If he had to guess, Bolan would go with the latter.

Watching the barren grid of broken brick and block after grassless, uninhabited block slowly rise to meet the plane, Bolan crossed his fingers and leaned against the glass as if it would support the insupportable.

As the plane touched down at Sandino Airport, Bolan stretched and ran through his cover again. He was unarmed in order to clear customs, but someone would meet him at the airport. He felt naked without a weapon and, when he thought about his situation, even worse, he felt stupid.

He stood before the plane stopped, ignoring the scowl of the flight attendant, and tugged his small suitcase from the overhead rack. He sat down only when the woman started toward him, waving her arms. The plane taxied to the terminal, its whole body shuddering as the pilot angled the nose in and urged it snugly home.

Bolan was on his feet before the engines stopped whining, and was the first one through the hatch. The accordion tube through which he walked bounced under his weight, and he felt like a novice on a trampoline. He followed the colored lines on the floor to the customs desk, attaching himself to a short line left over from another flight. The agents seemed efficient, if a little brusque. When it came his turn, he handed his papers to the smiling agent. The smile vanished almost at once.

"¿Norteamericano? Please state your business, señor."

"I'm in the electronics business. Parts, actually."

"You have clients here?"

"I hope so. I have an appointment with Señor Allende, of Centam Electronico. This afternoon, as a matter of fact."

The man nodded, but he seemed more interested in Bolan's bag. He pulled the zipper, but it was locked. "Open this, *por favor*," he said, turning the case for Bolan to reach the lock. He fished the tinny-looking key from his pocket, undid the small padlock and jerked it free. He started to open the zipper, but the customs man raised a hand. "*Uno momento, por favor.* I'll do it."

The agent spun the bag back and opened it slowly, as if he feared it might be full of snakes. He opened the lid a couple of inches, then closed it again. Taking the bag under his arm, he stepped away from the desk, nodding to a colleague to take the next person in line. "Come this way, please," he said, standing back and waving Bolan through the turnstile.

The customs clerk marched briskly toward a metal door set in one wall. Bolan was starting to worry. There was nothing in the bag that should have provoked this response. He knew it might be a subtle form of harassment, making one American pay for the sins of another, not uncommon in the Third World. The clerk pushed the door open, then stood aside for Bolan to precede him through.

Inside, the warrior found himself facing two more men in the dark green uniform of Nicaraguan customs. Like the first man, they were anonymous, wearing no name tags or badges with an identifying number.

The older of the two, who was also the shorter, said, "Sit down, please, Mr. Corday." Bolan registered the greeting without surprise, but wondered how the man knew his name, since the agent had said nothing. It was more than obvious they were expecting "Mr. Corday." What Bolan wanted to know was why and, more to the point, how.

"What's the problem, Señor...?" Bolan waited patiently, but the man didn't offer his name, and he didn't bother to answer the question, so he pushed on. "I can't imagine what the problem is."

The man laughed. "You're all alike, you gringos. You can never imagine the problem. That's because you *are* the problem."

"What are you talking about?"

"You come down here with your fat wallets and you look to buy trouble. Drugs, usually. Like you, eh?"

"Drugs? I don't know anything about any drugs."

"No? Then what's this?" He tossed a thin package, wrapped in translucent plastic, onto the table in front of him. It was the only furniture in the room. Bolan noted that there were no windows, either.

"I've never seen that before in my life."

"It was in your bag, Señor Corday."

"No, sir, it wasn't."

"You're calling one of my men a liar, *señor*. I should advise you to be careful."

"I'm not calling anybody anything. I'm just telling you that package wasn't in my bag. I've never seen it before. And it looks to me like it's never been opened. How do you know it's drugs?"

The man didn't answer that question, either. Instead, he walked to another steel door, pushed it open, then let it close behind him with a dull clank. He looked at the clerk who had processed him, but the man shook his head and turned away. The other man shrugged his shoulders.

Bolan was calculating the odds against the whole mess being a simple case of mistaken identity. They were astronomical, and he knew it. But that left only one explanation—someone had tipped off Nicaraguan customs, someone with a lot of clout, and a reason to put him on ice. Immediately he thought of Emiliano Rivera. But it made no sense. Rivera didn't need anything this elaborate to get him out of the picture. All he had to do was to tell Bartlett he wanted another man. Why go to all this trouble? But someone had, and that someone had a reason.

He had to get word to his contact man, but he had no idea how. And it looked as if it wasn't going to be easy, even if he had a way to do it. Before he had halfway puzzled through his situation, the officer was back, accompanied by two men in green fatigues. The new arrivals positioned themselves on either side of him, like bookends, and shoved him toward the far door.

On the other side of the door, Bolan found himself in a long, narrow hallway. Its walls were unpainted cinder block, and the right-hand wall was broken by a half-dozen doors as anonymous as the one he'd just come through. The soldiers prodded him with the muzzles of their AK-47s, striking him every so often just for the fun of it.

A third man, apparently a noncom, judging by the stripes on his arm, waited at the far end of the hallway. As Bolan drew close, he opened the door behind him and stepped back. In the surge of bright sunlight, he was reduced to a vague shadow, as featureless as those of the Hiroshima victims etched forever into the stone ruins after the bomb.

Bolan saw the rear end of a jeep behind the noncom. Everything shimmered in the heat, and the vehicle seemed as if it were about to dissolve in the wavering glare. Hustled into the jeep, he was handcuffed to a steel bar welded to the left side panel.

"Where are we going?" Bolan asked, switching to Spanish when the same question in English got no response. The Spanish was just as useless. The men ignored him completely. The noncom climbed behind the wheel, revved the engine, then popped the clutch. The jeep jerked forward, throwing Bolan back against the seat. The cuffs dug into his wrist as they took his full weight. The warrior righted himself, then turned his body slightly to wedge himself into the left corner, keeping his left arm half extended.

The road to Managua was littered with jerry-built shacks, mostly raw wood and tar paper, with rusty corrugated metal roofs. The skyline of the capital city in the near distance seemed out of place, but Bolan had seen it all before. It was always like this, people clinging to the last shreds of their dignity, living on the edges of big cities as if they stood in line at the gates of heaven.

The jeep roared into the capital and wound through back streets, mostly lined with tumbledown shops and makeshift houses. They sped through the narrow streets as if they were empty, sending pedestrians scurrying in every direction. The whole place smelled of rotting food and cheap spices. Under the hot sun the stink of bad fish swirled around them, mingling with the stench of poverty. The children, running in packs like small rodents, threw stones and rotting vegetables at the vehicle as it passed, a gentle enough expression of their frustration.

The jeep finally slowed, pulling between two tall buildings and stopping in a narrow alley behind what appeared to be an abandoned factory. Whatever it was, it wasn't a government building—it was the kind of place a man walked into but never came out of. Bolan knew he had one chance and that he had to take it. He shifted his weight, trying to loosen the cramped muscles of his back and shoulders.

The driver killed the engine, then turned to eyeball Bolan while the other man jumped down and walked to the back of the vehicle, fishing for the cuff key in his shirt pocket. He held it to the light as if to see whether it were the right one, then leaned over the back wall of the jeep to unlock the cuffs.

When the ring snapped open, the Executioner snapped his foot up, catching the soldier on the point of the jaw. The man's head whipped back, then he dropped like a dead mule. The driver started to move, but Bolan was ready for him. He lashed out with the cuffed hand, snaking the metal around the man's neck and grabbing the open ring with his free hand.

Putting his full weight into it, he hauled on the chain, shutting off the guy's wind. The chain scraped across the driver's larynx, and Bolan could feel the man's fingernails digging at the backs of his hands. He pulled harder, then twisted, forcing his victim's head sharply to the right. The guy started to gag, but Bolan couldn't slack off until he blacked out. The man was armed, and if he raised an alarm, there was no telling how many would answer.

The warrior took a chance. He let go of the chain and delivered a knockout punch to the driver's temple. He groaned and tumbled backward out of the jeep as Bolan scrambled over the rear. He stopped just long enough to grab an automatic pistol from the noncom's belt, then sprinted back down the alley toward the street.

He took the corner at full tilt, then slowed. People glanced at him, then looked away in disinterest.

He had to get off the street.

CHAPTER TWENTY-ONE

Vince Arledge was in a bad mood. The situation with Pagan was getting out of hand. He didn't like the bastard, but the money was too good to pass up. He'd seen too many guys buy the farm with nothing but a government insurance policy for the family. The kids never even knew what happened to their fathers half the time. That was cold, too cold. No way was he going to let it happen to him. Put some away, put a little more, then let it rain. He was covered.

He sat in Chico's Pub, watching the long legs of the waitress. He waved to her to hurry up with his drink. She glared at him, then threaded her way through the crowd with a tray full of glasses.

"What's your hurry?" she asked when she finally reached the table.

"A man could die of thirst, waiting for you, babe."

"Couldn't happen to a nicer guy," she replied.

"I'll bet you say that to all the boys."

"Not really. I save my good stuff for assholes like you."

Arledge started to answer her, then changed his mind. He was drunk and she was too quick for him. The real secret of staying alive was to know when to run away, he thought. He watched her, a lopsided grin smeared across his face while he fished in his pocket for his wallet. When he managed to get it out, she was already looking for the bouncer, tapping one toe on the floor with a sharp, insistent rhythm.

He plucked a ten out of the wad in his wallet and snapped it. She gave him a bored look, then reached for the bill, but he grabbed her wrist. "What do you say you and I get together later on, honey. I can make it worth your while."

"Dream on. You couldn't afford me even if you *were* worth it."

"You see that bill?"

"Barely."

Arledge laughed. "What would you say to fifty of those?"

"Piss off."

"High-priced, aren't you?"

The waitress leaned toward him, digging her long fingernails into his forearm. "I'm gonna count to three. If you're still holding my wrist when I finish, I'm gonna kick your balls all the way to Key West."

Arledge laughed again.

"One..."

"Two..." he said.

"Three..."

"All right, all right." He let go. "I was just kidding around, honey."

"You want to kid around, get a sense of humor first." She snatched the bill and turned in a single fluid motion. She was three steps away before he realized it. "What about my change?" he hollered.

"Try therapy."

Arledge shook his head. He was juiced again, and he knew it. He'd been hitting the sauce too hard for months. He worried it might be catching up with him.

When he worried, he drank. Then he worried about his drinking some more. It was a no-win situation.

He reached for the fresh drink, held it for a long moment, staring into the glass, then tossed half of the whiskey down with one swallow. He felt his head wobble, and he had a splitting headache. The music seemed to be getting louder. He ought to tell Monzon to find someplace else to meet. Mr. Clean wouldn't like it. But screw him.

He rubbed the circles of condensation into a puddle on the table, then dipped a finger in to draw another, larger circle. He couldn't get it right. Trying to fix it just made it look more like an egg and less like a circle. A nest egg, he thought, that was what it was. *His* nest egg. He rubbed it out and tried again, this time holding one hand in the other as if his finger were some kind of awkward calligraphy tool.

The new circle was no better, and he rubbed it out, then dried his hand on a damp napkin. He rolled the napkin into a ball and set up for a jump shot, tossed the paper and missed. He retrieved it, worked hard at rounding it out again and took another shot. The ball disappeared into a tangle of thick fingers. Blearily he looked up at Pedro Monzon, the big man's bald scalp electric blue and pink under the swirling lights.

"Hey, Pedro, my man, *qué pasa*?"

Monzon turned a chair around and sat down, crossing his arms on the back of the chair and resting his chin on a thick forearm. "You drunk again, amigo?"

"Who, me? Shit, no, man. I'm just getting loose's all. You know how it is. These late nights, man, they take a toll on me."

"You better watch your ass. Pagan's been hearing stories about you, man. He don't like what he's hearing, neither."

"Fuck Pagan."

"I'm gonna have to tell him you said that, Vincenzo."

"Fuck you, too, then."

"You ready, or not?"

"I'm ready, I'm ready."

"Let's go, then. This shit of yours is getting old real fast."

Monzon stood, backing away from the table as if preparing to leap over it. He turned abruptly. A petite blonde, her back to him, was dancing out of control. He didn't see her until he knocked her down. Her partner, ten feet away, said something Arledge didn't hear. But Monzon did.

He glared at the guy, flipped him a bird and brushed past. Arledge, finally realizing that Monzon was going with or without him, got to his feet. He moved around the table, lost his balance for a second, then stepped on the blonde's hand.

She howled, and her boyfriend took a step toward Arledge, who stopped in his tracks. He was weaving slightly, and that encouraged the hesitant Galahad.

"Hey, man, you stepped on her."

"Yeah, pal, and you're next if you don't get the fuck out of the way."

"You want some of me, man, that's cool."

"Yeah, asshole, I want some of you. I got to feed my dog." The boyfriend took another step forward, encouraged by Arledge's slurred speech. Arledge grinned. He held a hand in the air, fingers up, and wagged them. "Come on, tough guy. Come on."

Arledge was tilting over the edge now, and the guy sensed it. "Chill out, man. You should be more careful, that's all."

"Hey, if I want to step on your tart, I'll fucking step on her, all right?" The guy backed up, and Arledge followed him. "I said all right?"

Monzon stepped past the guy and pulled Arledge by the arm. "Come on, man, I've got to hang out here. Don't fuck it up for me." He glared at the white knight, who took one look at Monzon and lost interest in the confrontation. He bent over the girl, who was still trying to get up, and Arledge kicked him in the rear.

Monzon dragged him away, squeezing his upper arm so hard that it went limp. "Cut it out, Pedro," Arledge grated.

"You're pathetic, amigo. You know that? Pathetic..."

"If you were on time, I wouldn't get bored. Then I wouldn't have to drink."

"You drink because you want to, Vincenzo. No other reason."

"All right, save the goddamn sermon."

Monzon shook him once, then let go. "Behave now." They were at the exit, and the Nicaraguan nodded to the pair of monstrous bouncers standing guard. Then they were outside.

He opened the door of a Jaguar sedan and half helped, half shoved Arledge inside. He closed the door, shook his head and walked around to the driver's side.

"Amigo, you have got to get a grip. Guillermo is getting very upset about all these stories he keeps hearing about you."

"What stories? What's he hearing?"

"You know..."

"Well, maybe I do drink a little too much. It's not easy walking the edge of a sword, Pedro. I've got Gardner and Bartlett leaning on my ass, I've got Willie, I've got a bunch of assholes in Central America who are supposed to look like an army but not be one. Blah, blah, blah... It's old, man, old."

"It gets easier. Pagan takes over down there, and we're set, man. You can hang out at the beach and dissolve your liver if that's what you want. But you've got to hang on, man. We go way back, Vincenzo, you and me. Way back. More than once I've had to tell Pagan to let you slide. I tell him, 'Sure, he fucked up, but everybody makes mistakes.' I say, 'Look, we can't do it without him.' But he doesn't think we need you. I've got to make sure he doesn't make up his mind that way, you understand? But you've got to work with me."

"I appreciate that, Pedro. I really do. You know, we've worked together off and on for, what? Thirty years?"

"Next month."

"Okay, man. I won't blow it."

"Okay." Pedro seemed satisfied. "Look, this deal is the biggest yet. We've got fifty keys. At thirty per, you figure it."

"Mil and a half."

"Tonight, man. In one hour a million and a half dollars right in the trunk of this car. Now let's all be cool and make sure the deal goes down according to the script, all right?"

"What have we got for backup?"

"I've got four guys. They're already at the warehouse. I told DeCarlo don't bring more than three guys. He said okay, but I don't think he's that stupid."

"It doesn't matter. We're not gonna burn him. What's the difference?"

"The difference is these Italians, they can't see past their noses. He sees a way he can keep fifty keys *and* save a mil and a half, what do you think he's gonna do?"

"Nothing. If he wants the stuff to keep coming, he won't do anything. Like you said, he's not stupid."

"No, but he's greedy. Same fucking thing, Vincenzo. See, our problem is, we've got ideals. We want the money for some reason. All he wants is the shit and the money."

"He doesn't know who he's dealing with, does he?"

"No, man. He knows you and me. After that, he's just guessing. But no way he's guessing right, which isn't a good thing for us. See, if he knows he's fucking with Pagan and the goddamn CIA, he makes the deal and goes about his business. He thinks he's got a couple of spring chickens, he gets stupid. That's what I don't like."

"So maybe we drop a hint, make him think a little."

"Can't do it. Pagan would have our nuts for breakfast. He's already taking too much heat. You know what happened to his fucking house. The goddamn papers are starting to sniff around. And—"

"Look, I know all that. On my end, Gardner told me himself—keep it close. Nobody but nobody is supposed to know. Plausible deniability, all that shit. Bartlett doesn't even know. He'd shit a brick if he found out."

"Fuck him. Man likes to smoke a pipe and talk about theory. Who needs it?"

"But I have to handle him."

"Then handle him, man. What the hell do you think you're getting paid for?"

"You're right. I'll handle him."

"Okay."

Monzon concentrated on his driving. Their destination already loomed up ahead, a half-built warehouse that had been caught in the real estate bust. It sat on the waterfront like a reminder of just how easily aspirations could come up short.

Monzon wheeled the vehicle into the weed-filled parking lot, got out of the car and walked to the trunk. Arledge joined him in time to take the first Galil. Monzon took another one for himself, jammed in a clip, stuck two more in his pockets and handed three to Arledge.

"You ready?" Monzon asked.

"Let's do it, *compadre*."

CHAPTER TWENTY-TWO

Bolan felt conspicuous on the street. A man his size was a lightning rod for public attention, and when the population as a whole was on the short side, he was just that much more obvious. He had to find someplace to lie low until dark. Three blocks from the alley he turned down a side street, looking for an abandoned building.

The best he could do was a warehouse. Two vans were loading at a concrete dock, but the bulk of the building seemed deserted. Bolan edged along the side of the warehouse until he found a door. It was locked, and he cursed softly. He jogged around a corner and found himself staring into a broad expanse of waist-high brick walls. Weeds grew from the cracks in the walls, and vines hid some of the rubble on the ground.

A long alley, unpaved and clogged with cardboard and litter, ran the length of the warehouse. He made sure no one was watching from either end, then dashed forward, tumbling over the nearest wall.

He was in a box, and he knew it. He had killed one man and possibly a second. He had no papers—real or otherwise—a stolen pistol, and his "Corday" persona was a fugitive from something or other. Just what wasn't easy to figure out. He settled in for the long wait until sundown. His back against a wall, he watched the sky, keeping his ears open for the least unusual sound. He knew where to find his contact, but it wasn't something he wanted to risk until he knew where he stood.

The warrior was convinced that he'd been set up, but that didn't mean everyone in the operation was rotten. It did mean, though, that someone wanted to stop him from getting to Tony Gregory.

But that list of "someones" could be a yard long. Rivera had enemies by the dozen. If the CIA wasn't going ahead until Gregory was sprung, then any of Rivera's enemies had a motive. Guillermo Pagan was certainly at the head of that list, but someone inside the Agency could also have an ulterior motive in keeping Gregory on ice. That one was a little harder to figure, because motive was dependent on gain. Unless it was known what someone stood to gain, there was no way of guessing who it was who stood to make that gain. Once again, any of Rivera's enemies had to head the list. But how did he, whoever he was, get enough inside information to be able to blow Bolan's cover?

The only way to answer that question was to get out of Nicaragua, which was easier said than done, Bolan thought. He slapped a bug that was crawling down his collar, then shifted his back away from the vine-covered bricks.

He watched the sun creep across the sky, drifting slowly toward the Pacific. He could do nothing but watch and wait. Once in a while, to relieve the monotony, he would change his position, trying to ease the stiffness that seeped into his joints like some insidious fluid.

He heard a siren in the distance and was certain that someone had reported him. Pulling the stolen automatic from his belt, he examined it for the first time. It was a good weapon, a Makarov. As long as the odds were, he was still in the game.

Bolan could have used a map of Managua. His briefing had included a quick study of the city's layout, but there hadn't been time to commit it to memory. Unfortunately his map had been in the suitcase, which now sat in an office somewhere, probably still back at the airport. All he had was his wallet and a mix of local currency, U.S. paper and traveler's checks.

The siren faded away, and he relaxed a little. It was one thing to be a fugitive, but it was another to be treed like an opossum, a human noose slowly tightening around you, squeezing you until you burst from the pressure.

By five o'clock he was getting restless. He got to his knees, and a voice said, *"Hola, señor."* Bolan whirled around to find himself staring at a face with a scraggly beard.

"Hola," he replied.

"American, no?" The man grinned.

"How did you know?"

"The accent, *señor*. You gringos never get it right."

"What do you want?"

"I've been watching you for quite a while. I know things. I know you have been hiding. I know you don't want the police to know you are here. I don't know why, of course." He smiled, shrugging his shoulders. "But I think I know enough to feel secure, eh?"

"So what do you want from me?"

"Want? Nothing, señor. I don't want anything. Maybe, though, I have something you can use, eh? Maybe I can sell you something you need. Maybe you have some Yankee dollars in your pants."

"What have you got to sell?"

"What do you need? A disguise, maybe? A place to hide? Transportation?"

"Right. I pay you to hide me, then somebody else pays you to turn me in. Good business for you. No good for me."

"Amigo, do I look like that kind of man?"

"You look like a beggar."

Another siren sounded in the distance and Bolan gave a start. He knew the beggar had noticed it.

"Very well, I see plainly that you have no need of a place to hide. *Buenos días*, Señor Belasko."

"Hold on. How did you know my name?"

The beggar grinned. "I told you. I know things, *señor*."

Bolan jerked the stolen pistol out of his shirt. "You don't just *know* something like that."

"Forgive me. I guess my sense of humor got the best of me. It has been a long time since I have been able to use it." The man shrugged. "Actually, I followed you from the airport."

"What the hell's going on?"

"I don't know, *señor*. All I know is that you did not make it through customs. I have to think that someone had informed the government of your arrival. More than that I can only guess."

"Then guess, amigo."

"It looks as if there is a leak stateside. Señor Hoffman thinks he knows who is responsible. But he won't say."

"Hoffman's all right?"

"*Sí*, he's fine. He's waiting for you."

"We have to get out of here," Bolan said. "They've got to be looking for me."

"I have already made plans for that. We will stay here for a little while. A junk wagon will come through soon.

It will stop on the other side of this wall. We will climb in back and be taken to your destination."

"Who are you?"

"You don't need to know. It is enough for you to know that I am a friend. You can put the gun away now, I think."

"Not yet. Not until I know whose friend you are."

"Very well." The beggar got to his feet and stretched, looking for all the world like a hobo who had just awakened from a nap. He looked across the vacant lot, stretched again, then let his arms fall to his sides. He started to shuffle away.

"Where do you think you're going?" Bolan demanded.

"I think I should take a look around."

"Stay here."

"I don't think that's a good idea. It is better if I do what I normally do. People are used to seeing me around here. Why do anything to upset them, eh? I'll be back before the wagon gets here."

He turned his back and walked off. Bolan watched him helplessly. He couldn't shoot the man, and the guy might be telling the truth. He had to be. How else would he have known both his and Hoffman's names?

Another siren shrieked in the distance, and the warrior pressed closer to the wall. He didn't like the feeling of vulnerability that washed over him. He had to do something.

Bolan started moving along the base of the wall. About fifteen yards away another wall, no higher than the first, intersected at right angles. Reaching the corner, the warrior got to his knees and raised his head above the ruins, keeping the vines and tangled weeds in place like a veil. He could see the first intact buildings about two hundred yards away, but there was no point in trying to get to them. The back of a row of small shops was the closest, but they were probably open for business, and he wasn't about to walk in and ask to use a telephone.

Ducking again, he moved along the shorter wall, checking over his shoulder from time to time and taking it slowly. When he reached the end, he lay flat and peered around the jagged end of the stone just above ground level. All he could see was another wall about thirty feet away. It was like a maze, with the ruined foundations, most of them no more than three feet high, joining one another at odd angles. The rubble had been removed and the walls were all that had been left behind. It was eerie staring out over the expanse of weeds, knowing that he was crawling over hundreds of ruined lives.

Bolan slipped around the corner and found himself in the middle of a box canyon of ruined brick about two and a half feet high. He was better protected than he had been, but it didn't make him feel any less vulnerable. He looked up at the sun, which had finally started to sink in the sky. He was hot and sweaty, and the bugs swarmed around him incessantly.

Then, off in the distance, he heard a strange sound— a steady hammering as if someone were pounding on the cobbled street. It seemed to draw closer as he listened. Under the hammering was a more delicate sound, like the tinkling of small bells. Bolan raised his head above the wall and pushed some of the vines aside to peer down the empty street.

Wobbling slightly, a wagon glided toward him, its canvas cover shuddering as the iron wheels scraped over the uneven street. Two ragged horses, their hooves clip-clopping steadily on the smooth stones, pranced like circus animals. Sitting on a bench seat, an old woman held the reins in her hand, snapping them now and then to keep the gait steady. She looked like something out of nineteenth-century Europe, with a rag knotted under her chin and an apron draped over her chest and lap.

As he watched, the wagon slowed, finally coming to a halt near a break in the stone wall. Bolan turned the corner in time to see the beggar climb down from the back of the wagon. He tugged a canvas sack after him and stepped through the break in the stone. The old woman climbed down from the wagon and waddled after him.

The beggar broke into a grin when he saw the warrior, but said nothing. He knelt and spread the mouth of the sack open, waving Bolan toward it with a flourish. "Your coach, *señor*," he whispered.

Bolan slipped into the bag feet first. The beggar zipped it shut, leaving an opening at one corner, just large enough for Bolan to slip two fingers through. He would be able to open the bag himself if he had to.

The next thing Bolan knew, he felt the bag rise at either end. A moment later his head banged onto the wooden floor of the wagon and the tailgate creaked closed.

Then the wagon lurched into motion.

CHAPTER TWENTY-THREE

"Where's the stuff?" Arledge whispered.

"Van's coming in after we get inside." Monzon waved impatiently and moved toward a side door in the warehouse, which had been spray-painted with a variety of interesting graffiti. Arledge laughed at one of the lines. "Hey, Pedro, got a pencil? I want to write this broad's phone number down."

"Vince, don't lose it on me, amigo. We're walking on a very thin wire here. You step wrong, you slice off your foot."

"Relax, Pedro. DeCarlo's not gonna try anything. Just relax, man."

Monzon ignored him, yanked the door open and waved Arledge through. The interior of the warehouse was pitch-black, except for a large block of gray at the far end where a single freight bay was open to the air.

"DeCarlo?" Monzon shouted.

His voice bounced around the huge cavern, blurring into an unintelligible bellow that slowly faded away. There was no answer. Arledge shifted his grip on the Galil. He felt a trickle of sweat run down between his shoulder blades. It seemed to hesitate, stopping for a moment at every vertebra until it picked up enough extra moisture to push on down to the next. Every step made him tingle.

"DeCarlo," Monzon called again. Again the summons bounced around, then spiraled away into silence. No answer. "I don't like this."

"Maybe he's not here yet," Arledge suggested.

"He's never late. You know that. It isn't like him, man. I sure as shit don't like it. Back on out of here."

"Hang on, Pedro. Don't be so hasty. If we walk out on a million plus in cold cash, you better have a damn good reason to give Willie."

"Fuck Willie. He doesn't have to stand here and listen to the damn rats squeaking in the garbage."

Headlights suddenly sliced the warehouse in two. Arledge blinked away the glare, turning his head until his eyes adjusted to the harsh light.

Footsteps clacked on the concrete floor, and a figure passed through one beam, momentarily darkening the glare a bit.

"You got the stuff, Pedro?"

The voice was disembodied, seeming to emanate from a spot high up near the ceiling. Arledge recognized it as belonging to Frank DeCarlo, but the acoustics played such tricks that it still gave him the creeps.

"All set," Pedro shouted. He started to walk toward the car. Arledge hung back a little, then drifted to the left before following Monzon. DeCarlo didn't say another word. All Arledge could hear was the sound of his and Monzon's shoes on the dried paper and broken glass on the floor. Every step seemed to have a hundred tiny echoes.

After what seemed to be an eternity. Monzon moved in between the beams of the Mercedes. It was possible to see DeCarlo's features now, hazily but clearly enough to be certain it was he.

"Kind of a show biz entrance, isn't it, Frankie?" Monzon asked.

"Hey, I've got big bucks in the trunk. I'm supposed to come in here like Pinky Lee? You ought to know better than that, Pedro."

"Yeah, Frankie, I guess so."

"Besides," DeCarlo continued, "I been hearing things on the street."

"What kind of things?"

"Oh, you know. Rumors. The kind of shit that makes me nervous."

"You nervous, Frankie? I can't believe that."

"Don't bullshit me, Pedro. You got the stuff for me or not?"

"I've got it, I've got it. Relax."

"If I want to relax, I go to the beach. In here—" DeCarlo pointed at the floor "—I do business."

"All right, let's do it. Vince, get the van in here."

Arledge nodded, moving farther to the left and sprinting along the wall toward the open bay. One of DeCarlo's hardmen followed. The CIA man wanted to turn around, but didn't want to give the man the satisfaction. He stopped in the open bay, blinked his pocket flashlight one long, two shorts, then two longs.

He heard the engine rev, then the van jumped out of the shadows, careering through the bay door. Once inside, the van's lights went on, stabbing toward the rear of DeCarlo's Mercedes. It skidded to a halt alongside the car. The driver banged the door open and climbed out. "Okay, Pedro?" he asked.

"Get out of here, Chuckie. You're done for the night."

The driver, a slender black kid with a mustache that weighed almost as much as the rest of him, waved a skinny arm and snapped a badass salute. Then he skipped toward the door and was gone.

"Pretty sure of yourself, aren't you, Pedro?"

"Hey, Frankie. It's good shit. You know it and I know it. You want it, and we both know that, too. You change your mind all of a sudden, hey, no problem. I drive the van and Vincenzo here takes my car. No hassle, Frankie. At this price I can find somebody else."

"I didn't say I didn't want the stuff."

"What, then?"

"Forget it, Pedro. Just making conversation, that's all."

"No, it isn't all, Frankie. You were playing big shot. Like maybe you want it, maybe you don't. I don't have time for that crap. Check it out and let's get this over with, all right?"

"Take it easy, amigo. Take it easy."

"I'm a busy man, Frankie. I've got things to do." Monzon walked around the corner of the van and opened the rear door. Fifty plastic bags, stacked like bricks, five deep, stretched across the open doorway.

DeCarlo cocked his head to one side, nodding casually. "Fifty keys, huh?"

"Yeah, fifty. You count that high, Frankie?"

DeCarlo hefted one of the bricks. "Which one should I test, Pedro?"

"Doesn't make any difference, Frankie. They're all the same."

"That right?"

Monzon slammed the door. "Let's go, Vinnie. I've had it with this asshole." He brushed past DeCarlo and went to open the door of the van. One of DeCarlo's hardmen pumped a round into the chamber of his shotgun, but DeCarlo held up his hand. "Hold it, Dom.

Pedro is just trying to show me he's a serious man. He doesn't like wasting time. That's good, right? I mean, I don't like wasting time, either, so I can understand. He should lighten up a little, but no problem. He can work on that. A mil and a half will probably help him relax.'' He turned to Monzon. ''That right, Pedro? You relax a little, and maybe the next time you won't be so uptight, right?''

''Frankie, how can we have a next time when we don't even have a this time?''

DeCarlo nodded toward the rear of the van. Dom tucked his shotgun under his arm and opened the back door again. He clicked a switchblade open, jabbed one of the bricks in a middle row and took a little of the white powder on the tip of the blade.

He tasted it cautiously, a thoughtful expression on his thick features. He smacked his lips and nodded. ''Nice. Real nice.''

DeCarlo seemed to relax all at once. ''We've got a deal, then, Pedro.''

''Until I see the money we've got no deal.''

''Dom, show him the money.''

The hardman closed the van and walked to the Mercedes. He snapped his fingers and the truck popped open. ''Thank you, Richie,'' Dom said, waving at the driver's window of the Mercedes.

''Check it out, Pancho,'' he said.

''Pedro,'' Monzon snapped.

''Pedro, Pancho, Cisco. What the fuck's the difference?''

''Maybe you'd rather buy some Pepsi while you're here.''

''Pepsi, what are you talking about?''

"Coke, Pepsi, what the fuck's the difference?" Monzon said.

"I see your point."

He leaned in, pulled one of two identical briefcases out of the trunk and balanced it on the rear fender. Monzon opened it, clicking the latch and keeping one eye on Dom. When the lid swung up, he glanced at the money, then grabbed a stack of bills. All crisp thousands, they whispered as Monzon rubbed them with his thumb. Fifteen stacks all like the first. A quarter of a million dollars. Arledge edged a little closer, looking over Monzon's shoulder while the bald man checked the other stacks.

"They're consecutive," DeCarlo said, "but you said it was going offshore, so I figured it didn't matter."

"It doesn't," Monzon replied. He leaned in and grabbed the other briefcase, handing it to the hardman. "Open that for me, will you, Ron?"

"It's Dom. You know, Dominick."

"Yeah, yeah. Just open it."

When the second briefcase was opened, Monzon counted it, this time more quickly, closed it and said, "See you later, Frankie."

"You give me a call, Pedro. I can move all you've got."

"Same price?"

"Same quality, same price. No sweat."

"I'll let you know."

DeCarlo climbed into the rear of the Mercedes. He rolled the window down and waited for Dominick to start the van. Monzon stood with his arms folded across his chest as the Mercedes and the van made a tight turn and disappeared through the freight bay door.

Monzon set the briefcases side by side on the ground. "Get the car, will you, Vincenzo?"

Arledge sighed. "Yeah, I'll be right back, man." He walked toward the door, scuffing his feet in the trash on the floor.

"Take your time, Vincenzo. I mean, this is only money," Monzon called after him.

Arledge mumbled something but didn't change his pace. Monzon cursed under his breath. When Arledge stepped through the bay door, Monzon shouted. "All right, Kelly, you can come on down." His voice rumbled around the ceiling, coming back to him in a garbled mutter.

"Be right there, Pedro."

Monzon squatted on the floor next to the briefcases. He heard shuffling feet in the shadows. A flashlight clicked on against the wall, and he turned. "You guys can leave as soon as Vinnie gets back."

Kelly materialized behind the torch. "Piece of cake, huh?" he said, shifting the sling on the CAR-15 draped over his shoulder.

"Why not?" Monzon laughed. Two more men appeared and stood behind Kelly. Both of them carried automatic rifles. They all turned as headlights appeared in the open freight bay. The car sped toward them, skidded in a tight turn, then doused its lights. The men scattered like frightened birds.

Dirt and papers showered down around them. Monzon jumped up, brushing himself off and cursing. "Damn it, Vinnie! What the hell's wrong with you, man? You could have killed us all."

Arledge climbed out of the car, laughing like a loon. "Shit, Pedro. Just having a little fun's all. You got to kick back, man. Chill the fuck out, you know?"

"I'll chill *you* out if you try that again." He turned to Kelly. "You guys can split. I'll try to talk a little sense into Vincenzo. I'll talk to you later."

"You sure you're okay, man?" Kelly asked.

Monzon nodded.

"Whatever you say, Pedro." Kelly shrugged, then eased back into the shadows. His two sidekicks followed him into the darkness.

Monzon didn't say anything until he heard a car start outside. When the noise of the engine died away, he shook Arledge by the shoulders. "Man, what is with you? All that shit I told you earlier. Did you think I was kidding? Didn't you understand what I was trying to tell you?"

"I heard you, man. Don't worry about it. I'll be all right."

"Vinnie, I can't carry you much longer, man. You've got to pull yourself together. You want to get your ass in a sling, okay by me. But I don't want to go down with you."

"I said I'm okay, damn it. Now back off." Arledge turned away and walked toward the car. "Let's get out of here, man."

"You better let me drive, Vinnie."

"Suit yourself." Arledge crossed to the passenger door and climbed into the car. He slammed the door shut and sat there with his hands folded in his lap. The Galil sat across his knees, and Monzon reached in and took the rifle, tossing it and his own into the trunk. He set the briefcases on the floor of the trunk, slammed the lid and got behind the driver's seat.

As Monzon reached for the ignition, Arledge said, "I think I'd rather drive, amigo."

"Forget it!"

"I *said* I'd rather drive." Monzon turned to look at his friend in annoyance. His expression changed when he saw the pistol. "Vinnie, quit it now. Just stop fooling around. I'm tired of this shit."

"Me, too, amigo. Me, too." He squeezed the trigger.

The shot sounded impossibly loud in the interior of the car. He saw Monzon's head snap to one side, then slump forward. He reached for Monzon's throat and felt for a pulse. There was none.

Arledge shook his head. "I'm sorry, man. I really am." With his thumbs he gently, almost tenderly, closed Monzon's staring eyes. "But I'm getting too old for this shit. I've got to look out for myself, Pedro. Do you understand, man?"

CHAPTER TWENTY-FOUR

Bolan checked his watch. Hoffman was restless and kept pacing in a tight circle.

"I hate this crap," he muttered. "I don't like it and I never have."

"It'll be quick and painless," Bolan assured him.

"Easy for you to say. But I have a funny feeling. Arledge has blown this op wide open. Either that or something's going on that we don't know about."

"Take it easy, Gil. We're here, and there's nothing we can do about it. We'll get the job done and be in the air in three hours."

"Maybe. But Gregory was in the air when this all started. It didn't help him much, did it?"

"What, exactly, do you think is going on?"

"It's a gut feeling. Nothing I can spell out in so many words, but I've been in this game a long time. Too long, really. And after a while you learn to pay attention when your antennae twitch."

"What's your read on Arledge?"

"What's to read? The man is a typical cowboy. Power monger, really. But he's become unglued. He got too close to Pagan. I don't know how or why. It could be that Psychology 101 bullshit, identification or whatever. The company's full of assholes like that."

"You're sure he's in bed with Pagan?"

"No doubt about it, man. I saw it with my own eyes. And there's no way it was some kind of deep cover thing, getting next to the geek to burn him. He's on the team. Plain and simple."

"What about Bartlett?"

"Oh, hell, I don't know. Old money and all that. Tweed and horses. It's a goddamn game to guys like that. All they see is duty and kicks. Only they're too goddamn genteel to admit they get off on the power trip. So it's all theory and old glory."

"But you don't have any reason to suspect him of anything worse than ideological zeal, enlightened or otherwise?"

"Look, in this business you do your job or you cover your ass. You don't do both because it's not possible. Every decision you make, if you're paying attention to details, you're putting your ass in a sling if you fuck up. A guy who never got his wrist slapped hasn't been doing his job. Arledge hasn't been doing his job. Plain and simple. He's telling the jerks at Langley and the NSC what they want to hear."

Bolan shrugged, started to respond, then held a hand up. "Listen, do you hear that?"

"Yeah, that must be Rosario. It better be, anyhow." He backed away from the road, easing himself, butt first, into the dense foliage on the far side of a ditch.

Bolan leaped across the ditch and ducked down behind a water-soaked frond. The water showered down over his knees as he inched forward to keep an eye on the dirt road.

A moment later headlights stabbed through the mist as a jeep rounded a curve and careened into the long straightaway approaching the crossroads. The headlights meant that it was an army jeep, because no one, no farmer and not even the most foolhardy of the contra teams would dare use headlights in the middle of the night.

The vehicle slowed, its thick tires sucking at the muddy puddles filling the rutted dirt road. It stopped dead center in the middle of the crossroads, and a young Sandinista officer jumped down into the mud. The engine continued to run, but the headlights went dark. Bolan and Hoffman waited. Rosario was supposed to use a password, and they weren't going to expose themselves until they heard it.

Rosario lit a cigarette, then muttered something to the driver of the jeep. The driver replied, then gunned the engine, driving on through the intersection and coasting past the hiding men. Hoffman nudged Bolan, pointing to the .50-caliber machine gun mounted in the middle of the back seat. Rosario called out, *"Hola, gringos. ¿Como es Jim Baker?"*

Bolan turned to Hoffman and whispered, "Jim Baker?"

"It wasn't my idea," Hoffman answered. He straightened and pushed through the undergrowth. "Lieutenant Rosario, over here."

The young officer seemed startled by Hoffman's voice. He spun quickly, almost losing his footing in the slick mud. Hoffman walked toward him, conscious of the jeep fifty yards behind him, and even more conscious of the M-50 mounted in the rear of the vehicle.

Rosario moved warily. Bolan stayed behind, a CAR-15 in his hands. He kept the rifle trained on the Nicaraguan, and Hoffman was careful to avoid the direct line of fire. Rosario, too, seemed to realize the CIA man wasn't alone. He glanced nervously toward the bushes to Bolan's right, then at Hoffman, then back at the bushes.

"Do you have the money?" Rosario asked.

Hoffman nodded. He reached into his jacket and jerked out an envelope. He handed it to Rosario and said, "That's a down payment. You get the rest when we pick up Gregory."

Rosario reached for the envelope, backing off a step at the same time. "That wasn't the deal."

"It is now. You can't expect us to give you the whole thing up front. That's just a good-faith down payment. Don't worry. You'll get the rest as soon as we get Gregory."

"The papers?"

Hoffman shook his head. "After we get Gregory."

"I don't like it, *señor*."

"I've got news for you, Lieutenant. I don't like it, either. But you're new at this. You get used to it, if you live long enough."

Rosario flinched, then let his right hand drop to the holstered automatic on his hip. "It is not good to joke about such things."

"I'm not, Lieutenant. Believe me, I'm not."

Rosario seemed uncertain how to take it. He backed away another step, the cigarette still dangling from one corner of his mouth. He thumbed open the envelope, riffling the bills quickly, then repeated the rough count. He seemed satisfied, tucked the envelope into the thigh pocket of his fatigue pants and waved to the jeep. Hoffman heard the transmission whine and backed toward the side of the road, keeping one eye on Rosario and one on the muddy ground.

The jeep coasted to a halt, and Rosario climbed into the rear jump seat. He indicated that Hoffman should take the passenger seat in front, but the CIA agent waited. Rosario draped his left arm over the M-50, as if to make a point, and Hoffman laughed. "Lieutenant, you've been watching too many cowboy movies."

"Not at all, *señor*. It is just that there are too many cowboys in Nicaragua. One must be adaptable, no?"

"Not a bad idea." Rosario turned to see who had spoken and rose halfway out of his seat. He stopped when he saw Bolan, the CAR-15 directed toward him in a manner that was indirect but more than accidental.

"So, *norteamericano* cowboys come in pairs. Just like in the movies."

Bolan stepped toward the jeep, and Rosario moved to the far side of the M-50. Hoffman took the seat vacated by the lieutenant, and Bolan climbed into the passenger seat, the assault rifle resting on his lap. The driver glanced at the big man sitting beside him, then down at the trigger guard, where Bolan's finger curled lightly over the trigger.

"The road is very bumpy, *señor*," he said, nodding toward the rifle.

"Then you better drive carefully, *compadre*," Bolan replied.

"*Sí, señor*, I will."

He turned on the headlights and threw the jeep into gear. Rosario watched Bolan cautiously, as if he sensed that it was the big man who was the greater threat. Hoffman reached up and clicked the safety on the M-50. "Not a good idea to leave that off," he said. "You never know what might happen."

"That's why the safety was off, *señor*. Strange things happen in the jungle."

"How far?" Hoffman grunted.

Rosario shrugged. "Not far, maybe ten kilometers."

"Why are you doing this, Lieutenant? You're not supposed to be interested in money. You're supposed to be an idealist."

"Idealism is expensive. I didn't know that until it was too late to change my mind."

"What decided you?"

"When Daniel Ortega visited New York and brought back thousands of dollars worth of eyeglass frames. Expensive frames, 'designer' frames. I realized then that there are all kinds of bad vision. No glasses would cure mine."

"Hey, lighten up, Rosario. Even idealists should look sharp, don't you think?"

"They should see sharply, not look. I have a family. And your *contrarrevolucionarios* are not particular who they shoot."

"Were your people?"

Rosario didn't answer right away. Bolan stopped listening to the argument. It was one neither man could win. He tapped his knee with his free hand, scanning the foliage on either side of the road ahead. The jeep rocked through the ruts, the driver glancing from time to time at Bolan's lap, then shaking his head. Each time he looked, the finger was still there, still curled.

A small village popped up out of nowhere, a shabby collection of ramshackle buildings that seemed to stand only because there was no wind blowing. The jeep slowed abruptly, and the driver killed his lights, glancing at Rosario to make certain he had done the right thing. The lieutenant nodded.

"This is it?" Hoffman asked.

"This is it." Rosario tapped the driver on the back, and he nudged the jeep ahead, its tires sucking loudly in the mud.

"So where is he?"

Rosario ignored the question. He jumped down from the jeep and swaggered toward an abandoned butcher shop. The paint on the sign had half peeled away, but it was still possible to read the letters Carnicería. A low boardwalk, as gray as the rest of the wood in the village, ran the width of the butcher shop. Rosario clomped onto the boardwalk and rapped on the weather-beaten door.

Bolan stepped out of the jeep and moved around to the driver's side. The butcher shop door swung open, its ancient hinges creaking in the humid air. Rosario stepped aside and three men filed out. Bolan realized immediately that the man in the middle had to be Tony Gregory. He towered over the other two, both of whom carried the ubiquitous Soviet assault rifles.

Rosario spoke softly to one of the two guards, and Gregory looked around in bewilderment. The guard nodded, said something to his companion and veered off to the left. They disappeared around the side of the building, and a moment later an engine roared into life. A jeep raced around the corner and headed back the way Rosario had come.

The lieutenant reached into his pocket, and Bolan tensed. A black box, with a small red light winking on and off, sat in Rosario's palm. He covered the red light for a second, then yanked a small antenna out of the box. Bolan started to move toward him and stopped when a brilliant flash pierced the haze. A moment later a tremendous clap of thunder echoed through the trees. The warrior hit the deck, dragging Hoffman to the ground with him.

Rosario cackled. "It is nothing," he said. "Just part of my alibi."

Bolan started to get up, when a rifle cracked high and to his left. Gregory stumbled, falling on his face in the mud. The Executioner rolled to the left, his eyes searching for the location of the shooter. Hoffman scrambled to his feet and dived into the jeep.

Rosario stood rooted to the spot. He stared at Gregory, lying motionless in the mud. "It was not me. I swear. It was not—" A second rifle shot cut him off in midsentence. The slug caught him high on the back of the head, splitting his skull and spattering little chunks of gray matter into the puddles.

Bolan started toward the downed pilot as Hoffman raked the roofline with the M-50. Before he could reach Gregory, a third shot made the pilot jerk.

The warrior took one look and knew the pilot was dead.

CHAPTER TWENTY-FIVE

Bolan raced toward the abandoned hotel. It was the only two-story building in the village and the most likely spot for an assassin. Behind him he could hear Hoffman's M-50 hammering away. He was worried that the assassin might have backup.

The warrior put his shoulder against the door and shoved. He heard the screws groan in the old wood, but the door refused to yield all the way. He stepped back, keeping his eye on the roofline above him, and planted a boot squarely over the lock.

This time the double doors flew open. Bolan pressed back against the wall and peered into the darkness. He signaled to Hoffman that he was going in, and the man waved. The M-50 opened up again, raking the wooden parapet along the edge of the roof and showering splinters on Bolan's shoulders as he dived through the yawning door. Hoffman ceased fire, and Bolan could hear the squeaks of frightened rodents in the dark.

He stayed against a wall and waited until his eyes adjusted to the gloom. The room gradually filled with sculptured shadows. He could make out the outlines of scattered chairs, and a blocky bulk against a far wall. It took him a second to realize that it was probably the front desk.

He inched forward until he reached a corner. Litter crinkled underfoot with a damp rustle, and the floorboards felt spongy under his weight. Working along the second wall, he bumped into something about knee-high. He bent to feel it, recognized it as an ottoman and stepped past.

At the next corner he found a stairway and eased along the railing until he found the first step. The stairs were covered with papers and cardboard. His eyes had adjusted now, and it was possible to make out the wall above the first landing. The second flight led up at right angles.

Bolan stopped to listen for a moment. He was moving more quickly now, realizing that the assassins would have scouted their fire station and would know which way to run. He hoped Hoffman had sense enough to get to the back of the building in case there was a fire escape leading down from the roof, although he doubted it.

He was in the mouth of a hallway, but it was too dark to see anything except at the far end, where an uncurtained window glowed dimly under its coat of grime. There had to be a way to narrow the odds. As near as he could remember, none of the second-floor windows had been open, which meant the gunner had to have been on the roof.

But how had he gotten up there?

Bolan felt the wall with one hand until he found a door. He positioned himself squarely in front of it, kicked it open and ducked out of the way. The slam of the door against the inside wall seemed to rattle the whole building. The warrior stayed low as he crossed the threshold. Another window, this one in the back wall, caught his attention immediately. The window was closed and latched from the inside. He rubbed the dirty glass. A scaffolding of some kind was just visible below the window. He undid the latch and raised the sash, pulling slowly to muffle the sound.

He leaned out cautiously. The wooden structure, not really a scaffold but some sort of makeshift terrace, ran the entire width of the building. At the far end a ladder leaned against the wall, leading up to the roof. Bolan spotted Hoffman standing just off the corner, a CAR-15 in his hand. By hand, he signaled his intention, then climbed through the window as Hoffman stepped out from the wall far enough to give him a clear shot at the roofline.

Once on the shaky wooden platform, Bolan glanced up at the roofline, looking for any sign that someone was up there. When he saw nothing, he moved quietly but quickly along the rickety scaffolding. At the bottom of the ladder he paused. Then, holding the rifle ahead of him, his finger on the trigger, Bolan started up. The ladder was a hastily built contraption of two-by-fours nailed together with spikes. The spikes gleamed in the moonlight, evidence that they hadn't been exposed to the elements for more than a day or two at the most. Anything longer and they would already have begun to rust. Bolan wasn't sure whether that was a good sign or not.

When he neared the top of the ladder, he crouched to get his body higher without exposing his head to anyone on the roof. The ladder creaked ominously, and he felt the rung under his left foot begin to sink. He shifted his feet, putting his weight on the other end of the rung, and the board stopped shifting. He glanced down and saw that the rung had split. It was starting to tear loose on the left-hand side.

Bolan held steady, waving to Hoffman again to indicate that he was going to wait for a moment before attempting to gain the roof. He waited what seemed like an eternity, listening intently, but all he heard was a slight sighing of wind in the forest behind the village. There was something unsettling about the silence, as if everything were unnaturally hushed.

Someone was on the roof. There was no doubt in his mind. He counted in his head, and on five launched himself up and over the low wooden wall. He arched his body in midflight like a pole-vaulter, flattening himself to get just enough lift for the bar. A burst of automatic rifle fire, short and crisp, scratched at the wood just behind him as he fell. Tumbling over the wall, he landed on his stomach.

He started scrambling across the roof, conscious of his shadow on the white shingles, half rolling to keep the shooter off balance. The roof was almost empty of cover. Two cubes jutted up out of the center of the building. Even as he rolled he saw a door in one of them, the latch dangling loosely in the moonlight, glinting as he moved.

The other seemed to be unbroken. He reached it just ahead of a second burst. Chips of brick stung him as the chimney splintered. Sparks glowed as the slugs ricocheted off the stone and whined off into the night. Bolan climbed to his feet, crouching to keep his head below the chimney, which came only to his chest. Not much broader than he, it was just enough cover to keep him out of harm's way.

He dropped to one knee, then pressed closer to the stone. He was thankful he'd picked the right cover, angry that it gave him no offensive advantage. He stuck the muzzle of the CAR-15 out past the edge of the stone, and another burst chewed at the crumbling brick and decaying mortar. One slug glanced off the rifle's barrel, nearly knocking the gun from his grip.

He had to do something, but was pinned too tightly. With so little cover he couldn't even risk a peek around the edge of the stone. The chimney was so narrow that the gunner could see both sides of it without shifting his gaze more than a degree or two.

The rifle opened up again, and this time he heard the slugs splintering wood. He glanced toward the sound in time to see the last couple slam into the wooden parapet. Taking advantage of the diversion, he slipped around the chimney, the CAR-15 raking the edge of the other, larger cube.

The gunner heard his heavy steps and swung his weapon, but Bolan's fire clawed at the wood-and-asphalt edge of the cupola. The guy ducked back out of sight, but Bolan didn't quit. Instead of settling for a standoff on the opposite side of the cupola, the warrior continued around the far side. Hitting the roof in a roll, he came up firing, slicing across the center of the cupola with a 5.56 mm stream.

He saw the gunner start to turn, half obscured by the edge of the cupola. At the same time another burst, this one from behind, caught the shooter in the back. That burst sliced through the falling body, then gouged holes in the asphalt-covered wood.

Bolan moved cautiously toward the fallen gunman. Hoffman's head appeared over the wall, and he swung one leg up and over. The warrior knelt beside the body. There was no way the man could be alive, but he checked to be certain. He yanked the man's rifle out from under the body, a CQ assault rifle, released the clip, checked the chamber, then tossed the rifle aside. It landed with a dull thud against the wooden wall.

Hoffman leaned over his shoulder. He reached down and turned the shooter's face to the side. In the moonlight the shadows obscured the dead man's features. The CIA agent rolled him onto his back. "Uh-huh," he grunted.

"Recognize him?" Bolan asked.

Before Hoffman could answer, a rifle shot cracked behind and below. Bolan jerked around and scrambled to the wall. Rosario's driver lay on the ground behind the jeep. His legs still twitched, but there was no doubt that he was finished. A short man in dark clothing raced toward the jeep, and Bolan braced his rifle on the wooden wall. The little man dodged left and right, and the warrior fired a burst, leading him a little. The clip emptied, and the bolt locked open. The man stopped in his tracks, then cut to the right, diving in behind the vehicle.

As Bolan released the empty magazine, the man scrambled to his feet and dashed toward the nearest stand of trees. Bolan jammed the new clip into place and sighted just as the running man was swallowed by the shadows.

"Damn!"

"Gone?"

"Into the bush."

"Don't worry about it," Hoffman said. "I already know who it was."

Bolan turned to look at him.

"Felix Vasquez," Hoffman said.

"How do you know?"

Hoffman jerked a thumb over his shoulder toward the dead man behind him. "Because that's Tommy Arguello. You pinch one, the other says 'Ouch!'"

"Not anymore," Bolan said. "How do you know them?"

"Because they worked for Vince Arledge...." Hoffman stared at the jungle for a long moment before he added, "We've got to get back to the States. If Arledge sent these guys after Gregory, you can bet he's trying to cover his ass. I have to tell Bartlett about this. One on one. There's a hole in the dike somewhere, and I've got to find it before it's too late for all of us."

"Arledge?"

"You bet."

CHAPTER TWENTY-SIX

The flight to Tegucigalpa went smoothly. Rivera sat by himself, staring out the window as the sun began to set. Bolan watched the general with mixed emotions. There was something about the old man that demanded respect, but there was a history that couldn't be denied. It was the history that fascinated Bolan. How could a man with so much intelligence have allowed himself so easily to be used, he wondered.

The airport was almost deserted, and Bolan felt eyes on him at every turn. He wanted to turn and confront the stares, but felt he would end up whirling like a dervish.

Their greeting party consisted of Harry Martinson, an aide to the American ambassador. Martinson had dressed down for the occasion in an attempt, as he explained, to avoid calling attention to the general's arrival. As if that were possible in a city where every third person were occupied in keeping an eye on the other two. Bolan suspected Martinson was more than a subaltern of the diplomatic corps, but didn't want to raise the issue so publicly.

He noticed Bolan watching him, and gave his best State Department smile, but it stopped at his gums. The eyes behind it were as hard as marbles. They glittered with a cold light that the warrior knew only too well.

"Follow me, gentlemen, if you will," he said, keeping his eyes fixed on Bolan's face as if waiting for the big man to challenge him. The Executioner grunted and grabbed his bag. He'd dealt with the type before and, no doubt, would again. There would be time enough to take Mr. Martinson down a peg or two.

Rivera seemed distracted. He swiveled his head this way and that, trying to take the terminal in in one continuous survey. He seemed on the verge of saying something, then caught himself. He glanced at Bolan, noticed the big man had been watching him and smiled. "It's been a long time," he said. "I came through here on the way to Miami. It wasn't so quiet, then."

"I'll bet," Bolan said without smiling back.

Martinson led the way through a side door, past the customs office. He nodded toward it as they passed. "No need to trouble ourselves with red tape," he said. "And I should apologize for the ambassador. He's out of the country at the moment."

"How convenient," Bolan said.

"The ambassador's a very busy man. You have no idea how complicated things can get, even in a backwater like Honduras."

"That's not particularly diplomatic of you," Bolan pointed out.

"The people here have no illusions," Martinson said, giving Bolan another of those arctic sneers. "Without us they'd be up the creek without a canoe *or* a paddle. And they're well aware of it."

"I'll bet you're not backward about reminding them, either."

Martinson spun around, stopping in his tracks. His right hand moved toward his suit coat, then stopped just short of the lapel. "Look, buddy, I don't know who you are, but I don't have to take that kind of shit. I have a job to do. Why don't you keep your contempt in check long enough to let me get it done? Then you and I can talk it over when it doesn't matter which of us comes out on top."

"Suits me," Bolan replied with a shrug. "But why don't you keep that arrogant condescension under wraps?"

"Gentlemen," Rivera said, "aren't we all on the same side?"

"I'm not sure," Bolan said.

"Then let's try to get along. After all, I won't be in Tegucigalpa that long and neither will Mr. Belasko. I think we can all keep our tempers under control for twenty-four hours."

The glitter seemed to disappear from behind Martinson's eyes. He turned away, then resumed his quick shuffle toward a rear door. He hit the steel panel with his shoulder, shoving it wide open. It slammed back against the wall with a loud clap, and Bolan had to reach out and grab Rivera by the arm to prevent him from barging out right behind Martinson.

"Hold on, General. Let me go first."

Rivera smiled. "You're very contentious today. And more than a little suspicious."

"That's what I'm here for, General. You're not king of the prom, you know."

"Fate has no politics, Mr. Belasko."

"Maybe not, but it has helpers every now and then. I won't argue with fate, General, but I'll be damned if I'll stand around and let somebody give it a hand."

"I appreciate your dedication."

"Don't."

"I know you don't approve of me."

"You don't understand why, though, and that's what bothers me."

"On the contrary, I understand perfectly. I suppose that's why I—"

"Gentlemen, let's go, please," Martinson interrupted. "You'll have plenty of time after we get you tucked in for the night."

Rivera stared at Bolan for a moment, as if deciding whether he wanted to complete his thought. Then, with a sad smile, he shook his head and turned to Martinson. "You're right, of course."

Bolan stepped outside and took a quick look. There was nothing but empty space as far as he could see. The terminal was only two stories high in this area, and he watched the roofline for a minute, then jerked open the door of the waiting limousine. "Okay," he said.

Rivera moved quickly, ducking into the car with a grace that suggested it was a movement with which he was long familiar.

Bolan climbed in after him and locked the door. He made sure the far door was locked, then waited for Martinson to climb into the front passenger seat. The driver had the car in motion before Martinson managed to buckle his seat belt.

During the ride no one spoke. Martinson sat with one arm on the back of his seat, half turned toward the rear as if he wanted to keep an eye on Rivera. The general, for his part, leaned close to the tinted glass, and Bolan thought he might have fallen asleep.

"Where are we going?" Bolan asked.

"Don't worry, sport, it's safe."

"I'm supposed to worry."

The car rolled smoothly over the road, and Bolan leaned back against the seat. An occasional car passed in the opposite direction, its headlights momentarily filling the limo with light, then sweeping past with a rumble. The road ahead was pitch-black, as if they were speeding through a tunnel. After a half hour Bolan spotted a dim glow far down the road. As they drew closer, he realized an entire hillside was brightly lit. The closer they came, the more detail leaped out at him.

At the bottom of the hill a stone wall, topped with clay-colored tiles, disappeared in both directions. A twin row of trees wound upward, zigzagging half the width of the hill, and disappeared into a grove of trees. Above the grove Bolan caught a glimpse of the reddish tiles of a tall, broad building. Then, as they drew still closer, the car roof obscured his view. He ducked forward, but the house was no longer visible.

Two coils of razor wire encircled the wall, anchored to steel posts cemented in place atop the pilasters. A heavy gate stood just to the left of center, and the limo slowed as it rolled toward the opening. In one corner of the compound, half hidden by a stand of trees, Bolan spotted the dull ivory of a parabolic antenna. The driver lowered his window to identify himself to a pair of sentries, then cranked the window back up, tapping the steering wheel impatiently as the guards opened the gate.

"This is it," Martinson announced. "The ambassador's residence."

"I've been here before," Rivera said, startling both Bolan and the aide. "But it wasn't so inhospitable-looking in those days."

"Certain precautions are necessary. It's not like the old days, General."

"It never was, I suppose. We just didn't know any better."

The car passed through the gate, the driver moving slowly to allow for a series of speed bumps in the asphalt. The car jounced with every one, making conversation difficult. Since none of the men seemed inclined to talk, they listened to the creaking of the heavy limo's suspension.

When the car stopped at the front entrance, Martinson jumped out first, and the driver opened the door for Rivera. "Let's get you settled, General," he said, leaving Bolan to fend for himself. At the top of the broad stairway Rivera turned and waited.

When the big man joined him on the flagstone patio, Rivera said, "I suppose we'll be safe here for one night?"

"I suppose so," Bolan grunted.

Martinson led the way in, nodding to an attendant standing on tiptoe, ready to pounce as soon as he was given the word. Martinson ended the suspense. "Juan, please show the general to his suite." The small man nodded vigorously, wrenching Rivera's arm in his haste to take the general's bag.

Juan tugged on Rivera's sleeve, half dragging him toward a marble staircase. Bolan watched the two men ascend, then turned to Martinson. "We should talk."

Martinson nodded. "Follow me." He turned on his heel and moved through an open doorway on the left.

Bolan followed. He found himself in a lavishly appointed study. Bookshelves occupied two walls, and a massive desk stood at the far end of the room. Martinson closed the door and indicated a pair of chairs in one corner. "Have a seat."

Bolan nodded, set his bag on the floor and dropped into one of the big easy chairs. He waited for Martinson to begin, his head tilted to one side, his eyes trying to read the aide. But Martinson was so stiff that it wasn't possible to know what he was thinking.

The ambassador's aide dropped into the second chair. "You should know this isn't my idea," he began. "I don't like Rivera, and I think the whole operation is nuts."

Bolan shook his head. "Look, what we think is beside the point, isn't it?"

"Not to me. I've spent four years trying to piece things together down here. I think it's a pity they've turned away from Guillermo Pagan."

Bolan filed that one away for future reference. "Rivera's more tractable, and he's supposed to be more acceptable to the Nicaraguans. At least that's the theory."

"I know all that shit, but Rivera's not hard enough. When Ortega goes down, there's going to be a mad scramble to take his place. Rivera's not up to it."

"Goes down?" Bolan said.

"Don't be naive. What did you expect, a graceful resignation followed by a convention full of balloons and placards?"

"I was led to believe Rivera was going to spearhead a popular resistance movement and put pressure on the Sandinistas. He thinks he's here to open up the electoral process, to make himself available for the plebiscite."

"Is that what he told you?"

"That's what they told him."

"And you both believed it? Christ almighty... schoolboys, both of you."

"When?"

"Three days..."

"That's not much time."

"How long does it take?"

CHAPTER TWENTY-SEVEN

Bolan stood on the rear porch, watching the sun come up. It was only six o'clock, but he'd already been up for two hours. Tossing all night long, restless and nagged by a dozen nameless worries, he had lain there in the strange bed, reacting to every random sound. Twice he'd reached for his gun. Twice he'd gone back to bed, and still he couldn't sleep.

Now, with the chopper due any minute to ferry him and Rivera to the staging area, he wondered where the next threat would come from. He felt certain that Martinson was a blip on his radar screen. The guy had an edge, and he had those eyes that peered out at the world as if everything in it were designed specifically to annoy him. Martinson didn't like Rivera. That was plain enough. What was less obvious was why.

Bolan was convinced that Martinson was CIA. There was too much of the gunslinger in the ersatz diplomat for it to be otherwise. And in normal circumstances that would be enough to keep him in line. But the Agency was anything but monolithic. The real question was which half Martinson belonged to. Clearly he was a Pagan advocate. Whether he knew about the drug running was a toss-up, but Bolan wouldn't bet against it. He'd have to tell Hoffman to look into it.

The door behind him opened, and Bolan turned to see Rivera step out onto the patio. He nodded but said nothing. Already dressed for the trip in fatigues that looked lived in, Rivera looked faintly silly, like someone's grandfather ready for a masquerade ball. All that was missing was the mask. The old man was trim, and looked fit, but the loose clothing hid much of that, leaving the eye to concentrate on the slightly jowly face and the hint of sagging flesh at the collar line.

The general ignored Bolan and shambled to a corner of the patio to lean out over the rail. He seemed to be studying the neatly tailored gardens sloping away from the house, broken only by the asphalt apron of the helipad, then rolling on uninterrupted to the tree line at the base of the hill. Bolan looked down among the trees, where the razor wire shredded the sun's red light into shimmering bands. The wire moved gently in the slight breeze, and the fractured light seemed to throb like blood in stainless-steel arteries.

The scent of flowers was heavy in the damp air, wafting around the porch on the breeze. Bolan hoisted himself up and sat on the railing. Rivera seemed almost comatose, only a slight nodding of his head suggesting he wasn't a statue but a living, breathing man.

At the first thump of the chopper rotor Bolan dropped to the stone floor of the porch. The sound still made his pulse race a little. He knew where it would break over the hill, and was staring at the spot with anticipation. The whirling blades clawed at the sky, and the chopper rose as if it were screwing itself into the bottom of the sky. Out of the corner of his eye Bolan noticed that Rivera was still motionless.

The chopper hung in the air for a moment, then seemed to slip on a cloud and dropped to the apron like a stone. Bolan moved toward the door. He had his hand on the knob when Rivera broke his silence. "It's still not too late for you to back out, Mr. Belasko."

"If I wanted to back out, I never would have come this far, General."

"I know that. But..." He stopped as if searching for the right word, then waved a hand absently in the air. "Never mind."

Bolan jerked the door open and stepped inside for his bag. When he stepped back onto the patio, Rivera was no longer there.

He started down the winding gravel path to the helipad. Something about the chopper seemed strangely familiar. It was a Huey, and he had seen thousands like it, but there was something more, something he couldn't put his finger on. By the time he reached the apron, the pilot had shut the big engine down. He stood on the apron with hands on hips, watching Bolan jog toward him.

The warrior tossed his gear into the chopper. From behind mirrored shades the pilot watched him with a bored expression. Bolan leaned against the open door. Far up the hill Rivera stepped off the patio and started the downhill trudge. The old man moved gracefully. At this distance Bolan would have taken him for a man twenty years younger. Negotiating the turns smoothly, without lagging or apparent loss of wind, Rivera made it to the bottom of the path and walked over to the chopper with his gear balanced on one shoulder. He dumped the duffel bag into the chopper, then climbed in without a word.

"Friendly fuck, ain't he?" the pilot mumbled. Bolan didn't answer, and the pilot looked at him curiously. "Get's it from you, I guess."

He climbed into the cockpit, and Bolan hauled himself into the rear of the chopper. He noticed the Huey was loaded for bear. He hadn't seen one packing so much since Southeast Asia. The familiar minigun was lashed down, but loaded. Pods of 2.75-inch rockets, also full, hung from the undercarriage. The presence of so much high-tech armament was both comforting and disconcerting. It was nice to know it was there, but disturbing to realize it might be needed.

The general had already belted himself into one of the bench seats along the fuselage, and Bolan picked the jump seat just behind the open cockpit. He noticed a headset hanging from a peg and slipped it on. When he rapped on the pilot's helmet the man turned. Bolan pointed to his headset and the pilot opened his mike.

"What's the trouble?" he asked as the engine coughed, sputtered, then broke into a roar.

Bolan listened to the engines for a moment. When he felt the familiar shuddering of the floorboards, he said, "Just thought we should stay in touch during the flight."

"Good idea. You used to one of these buggies?"

"More than I'd like to be."

"Nam?"

"Where else?"

The pilot chuckled as he opened the throttle, and the bird started to lift off. "This is the closest to Nam I've seen, and I've been everywhere since."

"Combat here?"

"Hell, yes. Forget what you read in the papers. That ain't the half of what goes on down here. I've already lost two Hueys and three friends."

"Sandinistas?"

"One time, yeah. The other, I'm not so sure. It all happened so fast, but I'd swear it was a friendly."

"A mistake?"

The pilot shrugged. "I have to think so, don't I?"

"Why wouldn't you?"

"Our guys are crazy. They spend more time arguing among themselves than they do fighting the other side. And I'm talking live ammo. We had one guy, a captain or something from Somoza's National Guard, take a unit into Segovia Province to wipe out a whole village. There weren't any Nica troops for fifty miles, so I knew it wasn't an accident. Turns out the mayor of the village had insulted his mother's sister. Fifteen years ago. Can you believe that?" To prove he couldn't, the pilot shook his head in exaggerated mystification.

"What do you know about Guillermo Pagan?"

"Nothing." The answer had been too abrupt. But it was obvious the pilot would say nothing further. Bolan waited for him to redirect the conversation, but it seemed he was fresh out of subject matter. The warrior stared out the open door at the treetops a hundred feet below.

The Huey swept down the far side of the hill. Bolan could make out the rear of the hacienda for a few seconds, then it dropped behind the trees and disappeared. The road to the ambassador's residence dwindled to a rutted dirt road. The pilot trailed it for a quarter of a mile, then swept to the left over the trees to follow a sluggish stream that cut through the bottom of the valley.

Bolan watched Rivera, who seemed to be deep in thought. The general leaned back against the back of his seat, his eyes narrowed to slits. He felt eyes on him, turned his head away and closed his eyes completely.

The chopper lurched suddenly, and Bolan heard the engine cough at the same time. He jerked his head around and saw the pilot struggling to keep control. The steady thump of the rotors was gone, replaced by an intermittent fluttering as the engine rose and fell.

"We've been hit," the pilot barked.

Bolan climbed into the copilot's seat, and the pilot pointed to the left, where a pair of motor launches hugged the shore. A half-dozen men were firing automatic rifles at the crippled Huey. "Shouldn't have stayed so low, but I didn't expect trouble this close in."

"Can you get away from them?"

"Not sure. I think the fuel line's been ruptured. The engine seems okay, but I don't have control and I don't have full power. I don't want to go down in the trees. I'd rather ditch in the water."

"Take it straight up," Bolan ordered. He left his seat, crawled into the main cabin, jerked the headset loose and used the wall for balance as he moved to the open doorway. Belting himself in, he unlimbered the M-134 minigun and slammed the door gunner's headset on. "Swing her around," he told the pilot.

"What for?"

"Just do it."

The warrior waited for the crippled bird to pivot. It kept slipping as the engine labored to hold it stable. He swung the minigun around and opened up on the launches. The chopper climbed a little, and Bolan banked his fire. A hundred geysers suddenly erupted as the Executioner swept the 7.62 mm stingers across both launches. The men in the boats hit the deck.

The first belt was gone, and Bolan turned to look for another. Rivera slapped it into his hand. The warrior tossed the empty belt out of the open door, slammed the reload in place and opened fire. The lead boat had begun to drift into open water, and Bolan concentrated on its stern. Raking back and forth, the 7.62 mm slugs shredded the tail end. A puff of black smoke gushed through the floorboard, then spurted like a thin tube straight into the air. Bolan kept up relentless fire, pausing only once or twice to spray the second boat.

Then paydirt!

The fuel tank ruptured and an orange balloon inflated around the boat, swallowing it entirely. When the balloon deflated, the boat had been reduced to blackened slats, just barely staying above the waterline.

A sudden flurry of activity on the second boat caught his eye, and he swung the minigun around. One foot braced on the gunwale, a bearded rail of a man hoisted a LAW rocket to his shoulder. Bolan stitched him up and down with the minigun, and he tumbled backward. The LAW fell from his shoulder and he squeezed the trigger in a spasm as he fell. The rocket slammed into the small cabin, and the second boat was wrapped in black smoke and yellow fire. The flames had begun to recede when the rumble of the blast swept past. Bolan could barely hear it under the ragged cough of the chopper's engine. "Set her down," he barked over the intercom.

"Suppose the pontoons are ruptured?" the pilot asked nervously.

"Do we have a choice?"

In answer the pilot backed off, and the chopper began to descend, wobbling from side to side like a dying yo-yo on a tangled string.

Rivera slapped Bolan on the shoulder, and the warrior turned to see the old man grinning for the first time in days. He shook his head, then braced himself as the chopper touched down with a splash. The Huey listed a moment, then settled in. Bolan leaned out of the door to check the pontoons. There were no bubbles and no hiss. As far as he could tell, the pontoons were intact.

The chopper drifted toward the far shore, where Bolan and the pilot hooked the bank. They tugged the crippled bird in and tied up. The pilot opened the engine housing while Bolan kept watch. "Fuel line's okay," he said. "Still got to figure this out, though." Five minutes later he hooted, "Damn, there it is. Shit, just a couple of wires chopped in half. I can fix that in ten minutes." He went to the cabin and came back with a handful of tools and a couple of crimp splices. "Won't be long. Get you there by lunchtime."

While the pilot grunted and cursed under the open housing, Bolan watched the two blackened shells drifting in the current. He shook his head slowly, and Rivera asked, "What's wrong?"

"I'm not sure." In the quiet he could hear the water lapping at the pontoons. Through a gap in the trees on the far bank, he saw a bright flash of light, then heard an engine roar into life.

The whine of a transmission lurching over uneven ground snarled through the undergrowth, and Bolan caught a glimpse of a jeep bobbing among the trees. One of the occupants was there and gone in a flash. He looked familiar, but Bolan wasn't sure where he had seen him before. Then it came to him.

It was Harry Martinson.

CHAPTER TWENTY-EIGHT

Bolan eyed the small band skeptically. Rivera seemed more impressed, but Bolan wondered how much of it was feigned enthusiasm. One hundred men wasn't much of an army. But if the warrior had no enthusiasm, and that of the general was suspect, the men more than made up for it. They milled around Rivera like fans surrounding a movie star, pressing in on him until he was all but hidden at the center of the slowly tightening knot.

Rivera was the soul of patience, shaking each hand in turn, asking each soldier his name and once or twice asking whether a man was related to this Chamorro or that Gonsalvez. Bolan hung back, watching the entire performance through hooded eyes. Rivera made eye contact with him once, and the smile he flashed seemed real enough, but Bolan couldn't help but think of a dozen other such bands. What they were preparing to do would leave several of them dead, others crippled and, more than likely, all but a handful of them bitter and permanently disillusioned.

He knew Rivera couldn't be ignorant of that eventual outcome, and wondered whether it was the ability to blind oneself to the inevitable that made one fit to command an army of boys who wouldn't be men until it was too late for them to understand the difference.

The pilot, too, stood to one side, one hand resting on the scratched shell of the Huey. He glanced at Bolan, shook his head as if to say what a waste it all was, then climbed into the Huey and cranked up the engine.

The clamor of the still-celebrating warriors was suddenly swallowed by the rumbling engine, and as the chopper started to climb, the men all turned, their hands frozen in midair, their mouths open in childlike wonder. Rivera took the opportunity to extricate himself from the throng, threading his way through the astonished maze like a man pushing through a warehouse full of mannequins.

"It's very gratifying," Rivera confided. "I wasn't prepared for this."

Bolan noticed the tears in Rivera's eyes. In spite of himself, he was moved, glad for the old man. Rivera was turning out to be far more complicated than he had imagined. It wasn't enough to convince the big man that Rivera wasn't just one more cynical opportunist, but there was something real somewhere under the carefully cultivated exterior. But then, Bolan reminded himself, some people argued Hitler must have been a good guy because he liked children.

As long as they had blue eyes and blond hair.

As the chopper disappeared, a silence enfolded the camp. The soldiers began to drift back to their tents, strangely quiet, as if the excited chatter had exhausted their ability to make noise. Rivera, his arms folded across his chest, stood there until the last man was out of sight. He turned to Bolan, the tears gone now, and nodded.

He turned away, his eyes searching for the tent left for him. When he found it, he broke into a stiff trot, waving an arm over his head like a cavalry officer leading a battalion of one. Bolan followed.

Inside the tent, Rivera was already seated at a folding table. "Come in, come in," he said. "Sit down."

Bolan stood there, the canvas flap curled tightly in one hand.

"I said sit down. We have a lot to talk about."

"Oh, really?"

"Yes, we do. Or rather I have a lot to say and you have to listen because you're the only man here, beside myself, who will understand what I'm saying. And I'm not even sure about me."

"I don't really care to listen to some elaborate justification of your past, General Rivera. There's very little you can say that will change my opinion of you."

Rivera nodded. "Of course, you would feel that way. I know I would in your position. But there's a great deal you don't know. Not history, exactly, but also very much history. We're all products of our times, Mr. Belasko."

"Look, General, obviously I'm no fan of Ortega and his crowd."

"That goes without saying."

"Maybe. But, by the same token, I'm not shedding any tears over the late Mr. Somoza. As far as I'm concerned, whoever took him out did the world a favor. And Nicaragua, too."

"It's not that simple."

"It never is to hear guys like you tell it. There's always some excuse, some greater evil to be fended off. So you fry people, you torture them, you drag them from their homes in the middle of the night and put a bullet in their brains. Well, I've got news for you, General, that's not my idea of democracy."

"It's not mine, either." Rivera stood, walked to the tent door and looked out onto the empty square of parched earth. When he resumed, it was as if he were speaking to the air. "You know, when I received my commission in the army, it was 1953. I was a member of a small cabal of officers, all of them young like myself, wellborn and well-intentioned. We didn't like what the Somoza family was doing to our country."

"But you went along with the program."

"No!" Rivera whirled around. For a moment Bolan thought the old man was going to charge him. "No, we didn't. Not at first. We spent a long time, talking about what we were going to do, how we had to have a plan. It was no good just taking one eye for another. It was no good just to throw the old regime into a prison cell, or to line the members up against a wall and do to them what they had done to so many others. We wanted something real."

"So why didn't you do anything about it? What happened?"

"It's not enough for you to know that. First, you have to know what we had decided, the poor little rich boys... We decided on genuine reforms. Redistribution of wealth. Not all at once. Nothing Communist. It wasn't like that. But we wanted to allow the people to own land, let them farm their own property. But we knew it wouldn't be easy. There was too much power concentrated in too few hands. And, besides, we would be going against our own families. Do you have any idea how difficult that was for us, to even think about something like that?"

Bolan grunted. "Thinking comes easy, doesn't it, General? It's the doing that's hard."

"No, you're wrong. Thinking doesn't come easy. Not that kind of thinking. Not for men like us, with our backgrounds, our families, our...history. We would be turning our backs not just on the old way, but on the only way any of us had ever known. We were going to erase four hundred years, expunge it as completely as if it had never existed. You don't do that lightly."

"I'm sure." Rivera ignored the irony.

"For six months we argued. We considered dozens of proposals. It was like a contest, each man trying to come up with something more startling than the others. Everyone of us was trying to find some middle ground between the dictatorship we had and the future we knew wouldn't come overnight. It was important to set things in motion, but not too fast. It had to have momentum, but not enough to sweep us all into chaos. Wisdom, Mr. Belasko, that's what we were looking for. But we were too young. We didn't *have* any wisdom. We were idealists, plain and simple. And there was too much we didn't know. About ourselves, mostly."

"So you gave up."

Rivera collapsed onto a canvas chair, his body sagging as if under a great weight. For a long time he said nothing. He stared at the ground in front of his chair. Bolan held his peace, waiting for Rivera to speak again. When he did, his voice was that of a man confronting something he hadn't dared to think about for too long.

"So we did the only sensible thing. We asked for help. We asked the American ambassador for help. We sent a delegation to meet with him. He assured us he was sympathetic and that he would do what he could to help us. Two days later every single member of the delegation was arrested. They were tortured in ways I won't describe to you because I can't bear to think about it. But not one man broke. Not one man gave up a single name. Somoza was convinced there were others. There had to be. He was right, of course, but he was helpless to do anything about it."

"I still don't understand."

"No, of course not. You've never betrayed anyone. I know that. I can see it in your eyes. But if you look into *my* eyes, you'll see my betrayal, my victim. You'll see *me*. I turned my back on every thing I believed in, out of despair and self-loathing. If I couldn't change things, very well, then I would out-Somoza Somoza. I would hide my guilt in my zeal. He would never suspect me because I would give him no reason."

Rivera got to his feet with some difficulty. He looked Bolan in the eye for a long moment. "You know, Mr. Belasko, it's easier to fool yourself than it is to fool anyone else. After a while I told myself that I believed in what I was doing. That reform was an unworkable nightmare, that what was was the only way things could be. I had betrayed my ideals, sold them down the river for my own safety, and the only way I could justify that betrayal was to convince myself, and to convince everyone else, by brute force if necessary, that there was only one reality, that the world as it was was all that stood between us and the abyss."

"You didn't really come back here to recover the money, did you, General?"

"Of course I did. What kind of a fool do you think I am? I've lived too long, Mr. Belasko, far too long with a secret that I can't undo. And I now have what I didn't have when it counted—wisdom. I know that it's too late to change the past and that the future is beyond our power to change. Man reaches too far. *I* reached too far. But I won't make that mistake again." Rivera swiveled in the chair. "Now, if you'll excuse me, I'd like to be alone. With my past."

Bolan nodded. He pushed aside the flap and left the tent. Outside, it was high noon, but the sun had vanished. A swirling mass of black clouds had swept down from the mountains, pouring over the tops of the trees like a thick liquid. The first drops of rain splattered on the canvas like gunshots. Bolan felt a few drops on his shoulders and watched the small puffs of dust other drops kicked up from the bone-dry earth.

He didn't know what to make of Rivera. If the old man was an actor, it was a bravura performance. If he was on the level, it made for a whole new ball game. There was a passion in the man, but it could cut either way. If Rivera truly believed the past was a dead issue, that things couldn't be changed, then he just might be here for the fortune he'd left behind. But if, as Bolan was beginning to suspect, Rivera harbored long-hidden thoughts of setting right the past, it could be a long and dangerous path. Bolan didn't know which, and had to expect both. But how did you prepare for an earthquake triggered by a single footfall?

He looked up at the sky where the clouds had stopped swirling. A uniform sheet of charcoal now covered it, seeming to rest like a dark gray tent on the surrounding peaks. It was as if the entire world were confined to this single valley. They had already been shrink-wrapped in funeral garb, and the dying had yet to begin.

Bolan walked toward the trees, needing a solitude of his own. Among the green fronds, darkened by the absence of sunlight, he listened to the patter of the rain on the thick, fleshy leaves stretching high overhead. As if in response to his glance, the sky seemed to split open, and a clap of thunder signaled the beginning of a real downpour. Soon the leaves were too heavy to hold the water off any longer, and streams coursed down the trunks and branches, writhing silver bands wriggling like slender snakes toward the ground.

The steady drumbeat of the huge drops on the green canopy grew to a roar. Bolan stood under a thickly leaved tree and tried to keep dry. He watched Rivera's tent, then let himself slide to the ground. Resting his chin on his knees, he stared through the slashing rain. Rivera appeared in the mouth of the tent and stared at the sky, slowly slipping out into the open to spread his arms, palms up.

Rivera was smiling.

CHAPTER TWENTY-NINE

Gil Hoffman sat patiently, watching the motel across the road. Vince Arledge had been inside for two days without once venturing out, even for meals. He'd had a pizza delivered the first night, but had had no other visitors. It was getting tough just to sit there and watch. Hoffman was dog-tired. Twice he'd fallen asleep only to wake up with a desperate feeling that events were unfolding over which he had no control.

It was tempting to barge in on Arledge, but Hoffman was convinced he had to wait, to let the man make the first move. If Vince was in it alone, he thought, no harm done. If he wasn't, Hoffman had to know. Rapping the wheel impatiently, whistling through his teeth, Hoffman poured himself another cup of cold coffee from the thermos and swallowed another benny.

He thought back to the beginning of it all and his conversation with Ricky Vargas. He was certain now that he had been right. He *was* too old for this crap. He kept thinking of his wife and kids. He hadn't seen them in a month, and it had been the longest month of his life. Something kept nagging at him, telling him it might be the last month. He didn't want to believe it, but he knew himself too well to argue with a feeling like that.

Hoffman's stomach felt as if it were full of hot lead. The acid kept churning, and the coffee just made it worse. He tried another cheese sandwich, but his mouth was dry, the bread even drier, and the cheese wouldn't go down. He swallowed hard, washed the mouthful down with more cold coffee, then rolled down his window and tossed the last of the sandwich into the weeds.

More than anything in the world, Hoffman wanted to go to sleep. It wouldn't be the end of the world, he told himself. He'd planted a locator on Arledge's 4X4 the first night. He kept telling himself that even if Arledge left while he slept, he could find him again.

But that was only part of the problem. Arledge might just be the tip of the iceberg. Until he knew for sure, he had to stay awake. Hoffman fished another Benzedrine out of his pocket and washed it down with the last of the coffee. He felt his nerves pulsing just under his skin, imagining for a minute that he could hear them humming like high-tension wires.

The CIA agent got out of the car and stretched his legs, running a fistful of nervous fingers across his jaw. His whiskers grated on the skin of his palm. He stepped deeper into the woods to urinate, glancing over his shoulder to keep an eye on the motel. He zipped up again and sat on the hood of the car.

The Benzedrine was making it harder to concentrate. He knew the danger, but measured against so many other dangers it seemed like a small risk, one that at least gave him a return. Then Hoffman chuckled out loud. He remembered the first time he'd taken a benny. It had been Vince Arledge who had given it to him. "So much water under the bridge," he mumbled. Then, aloud, he said, "So much spilled milk."

The woods behind him grew even more silent. The flashing neon of the motel sign, a flamingo flapping its garish pink wings, hurt his eyes. He closed them, and in the darkness inside his own head he could still see the grotesque bird, its wings constantly flapping, making no progress at all. Like me, he thought. He rubbed his eyes, pressing them back into his skull hard enough to hurt.

The pain made him feel good somehow, made him more alert, pushed a lot of memories away. He and Vince had been through so much together. What the hell had happened to him? Hoffman wondered. Where had it all fallen apart? Whose fault was it, anyway?

Hoffman knew the answer even before the question fully formed in his mind. The fault belonged to Vince Arledge, and to no one else. Sure, there were temptations, but they were there for everybody. Sure, there were rotten choices to be made, but everybody had to make them. Arledge was no exception, and he was no victim.

Or was he?

Who knew? And in the final analysis what did it matter?

Hoffman recognized the signs. He was getting antsy. He was losing control, losing that analytical edge, that split-second advantage that perfect control gave him. It wasn't just a matter of reflexes, although that was part of it. It was a kind of second sight, seeing things before they happened, anticipating them just enough to compensate, to deflect them before they did any damage. But there was nothing he could do about it. He was what he was, just as Vince Arledge was what *he* was. And what they were, separately and together, had brought them to this point with an inevitability that was almost too perfect.

Hoffman eased off the car. He felt cold, even though it was a hot and muggy night. He wrapped his arms across his chest, hugged them to himself and rocked back and forth on his heels. God, he hated this shit.

How much he wished it could be over. But it wasn't. It was a long way from being over.

He climbed back into the car and sat in the passenger seat. He had a little more room, and he curled his legs and tucked his feet under him, leaning back against the door. Pouring the last of the cold coffee from the third and final thermos, he watched the motel out of the corner of his eye, but all he could see clearly was the flapping wings of the damn flamingo.

He choked the coffee down and crushed the flimsy paper cup into a ball. The little portable clock on the dashboard glowed a pale green. It said 2:17.

His eyes closed for a moment, and he felt a tremendous wave of sleep trying to suck him under. His lids were heavy, and they fluttered when he forced them open. He'd been chintzy with the bennies, and it was catching up with him. Hoffman screwed his head down into his shoulders and twisted his neck. The crack of his vertebrae felt good. He did it again, and this time the crack was less audible and less satisfying. He shrugged his shoulders and smacked his cheeks. The sting of his own hand on his face made him shiver.

He changed position and leaned across the seat, his head propped on the window ledge. He could see only half the motel now, just far enough down to watch the top of the doors. It was enough, but he felt negligent, as if he were slacking off. And he didn't give a shit.

He heard tires on the gravel of the parking lot and he sat up. Maybe Vince was having a visitor. He grabbed binoculars off the dash and sat up. A late-model Oldsmobile pulled up in front of number ten. Arledge was in number eight. The Olds was right next to his 4X4.

Two people sat in the front seat. They huddled together for a minute, then the driver opened his door.

The passenger was a woman. She slid across the seat, under the steering wheel, and climbed out behind the driver. Hoffman twiddled the focus, sharpened the image a bit and held his breath.

The driver walked to the door of number ten, which he opened, and stepped inside, leaving it open for the woman. She teetered slightly on high heels, entered the room and turned to close the door. Her face was clearly visible under the pale yellow light. Even at this range it was obvious that her lipstick was a little smeared. She closed the door, and that was that.

Hoffman allowed himself to sink back toward the car door, the binoculars in his lap. Nothing like a false alarm to get the juices pumping, he thought.

The agent was nearing the end of his tether. If something didn't happen soon, he was going to have to do something about it. He didn't know what he *could* do, but there had to be something. His options were limited working on his own. It would have been nice to mount a full-fledged surveillance operation, but that just wasn't in the cards. He didn't know who he could trust, if anybody.

He thought about the big guy in Nicaragua and wished Belasko was here. That was a man you could count on. But that would have to wait. There was business to transact, and besides, he reminded himself, Arledge was an open door. Somebody had set up the Gregory hit. Somebody had leaked the news about Rivera. Somebody, in fact, was running a full-fledged wire service for the other side.

It could have been Bartlett, but he didn't think so. Everything pointed to Vince Arledge. Of course, in the Byzantine logic of Winston Bartlett, anything was possible. But this seemed a little too convoluted even for the

DDO. It had to be Arledge, and the best way to find out was to take him out of the loop. Bartlett hadn't heard from Arledge in several days. That was suggestive, but not conclusive. But Arledge was plugged into all the wrong circuits on this one. Only things he knew had been leaked. To be on the safe side, Bartlett had cut him off, or so he said.

But the snowball was already rolling downhill, and it was up to him to stop it before it became an avalanche. A car door slammed, and Hoffman turned to see Arledge's brake lights go on.

Here goes nothing, he thought, reaching for the ignition key.

CHAPTER THIRTY

Bolan lay on his bunk, watching the bugs crawl up and down the mosquito netting. He stopped counting after he'd spotted two dozen species. If there were any more out there, he didn't want to know about them. He was uneasy with the way things were shaping up. The contingent of American advisers, just a dozen men, had seemed too aloof, too detached. They kept to themselves even at mealtime. It seemed as if they were trying to conceal something, either from the men they were there to advise, or from themselves.

The determined lockjaw, the tight mouths and immobile faces suggested an unaccustomed restraint. He'd seen that look before, and he didn't like the parallel. The CIA advisers training Hmong tribesmen in the mountains of Laos had had that look in the last days before they'd pulled out, leaving the people to fend for themselves. It was a mixture of resignation and contempt, but for whom was never clear, not even to the men themselves. They just knew that something had gone terribly wrong and that they were powerless to do anything about it, regardless of their feelings. So the next best thing was semiparalysis.

He knew Rivera wasn't a popular choice at the Agency. He was the candidate of desperation, the marginal player sent in when the game was out of reach. More often than not, the guy was on a bus back to the Texas League when he stepped out of the shower. Bolan didn't know if that was Rivera's impending fate, but he wouldn't bet against it. What had started out as a run at cocaine cowboys had turned into a political pipe dream. The warrior was backstopping a Company plan to win the hearts and minds of Nicaraguans in far less time than any reasonable man would think possible. It was a puppeteer's two-minute drill, and he kept tripping over the strings.

The heat sat on Bolan's chest like an anvil, and he had trouble breathing. He had to get out of the tent, get a little air, or he'd suffocate. The warrior grabbed an AK-47, standard armament in the camp, and slung it over his shoulder. Pushing aside the netting, he stepped out of the tent. The ground was as dry as if it had never rained, but clouds of smoky fog coiled among the trees, contorting like ghosts in a kid's Halloween nightmare.

It had cooled down a little from the afternoon's sweltering oppression, but it was still more than seventy-five degrees. A half moon drifted in and out of the ragged clouds. High above the camp, a dozen bats fluttered like black rags, their wings alternately flapping and dragging as they spiraled in tight circles after the bugs.

Bolan drifted aimlessly, crossing the makeshift parade ground at an angle toward a dim light that showed in one of the advisers' tents. Before he got halfway across the hard-baked square the light went out.

He slowed and watched the moon for a few seconds. It seemed to glow with inordinate brightness for a moment, then dimmed, and he realized there was a very thin overcast. He heard a guitar, some shuffling blues thing, as he drifted closer. The guitarist was good, bending notes and wrenching triplet clusters with painful restraint, building his lines slowly, patiently, a phrase at a time, letting space speak as eloquently as the strings.

As Bolan drew closer, the tent flap swung open. One of the advisers, a small black man shaped like a barrel with arms, stepped into the moonlight, a portable cassette player in his hands. He moved in time to the music, letting his body take its cue from the guitar. He moved away from the tent as an ironic Oklahoma drawl snarled, "Thank you, Homes."

The black man mumbled something Bolan couldn't catch and drifted toward the edge of the camp. The warrior moved after him, and at the first step the man swung around, a .45 in his hand. "You shouldn't sneak up on folks, cowboy."

"Sorry," Bolan said. He nodded toward the cassette player. "Luther Allison, right?"

The man shook his head. "Not bad. I'm surprised you ever heard of the dude, let alone recognize his style."

"A good bluesman is as recognizable by his instrument as by his voice."

"That's what they say. Especially those white folks who think they're cool 'cause they recognize B. B. King. My name's Caspar Washington. They call me Cazz." He stuck out a hand that felt as if it had been carved out of ebony, as hard as a rock. But he made no attempt to squeeze to show how macho he was. It was all there in the grip, and he knew it.

"Mike Belasko."

"Couldn't sleep or didn't want to?"

"I don't think I know the difference anymore."

"You're right. Maybe there isn't one."

"Listen, I didn't mean to startle you. I was just walking off a lousy mood."

"Don't walk too far. These woods are full of snakes. Good idea to hang close to the edge of camp."

"Thanks."

"Later..." Washington drifted off, cranking up the volume a bit as he left the tents behind.

Bolan moved toward the narrow road that entered the camp at one end and left it at the other. A winding gash in the forest that simply swelled enough to accommodate the tents, then closed up again, it was already losing the battle against the lush growth, sprouting patches of green and narrowing at the top where the canopy on either side reached out to heal the wound.

The warrior walked about sixty or seventy yards, just past the first curve in the road. When he turned to look back, he could no longer see the camp. The road itself looked otherworldly in the uncertain moonlight. At times the leaves, soaked by the day's rain, turned the color of skim milk, and when the moon receded, they faded to battleship-gray. If he didn't know why he was here, and what was going on every second in the forest all around him, it might have been peaceful.

But he knew too much.

He was about to turn back when a slight glimmer caught his eye. For a moment he thought it might have been a firefly, but as he let his eyes sweep the forest across the road, he realized there were no others. If there was one, there would be more.

The glimmer came once more, then disappeared. Bolan slipped the safety off the AK-47 and stepped into the trees. He had to go slowly, unfamiliar as he was with the terrain.

He swept tangled vines aside with his free arm, hefting the assault rifle in his right, his finger curled through the guard. The forest floor was a jumble of rotting timber and leafy mulch. Thorny vines wound around one another and everything else in their search for the scattered light that managed to sift through the canopy. His clothes kept getting snagged on the thorns, and he was growing impatient. He heard mumbled voices and stopped to listen. They were moving away from him out on the road, and he realized he had simply taken a short cut through a wedge of forest where the road doubled back on itself.

Bolan caught a quick glimpse of four men huddled over something on the ground in front of them. One man was pointing at it while the other three watched the movement of a small beam. As the warrior eased through a particularly dense clump of undergrowth, the conference broke up. The men straightened and shook hands. One man, his face bathed in silver light, looked vaguely familiar, but the combination of sheen and shadow distorted his features just enough to prevent recognition. He moved away from the others, keeping to the side of the road. A moment later Bolan heard the rumble of a jeep. It moved away slowly, as if the driver wanted to keep the noise to a minimum.

The voices were drifting away as the men moved freely without the impedance of the jungle. In the moonlight Bolan could make out the figures of three men. They were walking around the curve of the road, heading back toward the camp. Because of the angle, they were facing away from him. He picked up the pace, cutting at an acute angle to try to get in front of them without giving away his presence. It might just have been a few friends on a midnight stroll, but that didn't explain the fourth man, and it didn't explain the huddle.

It seemed clear that they had wanted to meet away from the camp and probable that at least one of them wasn't even from the camp. But why? Bolan moved out onto the edge of the road as the men rounded the curve and pulled out of sight. As long as they didn't know he was there, there was no need to do anything but keep hidden. Back at the camp, he could see which tent they went into and narrow the field considerably.

The men stopped abruptly, then dodged into the trees. He heard the footsteps behind him at the same moment and started to turn. Something nailed him high on the temple, and he went down without a sound. He lay there staring up at the clouds, only half conscious. He tried to get up, but his body wouldn't respond. As his last strength ebbed away, he fell back onto the ground, his cheek ripped by several thorns. The pain stabbed through him, and he reached up to wipe at his face when he heard the gunshot.

Then he blacked out.

CHAPTER THIRTY-ONE

Hoffman hung back, watching Arledge's taillights in the distance. The man was heading south, and there was no other traffic on the road. Hoffman felt Arledge was telling him something that he already knew. There was something final about this midnight run, and Arledge was driving as if he knew it.

Southwest of Miami, the population was sparse. Mangrove swamp and dark blue sky surrounded the two vehicles like a giant bowl. The stars were bright, and a piece of moon hung in the heavens like an inquisitive eye. Hoffman felt his nerves settle down. At last it was happening. This phase was about to close for both of them. After tonight neither man would be the same. One of them might even cease to be at all. But that was up to Arledge.

It didn't seem like a flat-out flight. Arledge seemed to have some idea where he was going. Hoffman wished he could say the same about himself. They were on Florida 27, heading toward the Everglades. Hoffman had figured the Keys, and was uncertain about the choice.

If Arledge wanted to disappear, this wasn't the best way to go about it. Unless he had a boat at Flamingo, it didn't make sense. The towns on the tip of the peninsula could be counted on the fingers of one hand. There were a few hamlets, clusters of shacks and that sort of thing, and the Miccosukee Indians had a few villages, some even the government didn't know about, sprinkled around the point, but that was about it.

They had done some training in the Glades years ago, before the Bay of Pigs, and Arledge might know about one of the camps, but there seemed little point in hiding out in a swamp. What did he expect to accomplish by that?

And how long could he stay there?

He remembered Belasko's story about the freighter, and slowly a germ of an idea began to crystallize in the back of his mind. A chopper had chased Belasko, appearing out of the blue. He wondered whether Arledge might have a little something going down here. They weren't that far off the sea lanes, and it had never made sense for Pagan to attack his own house, or to take down one of his own shipments. But somebody had known, and that somebody had access to some heavy artillery.

But before Hoffman had a chance to pursue his train of thought any further, the taillights up ahead winked out. He thought for a minute that Arledge might have decided to see who was pursuing him. He could stop, a sure sign that he had been following, or he could keep on going, doubling back if he had to. Hoffman slowed a bit as he debated. Finally, realizing that it was no better than a coin toss either way, he floored it again.

Keeping his eyes peeled, Hoffman searched both sides of the road, looking for some sign that Arledge had simply pulled over, perhaps into a clump of trees. It was difficult to gauge the distance between himself and the point where the lights had vanished, but he knew Arledge couldn't have been more than a mile or so ahead of him.

When the odometer showed that two miles had elapsed, Hoffman slowed the car and coasted to a halt. It was conceivable, but unlikely, that Arledge had simply turned off his lights and continued driving. The moonlight would have made it possible, although difficult, to stay on the road, but only at reduced speed. Hoffman knew he would surely have caught up to him by now.

Heaving a sigh, he jerked his car into a K-turn and started back the way he had come, this time moving slowly. He knew he was exposing himself to an ambush. All Arledge needed to do was pull off the road far enough to conceal his vehicle. At Hoffman's reduced speed, he would have been a sitting duck for a gunman hiding in the reeds on the far side of the ditch that paralleled the road on either side.

But Hoffman knew he had no choice. If he lost Arledge now, it was all over. Vince could go anywhere, and the odds against finding him again were astronomical. In the meantime he could sabotage the whole Nicaraguan operation. If there was any point in taking him at all, it had to be tonight. Tomorrow was no good; tomorrow was forever away.

Then Hoffman got lucky. He spotted a dirt road he had missed the first time. It was little more than a pair of ruts in the marsh grass. A mound of dirt, weedless and muddy, obviously of fairly recent vintage, had filled the ditch, permitting a car to drive off the road and head cross-country. How far was an open question, and Hoffman was reluctant to trust the tricky marshland. If Arledge had turned in here—and there seemed little possibility he hadn't—he had the advantage of knowing where he was going. Hoffman couldn't say the same. He pulled onto the makeshift road just far enough to get his car off the highway and left it astride the double ruts. It might make a difference if Arledge tried to bull his way out.

Hoffman shut off the engine and climbed out of the car. Walking to the trunk, he opened it and took out a web belt. In quick succession he attached a small first-aid kit, a couple of ammunition pouches, a couple of grenades and finally a canteen. He opened a leather case and removed an M-16, already fitted with an AN/PVS-2 Starlite scope. The rifle was bulky, but in these conditions the scope could be invaluable. With an eight-hundred yard range, he didn't have to get any closer to Arledge than he cared to. And with the lead Vince had, he might not get much closer than that in any case.

He wasn't eager, but he was ready. Leaning on the rear fender of the car, he used the scope to check the road ahead. As far as he could tell, Arledge was far ahead of him. He spotted a couple of small deer, far out in the marsh, so he knew the scope was working properly, but there was no sign of his former comrade-in-arms. Sweeping the scope across the tree line far ahead, nearly a mile as far as he could tell, he again came up empty.

Hoffman started down the road, his feet creating small pools of water with every step he made. He was glad he hadn't bothered to use the car. He'd have been hopelessly bogged down inside of fifty feet.

He stopped every so often to look for evidence of Arledge's 4X4. There were tracks all right, but the ground was so spongy that he couldn't tell whether they were minutes, hours or even days old. Every depression in the ground immediately filled with water. The telltale tread of a heavy tire left a pattern of oblique wedges in the mud under the bent weeds. Every so often

he stuck by a particularly perfect impression that caught
the slice of moon so precisely that it reflected it without a blemish on an absolutely calm, mirrorlike surface.

Hoffman stopped to listen, but he heard no evidence
of the presence of a human. The third time he stopped
he heard an owl far off in the distance. Its hoot was so
mournful that it made Hoffman second-guess his decision for an instant. The chill that had ran up his spine
made him feel old and vulnerable. Years ago, when he
was new at his business, such a noise was part of the
thrill, one of the accoutrements of his profession. Now
he felt differently. Now he knew the clichés were much
more deeply rooted in real soil than he had imagined.
And it made his spine tingle.

Two hundred yards in he found the Ranger, nosed
into a clump of bushes, its rear end blocking half of the
road. Hoffman took a quick look inside without opening the door. For a second he thought he saw someone
staring back at him from the back seat, then he realized it was his own reflection in the glass. He shook his
head as if to clear it, then pushed on. He searched the
grass for evidence of traffic, but as with the tires, the
footprints could have been there for several days.

Hoffman moved past the clump of bushes and
dropped to one knee. He used the scope again to check
out the road ahead. Straight as an arrow, it ran directly
toward the tree line, now no more than a thousand
yards ahead. Swampland was alien territory to him, but
he guessed the trees might mark water of some kind,
either a lake or perhaps a stream cutting through the
marsh.

He saw more than his share of nocturnal wildlife, but
there was still no sign of Arledge. The sun would be

coming up soon, and then the scope would no longer be an outside edge. He wished he'd thought to bring a daylight scope, but it was too late now. He started to double-time it, paying less attention to his feet and more to the approaching trees.

He listened to the sound of his gear slapping against his body, its rhythm spastic and irregular as his legs pumped through the grass and fought with the soggy ground. His muscles started to burn, and his lungs felt as if they were on fire. He wasn't used to this stuff anymore, and he kept telling himself that it would soon be over. Promising himself fifty yards at a time, he managed to get within a hundred yards of the trees before he had to stop.

He fell to his knees, struggling to keep his stomach under control. His chest felt as if it were ready to split open, and every breath burned his throat. His limbs trembled, and he knew he'd fall on his face if he tried to stand. The bennies were taking their toll. He'd been running on empty for too long. The chemicals could deceive him as long as he didn't try to push his body too hard, but the sprint for the trees was too big a lie. The truth spread along his neural circuits like flames tracing a network of gunpowder just under the skin. He tried to get his breathing back to normal. The pain in his chest subsided a bit, but his muscles were less cooperative. He had robbed them of stamina with the bennies, and they weren't about to be abused any further.

Hoffman dropped on his butt, ignoring the water sopping through his pants. Slowly his equilibrium was restored, but he could still hear his heart pounding in his ears. He placed one hand flat on his chest, and he could feel the insistent drumming on his ribs, as if some angry beast were hurling itself against the bars of its cage.

He looked stupidly at the rifle balanced precariously now on his lotused legs. With a shrug, and knowing that for the moment he was capable of nothing more strenuous, he raised the scope for one more look at the trees. He started at the left, about two hundred yards off the road. Slowly sweeping the Starlite, its objective scooping available light out of the darkness, he followed the irregular course of the trees. At a point directly in front of him he found a small break in the trees, but it was just one of several in the winding course he'd traced.

Scoping out the right, he moved the Starlite more quickly, as if he didn't really expect to see anything, anyway. He scanned nearly three hundred yards to the southwest, then doubled back. A hundred yards back toward dead center he stopped. Moving the scope back, he pressed his eye to the rubber, trying to cut out the seepage of glare from the slightly graying sky.

And there it was. At first he wasn't sure, but now he wondered how he'd overlooked it the first time. On the far side of the trees was a structure of some sort. Made of wood, its lines too regular, too sharply delineated, its edges too straight to be any natural growth, it was just discernible through the foliage. He wouldn't have spotted it at all if it hadn't been for the shifting branches. Whatever it was he was looking at, it didn't move when the wind blew, while everything else bent before the slight breeze.

"Okay, Vince," he whispered. "Okay, I'm coming, buddy."

Hoffman got wearily to his feet, levering himself erect with the help of the M-16. He moved much more cautiously now, keeping to the very edge of the road, almost flush with the reeds waving at shoulder height now that he had stepped off the slightly elevated road. He was reluctant to go any farther from the road. He'd heard things in the swamp on either side of him, and the marsh was full of sinkholes and alligator wallows. If one of the gators took a notion to run him down, it was all over. He was too far out of his element here.

When he reached the trees, he found the road intersecting another following the tree line in both directions. Hoffman headed southwest toward the structure he'd seen, this time staying close to the trees, where the ground was more solid underfoot. He had to estimate the location because he was too close to the trees now for the scope to help him pick it out. Twice he thought he'd gone far enough and eased his way among the trees only to find nothing.

He paused to listen. Still nothing.

Then he saw the light.

CHAPTER THIRTY-TWO

Bolan opened his eyes slowly. Staring straight at the sky, he watched the moon slide in and out through a tangle of dark gray shapes. He knew it was the moon, but wasn't sure what the shapes were. As his vision cleared, he noticed another, more solid shape to his left. He sat up sharply, and everything began to spin.

The hand on his shoulder pressed him back gently but firmly. "Stay down a minute," the voice ordered. Bolan vaguely recognized the speaker, but he was still disoriented.

"Who's there?" he mumbled.

"The old man," Rivera said. "Maybe not so old after all, eh?"

"What happened?" Bolan sat up again, this time more slowly. Rivera let him move.

"Somebody thought you saw something you shouldn't have," Rivera replied, a hard edge to his voice.

Bolan shook his head to clear it.

"If I were a suspicious man," Rivera said, "I might wonder what you were doing out here in the first place. I'm here, as you see, so perhaps I'm suspicious, eh? Maybe you would like to tell me what you saw."

"I didn't see much," the warrior replied. "I couldn't sleep. I took a walk and I saw a light. When I got close enough to see, four men were talking, looking at something on the ground. I don't know what. When they were finished, one went back to the camp, the others went the other way. I was following the one back to camp when somebody slugged me. So there was at least one other man out here.''

''Don't worry about him. Did you get a look at any of the others?''

''No. And I heard a shot after I got hit.''

''So you did. But it was my gun.'' Rivera shook Bolan's shoulder, then pointed. At first the warrior saw nothing but a fallen tree trunk. It took him a moment to realize the shadowy lump was the body of a man.

''Who is it?'' Bolan asked, getting to his knees. He was still groggy, but he had to move.

''The man who attacked you. The man who was about to shoot you when I beat him to the draw.'' Rivera chuckled.

''I guess I owe you.''

''I guess so,'' the general agreed. ''So, what do you think we ought to do about this?''

''If I had to guess what those men were looking at, I'd say it was a map, a diagram of some kind. Probably of the camp. One of your men was giving an update, or spotting targets for the others.''

''You think they plan to attack us, then?''

''What do you think?''

''I think we should assume the worst. I always do, and it's worked very well for me until now.''

''All right, what do you want to do?''

''I'll tell you on the way back. We better hurry,'' Rivera said. The playful tone was gone. He was all business now, and Bolan was getting a glimpse of yet another Emiliano Rivera, the no-nonsense military commander. Somehow he wasn't surprised. He was

starting to wonder, though, just how many men inhab-
ited that one body.

BOLAN MOVED into the first tent carefully, not wanting
to risk getting shot by a nervous soldier, and woke the
first man he came to after clamping a hand over his
mouth. He spoke softly, assuring the man that there was
nothing to fear. He told him what he wanted, and together they woke the rest of the men in the tent. Rivera
joined them, explaining that he feared an attack was
imminent. And he made it clear, with an emphasis that
caused more than a few quizzical looks and raised eye-
brows, that he wanted the advisers to be the last ones
awakened.

It took twenty minutes to rouse all the men. They
were armed and edgy. As Rivera outlined his plans, the
last traces of grogginess disappeared. This was what
they had been waiting for, training for, grinding themselves into powder for. All the weeks of lousy food and
insatiable bugs, the heat and the humidity, the isola-
tion and the tedium were all about this one moment—
combat.

Maybe.

If the general was right. But he had to be. They
wanted him to be right. He was, after all, their hero, a
man they admired. Rivera was their kind of soldier, just
as they were his. They all felt it; they all believed it. As
they slipped into the jungle around the camp, squad by
hastily organized squad, they were high. They smelled
blood and cordite, and they loved it.

The advisers weren't so sure. They had seen it all before. There had been too many duds masquerading as
live rounds, too many saviors who turned out to be
clowns. But this was Rivera's show, and the least they

could do was watch. Captain Thomas Robbins, the commander of the unit, watched quietly, his hands folded behind his back, a parody of parade rest. But it. was Rivera's parade, not his.

While Rivera outlined his plans, Robbins seemed to be bored, nodding once in a while, shaking his head slightly when he disagreed. Or was he just chasing a mosquito? Bolan watched him and wondered.

When the last unit had been deployed, Rivera turned to Robbins. "Captain," he said, "I'd appreciate it if you and your men stayed on the sidelines. Keep them out of the way. They're not to shoot unless directly threatened."

"You're the general, General," Robbins said. He didn't bother to conceal the smirk. His men chuckled, but Rivera ignored it.

"Very well, then. Shall we?"

Robbins nodded. He took his men up a steep slope overlooking the rear of the camp. Bolan and Rivera were alone now in the center of the camp. "I'm taking a great chance, here, Mr. Belasko. If this turns out to be a false alarm, I'll look foolish in front of these men. I can't afford that."

"You can't afford not to take the risk, General. At least the men will know that summer camp is over. This is the real thing, and their lives are on the line. I doubt if they realized that before."

"I hope you're right. But, God forgive me, I hope there's an attack. I'm afraid that I'm rusty. I need to know, and I need to know now. If I'm not fit to command these men, then there's no point in carrying this charade any farther."

"Charade?"

"You know very well what I'm talking about, Mr. Belasko. My reasons for being here are much more complicated than these men can understand. But I'm tired of deceiving people, using them. It's not how I was raised. I can't do it any longer, and I won't."

"General," Bolan said, "I think your reasons for being here are more complicated than *you* understand. But I can appreciate that. I've been there."

"Something tells me there are very few places you haven't been."

Bolan didn't answer right away. The general was on target, and nothing he could say would make any difference. "Watch your back, General."

"I don't have to. That's why you're here." Rivera laughed softly. "At least I can count on that." He turned and walked into the jungle opposite the approach road. He would soon see just how serious he was. And he was frightened that the answer might be one he hadn't expected.

Bolan looked around the deserted camp. It seemed pathetic that governments could stand or fall because of what happened in places like this. But they did just that, and he knew that there was no shortage of men like Rivera or Pagan willing to endure such humble beginnings for a chance at the brass ring. Few, if any, gave much thought to what they would do once they grabbed the prize, and that was the problem. Whether Rivera was any different remained to be seen. Despite his growing admiration for Rivera, Bolan didn't expect much. If he'd learned one thing over the years, that was it. Do your job and forget about it. Whatever happens happens.

He followed Rivera into the trees.

They didn't have long to wait. Bolan spotted them first. He tapped Rivera on the shoulder and pointed across the deserted camp. A handful of shadows moved among the trees. Rivera looked through his field glasses but couldn't make out any detail.

"Five, maybe six," he said, "but I can't tell if there are any more behind them."

"They'd have to be crazy to attack with only a handful," Bolan whispered.

"They'd have to be crazy to attack with this much moonlight," Rivera answered. He passed the word to hold fire, then used the glasses again. For a quarter of an hour nothing moved. Rivera handed the glasses to Bolan. "Here, you watch, I can't stand the waiting."

Bolan scoped the hillside where Robbins had gone. It seemed deserted. The mouth of the road glowed softly, but he couldn't tell whether it was moonlight or something else. Then he spotted movement among the trees again. More men were filtering in behind the advance unit, but it was impossible to gauge their strength. Rivera had opted for aligning his men on one side, leaving the forest on the far side free. He wanted to lull the attackers, hoping they would commit themselves. Taking them out would be a clear signal that he wasn't to be trifled with. It looked as if it was going to pay off.

"I make it at least thirty so far," Bolan whispered.

"What the hell are they waiting for?" Rivera snapped.

The warrior was about to answer when he heard the chopper. Suddenly it burst over the hilltop, opening up on the tents as it came down, hugging the slope. As soon as they heard the chopper's M-50, the men in the jungle on the far side opened fire. The chopper swooped down toward Rivera's tent and hung in the air while the door gunner tore it to pieces.

"Wait," Bolan urged, grabbing Rivera. "Let them go at it a bit."

"This is our chance," Rivera said, tearing free.

"No. That chopper gives them the edge. Just wait." He moved forward until there was a single line of trees between him and the edge of the camp. The chopper pivoted on its rotor, and Bolan caught a glimpse of the pilot. But first he wanted to shut down the M-50.

He waited patiently for the aircraft to make another half turn. The gunner was hanging back behind the doorframe, but if he were patient...

The Executioner slammed a burst from his AK-47 through the chopper's door. The M-50 tilted skyward, sending a stream of tracers off into the moonlight, then went silent. Bolan cut loose again as the gunner tried to crawl away from the open door. The troops on the far side had begun to move in. They seemed dazed and disoriented. It still hadn't dawned on them that there had been no return fire. They seemed confused, but kept coming, one reluctant step after another.

Bolan turned his attention to the chopper pilot as a grenade went off in the middle of the camp. "All right, General," Bolan snapped, "go get them."

With the door gunner down a big problem was solved. The rocket pods slung under the chopper nose were still trouble, but nothing Bolan couldn't handle. As Rivera's men moved into the open, the warrior snared a grenade launcher from one of the men.

Fitting the grenade in place, he moved sideways. The pilot seemed aware that his gunner had stopped firing and spun the chopper in a tight circle, then started to climb. Bolan held his breath, waiting and suddenly there it was, the opening he needed. The grenade just slipped through the open doorway and slammed into the rear of the helicopter. It went off with a muffled thud. A burst of white light seemed to spill out of the aircraft as it split open. The tail rotor was gone, and the pilot could no longer control the ship. The more he gunned his engine, the more the main rotor torque took command. The chopper fell straight down. Trailing burning fuel like the tail of a comet, it plunged into the center of the camp. Men scattered as the rest of the fuel went up, sloshing over the tents and the milling soldiers.

Bolan rushed toward the wreck, looking for Rivera. The general was up front, alternately sprinting and stopping to sweep the ground ahead of him with a burst of gunfire. Several of the tents were ablaze now, and grenades thrown by both sides were hurling clods of earth into the air. Bolan glanced up the hill and saw Robbins watching through binoculars. He was talking to a man beside him, but the warrior didn't have a chance to see who it was. The smoke and dust half obscured the combatants, and Bolan turned his attention back to Rivera.

He raced after the general and grabbed him by the arm. "I think you should back off. Get out of the fire," Bolan shouted.

Rivera laughed. "I know I should."

"Then do it," the warrior snapped.

Rivera looked at Bolan in surprise. "You really mean it, don't you?"

CHAPTER THIRTY-THREE

Hoffman slipped through the trees. He felt his feet sinking into muck past his ankles, but this was it. There was no time to lose. He pushed the branches aside, tripping on underbrush and half stumbling toward the small gleam on the far side. As he neared the far side of the trees, he caught the glimmer of moonlight on water. Breaking through the last line of underbrush, he found himself face-to-face with a broad expanse of standing water. Patches of tall grass dotted the smooth surface, but it stretched away as far as he could see.

An engine roared into life, and he turned toward the sound with a startled jerk of his head. The engine noise gradually diminished and was swallowed by a hum like the wings of a giant insect. He moved out toward the water's edge to look around a clump of head-high bushes. The sound was coming from somewhere ahead of him, but he saw nothing.

He shoved his way through the bushes and broke into the open as the engine started to whine again. It was still too dark to see clearly, so he swung the Starlite up and swept it along the waterline as the humming grew louder.

Then the scope picked out the source of the sound. An airboat, its huge propeller a blur in the pale moonlight, sat at a bare wooden dock. A figure was bent over the side of the boat, his hands full, busily lowering something onto the small platform behind the bench seat. He knew without seeing the face that it had to be Vince Arledge. A second airboat lay idle behind the first.

Hoffman started to run as the man turned back to a thatched lean-to at the other end of the dock, but he slipped and fell to his knees, landing with a tremendous splash just past the waterline. He stumbled getting to his feet as the blurred figure turned toward him. Hoffman swung the rifle up, but lost his footing again as the mucky bottom slipped out from under the soles of his boots.

The figure fired a shot, but it sailed harmlessly over his head. With nothing to stop the sound, it seemed to fade slowly away, then came back from a great distance, sounding like a handclap in the darkness.

"It's over, Vinnie. Give it up."

"Fuck you, Gil!"

Arledge fired again, but he couldn't see Hoffman any better than Hoffman could see him. And the handgun was less than accurate at that range. Hoffman struggled onto the bank and started to run again. Arledge turned and ran toward the airboat, bending to untie the rear line, then scrambling forward. Instead of working on the bow line, Arledge snatched a rifle from under the seat. He crouched on the end of the pier and fired a short burst. The slugs swarmed around Hoffman, kicking up spouts of water on the lake side and snapping twigs and branches on the land side.

Hoffman hit the deck.

"You should have left it alone, Gil," Arledge shouted. "It was none of your business, man."

"Couldn't do that, Vinnie. You know that."

Arledge cut loose again, a shorter burst this time, as if trying to buy himself some time. "You're a fool, Gil. I knew that or I would have offered to cut you in."

"It isn't worth it, Vinnie. No way is it worth it."

"You have no idea just how worth it it is, man. Millions, that's what it's worth."

"To Pagan, maybe. But not to you." Hoffman, aware that Arledge couldn't see him clearly, squirmed forward every time the man spoke. It was slow going, but he wanted him alive if it was possible. Somewhere deep inside he knew it wasn't, but he had to make the effort.

"Screw Pagan. He's an animal like all the others."

"Then help me bring him down."

"No can do, Gilly. No can do. It's too late for that. The wheels are in motion, man. You, Belasko and Rivera, even Bartlett, you're all history, man. Smoke."

"Bartlett? What about Bartlett?"

"What do you think? Pagan wants to waste him. I set it up. It might already have happened."

"He never did anything to you, Vinnie. Why Bartlett?"

"Hell, why not? All those pipe-smoking assholes sitting there in their nice little offices. What the hell do they know? What do they know about the real world, Gilly? They don't know shit. They push us and push us and push us. Then they throw us away."

"Bullshit. They have a job to do. So do we. We both do what we can."

"Save it, Gilly. That's a crock, and you know it." He fired a single shot, then started yelling again. "Ever stay up at night and count your dead friends, Gilly?"

"Yeah, sure."

"Me, too..."

"It goes with the territory. You knew that when you signed on."

"Maybe. But how come all your dead friends don't include a single Langley asshole? Why are they always grunts like us? You ever ask yourself that?"

"No."

Arledge laughed.

"What's funny?"

"Nothing. I was about to say maybe you should. But what's the point? You aren't walking away from this one, Gilly. No way. I can't afford it. I can't let it happen."

"It's not too late. You can call it off."

"I don't mean Bartlett, man. It's Pagan. I burned him for more than a mil. Took out his right-hand man. No way he'll let me walk, and there's no way to take him down. He's got too many friends. Friends in high places, man. Higher than Bartlett even."

The wheels started turning in Hoffman's head. Why wasn't Arledge running? He seemed anxious to talk, too anxious. Why? And then it hit him. The second airboat. Why was it there? Who was it for? He heard the noise behind him at the same instant. He started to roll even as understanding dawned. Then he rolled again to his left. The ground beside him exploded as he rolled, and he swung around the M-16. He heard footsteps behind him, and Arledge was running toward him. The figure in the trees lunged forward as Hoffman squeezed the trigger. The M-16 stuttered, bucking in his slippery hands.

The shadow zigzagged sideways, and he cut loose with a lateral slice. This time he found his mark and the shadow slumped forward. It landed with a soggy thud, and Hoffman rolled again, this time landing on his stomach and starting to scramble to his feet.

"Forget it, Vinnie. The cavalry's not coming, man," Hoffman shouted.

The thudding steps stopped for a moment, then began to recede. Hoffman still wanted Arledge alive. Now more than ever. If Bartlett was at risk, he had to find out the details. He raced toward the dock. He could see Arledge bent over the bow, his arms pumping as he struggled to untie the line.

Hoffman fired a burst in the general direction. Arledge winced as two slugs slammed into the propeller blades, scattering sparks in every direction. But the engine continued to pulse and the prop to spin.

Then Arledge was on the boat, kneeling in front of the bench. He banged a pair of shots from a handgun in Hoffman's direction. Hoffman dived to avoid the slugs, and Arledge gunned the engine and swung the boat around. The engine roared and the terrible hum grew thunderous.

The airboat started to edge away from the dock. Arledge wasn't skilled in its use, and it kept swerving too far left and too far right as he overcompensated. Hoffman raced toward the dock, the mud on his boots slowing him down. His legs felt like lead, but he was closing the gap.

"Vinnie, stop!" Hoffman tried to shout, but he didn't have the strength. It came out as a croak, and he knew Arledge didn't hear him. But he also knew Arledge would ignore him, anyway. The boat started to speed up, and Arledge swung the rudder, still on his knees and staring back into the near darkness through the propeller.

Hoffman fired again, aiming low to avoid hitting Arledge. He chopped at the waterline, trying to riddle the hull and sink the airboat before Arledge got too far from shore. If Arledge had to swim for it, he'd never make it. Already the angry bull gators were grunting, and a series of splashes along the shoreline past the dock signaled the entrance of several of the big animals into the water.

Hoffman hacked at the airboat until his clip ran out. He jettisoned it, slipped another clip home and opened up again. This time he aimed a little higher, going for the engine. Bullets spanged off the metal and snarled off into the night. Sparks showered in gentle arcs away from the whirling prop, but the engine continued to roar. Then a small flame popped up just about deck level. It grew larger, and Hoffman could see smoke.

"Turn it around, Vinnie," Hoffman bellowed. The engine coughed and sputtered. The hum of the prop rose and fell, then wound down as the engine died.

"Come back before it's too late," Hoffman shouted.

"Forget it, Gilly," Arledge answered.

Hoffman worked his way along the shoreline, back toward the fallen gunman. He found the body face-down in the muck and knelt to turn it over. It was Felix Vasquez.

The boat was drifting his way, and Hoffman watched through the scope. Arledge worked feverishly at the engine, then pushed the ignition button. The engine coughed and sputtered. A spurt of burning fuel geysered out into the water. In its glare Hoffman saw Arledge freeze. He'd made a mistake, and he knew it, but it was too late.

Hoffman pulled his eye away from the scope as the boat caught fire. Orange flames sprouted in every direction. Arledge was etched like a lump of coal against the brilliant light, then cartwheeled through the air as the fuel tank blew, outlined in bright yellow where the burning gasoline coated his body. He landed with a splash, one among many as bits and pieces of the boat started to fall back into the water.

Then a series of explosions rocked the night as several grenades went off. High in the air an oblong shadow disintegrated, and Hoffman watched in fascination as rectangular confetti spilled out of the oblong. Some of it fell into the water and some fluttered away on the current of heated air above the burning hull. Hoffman turned away as the first grunting gator reached the body.

He wanted to do something, but there was nothing he could do. He thought for a moment about taking the other airboat and trying to recover the body, but he knew there would be nothing left by the time he got there. So he stood quietly on the shore, sadly shaking his head. The body disappeared underwater with a burst of bubbles. A tail swished in the water, and then it grew quiet. The flames had begun to die down, and the water lapped at burning wood, hissing and sputtering away to silence. The sky was getting brighter now, and he could see the charred hull floating quietly. The wind was picking up, and it felt cool on his neck and face.

As he turned away, the last few bits of Vinnie's nest egg rained down on the silent swamp.

STILL WONDERING whether he should have answered the phone, Bartlett settled back into the car with a stack of newspapers on his lap. His driver, accustomed to a certain distraction on the part of his employer, closed the door without speaking, climbed into the driver's seat and started the car.

The highway was almost empty, and they moved easily into the right lane, where Perry set the cruise control, then let his foot sit beside the gas pedal. At sixty-five he was doing ten miles over the limit, but the car was known to the highway patrol who, in any case, were disinclined to bother anyone who wasn't weaving or behaving in some outrageous manner.

Charlie Gardner had been hot-wired on the phone, and Bartlett wasn't looking forward to their meeting. He knew it would be nothing short of a confrontation, but the gentleman in him refused to acknowledge the fact. Every paper carried the story on the front page, and Bartlett devoured each one. It struck him as odd how closely the details corresponded from paper to paper. Even though it wasn't a wire service pickup, and had been filed by separate journalists or, in some cases stringers, the details were a perfect fit, as if each reporter had spoken to the same source or sources, none of whom had been named.

That anomaly troubled him more than the substance of the stories themselves, which accused General Emiliano Rivera and unidentified CIA support personnel of having destroyed a fishing village on the Nicaraguan coast. Several lives had been lost, all fishermen or their families, and the entire commercial fishing fleet of Chenango—such as it was—now sat underwater, charred hulks beyond salvage.

Gardner had read the entire text of one story over the phone, screaming phrase after phrase into the receiver. In his mind's eye Bartlett had seen the prominent vein in Gardner's left temple writhing like a snake. That the story was a plant, a not-so-subtle piece of disinformation, seemed beyond dispute. What intrigued Bartlett was who had planted it. The why was clear. And that, of course, would narrow the field of possible candidates to a few. Gardner, as obtuse as he was, would eventually realize that. But, in the meantime, the story had already achieved one of its desired purposes: it had disrupted a delicate balance within the Agency.

Bartlett also had a sick feeling in his stomach. He wanted to believe that the entire story was a fabrication, but there were pictures. He hoped, and wanted to believe, that the pictures themselves were frauds, subtle contrivances manufactured solely to suit a perceived need for documentary support. But he knew it wasn't so. He knew that whoever had been so crude as to manufacture this seamless web wasn't subtle enough to do that.

This was a fabrication of the most basic kind. You want dead bodies? Here are your dead bodies. You want sunken fishing boats? There they are. Give them the real thing. That was the thought behind this abomination, and he feared that he had somehow helped in creating the monster behind it all.

It struck Bartlett as a kind of poetic justice that one of the Agency's own techniques had been crudely but effectively turned on its head and used against its past masters. He wished he'd been able to reach Vince Arledge, but there would be time enough for that later. For the time being, he'd have to stand into Gardner's wind and bear the brunt of the storm on his own. When it blew over, as it surely would, Gardner would owe him one. It was a good feeling.

At the next intersection Perry eased into the cloverleaf, then down into the merge lane on I-95. When he slipped into the main lane, he let the cruise control take over again. A red camper parked on the shoulder up ahead started to move out, stuttered for a moment, then pulled back onto the shoulder to let the limo by.

Perry glanced in the mirror to see if the camper needed help, but it seemed all right as it picked up speed on the shoulder, then slipped into the slow lane. The sun was almost down, and the reddish light on the hood made it difficult to see, even through the tinted glass. Perry pulled his sun visor down, which helped to block out the direct light. But the glare still bothered him, so he averted his eyes and managed to see well enough to continue in the sparse traffic.

Clicking on the stereo, Bartlett pushed the scan mode until he found a classical station. He ignored the papers for a few minutes, listening to the music with his eyes closed. It had been a long day, and he was annoyed that he couldn't place the piece. It was definitely Mozart, one of the string quartets, but he wasn't sure which one. It was one of those precise details that mattered so much to him, as if the music had no value without a name. He remembered Milton exploring the significance of Adam's role in naming the beasts of Eden. Nomenclature was power. It made control possible, categorization easy and, ultimately, made the one who controlled the names the master.

The movement ended, and Bartlett stared at the speaker as if he expected someone at the radio station to indulge him, but the next movement began and still he couldn't place the piece. Annoyed, he considered the possibility that the announcer wouldn't name the piece at its conclusion. Nothing about radio infuriated him more. He would rather endure untrammeled profanity in exchange for a requirement that all pieces be named both before and after being aired.

As the second movement came to a close, he listened harder, not sure where he had come in. The themes hadn't been familiar. But once again another movement began. He punched the button, looking for another station, one that had more respect for his need to know. He settled on the rather syrupy tones of a woman announcing a Beethoven sonata. He hated Beethoven, but at least he would know what it was he was hearing.

Picking up the *Washington Post*, he started the article on the atrocity at Chenango. Even the usually impeccable *Post* seemed somewhat sketchy on exactly what had happened. The same language was there about the "ruined hulks" of the fishing fleet, and the "unprovoked" assault by dozens of soldiers.

It was interesting to note that none of the nine articles he had with him contained an allegation that Rivera himself was actually present. That seemed to demand that one ask how it was known that the attacking force, if indeed there even was such an event, was under the command of Emiliano Rivera. Did the soldiers announce it? Did they leave something behind?

It couldn't have been that an associate of Rivera had been recognized, and the witness made the leap to Rivera, because Rivera had just arrived in Nicaragua and *had* no associates, known or otherwise, of any prominence whatever. No, there was something rotten here, and Bartlett had to know what it was.

Then, too, there was the peculiarity of such an event having been so closely timed to Rivera's arrival. If it was a fabrication, there was a strong likelihood that the fabricator was someone who knew that Rivera had gone to Nicaragua. That fact alone narrowed the field to perhaps a dozen or two. More than half of those were in the Agency, so it shouldn't be difficult to isolate them.

The disturbing thing was that someone with a need to interfere was aware of Rivera's presence. That posed a danger, not only to Rivera himself, but to the new game plan. Reluctant to continue a war that had been officially put on hold by Congress, Bartlett had fought against the plan until he was out of objections. Gardner knew what he wanted, and he didn't give a damn whether it was legal or not.

In Gardner's view the rules didn't apply to the Agency. How could you fight in secret if you had to tell every third blabbermouth on the hill? For that matter, how could you fight against an enemy who knew no rules if you had to abide by so restrictive a set of your own? There was something to be said for that, Bartlett would be the first to admit. But the Agency had gotten into trouble in the past by waltzing blindly down that logical dead end, and the rules that fitted like a custom-tailored straitjacket were the result. They had ordered the suit; now they had to wear it.

It wouldn't hurt to give the *Post* a call to see if they were sitting on something more, something they weren't confident about running. It might be possible to provoke some sort of disclosure simply by complaining about the story having been run at all.

Bartlett folded the paper into a rough square and smoothed it on his lap. It was dark now, and the sky was full of the urban haze that made stargazing all but obsolete from D.C. to Boston. At 602 the limo slowed and ducked into the last straightaway before the approach road to headquarters. Bartlett leaned back against his seat, easing the volume up a little, letting the music wash over him.

The car lurched as a van sped by on the left, its slip-stream buffeting even the heavy Cadillac. And then the car seemed to hesitate. It started to rise in the air, slightly at first, and then with a deafening roar it began to cartwheel. Bartlett looked at the back of Perry's head as if to accuse him, and then the car began to roll. It split in two, spilling men, newspapers and parts of the machine itself along the highway.

But by then Winston Bartlett was already dead.

CHAPTER THIRTY-FOUR

As Bolan stared at the ruined chopper, Rivera came up beside him. "How did the Sandinistas know so quickly?" Rivera asked.

"What do you mean?"

"I mean, know that I was here and which tent I was in?"

"Come on, General, you know the answer to that as well as I do."

"Oh?"

"To begin it, it wasn't the Sandinistas."

"How do you know? The weapons are Czech."

"Look, East Bloc hardware is a staple on the arms market, and if you want to pretend you're something you're not, you buy weapons that don't connect you. It's done all the time."

"Still, the other side knows this, so why not use East Bloc weapons on the assumption that people will think you're CIA when you're not?"

"Too devious to bother with. All you really want is to obscure your own presence. But the thing that seals it isn't the assault rifles, anyway. It's this...." Bolan pointed to the still-smoking hulk of the chopper. "If this was a genuine Sandinista unit, they'd have used regulation hardware. They don't have to hide anything, because we're on their turf. Why not use a Soviet Hind?"

"So what are you saying?"

"I'm saying that whoever was behind the raid was plugged in. The chopper was probably supplied by the CIA. I'd love to know to whom, but I think I can guess."

He moved closer to the wreck. The body of the pilot was charred beyond recognition, but the gunner wasn't in the wreck. If he could find the gunner's body, it might tell him something. In the meantime he wanted to sift through the chopper as soon as it cooled down enough to let him get inside.

"We came out of this in pretty good shape," Rivera said. "We only lost four men. Some are wounded, but only one seriously. The medical evacuation team is on the way. I think he'll make it."

"What about the other side?"

"So far we've found fourteen bodies. The men are still combing the woods. We'll have to bury them quickly. In the tropics it doesn't take long for a body to become a danger."

"Tell the men no burials until I get a look at the bodies."

"Are you looking for someone in particular?"

"I don't know what I'm looking for, General."

"But you'll know when you find it, eh?"

Captain Robbins watched Bolan with interest. He edged closer, then dropped to one knee beside the big man. "You look like a rag picker, Belasko. What the hell are you doing?"

"Research, Captain."

"What the hell for?"

"I want to know what happened here."

"Hell, I can tell you that. Some Sandies got lucky. They found the camp and tried to tear us up. What more do you need to know?"

"You heard me."

"I just told you what happened."

"You didn't tell me anything other than what this is supposed to look like. That's all."

"Shit, you can have a copy of my report if you want to know the nitty-gritty."

"No, thanks. I don't read much fiction."

"What the hell's that supposed to mean? You sayin' I'm a liar?"

"Either that or you're a fool, Captain. Maybe both, for all I know."

"You better watch your mouth. I don't like being called a liar."

"Then don't lie. It's really not that difficult."

"Look, if you know something I don't, maybe you and me should have a talk."

"What for? You already have your report. I can live with that."

"Belasko, I'm warning you. I'm in charge here. You mess with me, you'll be one sorry son of a bitch. Believe it."

Bolan shook his head. "I'm busy, Captain, if you don't mind..." He moved closer to the chopper. He could still feel the radiant heat on his bare skin, but it was possible to pick around in the outer fringes of the wreck.

In the ruined cabin he found a charred wallet. Using the stock of his assault rifle, Bolan raked the blackened leather lump toward him. Part of it flaked away from the pressure, but it remained largely intact. It was warm to the touch, and he dropped it once, trying to fold it open.

"What have you got there?" Robbins demanded.

"I don't know."

"Better let me have it."

"Like hell."

"I'm just about at the end of my rope with you, hot-shot."

Bolan straightened. "Then you better hold on and hope I don't kick the chair out from under you, Rob-bins."

The captain took a step forward, but Bolan was too fast for him. He ducked in with a quick left-right-left combination, the blows sounding like a drumbeat on Robbins's rib cage. The captain doubled over, then vomited loudly. Dropping to one knee, he gasped for air, then spit to rid his mouth of the residue.

"That's it, you bastard," he snarled. His men had begun to gather around. He struggled to regain his feet. "I want this son of a bitch locked up. If he gives you a problem, shoot him."

The men looked at Robbins, at Bolan, then back at Robbins.

"I mean *now*!" Robbins barked.

"Captain, we don't have any authority to—"

Robbins slugged the man who had started to object, wrested his rifle away as the man fell and turned it on Bolan. Rivera heard the commotion and raced over. "What's going on here?" he demanded.

"Your butler here is under arrest," Robbins said. He grinned at the general.

"On whose orders?"

"Mine."

"You're not in command here, Captain. I am."

Robbins seemed surprised. "But I—"

Rivera stepped between Bolan and the captain. He grabbed the rifle and pushed it aside. "You take your orders from me. You'd do well to remember that."

"General Rivera, this is an internal matter. This man is a U.S. citizen. I have every right to—"

"Captain, you have no right I don't want you to have. Do you understand that? None! I'm in command of this unit. This is my soil on which you stand, not yours. We're in Nicaragua and you're a guest here. This isn't a military base of the United States, and this man isn't in your army. You've got nothing to say about what he does or doesn't do. Now, can I make it any more explicit than that, or will you go on about your business and let Mr. Belasko go on about his?"

Robbins glared at Bolan. "This isn't over," he snarled.

BOLAN LAY on the slope, watching Rivera's tent. He felt guilty using the old man as bait, but there was no other way to do it. Somebody in Robbins's unit was a pipeline to the other side. So far they'd been able to run nothing through it, nothing that did them any good. The schedule was evaporating. There just wasn't that much time left. Subtlety hadn't worked, and they couldn't afford to wait much longer.

Who "they" were was still up for grabs, but at the moment it didn't matter. Bolan had to keep Rivera alive. They could put the pieces together later. He kept coming back to Harry Martinson, but it didn't make sense. He knew he'd seen Martinson on the riverbank when the two launches had gone after Rivera's chopper. But Rivera had Bartlett's blessing, and if anybody in Central America was certain to know that, it was Harry Martinson. So why would he deliberately run against policy? What was in it for him? Money? From whom? Power? What kind of power could anyone give him that would make any sense?

And the questions just kept on coming, rolling over and over in his head, like Ping-Pong balls in a lottery basket. But what was the winning combination, and how would he know when it came up?

The advisers' tent was quiet. A small light glowed in one end, just enough to throw shadows on the canvas, but enough for them to have shape. All he could detect was motion, and so far, there was none. But there would be. He was convinced of it. There had to be, or the puzzle was even more hopeless than it seemed.

Above the camp, isolated from the few human sounds the sleeping men made, the snores and the unconscious coughs, the twisting and turning under rough blankets, the creaking of the cots, it was possible to imagine the camp was deserted. Out in the darkness, he knew, a handful of sentries had been posted, but they were invisible. Motionless shadows among other motionless shadows, they might as well have been in another jungle.

Bolan tried the handset again. "General," he whispered, "are you there?"

"Where else would I be, Mr. Belasko?"

Even in the dark it was possible to see Rivera's sardonic smile. The man seemed unflappable, as if he had some peculiar notion of fate and accepted all its implications. He seemed to feel that he was destined to win but, if not, there was nothing he could do about it. At first Rivera had been reluctant even to consider Bolan's plan. But an hour's discussion had broken his resistance. Bolan still believed Rivera agreed to go along just to humor his American bodyguard, but at least he had agreed. In Bolan's line motive was less important than result.

They were down to three days on the timetable, and seventy-two hours didn't seem like much time to change a country's history. In fact, it often happened in less time than that, as Bolan well knew. But he found the notion unsettling. It seemed to fly in the face of everything he believed in. If the good guys could topple one government and replace it with another, then so could the bad guys. In fact, the bad guys could probably do it better because they had fewer restraints. Where was the stability?

More to the point, why bother to do something another handful of men could undo just as readily? But that was a question Bolan didn't dare consider. He believed because he had to believe, that good was better, that good would endure because somewhere there really was justice. But it was a justice that relied on something other than a gun. It staked a claim on men's souls, and they hugged it to themselves because they knew it was right.

The light went out in the advisers' tent. Bolan felt himself coil a little tighter, and he edged down the hill a bit. The moon was behind him, and he could see his own shadow sliding slowly along the grass ahead of him.

The light flashed on in the tent again, just for a moment, and the warrior froze. He held his breath as if a single inhalation would be fatal. The light was out in the tent again, and this time he saw a figure slip out of the tent. It darted like the shadow of a bat, back along the canvas wall, then disappeared into the trees at the foot of the hill. Whoever it was was heading straight toward him. Bolan scurried to the left, found a cluster of boulders overgrown by tangled vines and lay still, his arms covering his head.

He heard music, as he had the night before when he'd bumped into Caspar Washington. It was the blues, and Bolan held his breath as the tinny sound drew closer, trivialized by the earphones. The warrior pressed himself into the vines, ignoring the hundreds of thorns slashing at his skin and piercing his clothing.

When the music passed, he took a shallow breath, then raised his head. The man had gone past and was now standing among a clump of trees near the crest of the hill. But it wasn't Cazz Washington. This man was too tall and too thin. He seemed confused, standing there among the shadowy trunks, twisting his head from side to side, as if trying to get his bearings.

Bolan craned his neck, but the man's face was hidden from the pale wash of the moon. A moment later he was gone, passing over the crest of the hill and moving down the far side. The warrior told Rivera what was going on, then got to his feet and started after the man.

The moon disappeared behind a massive black cloud. Bolan looked up at it to gauge how long he had in darkness. The cloud was moving slowly, its edges a brilliant white, the rest as black as coal. Picking his way from cover to cover, he reached the crest of the hill in ninety seconds. He hit the ground, breaking his fall with stiffened forearms and crawled another ten yards. It was starting to brighten again when he crawled in behind a stand of trees just below the far side of the ridge.

His quarry was nowhere to be seen.

Bolan didn't want to move until he knew where the man was. But if the guy was on the move himself, he'd never be able to catch him. The Executioner decided on action. He got to his knees and peered out from behind a slender tree. The far side of the hill was more heavily wooded, shading down into genuine forest about three-quarters of the way down. The terrain of northern Nicaragua was a strange mix of grassy hills and valleys clotted with thick rain forest. The dark green seemed to flow like water in the valley bottoms, lapping up the hillsides just so far, then running out of steam.

Easing downhill, he kept his eyes on the tree line, about a hundred yards below. Working on the assumption that a beeline was the most logical route, he confined himself to a swath no more than twenty-five yards wide, trying to keep to the center. The grass was stiff and dry, but he thought he saw a couple of places where it had been recently broken. Bending low to cut his exposure, he searched the dry grass ahead, found another slight indentation, then another just beyond it.

They were just short of his own stride, and he put his quarry's height at an inch or two under his own six-three, so it was a decent match. In places, the hillside was too dry and nearly barren. The earth itself showed no signs of recent passage, and he skipped on to the next patch of grass. Once again, he had to search for a few moments before he found the next footfall.

Only fifty yards from the trees now, he worried that he might be seen. The moon was back, bathing the hillside in milky light, and he was a sitting duck for anyone among the trees. Shifting his AK-47 to his left hand, he raked his fingers through the dry grass until he found a few snapped blades. The next patch was canted to the left, and Bolan shifted direction.

He walked right into it.

The slug slammed into his left side just above the hip.

CHAPTER THIRTY-FIVE

Bolan lay on the ground. He had landed heavily, winding himself. The wound wasn't serious, but he could feel the sticky blood seeping down his hip. Even in the dark the insects sensed it, and several flies began to buzz around him. The warrior slapped at them, trying to keep them away, but they were too persistent for so simple a defense.

He hadn't heard the shot and considered himself lucky to be alive. What he couldn't figure was how the shooter had missed him. He tried to pick up some movement among the trees to pinpoint the location of the gunman, but it was impossible to make out any detail in the darkness.

The AK-47 had skidded away when he'd fallen, and he patted the ground now, trying to find it. Finally his fingers found the barrel and closed over it. He pulled the weapon toward him with his fingertips, then found the trigger guard and curled a finger through it.

Then it hit him—they hadn't killed him because they didn't give a damn. He'd been decoyed. All they wanted was to get him out of the way while they went after their real target—Rivera.

Bolan got to his feet, sending a jolt of pain rocketing across his hip. The slug had gouged through the flesh between hipbone and rib cage, leaving a furrow deep enough to feel through the cloth of his shirt, now sticky with blood.

Ignoring the pain, he ripped the sleeves off his shirt, knotted them together, then twisted them into a tight band and cinched them around his waist. It hurt to put pressure on the wound, but he had to stop the bleeding. As he started back up the hill, he called Rivera on the handset but got no response.

Bolan cursed and started to run. His strength had seeped away with his blood, and the going was tough. His feet felt as if they were encased in concrete, and every breath stretched the sore muscles over his hip. At the top of the hill he looked down on the camp, which seemed to be as peaceful as it had been earlier.

Angling across the hillside to a spot that would bring him halfway between Rivera's tent and the advisers' tent, he picked up speed. As he ran, he took the safety off the AK. The moon was covered with clouds, and the sky was completely dark. Wisps of fog coiled among the trees as he entered the narrow strip of forest at the bottom of the hill, and he could no longer see either tent.

He picked his way through the snarled undergrowth until he could finally see the dark bulk of a tent. But it wasn't Rivera's. It was his own. He charged straight ahead, finally tearing into the open and stopping, breathless, to get his bearings. A small circle of light appeared on the wall of Rivera's tent, then vanished. Ignoring the fire in his side, Bolan broke into a run.

He was in the center of the camp now, his feet kicking up clouds of dust as he pounded across the parade ground and through the primitive obstacle course. He stopped again beside the palisade. He could see Rivera's tent, its flap open, but nothing moved.

Charging across the last open space, he burst into the tent, the AK up and ready. He heard a thump in one corner and dived to the ground.

"That you, Belasko?"

"Who's there?" Bolan whispered.

"It's me, Cazz."

"What the hell are you doing here?"

"I had a funny feeling. I came to check things out, but somebody slugged me. I don't know, man. I don't like it. Rivera isn't here, and—"

"Put on a light."

"That's what I'm looking for. I dropped my flashlight and I can't see squat in here."

"You got a match?"

"Yeah." Washington cracked a match on his thumbnail. "Here it is." The match went out and, a moment later, was replaced by the small beam of a pocket flashlight. "They must have taken him," Bolan said, "Let's go."

"Go? Where the hell we gonna go, man? You don't know where they took him."

"Suit yourself," Bolan snapped. "Give me the light for a second." Washington stepped close enough to hand him the flashlight. The warrior dug into the mound of clothing and equipment in one corner of the tent.

"What're you lookin' for, man?"

Bolan's hand closed over the infrared glasses. "These," he said, holding them up for Washington to see. He slipped the strap over his head, crammed a couple more clips for the AK into his shirt and dashed out of the tent.

He heard Washington right behind him. "Look, man, if you're gonna do something stupid, I guess I got to go along and bail you out."

Bolan held up a finger. The sound of a jeep cranking up drifted toward them. He swiveled his head, trying to get a fix. Then the engine caught and the transmission whined.

"There." The warrior pointed at the hill. "It's on the other side. Damn! I was right there." He started back toward the hill. Washington sprinted past him, his stubby legs pumping like pistons. Then the man veered to the left, and Bolan charged up the hill. He was a third of the way up when he heard another jeep, this one behind him. He turned to see what was happening and saw the jeep lurch out of the shadows by the motor pool. A moment later it spun to the left, kicked spurts of dust behind it and bounced toward him up the hill. Men started to shout, and Bolan saw three or four shadows rush out of the tents, rifles in hand. He debated organizing a team but decided against it. Speed was going to be more important than firepower.

The jeep slowed, and Washington downshifted, backing off on the clutch to hold it steady while Bolan jumped in. Then, jerking the shift lever, Washington floored it. The back wheels spun on the dry grass for a few seconds before the treads bit into the earth and the jeep darted forward. At the top of the hill they stopped to get their bearings. Headlights slashed through the trees a quarter mile away.

Washington gunned the jeep all the way downhill, controlling the vehicle with some fancy gearshifting. At the bottom he nudged it through a narrow break in the trees. A sharp turn halfway through caught Bolan by surprise. Both men ducked under the overhanging branches, and then the jeep was in the clear. A narrow field of plowed earth stretched away in both directions. Across the dusty furrows Bolan saw tire tracks heading off to the left.

Washington saw them at the same time. Jerking the wheel, he pushed the jeep out into the open. It rocked through the deep ruts, nosing up, then down like a small boat in heavy seas.

The headlights were gone, but Washington seemed to know where he was going. He let the vehicle settle into a pair of furrows, then gunned the engine, ignoring the earth scraping at the undercarriage.

They picked up speed, but still couldn't run flat out. There was just too little clearance. Washington fought the wheel to keep the jeep under control in the uneven furrows. Twice it canted over as the tires climbed the side of a furrow, but Washington was equal to the challenge. The trees on either side of them began to narrow to a point, as if jeep were speeding into a funnel. The first burst of rain splattered the windshield, and Washington cursed. He clicked on the wipers, but the dust and rain just coated the glass with a veneer of thin mud.

"If I had my Caddy, I'd just squirt a little water on those suckers and we'd be able to see." Washington reached forward to knock the windshield down. "Better to get a little water in the face than one of those damn trees," he said through gritted teeth.

They bounced out of the plowed field and slammed into the stem of the funnel with the engine beginning to snarl as Washington opened it up. "This road heads deeper into Nica. I hope those guys know where they're going, because we can get hung out to dry with no sweat."

"They know. They've been trying to get to Rivera since he got here. Everything's been carefully planned. What I don't get is why they decided to capture him instead of kill him."

"Maybe it isn't the same guys. You ever think of that?"

Bolan shook his head. "No, I didn't. You might be onto something."

"Yeah, but what? Unless we know, it isn't gonna help us much, is it?"

"You have any idea what you're letting yourself in for?"

"Do you?"

"Not really."

"There you go, then. A couple of dumbass soldiers of fortune. What the hell? Life's too short to worry about it, man. Besides, it isn't often you meet a white boy who knows who Luther Allison is. I expect you must be some kind of rare specimen who's got to be saved from extinction. You know, like the snow leopard."

"Whatever you say, Cazz." Bolan grinned.

"What *is* your story, anyhow?"

"I'll tell you sometime."

"Hey, I know how it is. I been there. I won't ask again."

"Can you think of anyplace they might be headed?"

"Just one. There's an abandoned cantina about two miles ahead. Just a dirt intersection, but the place used to do a good business when we first got here. But some of the boys got a little rowdy, you know. The locals didn't like it, and they stopped coming. Then Robbins put his two cents in when he got here. Said it was making it too easy for the Sandies."

"Makes sense."

"Yeah, but where's a man supposed to get a drink?"

"How long has Robbins been here?"

"About a month or so. Maybe five weeks. Hard-assed mother, he is. Knows his shit, though."

"What's his story?"

"Listen, you didn't tell me yours, he didn't tell me his. Guys like us, we either have a dozen stories or we don't have any. My guess is Robbins has a dozen easy. Probably twice that."

"He doesn't like Rivera, does he?"

"Hell, do you?"

"I don't know. I didn't, but I'm starting to second-guess myself."

"Bad idea, my man. Go with the gut, that's my philosophy."

"You're right, Cazz."

"I know it."

"Let's work on the assumption they went to the cantina, then. At least as a first stop. They probably don't want to keep him there. It's to close to camp. But they might use it as a staging area. Maybe an airlift."

"Could be. There's a big open field behind the place. Perfect LZ."

"Let's take the last half mile on foot."

"You up for the hike?"

Bolan grunted.

They rode another mile in silence, Washington trying to keep the engine noise to a minimum. He pulled off the road into a small patch of weeds just big enough to accommodate the jeep. "End of the line. We better go on foot from here on."

"We have to assume they left an ambush to cover their asses," Bolan said.

"I was thinking the same thing."

"Let's do it, Cazz."

Bolan jumped down from the jeep. The landing jolted his injured hip, but he bit his tongue and said nothing. Washington jerked the key loose and tucked it under the driver's seat. "It's up under the springs in case you need it, man."

"We're going in together and we'll come out together."

"Let's hope so, my man."

CHAPTER THIRTY-SIX

The cantina sat back off the road like a box of bleached bones. Its front was a dirty gray window, its parking lot a dust bowl. Two jeeps were parked at the rear of the structure. Bolan and Washington crouched in the trees and watched.

"Bingo," the warrior said.

"Maybe, maybe not. Everybody in camp knows about this place. For all we know it's just some weed-heads come down for a smoke without the man peeking over their shoulders."

"You don't believe that and neither do I."

"Just touching all the bases."

"See the four men in the trees across the road?"

"No. Where?"

"There," Bolan replied, extending his arm through the bushes.

Washington followed the point. "Looks like they're expecting some company."

"We're here, and we have to take them out first thing. I don't want to go up against the building with four guns at my back."

"Deadly force?"

"Not if we can avoid it. I want Rivera, but I don't give a damn about the others. They can walk if they want. But we can't move until they're out of the picture."

"Got any ideas?"

"Just one. Follow me."

Bolan eased back away from the road. The farther away he got, the thicker the vegetation. Another ten yards and they were completely hidden from the road.

The warrior crouched beside Washington and whispered, "We have to go back past that last bend in the road. I want to come at them from behind. That means we've got to move fast. It's a big detour."

Washington nodded.

It took nearly fifteen minutes to reach the bend and another five to work their way back to the road itself. Bolan was the first one to cross. He crouched, checked both ways, then waved Washington across.

As they doubled back toward the cantina, Bolan stopped every fifteen or twenty yards. Somewhere up ahead four men with automatic rifles waited for him. It wasn't his intention to kill them if he didn't have to, but he had no such illusions about their intentions. One mistake would be all he'd get the chance to make.

The ambush was just ahead. The men lying in wait had made a mistake, gathering in a tight knot instead of stringing themselves out. Bolan understood that. Nobody wanted to die, and it was easy to fool yourself into believing that you could only die if you were alone. Nothing could be farther from the truth.

"We can't afford any noise. One shot and the game's up," Bolan whispered. "We have to surprise them and hope they're too stunned to put up a fight."

"And if they're not?"

Bolan shrugged. "Play it by ear."

Using hand signals, employing words only when absolutely necessary, he explained what he wanted Washington to do, then what he planned to do. It was critical that they work in tandem. It was only in a joint effort that success, with the requisite silence, was possible.

Washington nodded his understanding, and the Executioner slipped away, making a wide circle to move in behind the group of men. Washington inched closer, every painstaking step as precisely planted as if he were moving through a mine field.

Bolan reached his destination sooner than he expected. He could see the individual shadows of the four men huddled together like kids playing touch football. He waited for Washington to reach his own position.

Checking his watch, he frowned when he realized it was more than an hour since they'd reached the cantina. The two jeeps were still there, but if Rivera wasn't, they had wasted a lot of valuable time. Perhaps too much.

The warrior edged closer. He could almost reach out and touch the nearest man. It was so tempting to use the Beretta and take them out. But for all these men knew, they were doing the right thing. How could you blame a soldier for following orders when nobody seemed to know what should be done? Scratch two congressmen and you got two speeches on what was wrong with U.S. Central American policy. It was so much easier to let somebody else decide, go along with the program, follow orders. At least nobody could accuse you of shirking your responsibility.

Bolan heard the sharp crack of a dry stick. It had the desired effect as all four men turned to stone for a moment. He slipped up behind the nearest man, held the Beretta at his temple and wrapped an arm around his neck. Even in the dark the warrior knew he was young.

He could feel the kid's downy whiskers against his forearm.

"Everybody take it easy and nobody gets hurt. Understand?" Bolan asked in Spanish.

"Yes, sir," the young man replied, his Adam's apple bobbing against the pressure of Bolan's arm.

Washington stepped through the undergrowth on the far side of the small clearing. One by one he took their weapons, then pressed each man to the ground.

Working quickly, Washington bound their hands behind their backs with lengths of a tough, ropelike vine, then tied their feet, running a line from ankles up to wrists and jerking their feet into the air. Cutting strips of duct tape from a silver roll, he taped their mouths closed, making sure each man could breathe before moving on to the next.

"You'll be all right," Bolan whispered to the captives. "When we're finished we'll come back and set you loose. In the meantime just stay calm. Don't try to get loose. You can't, and you'll only make things more difficult for all of us. Understood?"

All four nodded.

"Let's go, Cazz."

Bolan sprinted out of the trees and across the road. He ran straight for the side wall of the building, between the two jeeps. When he had his back against the wooden wall, he waved Washington across. Cazz joined him, puffing slightly from the long sprint. Bolan's side was beginning to throb, and he felt a little weak.

The flimsy walls of the cantina looked as if they would give way under the first strong breeze. There was no window on that side, and he had to get a look inside before deciding what he could do. If Rivera wasn't there, then they'd be back to square one. He whispered to Washington that he was going to find a window. The man nodded and moved toward the front corner, where he could watch the door.

Bolan moved the other way, waiting for Washington to get in place before he slipped around the back. Two windows, one toward either corner, threw dim light onto the wet grass. He raised his head to the sill and listened. A low mutter from inside was unintelligible. Continuing on past, he stood on the far side and eased back just far enough to look into the room. Two men sat at a scarred round table, playing dominoes. They were talking quietly, absorbed in the game. There was none of the usual banter that accompanied the slapping of tiles in place, none of the insulting challenges, the triumphant celebrations.

Bolan tiptoed along the wall to the far window. Knee-high weeds at the base of the building hampered his progress, but the farther away from the wall he got, the more likely someone would spot him from inside.

At the far window he stopped again. This time he looked first before listening. He could hear someone talking, but he couldn't see anyone. The angle was all wrong. He ducked beneath the sill and moved to the far side of the window. Looking back toward the middle of the building, he could see the speaker now, leaning over someone seated in a chair. The conversation was in Spanish, but Bolan caught scraps of it each time the speaker's voice rose.

Berating the seated man, the speaker was urging him to sign something. The speaker's broad shoulders blocked everything at the table from Bolan's view. A fist pounded on the table, and the speaker turned away in disgust. "You stupid pig," he was saying, raising his voice for the first time. "Don't you understand that you have no choice? You *have* to sign."

The seated man said something Bolan didn't catch. Whatever it was, it enraged the speaker. He whirled around, reaching for his pistol at the same time. With the gun drawn, he leaned forward again, pounding on the table repeatedly with an open palm. As he pounded, he moved gradually around the table toward the front of the building. Slowly the seated man came into view. And when the speaker finally stopped pounding, he was across the table from the seated man.

Emiliano Rivera shook his head again. "I won't sign it," he said. The standing man leaned closer, raising his pistol until the muzzle was pressing against Rivera's chin. "You think we'll kill you if you sign it, don't you, old man?"

"I know you will," Rivera replied.

"Wrong!" The standing man pounded the table with a fist to emphasize each denial. "We'll kill you if you *don't* sign. You can save your life."

"And lose my soul? And betray my conscience and my country? No, thank you."

"The butcher of Matagalpa has a conscience?" The man laughed. "You must be joking."

"That was a long time ago. I've learned a great deal since then."

"Not enough, old man." The speaker was losing his grip. Bolan could hear the rage in his voice. He wasn't used to being defied. The gun pressed harder against Rivera's chin. Bolan had wanted to frame some sort of plan, but there wasn't time.

He banged the stock of the AK-47 against the wall. The thump echoed in the room and the speaker backed up a step. He looked toward the window, jerking the pistol away from Rivera's chin and pointing it at the wall. Bolan cut loose with the AK at the same instant. The shattering glass obscured what happened next, but when Bolan could see into the room again, the speaker was on the floor. Rivera was standing, backing away from the table. The warrior stuck his head through the shattered window frame as two men rushed into the room, probably the same two who had been playing dominoes.

Bolan took them out of the play with a tight figure eight as they barged in, the second man tripping over his comrade and falling through the deadly hail. Rivera hobbled toward the window. The Executioner heard the rattle of chains and realized the general was in shackles. His hands were manacled.

"Stay out of the line of fire," Bolan barked, and Rivera slid to one side, the awkward penguin strut imposed on him by the chains almost comical. At the same instant a burst of gunfire erupted around the front of the building.

A third man charged through the door, but before Bolan could raise his rifle, the man stumbled and fell, ripped from behind by a tight burst. He sprawled facedown, half a dozen holes across his back from shoulder to shoulder.

"It's me," Washington shouted. "Don't shoot." He stepped over the carnage in the doorway, ramming another clip into his rifle. He looked at Bolan with a lopsided grin. "You don't believe in foolin' around, do you? Next time give me a shout or something first, okay? This John Wayne shit almost gave me a heart attack."

"There wasn't time, Cazz."

Bolan turned to Rivera. "Where's the key?"

Nodding toward the body on the floor by the table, the general said, "In his pocket. There are four more of them. You better hurry."

"Already taken care of, General," Washington said, snapping off a mock salute. "Who the hell are these guys, anyhow? They don't look like Sandies."

Bolan interrupted them to open the locks on the shackles and manacles. Rivera watched silently as the chains came free. He rubbed his wrists for a second, then walked to the table and picked up a sheet of paper lying under a ballpoint pen. He read the paper to himself, then spit into it and crumpled it into a ball. Tossing it onto the floor by the dead speaker, he said, "They're not. They're former members of the National Guard."

"Somocistas, huh?"

"No more. Now they're worse than pigs. They're Paganistas." Rivera looked at Bolan. He nodded, then answered Bolan's question before the big man got a chance to ask it. "I'm sure."

CHAPTER THIRTY-SEVEN

A blade of light slashed through the narrow opening at the door of the tent. Bolan turned in his sleep, and the light fell across his face. Instantly awake, he blinked and sat up. Gil Hoffman was sitting at the foot of the cot, his back to Bolan and his arms propped on the small table.

"What's up?" the warrior asked.

Hoffman didn't answer him immediately. He took a deep breath, then turned to look at the big man as he swung his legs over the edge of the cot. Bolan watched him without speaking.

The CIA agent stood, bumping his head on the taut canvas, then moved to the center of the tent where he could stand upright.

Bolan ran a hand through his hair, then took the Desert Eagle's holster from the end of the cot and slipped it on, wincing as the pain shot through his side.

Finally Hoffman spoke. "Bartlett's dead."

"What did you say?"

"Bartlett's dead. Murdered. Blown to fucking bits."

"What the hell happened?"

"Arledge set it up. I found out too late to do anything about it. And I've got news for you. I think that asshole Gardner's in Pagan's pocket.

"But why?"

"Search me. I just don't know. But I've put it together every way you can and it always comes out the same. Arledge knew too much. He knew shit Bartlett and I were doing, and I know Bartlett didn't tell anybody. At least he said he wouldn't, and I believe him. I didn't like the guy, but I trusted him.''

"That explains it, then.''

"Explains what?''

"How they knew we were here. We had a little excitement while you were away.''

"I know. Rivera told me.''

"What about Arledge?''

"Eighty-sixed. I blew him to hell, along with his blood money. I think the gators will probably get ptomaine. At least I hope so.''

"Gators?''

"I'll tell you about it sometime.''

Bolan knew not to press. He pushed open the tent flap. "Be right back.''

Hoffman sat down again, this time facing the mouth of the tent. He stared at the crack of brilliant sunlight until his eyes hurt. He'd seen a little too much in the past few days. Maybe he needed a little down time, he thought. Maybe seeing wasn't so good. Maybe if he seared his eyes with something other than the truth, he'd look at the world differently. Maybe...

When Bolan returned, Hoffman was still staring at the blade of sunlight.

"You okay?''

Hoffman nodded. "Yeah. But we're blown. I know that as sure as I know my mother's name.''

"We can handle it.''

"I hope so.''

"Does Rivera know about Bartlett?'' Bolan asked.

"I told him when I got in. He thinks it's Pagan. Says he wants to even the score.''

"Easier said than done. If you're right about Gardner, we're bucking both ends. They cut us loose."

"Like you said, we can handle it."

The tent flap moved aside, and Rivera stood in the light. "We have a few things to discuss," he announced.

Bolan nodded. "Come in, General."

"So formal, Mr. Belasko. That's not like you."

"It's his postmortem style," Hoffman said. Rivera glanced at him, then at Bolan.

"You know about Mr. Bartlett, then?"

Bolan nodded, then sat on the bunk. "What did you want to talk about?"

"I've had a long, restless night. Soul-searching is the term, I believe. I'm long past believing in so elusive an entity. But the process is useful, nonetheless. I think it only fair that you be the first, and so far as I am concerned, the only ones to know what I'm about to tell you."

"Secrets have a short half-life these days, General," Hoffman said.

Rivera looked at him sharply. "If you can't keep one, then perhaps you should leave me alone with Mr. Belasko. I have no qualms about him."

"You don't have to have any about me, either." Hoffman's voice was sharp. "I just meant that it seems difficult to keep them secret for very long."

"Be that as it may, I have one I expect you to keep. It seems that Guillermo Pagan is determined to keep me from running in the election, whatever he has to do. But I don't think Señor Pagan is what Nicaragua needs. Not now. Not ever."

"He's got a hell of a head start on you, General. Not to mention the fact that he's holding all the aces," Hoffman said.

"I suspect Señor Ortega has a few of his own." Rivera smiled.

"So did Wild Bill Hickok," Bolan added.

"I don't understand the reference."

"Aces and eights, General," Hoffman explained. "It's what Hickok was holding when he was killed. Dead man's hand, they call it."

"Do I understand you correctly, Mr. Belasko? Do you mean to tell me that part of the operation involved assassination?"

"According to Harry Martinson, it does."

"That bastard," Hoffman exploded.

"You know him?" Bolan asked.

"Yeah, I know him."

Rivera and Bolan both looked at him, waiting for an explanation. Hoffman seemed reluctant to follow up on his outburst.

Under the insistent stares, Hoffman shrugged. "Let me put it this way. If he were KGB, he'd be a specialist in 'wet affairs.'"

"I've seen evidence of that myself," Bolan said. "He was part of the attack on the chopper, General."

"Why didn't you tell me?"

"I wasn't quite sure. Besides, what was the point? It was over. If there was another attack, we'd have to be ready. And we were. There was no reason to assume Martinson would be involved in it, anyway. If they're out to get you, you can bet there's more than one executive action team roaming around."

"I'm not sure about that," Hoffman said. "As near as I can figure it, this was in a pretty tight box. I don't think Gardner wants half the Company to know about this. I wouldn't be surprised if the whole thing was off the books. Bartlett seemed to think so.''

"How do you know that?" Rivera demanded. "Why have you been holding out on me, both of you?"

"It seems we've all been keeping our little secrets, General," Bolan said.

Hoffman kept silent for a minute. Finally he stood. "I pulled a couple of strings. After they got Bartlett, I got in touch with an internal security man. He got me into Bartlett's house. I found a few things in his desk— a file on Pagan, one on Arledge. It looked as if he was cross-referencing things, piecing things together, sifting through what he knew from me and what Arledge had been telling him. My guess was that he was onto something, and Arledge guessed it. He probably pushed the button for Pagan.''

"We're in a deeper hole than I thought," Bolan said.

"Without a ladder," Hoffman added.

"Then we'll do what any good soldier does in such a situation, gentlemen.''

"What's that, General?"

"We'll take the offensive."

"Good luck."

"The just man doesn't need luck, Mr. Hoffman. All he needs is courage."

Hoffman looked at Rivera then at Bolan. "The way I see it," he whispered, "we don't have a whole lot of just men in this tent."

"On the contrary, we have two, and I shall do my best to atone for my past. Perhaps I can become a third." Rivera sighed. "But I can't participate in a fraud and I can't be a party, however remote, or a beneficiary, however indirect, of assassination.''

"We can't do anything about it, General. The ship has sailed."

"Ships can be recalled or, if necessary...they can be sunk."

"What the hell are you going to do?" Hoffman asked. "Call Ortega on the phone and tell him to look over his shoulder?"

"Only as a last resort," Rivera said. "I would rather we just handle it ourselves."

"You're joking..."

"I don't think so," Bolan said quietly. Turning to Rivera, he continued, "You know how long the odds are, don't you, General?"

"I do."

"All right, let's do it, then. Let's lay it all out. This is no time to hold back anything. Agreed?"

"Agreed," Rivera said.

Hoffman nodded. "What the hell?"

"All right, Gil, tell us everything you got from Bartlett's files. The more we know about Martinson and Pagan, the better chance we have to pull this off."

Hoffman talked for the better part of an hour. When he finished, he stared at his audience of two, waiting for their reaction. Bolan ran a hand over his unshaven chin. Rivera just rocked back and forth on the bench where he had sat the whole time as motionless as a painting.

Bolan was the first to respond. "I think we have to assume that the general is also a target. I think we can also assume that Martinson knows the plan Bartlett had devised for the general's approach to Managua."

"What's your point?" Hoffman asked.

"The point is, we know where to find them because they'll be waiting for us."

"That doesn't help on the Ortega end."

"It might. I think we have to make one more assumption. I might be reaching a bit, but I don't think so. If I were in their shoes, I would make sure the general went down before taking Ortega out. Otherwise you run the risk of the public throwing its support behind the general. So Ortega is safe at least until an attempt is made on the general. They might cut it very close and move on Ortega at the same time, but they'd want confirmation, I think. I know I would."

"So what do you propose, Mr. Belasko?" Rivera's voice showed no emotion despite the fact that Bolan had just spoken about a probable attempt on his life. He was all business, and the warrior had yet one more angle from which to view the man. He was beginning to wonder whether there was any limit to the colors of this strange chameleon.

"I think we go ahead with the original plan, with one simple modification. I'll explain that in a minute. General, how many of these men can you really trust?"

"Two dozen, I think. Why?"

"You better go get them."

CHAPTER THIRTY-EIGHT

"Cazz," Bolan said, "I know this isn't an easy thing I'm asking you to do, but it's important."

"No sweat. I never liked Robbins, anyhow."

"Look, don't take any chances. All you have to do is keep them in the tent and make sure they don't contact anybody. Roberto here will give you a hand."

"Check." He reached into his shirt and pulled out two small printed circuit boards. Holding one in each hand, he tapped one against the other. "Don't worry," he said. "I've got a feeling the radio's busted and somebody stole the spare parts for the damn thing, Wouldn't you know, a goddamn snafu just when we can't afford it. Some crazy men are tearassing through hell and we can't even tell anybody." He smiled.

Bolan looked at Hoffman and Rivera. "You ready?"

Hoffman nodded, but Rivera took longer to answer. He seemed to be giving himself one last opportunity to change his mind. Redemption wasn't easy to contemplate, maybe harder than actually doing it. Finally he nodded. "I'm ready."

"Let's go, then." Bolan shook Hoffman's hand. "Gil, watch yourself. And remember, you don't have to take them down. Just keep them busy. If we leave now, we'll be there in two hours. It should take you about four hours, so I guess you better hit the road."

Hoffman climbed down from the table he'd been sitting on. He clapped Bolan on the shoulder, then shook

Rivera's hand. "General, you better deliver. I'm too damn old for another disappointment. I'm not even sure I'm doing the right thing. If I put my ass on the line, there better be a payoff at the other end."

Rivera held on to Hoffman's hand. Looking him in the eye, he said, "I have a feeling my watchdog will see to it there *is* a payoff."

Hoffman pulled his hand away and walked out of the tent, followed by Bolan and Rivera. The CIA agent climbed into the waiting jeep and waved casually. Then the vehicle lurched, groaned across the dirt square and was gone.

Bolan stood and watched until Hoffman was out of sight. He looked at Rivera then, a thoughtful expression darkening his features. "You better believe I'll see to it," he said.

Rivera turned to him. "Mr. Belasko, if you have any doubts at all, we'd better clear them up right now. Once we leave here there's no turning back. We both know that."

Bolan sighed, then spoke to Washington. "Okay, Cazz, you're up."

Washington grabbed the warrior's hand. "Good luck, my man. I'll be rooting for you."

"Maybe you should pray," Rivera suggested.

The man looked at Rivera. "General, that's something I stopped doing a long time ago. I don't think God's home when any of us call." He nodded to Roberto and walked across the compound to the supply tent.

Bolan waited until the men reappeared with AK-47s, then tapped Rivera on the shoulder. "The jeep's out back," he said. "We better move or we'll miss the chopper."

The two men slipped between Rivera's tent and the woods on the far edge of the camp. Bolan led the way through the trees to a small clearing, where two men waited in a second jeep. While the general climbed into the passenger seat, the Executioner slid behind the wheel, started the engine and kicked the jeep into gear. The vehicle struggled through tangled weeds and small bushes, jolted over a fallen log, then cut into the road about fifty yards past the far side of the camp.

Over the roar of the engine, Bolan shouted, "You know this is a long shot, General, don't you?"

Rivera shouted back, "The longer the odds, the bigger the purse. But I'm not a gambler. If I didn't think we could pull this off, I wouldn't be in this jeep right now."

Bolan lapsed into silence and crossed mental fingers, hoping the chopper would be at the rendezvous. The operation was a shoestring affair, hastily assembled and precariously balanced. One small glitch would tear the whole thing to pieces. Both men knew it, and neither one seemed disposed to discuss the fact.

Twenty minutes later Bolan heard the unmistakable sound of a helicopter. He turned to the two men in the back of the jeep. Carlos Ingrazia, a man Rivera had taken a liking to on sight, patted the M-50 between him and Joaquin Cruz. "Ready," he said, "just in case."

They all knew it could be a Sandinista chopper and also knew that the smallest delay might wipe out their plans. Ingrazia raised crossed fingers. "I think it's ours," he said. "The Hinds sound different."

The rendezvous point was about a mile and a half ahead. The sound of the chopper faded, and Bolan goosed the Jeep. Even while in the air they wouldn't be safe, but they'd have a better chance. A jeep on the ground stood little chance against a fully armed Hind. They could run for cover, but the forest on both sides of the road was too dense for the jeep.

The road swept to the left about a hundred yards ahead. Bolan slowed a little, downshifting to give himself more control, and hit the curve with the jeep wound out. The transmission whined like a buzz saw and the vehicle sideslipped into the near leg of the hairpin. A clearing on the left exploded like a disturbed anthill, and Bolan cursed under his breath. Two jeeps—carrying eight men wearing the light brown uniform of the Nicaraguan army—buzzed in circles as the jeep flew by. They had been eating lunch, and the sudden appearance of the vehicle had disoriented them.

Scattered gunfire broke out, but Bolan swept his vehicle into the second half of the hairpin and was out of sight in an instant, knowing that the patrol would be on their tail in minutes.

Cruz unlimbered the M-50 and knelt on the floor. He made sure the safety was off and swept the machine gun back and forth in silent practice. They were in a long straightaway now, and by the time they neared the far end of it, one of the Nica jeeps had already entered the back end.

Bolan heard gunfire, but it was as if he were listening to a sound track. The jeep was untouched, and he saw nothing to indicate that the shots were near misses. Heading into the next turn, the warrior had to back off the gas to keep control. Then he floored it again as the sharp curve flattened into a broad, gentle arc. As long as the road continued to wind, they'd be safe unless the pursuers got too close. On the straightaways it was another matter.

Rivera seemed curiously detached from the excitement, as if he hadn't even noticed it. On the next straightaway Bolan glanced back. The four-hundred-yard lead had shrunk to less than three hundred. Cruz opened up with the M-50, its thunderous rattle shaking the jeep. Their pursuers returned fire, sporadic bursts that popped like distant firecrackers. This time, though, they came a lot closer. Dust geysers sprouted in front of the jeep, and a hail of shattered twigs and bits of bark clattered down from the branches overhead. It was only a matter of time before they found the range.

Bolan started to juke the jeep, jerking the wheel left, then veering back to the right at irregular intervals. It cost them a little time, but the trade-off was a good one. Cruz hammered away now, firing in short, choppy bursts. The belt clattered on the floor of the jeep, and Ingrazia opened up with his AK. Rivera had turned and now knelt on the front seat, bracing himself with one hand and firing his side arm. The pop of the Browning automatic sounded frail and puny alongside that of the larger guns.

"They're gaining," Rivera shouted, tossing an empty magazine into the trees. He slapped a second in place, then nearly lost his hold on the seat as Bolan wrenched the wheel violently to the left to avoid a fallen tree sticking halfway into the road.

Cruz shouted, "Bastards won't stay still, damn it." He held the trigger down almost constantly, wasting ammo in his frustration. Then he cried in exultation. "Take that, *maricón*."

Bolan heard a sharp explosion and looked back for a second, just long enough to see the lead jeep nose over, then fall onto its top. A sheet of flame shot up from the shattered vehicle, and the spinning wheels disappeared in black smoke.

Ingrazia shouted, "Here comes the other one."

Cruz was busy slapping a new belt into the M-50 as Bolan rounded the last curve. They careered into a straightaway, the jeep skidding into the turn and sending rooster tails of dry sand off into the trees. Up ahead a Huey sat on the ground, its rotor turning slowly, the blades sagging a little.

"There's the chopper," Bolan shouted as the machine gun started hammering again. The second jeep was too close for comfort. The warrior braked just outside the reach of the whirling blades and jumped down, followed by Rivera.

"You guys go ahead," Cruz shouted.

"Come on, Joaquin," Ingrazia shouted, pulling his friend away from the big machine gun.

But Cruz shook him off. "Get in the goddamn chopper, Carlito. I'll keep them busy."

Bolan shoved Rivera into the open chopper. The pilot waved his arms frantically and shouted something, but his window was closed. The warrior knelt and began to fire his AK as Ingrazia rushed past him, still looking back over his shoulder.

"We can wait," Bolan shouted. "Get in!"

The Sandinista unit had swung its tail end around and was using its own machine gun now, a Soviet PKS mounted in the rear of the vehicle. Three of the four men had taken cover behind the jeep, while the fourth knelt behind the PKS.

Cruz raked the jeep, and Bolan saw sparks flying off the fenders and tailgate. He climbed into the chopper, and the pilot started to rev the engine. Cruz poured it on. He raised a fist in the air when both rear tires blew, then he sprinted for the chopper. Bolan unhitched the chopper's M-60 as Cruz ducked under the rotor. The chopper started to lift off, and Bolan slammed the Sandinista jeep with a quick burst. He let go of the machine gun and reached down for Cruz, locking his hand around the smaller man's wrist. As the chopper climbed, Cruz dangled from the big man's arm.

Ingrazia had taken over the M-60, keeping the soldiers pinned. The PKS had fallen silent, and Bolan spotted the gunner draped over the tailgate of the jeep, his arms swinging gently.

The warrior hauled Cruz up far enough for the younger man to grab the doorframe with his free hand. Rivera dropped to the floor alongside Bolan, and together they hauled the little man up into the chopper, which was now two hundred feet above the ground. It spun into a bank, then nosed forward as Cruz collapsed on the floor.

He looked at Bolan with a weak grin, then vomited on the floor. His body jerking spasmodically. He shook his head, then spit as he rolled away from the mess.

"Can't take you anywhere, man," Ingrazia complained.

CHAPTER THIRTY-NINE

The second rendezvous went off without a hitch. Huddled in the back of the truck, the four men kept their own counsel. Bolan wondered how Hoffman was doing. He knew that they were paying out a very fine wire. It wouldn't take much to snap it, and if it snapped, the backlash of the razor-thin line would cut them to pieces. So much depended on finding one tiny needle in one gargantuan haystack.

They were close to the capital, and the truck rolled smoothly over asphalt for the first time since boarding. Traffic was much heavier, and Bolan took comfort in the crush of vehicles. They no longer stuck out like a rodeo clown's nose. He didn't kid himself. Things could still go very wrong very quickly, but at least they were getting close. Ironically so much depended now on Daniel Ortega. He was scheduled to give a major speech about the upcoming election. But Ortega was notoriously unpredictable. He changed his schedule with almost perverse whimsy.

If they didn't get to Pagan's assassins today, they would never get to them at all. Never had a second's timing been split so fine. Bolan watched the general, who seemed lost in thought. Almost hidden by shadows at the front of the truck bed, Rivera leaned against the side of the big van, rocking from side to side as the truck bed shifted on its springs. He seemed detached, as if he were a small wheel in a huge machine rather than a key player in a complex and deadly game. It might just be the way he controlled his emotions or, Bolan realized, he might not have any emotions at all. The man was almost impossible to read, no matter how carefully you studied him.

Cruz and Ingrazia whispered softly to each other, trying to calm their own nerves with small talk. Bolan got up and took a seat on the floor of the truck alongside Rivera. "Have you decided what you want to do, General?"

Rivera laughed without enthusiasm. "You ask that as if it were up to me, Mr. Belasko."

"Isn't it?"

"No, it isn't. And I won't bore you with my speculation, either. I just want what's best for Nicaragua."

"Isn't that what you're supposed to be? The best man for Nicaragua?"

"How does one ever know that? What are the signs? Snow, perhaps? That would truly be a miracle in Nicaragua, would it not?"

"Who said anything about miracles?"

"We're talking about what my country needs. And what it needs is not a man, but a miracle."

Bolan didn't say anything for a few minutes. He sat there, rocking in rhythm along with the truck. Finally he asked the one question that had haunted him since their first meeting. "General, there isn't any hidden fortune, is there? You didn't come back here for money."

"No, there's no money."

"Then why?"

"Because I love my country. And because I, like you, am wary of men who say such things too easily. I didn't want to sound too much like a missionary. I mistrust that kind of zeal. I think you know why. I think you mistrust it, too. But it's true. Not the zeal, I'm too much a realist for that, but the love. That's genuine. And I couldn't sit back and watch a beast like Guillermo Pagan take control. I have no love for Ortega, but replacing him with Pagan is like trying to cure leprosy with cancer. Do you understand?"

"I—" He was interrupted by a rap on the window between the cab and the truck bed. Bolan moved to the tailgate and looked out as the vehicle began to slow. They were turning a corner, and the truck wobbled as it eased over a curb and down into an alley. Weathered brick pressed in on both sides, then the truck turned again and stopped.

Bolan heard the driver open his door and jump down to the pavement. A moment later he rapped on the tailgate and jerked the pins loose to let it swing open. The canvas top was still pulled across the back, and the warrior peered out from under it. He lay flat on the bed and slipped out to the ground. They were in a courtyard of some kind surrounded by walls. Only the mouth of the alley broke the encirclement.

The Executioner reached back into the truck for his weapons, then stepped aside to let Cruz and Ingrazia climb down. Rivera came last. He lay on the bed, staring at the four men. Tentatively he let one leg slide over the edge and dangle toward the ground. When both feet touched the pavement, he looked up at the bright blue sky overhead. He was overwhelmed, and it showed. He watched a cloud slide by, the way a man at the bottom of a well would see a bird fly past—with a mixture of envy and admiration.

The driver tapped Bolan on the shoulder. "We have to get out of sight, *señor*. Quickly." He stepped away, and Bolan turned to follow him. Cruz and Ingrazia fell into line behind him. The driver stopped at a metal door, rapped twice, once, then waited. Metal ground on metal, and the door swung out into the courtyard.

"Quickly, *por favor*," the driver said, pushing Cruz and Ingrazia through the doorway.

"We have to hurry, General," Bolan whispered.

The warrior waited for him to enter the building, then stepped in and closed the door. They were in a dimly lit, windowless room that resembled a basement. A kerosene lamp burning on a table in a corner failed to dispel the gloom.

A man sitting on a folding chair at one end of the table nodded as Rivera approached. The man had long gray hair and a snow-white beard. His hands, orange in the lamp light, were wrinkled and leathery. His face, the little of it that was visible behind the beard, was like parchment.

He extended a hand to the general, who took it hesitantly. The old man smiled distantly. "Emilito, you've gained weight."

"Yes, the weight you've lost, my friend."

"Cancer, Emilito, has taken my weight. Not you."

"I heard. I'm sorry, Juan. I wish there was something I could do."

The old man waved one leathery hand. "Too late for that. I have the information you wanted. We better talk." Juan patted the opposite end of the table before unfolding several sheets of paper and pressing them flat on the chipped wood.

Rivera turned to Bolan. "If you'll excuse me, I'd like to be alone with my old friend for a while."

Bolan nodded. He understood perfectly.

The driver took the warrior's arm. "This way," he said, leading him into another room. Cruz and Ingrazia were already there, changing into peasant clothes, stained canvas pants and denim shirts. Both men already wore sandals.

The driver handed Bolan a pair of jeans and a denim work shirt. "These should fit," he said. "Not so easy to disguise a gringo your size...." He shrugged. "Maybe the Virgin will watch over you."

Bolan took the clothing and changed quickly, first donning the harness that would hold his weapons.

When he finished changing, the driver handed him an Uzi. "Four extra clips are all we could get our hands on," the driver explained. "You'll each have one, and the same amount of ammunition. If you have to shoot, shoot straight and sparingly."

He handed Cruz and Ingrazia Uzis fitted with slings made out of insulated wire. "Wear these under your shirts," he instructed. "They slip off the wire like this." He jerked on a spare gun, also on a sling, and the wire parted. "It'll hold the weapon securely, but you can get it quickly when you have to."

Cruz slipped his over his shoulder, then pulled on the shirt. Nestled under his arm under the loose blue cloth, the weapon wasn't at all obvious. Ingrazia followed suit, buttoning his shirt only halfway up.

"Come with me," the driver said.

He led them back into the other room, where Rivera and Juan were deep in conversation. The old man acknowledged them with a slight dip of his head. Rivera didn't turn around.

"You're sure of this, Juan? Absolutely sure?"

Juan shrugged. "As sure as I can be of anything. Who knows how sure that is? I don't."

"That's good enough for me."

"It's not as if you have any choice, eh, Emilito?" Juan laughed, and the sound of it was full and rich, despite his fragile appearance.

Rivera joined him in the laughter. "Juan, I didn't know until this minute how long I'd been away, and how much I missed you, my friend."

"Lucky for you I stayed here, or you would be in one deep hole."

The general agreed. He tugged the old man to his feet and embraced him warmly. "If I succeed, old friend, things won't change for you. You understand that, don't you?"

"It doesn't matter. I'm past saving, and too old to celebrate with the *señoritas*. But there has been enough killing. The best thing you can do for Nicaragua is to show her there's another way. And to show the world we Nicaraguans know it." He looked at Rivera for a long time, then turned away. "Forgive a sentimental old man, Emilito. You better go now. God be with you."

Rivera reached out and patted Juan on the shoulder. "And with you, too, Juanito. With you, too."

He turned abruptly. "I have to change," he said, and followed the driver into the other room. When he returned, he was transformed. The illusion of softness that seemed to cling to him was gone. He looked like a man who had worked the earth unceasingly all his life. The hardness of the man, the steel frame over which the deceptive flesh had been stretched, was evident.

Without looking at Juan again, he headed toward the door, leading now instead of following. Cruz rushed after him, followed by the driver. Ingrazia hung back and looked at Bolan. "Go ahead," the big man said.

Juan watched Bolan quietly. "Is there something you want?" he asked.

The warrior shook his head.

"Take care of him," the old man whispered. "He's his own worst enemy. More courageous than you might think. He can get himself killed if he's not careful."

Bolan shook the old man's hand. He marveled at the strength in a limb so light that it felt like rice paper in his hand. "I'll do what I can," he replied, then he turned to join others in the courtyard.

HOFFMAN SAT QUIETLY in the jeep, tugging the tarp a little more snugly in place. It was a makeshift arrangement, but there was no other way to handle it. He knew that Pagan and Martinson were aware of the itinerary Bartlett had planned for Rivera. He remembered reading the files and thinking then it was almost eerie how prescient they seemed. It had struck him that Bartlett had written notes expressly for him, as if the DDO expected trouble and wanted to make sure that someone knew.

Ever the gentleman, though, Bartlett had refused to point a finger at the DCI. Ever the intelligence officer, however, he had left enough tantalizing implications between the lines, almost like a separate text for the cognoscenti alone. Hoffman smiled wanly when he re-

alized that Gardner himself would have missed the indictment that in the right hands could hang him.

The supreme irony was that the indictment would
never be handed down. No matter what happened, it
wouldn't be possible to call Gardner to account. If
Rivera was successful, it would make no difference. If
he failed, the chances were better than even that Hoffman, Rivera and Belasko would be reduced to nothing
more than minor footnotes in an inconsequential history of Central American politics.

Hoffman felt guilty not telling his men they were bait,
but if the deception was to work, it had to be secret.
They couldn't risk an accidental leak, not even at this
stage. If they were ambushed—and there was always the
expectation that they would be—it was an unaccepta-
ble risk for anyone to know where Rivera was. Hoffman was sorry that he knew himself. It was only too
easy to extract information from an unwilling infor-
mant.

The scenario called for the unit to enter Managua no
later than three o'clock. So far they were right on
schedule. There were a dozen ways it could go wrong, a
hundred reasons why it should, and a thousand why it
better not. Those numbers kept rubbing against one
another in Hoffman's head, like gemstones in a tum-
bler. The more often he thought about them, the more
luminous they became.

He wasn't all that worried about being stopped. After all, it was supposed to be Rivera's jeep. They were
being monitored, he was certain, but there would be no
routine check of papers, no overzealous lieutenant interfering. As long as they thought it was Rivera's jeep,
they would leave it alone. And that was fine with Hoff-

man. As long as they thought they were already watching the general, they wouldn't be looking for him. But in the back of his mind was the certainty he couldn't confront but couldn't avoid. They wanted him to go so far.

But no farther.

The sun beat down on the jeep's hood. Even the dull mat finish was too reflective to kill the glare. Hoffman's eyes hurt, and he was fighting a killer headache. The tension did nothing to make it more endurable. Glancing at his watch, he wondered whether Belasko and Rivera were holding up their end. He knew that the same odds against success applied to them, but it pained him to think that he might be doing all this for nothing.

As they drew closer to the capital, he felt less and less confident that the masquerade would succeed. It seemed too transparent by half. The uniforms were legitimate Nica issue; the paint job was bogus. But he knew that most deceptions were in the eye of the beholder. People seldom saw through flimsy veneers because they saw what they expected to see. It was an axiom of his trade, and he prayed to God it would hold true just one more time. After that he really didn't care. He promised himself he would spend the rest of his life in some quiet suburb. Nine to five. The grind that once had seemed too tame now seemed like heaven.

And if he failed, he at least wanted his wife to know that he had meant well, and his kids that he really had wanted to coach Little League. When he thought about the possibility of dying that was what troubled him the most—that he would take his good intentions to the grave with him unspoken, his last and most unforgivable secret. It seemed almost too cruel to consider the possibility that he would be deprived of the chance to be bored stiff at the office at least once before he passed on.

The men with him in the jeep seemed wrapped in their own thoughts. Silvio Collazo, Raul Rodriguez and Victor Chamorro all kept their own counsel.

One of these days, Hoffman thought, he'd have to set this all down on paper, a private diary, something for the grandchildren to find in the attic one rainy afternoon when he was long in the ground. It amused him to think that he might have a chance to spill every last secret he knew, even if it brought no one to justice, toppled no government. Just the telling, that was the thing. And he knew he would do it.

If he got the chance.

Ten miles out they had a close call. A Sandinista militia unit, three truckloads of trainees and a jeep full of regulars, had to pull off the road to let them by. Hoffman could feel the eyes on him for half a mile. It was bad enough waiting for the other shoe to drop. Knowing that both of them might land on him at the same time made the trip almost unendurable. At seven miles they passed through an abandoned village.

Hoffman stared at the ruined buildings as if he expected to learn something from them. A handful of shacks announced the hamlet. At a crossroads there were buildings on both sides, a cantina and a store that sold farm implements the largest and most prominent. In the window of the latter merchandise leaned against the glass. Even from the moving jeep Hoffman could see the cobwebs spun between them, knitting them into a single tableau like a monument to a vanished culture.

It reminded him of a museum display, except for the absence of costumed mannequins.

The first shot ripped through the canvas cover before he realized it. The driver reacted late, hitting the brake rather than the gas, almost stalling the jeep before realizing his mistake. It was the mistake that saved them, at least for a while. Anticipating an acceleration that didn't come, a burst of machine gun fire tore up the dirt road in front of them, detonating the first mine. It triggered two others, and it seemed for a moment as if the entire world were about to be torn out from under them.

Shrapnel from the mines took out the front tires and starred the windshield in a dozen places. Rodriguez tumbled from the jeep, landing on his back in the road. Hoffman thought he'd been hit, but the man crawled under the vehicle, narrowly avoiding a snake of dirt geysers coiling toward him. The CIA man dived out of his side of the jeep, landed on his knees and started running.

The machine gun hammered incessantly. Hoffman heard the slugs tearing through the side of the jeep, and the footsteps of two men behind him. The machine gunner shifted his aim, and the window in front of Hoffman exploded in a thousand pieces, the glass cascading into the store.

Hoffman launched himself as he got within range, cartwheeling through the show window and landing on his back amid shards of glass and rusted tools. His heel slammed into an antique plow, and he thought for a second that he'd broken his ankle. Collazo and Chamorro dived in after him, the latter kicking Hoffman in the back as he rolled by. The CIA man turned, his arm tangled in the AK sling, and tried to get to his knees.

Rodriguez was still under the jeep, his hands clasped over his ears. He was wriggling, trying to kick himself out from under the vehicle, and Hoffman saw the dark pool in the dirt beside the struggling driver. At first he took it for blood, then realized it had no color of its own. Rodriguez got to his knees as Hoffman realized it was gasoline. The machine gun opened up again, igniting the fuel just as the man got to his feet, his pants and shirt soaked with the volatile liquid. But he was too late. His clothes burst into flame and he spun in a circle, beating at his clothing with his bare hands. Then he started to run, ignoring the fire. His flight only fanned the flames, and he collapsed in the dirt after a few yards. Seconds later the screams died away, lingering only in the back of Hoffman's mind as Rodriguez finally lay still.

Across the street, Hoffman found the first gunner, a rifleman, in an alley between the cantina and a nondescript building. He sighted in and squeezed off a steady stream of 7.62 mm slugs as the gunman turned to run. Hoffman watched just long enough to see the guy's legs buckle, then looked for his next target.

The two men who had tumbled through the window after him scrambled back to the frame and took up a position on either side of him. Hoffman pointed to the machine gun on the roof. It looked like a PKS on a bipod, but appeared to have been deserted. He didn't understand why a cross fire hadn't been set up. It was the most sensible way to do it. Then, as if a light went on, he realized that it might have been, after all.

"Watch the MG," he said, backing away from the window. "Shoot anything that moves out there."

Hoffman stood and rushed toward the back door of the one-room store. Several empty display counters transected the floor, like hurdles on a track. He moved to the left and ran along the wall just as the back door flew open.

He heard the grenade land, but couldn't see it in the darkness. He shouted to the men at the window, then dived between two counters as the thunder of the exploding grenade filled his ears.

Hoffman crawled the length of the aisle, then concealed himself behind the end of a counter. As he brought his rifle up, two shadows darted through the rear door. The CIA man got off a short burst, and the second man through went down. The lead man vanished in the smoke and shadows. Hoffman could hear him moving but couldn't see him.

He listened to the stealthy movement, trying to pinpoint the location. Moving left, Hoffman gave himself a clear shot down the next aisle, leaving a single counter between himself and the back door. A shuttered window on the rear wall leaked light around its edges, but not enough to help. Hoffman pulled a new clip for the AK out of his ammo pouch, then emptied his rifle through the window. The shutters shattered, and a broad swath of light cut through the swirling dust. He changed magazines before the glass stopped tinkling.

The shadow ducked, but not soon enough. Hoffman dived into the next aisle, the AK held out in front of him. His extended arms absorbed most of the shock, but he almost lost his grip on the weapon. The shadow scrambled backward as the CIA agent found the trigger. He squeezed off a short burst, but he was too late.

The gunman was in a position to backshoot the two men at the front window. Hoffman started down the aisle, but the man heard him and drove him back with a quick burst. Collazo turned just as the gunman aimed, and he rolled to the left, bringing his gun around. Hoffman zeroed in on the end of the counter as Collazo returned fire. And the gunman, intent on avoiding gunfire from that direction, backed away from the counter. Hoffman drilled him.

Collazo gave Hoffman the thumbs-up and continued his surveillance of the street. They were safe for now, but the back door was a problem. Hoffman didn't know how many men were outside, and if another grenade was tossed in, he might not be so lucky. While he tried to decide what to do, another shadow blocked the doorway.

"Forget about it, Hoffman," the apparition shouted. "Give it up, man. We don't want you. We want Rivera. Where is he?"

"Go to hell!"

"Come on, Gil, be reasonable."

"Harry, is that you?"

"You know it is. Come on, where is he? Just tell us and we'll leave you alone."

"Sure you will."

"Gil, I've got no beef with you."

"You had no beef with anybody you killed, did you, Harry?"

"Be nice."

Hoffman cut loose at the door, but Martinson must have sensed it. He was already moving as his adver-

sary's finger closed on the trigger. He was outside just
ahead of the burst. The doorframe splintered from top
to bottom and halfway back up, then the well went dry.
Hoffman changed clips again.

"That wasn't smart, Gil. I'm getting pissed off now."
Hoffman didn't bother to answer.

"Gil, you still there?" Martinson shouted.

Hoffman eased out from behind his cover. He
climbed onto the last counter, took a trial step, then
launched himself through the shattered window. He saw
Martinson out of the corner of his eye as he arced
through the opening. The man looked stunned. While
still in the air, Hoffman swept the AK in a broad arc, his
finger locked on the trigger. Martinson's expression
changed as his hands came up. As if in slow motion,
Hoffman saw it all—the gun falling from Martinson's
hand, the puzzled look on his face, the sudden puff of
his cheeks as the first 7.62 round hit him in the chest,
the bright red flowers opening in a drunken row across
Harry's shirt—and then he hit the ground. He rolled
over, feeling the glass slicing through his clothes, his
weight pressing him against the razor-sharp edges.

He stopped moving, his eyes still locked on Martinson, who lay on his back beside the open door. Hoffman started to get up, pulling his arms back and
climbing up on all fours, like a sprinter in the blocks.
Maybe I'll do that diary yet, he thought. Listening to his
own inner voice, he heard the other noise only dimly.
He started to turn toward the sound when the first bullet slammed into his shoulder. He rolled over as one arm
went out from under him and he lost his balance. He

was staring up at the sky now, and at the gunner on the roof.

He started to shake his head, but he didn't finish.

CHAPTER FORTY

The Plaza de la Revolución was already crowded when the truck nosed its way through the traffic and into the market square two blocks away. The driver pulled in between two stands and shut off his engine. Bolan was riding in the front seat; Rivera, Cruz and Ingrazia were in the back. The big man jumped down and thanked the driver as if he had hitched a ride.

Bolan sauntered toward the plaza, unhurried as if he were a tourist. He towered over most of the milling crowd that was drifting toward the heart of Managua. He stopped at a cart selling flavored ices and bought a coconut-pineapple concoction in a flimsy paper cone. He carried the shopping bag in his left hand, the ice in his right. Sucking the thick, sweet juice out of the shaved ice, he drifted casually along.

Far down the street he saw Rivera and Cruz moving his way. They argued as they walked, doing their best to look like concerned citizens on the way to a political rally of some consequence. Juan's information was the linchpin of their plan. If the old man was wrong, they were so far up the creek even a paddle wouldn't help them. If he was right, they were still shooting in the dark. Of the four men, only Rivera had ever seen Pagan face-to-face. Bolan had seen photographs, but they were more than three years old. A man's appearance could change a lot in three years, especially if it had to.

Juan had learned that the assassination was to be done by means of a bomb hidden under the podium. The fallback was a suicide hit squad of three men who would be among the crowd near the front edge to give them a clean shot. The bomb was to be detonated by radio, since Ortega was so unpredictable. Unlike Castro who, once having attained the microphone, often spoke until it seemed he would die there of old age, Ortega was a hit-and-run speaker. He might take an hour, or speak his piece in five minutes. A timer was out of the question for such a target. You had to be there and you had to push the button.

Bolan knew enough about radio detonators to know that the button man would want to be within a couple of hundred yards. But that covered half the plaza. How did someone find a black box no bigger than a cigarette pack that might be in any one of thirty thousand pockets?

Given the range, and given the premise that the button man wouldn't want to kill himself, he was probably going to be on the outer edge of a hundred-yard semicircle, close enough to do the job and far enough away to stay clear of the debris. At the back of the square Bolan stopped and leaned against a truck, sucking on the ice and scanning the throng, hoping to get lucky.

Rivera walked past him, still arguing with Cruz. Ingrazia sat on the ground five feet from Bolan, leaning against the front wheel of the same truck. All four of them wore straw hats with large blue feathers to make themselves more visible in the throng. Ingrazia glanced at the warrior with a neutral expression. The big man nodded slightly to indicate that he'd seen him. Bolan's side ached, more from the tension than anything he had done to aggravate the wound. He pressed on the injured side with the flat of his hand, letting the shopping bag dangle from his forearm.

He wished for a break and knew he'd have to make his own. In the button man's shoes, what would he do? What would he need? If he could answer those two questions, he could narrow the field. Then it dawned on him—the radio signal might be blocked by a dense crowd, so the best place to be was at the front, which was suicide, or above it, which made more sense, but which wasn't easy to do. The nearest buildings to the platform were all more than a hundred yards, except for the government buildings directly behind it.

If the detonator was in one of those buildings, Ortega was as good as dead, because there was no way Bolan could get inside without being pounced on immediately. He heard a horn blaring in the street behind him and turned to see a van trying to nose through the thickening crowd. Then he faced the plaza again. This was a no-winner. It was nearly impossible.

He saw Rivera slipping through the crowd, getting close to the front. He and Cruz had separated, as each tried to squeeze ahead of the mob and get close to the podium. As Bolan watched, Cruz got into a shoving match with a couple of farmers who resented his impertinence in crashing the front. The warrior thought for a second that there would be a fistfight, the last thing they needed. If the police were called, they'd find the Uzi under Cruz's shirt, which would probably be enough to cancel Ortega's appearance. One of the fundamental axioms of protecting heads of state said that if you found one gun, you had to assume there were others.

The blaring horn continued as the van fought its way into the plaza, drifting to the left and literally bumping people out of the way. People beat on the sides of the truck with the flats of their hands, setting up a drumming sound like small thunder. Bolan was intrigued by the big black vehicle. He couldn't imagine why it had chosen to cut across the congested plaza. Suddenly the truck braked, then stopped altogether.

Bolan watched three men scurry out of the vehicle and rush toward the rear doors. They opened the back and began to haul out glittering aluminum piping. When several sections of the piping had been removed, two men began to assemble it as the third continued to unload. In no time a scaffolding began to ascend the side of the van, then spread out across its top.

The warrior drifted closer to the van, more than curious now. It began to look as if a possible nest for the button man were being assembled right in front of his eyes. A car started honking at the edge of the plaza, and Bolan turned as it swam through the crowd like a shark in a school of minnows. The car bore some sort of insignia on its side, but the crowd was too heavy for Bolan to be able to read the inscription.

Finally the car managed to nose in behind the van, and a stylishly dressed young man with blow-dried hair climbed out. He carried a clipboard and sported designer sunglasses whose cranberry frames were the same color as his tie. Two men got out of the back seat of the car and rushed to the van. The smaller of the two climbed into the truck while his companion waited at the open rear door. Several coils of black cable were passed out of the truck and on up to the man atop the scaffolding. Bolan didn't need to see the camera to realize he was watching a mobile video crew set up, presumably to broadcast Ortega's speech.

All perfectly logical, and perfectly innocent, but Bolan had a hunch. Moving still closer, he pretended to be looking past the van toward the podium area while taking stock of the video unit. It was the perfect location—a guaranteed line of sight to the podium, the normal activity of a perfect cover, and no one would raise an eyebrow at a blinking red light or a black plastic box with a red button. It was electronic camouflage at its finest.

Bolan pushed the brim of his hat farther down his forehead, shading his eyes with it. He saw Rivera at the far left corner of the podium, about five rows back. The general was scanning his immediate neighbors in the throng, and the telltale blue feather on his straw hat bounced like a fishing bobber on a turbulent stream. Cruz, too, was checking his sector. Bolan would have to watch them carefully to know whether they had spotted anything. The signal would be a shift of the blue feather from the left side of the hat to the right. The warrior stroked the feather with his left hand to make sure it was still securely in place.

The odds were long, even though Bolan was convinced he'd found the location. Six men were candidates, none more likely than any of the others, although if he had to eliminate one, it would be the journalistic fashion plate. The man would handle a mike and, most likely, handle no other electronic gear. It would be too noticeable if he did. But that still left five.

The crew continued to work at a feverish pace, which could only mean that Ortega's arrival was imminent. The camera crew set up with brisk professionalism, one man on the scaffolding to provide podium coverage, while the other strapped himself into a minicam backpack. One of the techies screwed the battery pack cable into the camera, then climbed into the truck.

Bolan was only twenty-five feet away now and able to see everything very clearly. His height, which called attention to him, also enabled him to see over the bulk of the crowd. He was gambling on logic. It was his only ally at the moment, but it had a reputation for subtlety he had no time to consider. The minicam cameraman would have his hands full, which seemed to rule him out. But that still left the three techies and the platform cameraman. One out of four with the stakes this high were lousy odds.

Positioning himself behind the reporter's car, he watched the four remaining candidates intently, looking for anything to whittle the odds a little more to his liking. The crowd was beginning to buzz, and he glanced toward the speaker's platform. Three or four men huddled behind the podium now, the tops of their heads visible behind the bunting-draped partition bracketing the rostrum.

One of the technical men climbed back up on the van, while the other two sat on the tailgate and opened brown bags that contained nothing more lethal than hunks of bread and cheese. Despite the open air, the crowd and the heat made Bolan feel as if he were in a box. He found it difficult to breathe, and his ribs still ached from the bullet wound. Adding to the tension was the fact that he was going to have to stop the button pusher without giving himself away. He couldn't afford to be captured, even by police inclined to be grateful. Not here, not under these circumstances. No matter what happened, he had to get away clean, or he wouldn't get away at all. An American on the scene of an attempted assassination of the Sandinistas' best known spokesman would be a propaganda plum too juicy to ignore.

Bolan noticed a bulge in the rear pocket of the techie on top of the truck. It was bulky enough to be a detonator, but its contours were so nondescript that it could have been a wallet or a key case, even a handkerchief. Moving around to the side of the van, staying far enough away not to attract the attention of either man atop the van, he checked the cameraman. The guy's shirt pocket also hid a small rectangular bulk.

The crowd started a chant *"Viva Sandino, Viva Sandino"* louder and louder as more and more voices picked it up. Hands started to clap, punctuating every syllable, and stamping feet took up the rhythm as Bolan tried to get a clear look at the two men from another angle. The crowd around him pressed forward, chanting louder and louder. The clapping hands and stamping feet sounded like thunder now, the words all but drowned out by the rhythm, reduced to an elemental surge.

The crowd pressed on to the platform, and the warrior had to struggle against a tide of human flesh to avoid being swept away from the van. The cameraman seemed to be absorbed in his work and kept his eye glued to the viewfinder. As Bolan tried to make his way toward the van, the cameraman reached into his pocket and the warrior tensed until he saw the familiar red-and-white of a Marlboro pack. Without taking his eye off the viewfinder, the cameraman tapped a cigarette out of the box and stuck it into the corner of his mouth. The box disappeared and a lighter took its place. That left the techie, who hadn't reached for his back pocket yet.

A tremendous roar erupted from the crowd, sounding like a tidal wave rushing toward a stone wall. As the pressure built, the sound seemed to rise in pitch instead of in volume, then grew louder as a hiss like breaking surf sizzled over the plaza. Bolan was near the rear bumper of the car now and shoved two men aside to leap onto the trunk. Hands clutched at his pant legs and the reporter turned to shout at him, but the warrior couldn't hear anything over the roar, which seemed to have gotten a second wind.

Bolan jumped to the roof as the two techies dropped their lunch bags and stood up, waving their arms. Bolan leaped toward the scaffolding alongside the van. The techie on the roof glanced back at him, letting go of the bunched cables in his hand. Bolan scrambled up the aluminum rungs of the scaffold as the two techies below him tried to pull him back. The warrior lashed out with a foot, catching one man in the face. When the techie on the roof made a move to intercept him, Bolan knew the cameraman was the assassin.

A speaker announced Ortega, then the sound system crackled like lightning. Through the cameraman's legs, Bolan could see Ortega stepping toward the microphone. A slender silver antenna protruded from the cigarette lighter, catching the sunlight as the cameraman reached out. Bolan swept the techie aside and drew the Beretta. He saw the cameraman's thumb fumble for a small, shiny switch on the side of the bogus lighter and swung the Beretta around.

The cameraman started to turn as his thumb slid along the surface of the lighter. Bolan fired twice, the suppressed sound completely inaudible in the bedlam sweeping toward the platform. Two bright red flowers blossomed on the cameraman's shirt as he spun away from the camera. The lighter spiraled high into the air as the assassin flung up his arms in reaction to the punch of the slugs.

Bolan scrambled over the lip of the van, reaching for the detonator. The techie seemed stunned, as if he were starting to understand what was happening, but didn't know whose side to be on. As the detonator fell toward the roof of the vehicle, Bolan leaned forward, launching himself across the polished metal, his arm extended. The detonator struck him on the wrist and started to skid off the roof when the techie stopped it with his foot. Bolan's fingers closed over it carefully.

He looked at the techie, who watched in slowly dawning comprehension. He shook his head, as if to say he wouldn't interfere, and Bolan slid the lock in place, then pushed the antenna back into the detonator. Police from around the perimeter of the plaza were beginning to surge toward the van as Bolan slipped off the roof and down into the crowd. He pushed and shoved his way to the car and climbed in through the passenger's window. Slipping behind the wheel, he started the engine.

The warrior leaned on the horn and gunned the engine, his foot still on the brake. As the crowd began to part, he jerked the wheel and headed toward the speaker's platform. The reporter ran alongside the car, trying to drag Bolan's hands from the wheel, but the big man stiff-armed him and lifted his foot off the brake. The reporter lost his grip on the window frame and fell to the ground.

Up ahead, the platform floated above the heads of the parting sea like a vision of the promised land. Bolan hoped he had better luck than Moses.

CHAPTER FORTY-ONE

The platform was deserted now. Directly ahead of the car people scurried like ants to get out of the way. The crowd behind them pushed back, and Bolan could feel the near misses as hands and elbows, knees and feet bounced off the car. He couldn't stop, because the crowd would press in around him and he'd have to run someone over to get moving again.

Trapped in the car, he couldn't see Rivera or Cruz. They would have been hard-pressed to hold their ground. Then the first gunshots rang out. Bolan gunned the engine. The crowd seemed to sense his urgency, and the channel grew a little wider as panic sent adrenaline coursing through those closest on either side. The engine roared, and Bolan rode the brake. He could smell the burning shoes of the rear brakes, and the transmission's wild snarl sounded as if a beast were trapped under the front seat.

Bolan swung the wheel and headed straight for the platform. He'd have to rely on Rivera or Cruz to find him once he got close enough. More gunshots boomed, and several of the microphones were blasted to pieces, leaving brightly colored wires peeking out of the cable ends.

One of the blue feathers suddenly broke into the channel thirty yards ahead. Gesturing wildly to the left, Cruz jumped out of the way of a careening body, giving it a shove as it flew by. Then the mob closed around him again. Bolan lifted his foot off the brake, and the engine throbbed, set free once again. The throng dissipated as the big car roared straight head.

The blue feather bobbed into view again, and Bolan reached behind to make sure the rear door was open. Cruz struggled to stay on the leading edge of the crowd. The car slowed a little, and Cruz leaped onto the hood as Bolan went by. The scramble of limbs on the top of the car settled into a steady rhythm as Cruz pounded the roof to tell Bolan he was secure.

"Right, right, right," Cruz shouted. Bolan eased the wheel around, and the second blue feather bobbed into view. Bolan spotted it at the same instant Cruz shouted, "There he is!"

Rivera was grappling with two men, neither of whom seemed to be police. The general swung his fist and connected with one man, who stumbled backward. But the other took advantage of the distraction to grab Rivera in a headlock, knocking the hat away at the same time. The feather disappeared, and Bolan shouted, "Keep an eye on him, Joaquin."

Suddenly a circle appeared around Rivera, who was lying on the ground. The circle widened as Bolan watched, people on the perimeter backing away. Women covered their eyes and turned away. The men, their faces contorted, were screaming, but Bolan couldn't make out the words. As he nudged the car through the crowd, which was thinning again, two men stepped through the circle, automatic weapons in their hands. Bolan let the car go under a full head of steam. The roof above him vibrated as Cruz opened up with his Uzi. Using short, tight bursts to avoid the innocent bystanders, he got the attention of the two gunmen, who ignored the prostrate general to face this new and unexpected threat.

The men dropped into crouches, like armed bookends, and aimed their weapons at the car. Bolan floored it, charging straight at them. Cruz opened up again. The Uzi, braced on the roof, pounded on the metal as if it were trying to get in. One gunner went down, his weapon skidding away and into the crowd. The second man cut loose, and Bolan ducked under the dash, jerking the transmission into neutral at the same time.

A shower of broken glass cascaded over his head and shoulders, then Bolan heard a loud thump. Looking through the back window he saw Cruz slide off the roof and bounce once on the trunk before disappearing. The back window went out, too, and Bolan kicked at driver's door with both feet. Without power, the car was slowing down.

The door flew open, and the warrior rolled onto the pavement, unslinging his Uzi on the fly. The gunman was running sidewise, trying to ram another clip into his weapon. Bolan brought his Uzi to bear and let loose a tight stream of 9 mm parabellums. He nearly cut the gunman in two, catching him just above the bent knees and slicing across his midsection. The man folded like a ventriloquist's dummy and fell to the ground.

The crowd continued to back away as Bolan started to get up. Another burst of gunfire grabbed his attention, and he spotted Rivera, on his knees, trying to get up. Two men charged out of the mob toward the general, automatic rifles up and ready. Rivera weaved the Uzi left and right, holding the trigger down until the magazine was empty. One of the gunmen fell on his face, skidding a couple of yards until the friction caught him and he lay there, arms stretched like a man trying to surrender.

The second gunner fired a single shot from his AK-47. Bolan saw the spurt of blood where the slug struck Rivera high in the chest, and the old man fell over backward, the empty Uzi waving in the air like a black metal flower. Bolan stopped dead and stitched the advancing gunman from groin to chin. The guy staggered backward several paces then collapsed in a heap.

Bolan sprinted to Rivera, who lay on the ground moaning. By now people had begun to recognize the old man. The word spread, and the crowd started to surge back in, surrounding the general and cutting Bolan off as he tried to reach the man.

Even the weapon in Bolan's hand did nothing to deter them as they pressed forward. Using his size to advantage and rapping defenseless shoulders with the Uzi, the Executioner managed to clear a path.

The general lay on his back. His chest heaved, and with every breath a small bubble of bloody foam appeared and disappeared over the hole in his chest. A thin dribble of bloody water ran down his chin. Bolan could hear the hoarse breathing as he knelt beside the old man.

"We stopped them, eh, Mr. Belasko?"

"Yeah, general, we stopped them."

"I think we got here in time. They took Ortega off. There was some shooting, but I don't know what happened."

"Save your strength. We have to get you out of here."

"Too late for that, my friend. I know about bullet wounds. I know which ones kill and which just look bad. I . . ." His words trailed away in a phlegmy cough, and more foam appeared at his lips. Rivera wiped his chin with the back of his hand, then looked at the bloody smear on the skin. He smiled weakly. "We stopped them, anyway. Better to lose like a decent man than to win like an animal. You remember that."

"I will, General. Don't talk. You have to save your strength."

Rivera put a finger to his lips. "I have nothing to say," he gasped. He closed his eyes just as the loudspeaker squawked into life. Bolan turned to see a man backing away from a newly installed microphone. Then a bushy head of black hair appeared behind it.

Rivera tried to sit up, pulling on Bolan's arm for support. "Pagan," he whispered, pointing. "Pagan . . ."

Bolan looked back at the podium and realized Rivera was right. Guillermo Pagan was on the platform, leaning toward the microphone. *"Amigos y compadres,"* he began, raising his hands high over his head and urging the crowd to keep quiet. Feedback howled throughout the plaza, and Pagan covered the microphone. He turned to someone behind him.

"Don't let him speak, Mr. Belasko. Thousands of people will die for nothing. You can't let him speak."

But they were fifty yards away, and Bolan was alone in the middle of a terrified throng. He pressed Rivera back to the ground.

Someone knelt beside the general, and the warrior looked up to see Carlos Ingrazia leaning toward Rivera. The young man leaned forward, a cigarette between his lips trailing a thin stream of smoke into the sunlight. The public address system squawked again, and Guillermo Pagan again called for the attention of the crowd.

The Executioner reached into his pocket and jerked out the cigarette lighter, pulling the small antenna to its full length. Rivera saw the glittering silver wand, and smiled as the warrior freed the lock and stood.

"Amigos y compadres," Pagan began again.

Bolan pushed the button.

TAKE 'EM NOW

FOLDING SUNGLASSES
FROM GOLD EAGLE

Mean up your act with these tough, street-smart shades. Practical, too, because they fold 3 times into a handy, zip-up polyurethane pouch that fits neatly into your pocket. Rugged metal frame. Scratch-resistant acrylic lenses. Best of all, they can be yours for only $6.99.

MAIL YOUR ORDER TODAY.

Offer not available in Canada.

Phoenix Force—bonded in secrecy to avenge the acts of terrorists everywhere

SEARCH AND DESTROY $3.95 ☐

American "killer" mercenaries are involved in a KGB plot to overthrow the government of a South Pacific island. The American President, anxious to preserve his country's image and not disturb the precarious position of the island nation's government, sends in the experts—Phoenix Force—to prevent a coup.

FIRE STORM $3.95 ☐

An international peace conference turns into open warfare when terrorists kidnap the American President and the premier of the USSR at a summit meeting. As a last desperate measure Phoenix Force is brought in—for if demands are not met, a plutonium core device is set to explode.

Total Amount	$ _____
Plus 75¢ Postage	_____.75
Payment enclosed	$ _____

Please send a check or money order payable to Gold Eagle Books.

In the U.S.	In Canada
Gold Eagle Books	Gold Eagle Books
901 Fuhrmann Blvd.	P.O. Box 609
Box 1325	Fort Erie, Ontario
Buffalo, NY 14269-1325	L2A 5X3

Please Print

Name: _____

Address: _____

City: _____

State/Prov: _____

Zip/Postal Code: _____

SPF-A

Vietnam: Ground Zero is written by men who saw it all, did it all and lived to tell it all

"Some of the most riveting war fiction written..."
—Ed Gorman, *Cedar Rapids Gazette*

SHIFTING FIRES $3.95   ☐
An American Special Forces squad is assembled to terminate a
renowned general suspected of directing operations at the siege
of Khe Sanh, where six thousand U.S. troops are pinned down
by NVA regulars.

THE RAID $3.95   ☐
The Pentagon calls in experts in unconventional warfare when a
Soviet training contingent is discovered in North Vietnam. Their
mission: attack and kill every Russian in the place... and get
out alive.

Total Amount	$ _____
Plus 75¢ Postage	_____ .75
Payment enclosed	$ _____

Please send a check or money order payable to Gold Eagle Books.

In the U.S.	In Canada
Gold Eagle Books	Gold Eagle Books
901 Fuhrmann Blvd.	P.O. Box 609
Box 1325	Fort Erie, Ontario
Buffalo, NY 14269-1325	L2A 5X3

Please Print

Name: _____

Address: _____

City: _____

State/Prov: _____

Zip/Postal Code: _____

GOLD EAGLE ®

SV:GZ-AR